Medical ethics in literature

In the privacy of general practices and hospital clinics a million people a day in the UK share stories of personal moment with healthcare professionals. Fragmentary and often tangled, their accounts may feature bizarre experiences, unpleasant sensations, weird situations, complex relationships, difficult choices, conflicting interests and extreme emotions.

This refreshingly different series of novels conjures up some of these lived realities, especially their medical and ethical dimensions. The stories draw us deep into moral quandaries alongside people grappling with health issues and difficult choices; they are tales of passion, perplexity and crime that hold the reader spellbound amidst the thoughts, emotions, plans and actions of their characters.

Hazel McHaffie, already an award-winning author, has woven together authentic clinical details and ethical dilemmas with a lightness of touch that transports the reader effortlessly into the world of scientific medicine. In *Paternity*, the second of the three books which launch the series, she tackles the emotive issue of male infertility. The ethics and consequences of assisted reproduction are rarely out of the headlines but this book challenges preconceived ideas and drives us to reflect on what is done in the name of modern medicine and what, in similar circumstances, we would choose for ourselves.

'Ethics is a complicated matter' writes the philosopher and educationalist, Mary Warnock: 'it is partly a matter of judgement and decision, of reasoning and sentiment, of having the right feeling at the right time, and every time is different'. These novels cogently and evocatively embody that heady mixture of elements, bringing ethics to life. They are accessible and compelling and will be enjoyed by general readers as much as by philosophers and health professionals.

Brian Hurwitz
NHS GP
Professor of Medicine and the Arts, King's College, London
Series Editor
February 2005

Website resource

Medical ethics is a fast-moving, constantly evolving hotbed of challenges. You can stay up to date with current controversies, laws and guidelines by visiting a website created to offer useful background information about the series and about the ethical and medical challenges these novels address.

For those who will use this unique and exciting resource to bring medical ethics alive in their teaching, additional educational material and references are also available free on this website:

www.radcliffe-oxford.com/livingliterature

About the author and series editor

Hazel McHaffie's first novel was published in 1994 and 2005 sees the publication of three more. She began her professional life as a nurse and midwife and later gained a doctorate from Edinburgh University. During her career as a Research Fellow in medical ethics she was the author of almost a hundred academic papers and books. One of her books *Crucial Decisions at the Beginning of Life* was voted BMA Medical Book of the Year in 2002. In her new novels she has woven an extensive knowledge of ethics and moral conundrums into gripping tales of passion and tragedy.

Brian Hurwitz is Professor of Medicine and the Arts at King's College, University of London, and a NHS general practitioner in London. He is a member of the UK Association of Medical Humanities and serves on the Editorial Board of the *Journal of Medical Ethics*.

Acknowledgements

It was with some trepidation that I first handed an early draft of this book to my daughter. Thanks to her enthusiasm I was emboldened to relinquish it to others, and through its evolution it has benefited greatly from the wise advice of many people.

Dr Mary Porteous contributed expert genetic information, and Dr Martin Lees scrutinised the obstetric components. Dr Andy Lyon and Professor Rob Hume, long-time friends and allies, supplied medical detail and accuracy checks. Professor Kenneth Boyd, a colleague for almost 20 years, read and critiqued the first draft with his usual quiet wisdom and insight. Professor Brian Hurwitz and Gillian Nineham gave valuable editorial suggestions and their enthusiasm for the series of novels in medical ethics made publication possible.

My family, Rosalyn Crich, Jonathan, Camille and David McHaffie, read the manuscripts with affectionate bias, discussed the issues from helpful perspectives, and supported my venture into uncharted territory in a variety of ways.

I am indebted to them all.

Hazel McHaffie
February 2005

ONE

The first hairline fractures appeared without warning on their wedding night.

From the moment they left the reception, time seemed to Declan to have entered into a conspiracy to thwart him. No driver had surely ever driven so slowly through the city. No hotel receptionist had been so meticulous about form filling. No porter had taken so long to carry cases upstairs.

Judy seemed to feel no such frustration. Her eyes darted everywhere, her laughter only half stifled as she shared her irreverent thoughts in furtive whispers. Once in their suite she flitted from place to place exclaiming over the detail, feeling the bathrobes, smelling the soaps. In spite of his impatience, Declan smiled at her girlish excitement.

The first time he slid his arms around her waist, she wriggled free and rushed across the room to examine a bowl of exotic fruit, 'compliments of the manager'.

'Wow! Fruit, champagne, Belgian chocolates – enough for a midnight feast!' she giggled, her eyes still restlessly exploring.

'You're the only feast I want!' He grinned. 'Come here, Mrs Robertson.'

Instead she took a step away, flinging her arms wide to take in the whole room.

'I've never *seen* such magnificence before, much less *stayed* in it!'

'Well, don't get too used to it. It's merely honeymoon extravagance. Poverty will all too soon be the order of the day!'

'You mean you've got me here under false pretences?' She shot him a look of mock indignation.

'For better, for worse. You promised – let me see, eleven hours and twelve minutes ago. Don't tell me you're regretting it already!'

'Well …'

He stopped the banter effectively with his kiss. Hunger for her surged as he held her hard against him, letting her feel his desire.

He chuckled as she pulled away from him.

'Only joking! I'll treat you like a princess till death us do part. Promise!'

But her laughter had been suddenly extinguished. She was trapped by his arms but now remained there tense, unyielding, her face resolutely hidden against his chest.

'Jude?'

In the sudden silence he felt the shallowness of her breathing, the trembling of her body.

'Jude? What is it?'

With both hands he turned her face up to his but, barely suppressing a shudder, she closed her eyes, shook herself free and buried her head on his shoulder.

'Heey,' he soothed, stroking the thick auburn curls. 'Tell me what's going on here.'

'I just ... need ... some space.' It was muffled and somehow breathless.

Releasing his hold, he said lightly, 'Fair enough. I'm hot and sticky from all that dancing, anyway, I could do with a shower. Want to come with me? Or would you prefer some privacy? It's fine by me either way.'

'D'you mind if ...? I'd rather ... go ... on my own.'

'Absolutely. You go first. I'll slump here and try out this king-size bed. Feel free to wake me up if I disgrace myself by falling asleep before you come out!'

Declan threw himself face first onto the bed, stretching and yawning expansively.

The sound of the shower conjured up vivid images of water cascading over her body. He dragged his mind onto safer ground. She'd fired the warning shots. Slow down. Proceed with caution.

His eyes roamed around the deliberate opulence of the room. Stray pieces of confetti littered the carpet; his new jacket lay where he'd tossed it carelessly onto the chair. Was it all too oppressively bridal? Should he have gone for something more low-key?

He tried switching off different lights. Yes, the dimness was more reassuring. Or ... was it too suggestive?

When she finally emerged he was sitting nonchalantly on the edge of the bed, apparently reading. All his calming techniques were forgotten in an instant as she stood in her nightdress silhouetted against the light. But her eyes were darting around the room, taking in the dimness, the turned-down bed, the unopened champagne; looking everywhere but at him. Taking long slow breaths he willed himself to sit perfectly still until she'd moved to the dressing table and was rifling through her cosmetics bag.

The room was already in darkness by the time he had showered. Fair enough. It was early days. The ambient light was sufficient for him to see she had chosen the far side of the bed.

Her subtle perfume enveloped him as he slid between the sheets.

'Mmmmmm, you smell wonderful,' he murmured, inching closer.

But as soon as his body met hers, the violence of her reaction made him recoil instinctively. She was suddenly an inflexible no-go zone; knees tightly up against her chest, both arms clenched around them.

'Jude?'

'No ... please ... no.' The strangled words were barely audible.

Declan lay motionless. The trembling continued.

'Jude ...' He slipped one arm around her.

She was instantly rigid.

'Please ...' It was no more than a whisper.

He propped himself up on one elbow and peered in the direction of her averted face. It was too dark to see her expression but her panic was palpable.

'Hey, speak to me. What's up?' he said.

'Please ... please, don't.'

Declan lay still, completely nonplussed, inwardly cursing his own inexperience. What was a guy supposed to do next?

He felt rather than heard the stifled sob.

'Jude, what is it? Tell me what's wrong.'

Firmly now, he turned her towards him but she remained hunched like a child newly woken from a nightmare, rocking to and fro, her knees and elbows holding him at arm's length.

When she finally spoke, her words were thick with tears.

'I'm sorry, Dec, I'm sorry. I've spoiled everything.'

'Forget that. Tell me what on earth's going on here.'

'I know you want to ... but ... I ... I can't ...' Her voice petered into another choked sob.

'Well, of course I want to. Desperately want to. Not much point denying it, eh?'

'I know.' A fresh wave of crying sent her burrowing into her tissues.

'Hang it, Jude, any normal man with half a hormone would want to make love with a bundle of loveliness like *this* in his bed!' He tightened his arm around her waist. 'After all these months of waiting. On his wedding night of all nights! So why do I feel like some kind of a monster here?' He tried for a teasing tone but knew immediately he'd failed miserably.

For the first time she half-turned her head towards him.

'You're not ... it's not you ... I ... I ... just ... can't ...'

'Did I do something wrong? You'll have to give me some guidance here.'

'No, it's not you. It's ... it's ... I can't say ...'

They lay in silence in the vast bed, the tension between them impenetrable.

'Look, I haven't a clue what's going on here but, for goodness sake, this is our first night of married life. We can't let it end like this. Will you at least let me hold you – like I used to? I won't press for more. Promise.'

Even as he said the words everything about their circumstances shrieked in derision. Two young healthy people, in love, in a warm bed, one of them wearing nothing but a brand new wedding ring, fuelled by aching months of self-imposed chastity, licensed by law that very day. Talk about farce!

He turned to lie prone, leaving one arm still lightly around her waist, as safe a distance from temptation as he could achieve.

'This OK?'

'Uhhuh.'

They both lay perfectly still, surrounded by the appalled silence. In all the months of courtship, they had never had an argument, always parted with avowals of love. And now on the very day when they had sworn undying love in front of witnesses, promised to be all things to each other, there was only tension between them, an unseen, unknown barrier even to verbal communication.

'Jude,' he whispered tentatively.

Nothing.

'I love you.'

Still nothing.

The old clock outside on the landing ticked slowly towards daybreak.

TWO

Austria had been Declan's choice for their honeymoon – a secret until they were checking in at the airport. The hotel in Wolfgangsee was everything the brochure had promised, with stunning views of the mountains and lake and easy access to the surrounding countryside. Even the weather was idyllic. But in spite of his best efforts to be patient, for Declan, the shadows lengthened.

In the aching silence of the night his restless mind relived the past, searching for clues.

They'd met on Shotton station.

The light was already fading when he arrived there and found no sign of a connection to Wrexham.

'Over the bridge,' the official said dismissively when Declan asked the way to the right platform.

Eight people huddled together in the shelter on the opposite side of the track. A middle-aged woman shouted across to him, stabbing her finger into the darkness.

'You just have to go down there. Cross the line where it's narrow.'

Large notices in bold capitals warned that no passengers should trespass on the line. There were penalties. Death, I shouldn't wonder, he thought grimly. But there seemed to be no alternative.

When ten minutes later a young woman hurried across the bridge and stood hesitating on the far side, he immediately cupped a hand to his mouth to call across to her.

'It's OK. I came over the rails too. Walk down a bit further and cross when I say so.'

He walked parallel to her away from the lights on the platform, down into the darkness. He strained his ears, listening on her behalf. Only silence along the track.

'OK. Cross now!'

She crossed jerkily, stumbling at the edge of the platform in her haste.

'Horrible feeling, eh?' He smiled, reaching out to steady her. 'Didn't like it myself. But you're fine. You made it safely.'

She sounded breathless and her smile was shaky.

'Thank you so much.'

'No problem. I'm Declan, by the way, Declan Robertson.'

'Judith, known as Judy – Judy Burrows.'

'Hello, Judy. Going far?'

'Just to Wrexham – for a conference. Midwifery conference.'

'I'm going to Wrexham myself to see a client. I'm in computing – like half the world these days!' He grinned.

The train was half empty but he took a seat opposite her. She was easy to talk to. It seemed natural, polite even, to give her his card, ask for her email address.

He didn't expect to see her again. His business in Wrexham would take only one day, her conference was for three days. She would return to Edinburgh, he to Bristol. There was little chance of their paths crossing again.

His email was brief.

Hi Judy. Hope you're back safely. No track to cross coming back, eh? Declan.

He didn't really expect a reply.

Hi Declan. How kind of you to remember. No problems, thanks. Judy.

It was encouragement enough to contact her again. The brief exchanges continued. He found himself anticipating her replies.

Four weeks later he found the courage and the excuse he was looking for.

Hi Judy, I have to come to Edinburgh on Thursday this week to meet colleagues in our office up there. Any chance we could meet? Declan.

Hi Declan, That'd be good. I'm working an early shift. Finish about four. Some time after that any good? Or do you have to get back? Judy.

He hadn't realised, in that first brief meeting, just how slim she was. Good legs too. She seemed more shy than he remembered, but he liked that; it increased his confidence. In repose there was something melancholic about her expression. He found himself consciously working to bring a smile to her dark eyes, to make the shadows recede. Encouraged by her response, he told a few stories against himself, making her laugh. She was attractive when she laughed. Good even teeth, a suggestion of dimples in the clear complexion. And those eyes – he was mesmerised by her eyes. Huge unfathomable darkness one moment; kaleidoscopes of light and merriment the next.

He was perfectly aware of her surreptitious scrutiny too. What would she see? Would she look beyond the thick dark hair, the square-cut face, the lean frame, to the insecurity? What was she expecting? Simple friend-ship? Flirtation? Seduction? Was she disappointed? He couldn't tell.

He told her frankly two weeks later he'd like to come up expressly to see her – by email so that it'd be easy for her to turn him down. She didn't.

The first few times he made his own arrangements and stayed in a nearby hotel. She made no comment, so he took it as encouragement when she volunteered a change.

Hi Declan. Seems a shame to waste money on a hotel when I have a perfectly usable – if girly (!) – spare room. It's up to you, of course. Judy.

Hi Judy. Thanks. I'd love to. And I can cope with girly – had two sisters after all! Declan

It had taken five months before Judy had taken him to meet her mother. Everything about the house was meticulous. Mealtimes were punctual to the minute. Books were ordered by size. Home-made preserves were lined up in perfect rows, labels all exactly the same distance from the lids. The front path was swept daily. Betty Burrows presided over this precision with co-ordinated twinsets and unremitting vigilance. Even conversation seemed to run by her rules. Judy had given him prior warning that the subject of her father was off-limits; he'd never been mentioned since he'd left home suddenly without warning when she was thirteen. But Declan felt unspoken taboos on every side. It was a relief when the visit ended. He had seen enough to know that he'd be unlikely ever to earn approval from her mother, and he had an explanation for Judy's previous reticence about her early years and background. Who wouldn't want to push such repression out of sight?

Those few days hedged about by disapproval had made him long to share with her the warmth of his own family, but they were now so scattered. Only his twin, Georgina, was in the same country; and even with her he had reason to hesitate before introducing Judy. As twins they had shared an exclusive closeness that Declan had sometimes found discomforting – certainly in some of his early youthful forays into the world of girls. By the merest inflection and look Georgina could make everyone else feel like an outsider. And she was nothing if not forthright in her opinions.

But perhaps the risk was worth taking to show Judy something of his own early advantages, his personal ambitions for a family. Georgina's reaction took him by surprise. Her warm friendliness embraced Judy as well as her brother, and in private her spontaneous endorsement gave unexpected encouragement.

'This one's different, eh, bro? Easy to see you're besotted.'

'That obvious, eh?'

'To me. Remember – I've known you since we were blastocysts!'

'Very poetic!'

'Judy feel the same way, d'you think?'

'What do *you* think, Miss Perspicacious?'

'Well, she doesn't give too much away. But I hope so. I'd like her for a sister.'

'Wow. High praise indeed.'

Looking back now it all held undercurrents. At the time it had seemed perfectly understandable – even in part of his own making. There had been an awkward moment early on in her flat, when he'd sensed a sudden tension. He'd quickly reassured her: he was old-fashioned about sex outside marriage. He'd mocked himself, keeping his tone light, and the moment had passed. He was happy to go slowly.

And even as their relationship developed he'd been careful to stay on the safe side of unmarked boundaries. Two incidents had reinforced the need for caution. Kissing her goodbye in the car one night his hand had strayed to the smooth silk of her shirt stretched across her breast. She'd almost wrenched herself away and gone indoors with only the briefest of farewells. Then in the following summer, they'd been happily swimming together in the sea, diving through each other's legs in a game of inverse leapfrog, when he'd spontaneously pulled her close, laughing in the warmth and innocence of their fun. He'd been unprepared for the sudden arousal. Before he could register what was happening and pull away, she had made an excuse about getting cold and swum for the shore. She'd been engrossed in her book by the time he dared to emerge himself. Nothing was said but he'd stepped up his own vigilance from then on.

It had seemed fair enough at the time, even if it nudged the edges of paranoia. One thing could easily lead to another. And in her job she knew all about unwanted babies. Besides, the straitjacket of religion that had moulded her early ideas must have left its own legacy.

But now ... ? Had her prudery been more than natural protection? Was her repressed childhood extending its tentacles beyond the realms of courtship into marriage? Could a girl grow up in that suffocating atmosphere and *not* be marked? But apart from those few occasions where he'd betrayed his desire for her, she'd been so warm, so loving, before and ... yes, so responsive with her kisses, her affectionate embraces. But, of course, then she'd been secure. The boundaries, the expectations were fixed. Had he himself unwittingly provided a smokescreen to protect her inhibitions? Should he have seen this coming? But even if he'd been hoodwinked, *she* must have known. Why agree to marry him?

There had been no hesitation.

Venice, standing in the crisp night air in St Mark's Square, listening to the bells ringing in a New Year – it had seemed like the ideal moment to propose.

14

'What a romantic you are!' she breathed, nestling against him as they walked along the waterways festooned with fairy-lights.

'Well, I had an ulterior motive really. I guessed you'd be less inclined to say no in this enchanted place!' he teased.

'What would you have done if I *had* said no?'

'Packed you off back to the UK and asked the waitress at the hotel instead!'

Their laughter disturbed an old man crouched on a wooden seat dozing, his breath visible in the cold air.

'No, I'd have taken you to Oslo and Salzburg and Florence and Paris – around the most romantic cities in the world! – and asked you again and again and *again* until you said yes.' Declan pulled her close against him as he spoke.

'So I've saved you a lot of expense then.' Judy grinned up at him.

'Ah, I see you're going to be a frugal wife. Excellent! I approve of frugal wives!'

'And they call the *Scots* miserly!'

No, even with hindsight, he could detect no warning signs there. But lying now inches from temptation, doubts assailed him.

THREE

Conflicting emotions jostled for position in his head as he stared now at the hunched figure on the far edge of the bed. Could it be less than two short weeks since he'd watched this girl walking down the aisle towards him with a lump in his throat and unclouded promise in his thoughts? How could happiness dissolve so rapidly?

He closed his eyes and saw again that first glimpse of her as his bride. Each step towards him in time with the beautiful chords of Bach's Air from Suite No 3 in D. The pearls and crystals on her dress catching the light with each flowing movement, her shape perfectly silhouetted in the soft drapes, her dark eyes alert for his reaction.

He'd been the emotional one with a quiver in his voice. But she'd seemed so calm herself, her gaze steady, her fingers twining through his reassuringly. Her own vows spoken with confidence.

All the preparation had been fun up till then. They'd laughed together as they'd worked out a form of service uniquely theirs. She'd teased him about wanting to incorporate the English declaration that they knew of no lawful impediment to their union; did he suspect a skeleton in her cupboard? He'd teased her about wanting to promise to obey him. Oh yes, he'd happily rule her with a rod of iron, he'd promised then. But the real thing – making those solemn vows 'before God, and before this congregation' ... 'to love you with all my heart; cherish you through bad times as well as good; do all in my power to help you to be all you can be' – he'd been overwhelmed by the huge commitment, the wealth of promise.

Had it all been a sham? Neither of them was laughing now.

Less than two weeks ago! It seemed unbelievable now.

He'd been so happy even Betty Burrows' fluttering and inconsequential chatter fading in and out of his consciousness had failed to irritate him.

'I'll have to have words with that florist – I mean, I definitely ordered cream roses – these are too pink for my suit. I *told* her champagne silk. ... Oh, and I must check to see if Aunt Minnie's got the right food. The chef wasn't at all accommodating when I rang him yesterday about that. But of course, she *has* to have the right diet. I dread to think what would happen if they put onions in her salad ... I've never had mildew like it on my gooseberries before! Of course, I still made my usual jam and chutney for the village sale ... She was new. I mean, I go to the library every week, and she wasn't one of the regulars. But even so, what a cheek – to tell me she wasn't my personal slave! The audacity of it! I mean, I only asked how much longer would it be before I got the book. Libraries are *supposed* to get the books you want, aren't they? It wasn't as if I was expecting anything out of the ordinary …'

He'd watched with wry amusement as even Betty's brittleness softened in the warmth of the pervasive happiness. She'd originally tutted about their decision to involve children – 'They're sure to make a noise and get dirty' – but she had grudgingly to admit they had behaved impeccably. Indeed she'd taken a photograph herself when the flower girl, Emma, stole the show, marching up to the top table and climbing up onto Declan's knee, where she snuggled down, thumb in her mouth, for a rest from the labours of high office. He'd cuddled the child close, smiling over her head into Judy's eyes. Dreaming of a future.

In the darkness now the seeds of doubt germinated and began to erode his confidence. Had she actually been sharing his dream? How well did he really understand her needs, her wants? What did he really know about this woman he'd bound himself to?

The English guests had been enchanted by the Scottish traditions – the castle, the kilts, the country dancing. Overhearing their comments, Declan had smiled at the memory of battles fought between Judy and her mother during the weeks of preparation. Mostly Judy's tact had won the day but on one point there had been tears. She would not – no, not under any circumstances – be piped in to the meal. Yes, she accepted that bagpipes were splendid in their place and part of her heritage, but she really couldn't stand them in a confined place. Declan had watched from the sidelines Betty wheedle and cajole, Judy counter and parry. He'd seen for the first time a steely determination beneath that deceptively gentle smile.

Would she be as resolute and persistent now? Would he be any better able to change her mind than her mother? Betty had had a lifetime of experience, and she hadn't won.

He lay still, breathing evenly, pretending to sleep, fighting to stem the trickle of doubt bleeding into his mind.

It was early days. Plenty of couples took time to adjust to each other. She was still her old self during the daytime – well, almost. They laughed and teased and shared loving moments. But … no. It wasn't the same. There were new constraints. He had to admit it. They were tiptoeing around each other at times; he was nervous, not wanting to stir that hidden well of coldness. He must just be patient. Yes, that's it. Patience. Give her time. Let her know how much he loved her. Patience.

Easy to say. Not so easy in practice. Especially when she was responsive. Most of all then.

It was not yet nine when he woke that first morning, but she was already up and dressed. He watched her for a while through half-closed eyes. When she looked up he stretched lazily.

'Good morning, Mrs Early Bird. Have you eaten all the worms?'

'Not so much as half a worm.'

'Yuck! So much worse than a whole worm! Are you starving?'

'Not starving but ready to eat when you are.'

'I'm sorry. I didn't order … breakfast …' His voice tailed off.

From then on he skated unfettered on the thin ice. The naked dash to the bathroom became an ordeal. Excusing the absence of breakfast held only reproach. Touching her seemed dangerous; not touching her worse.

The very seclusion of their table in the dining room underlined his own unfurling discomfort. He reached across to lay a hand over hers, vaguely sensing fault lines widening, clutching at any chance of bridging the gap. She held his gaze, a slow smile conveying all the old tenderness. On the way back upstairs to their bedroom he slipped an arm around her and his spirit soared when hers circled his waist. Neither spoke as they re-entered the room but as soon as the door closed, he turned towards her. In an instant she was out of his clasp and busy packing her case. Declan stood for a moment, uncertain, then walking over to her, he reached out to lay a hand on her shoulder.

'Jude, you can trust me. I love you.' He knew the hurt was in his voice. He couldn't disguise it.

She threw her arms around him, and held him tightly to her. But her tension was unmistakable.

'I know, Dec. I know. I'm sorry. I love you too.'

'Please don't be scared of me. I couldn't bear it.'

'I'm not …'

She remained in his clasp for a long moment, but over her head Declan surveyed the bridal suite with a strange sense of loss. Something innocent and precious, something almost undefinable, had seeped out of the room. He felt a sudden need to be alone to fathom this mystery and that very thought clutched at his heart, even as he loosened his hold on his new wife. Solitude? *Now?* On his honeymoon?

'Thank you, sir. Everything to your satisfaction, I hope?' the man at the desk said obsequiously when Declan handed in the key and paid the bill. Unfortunate choice of words.

'Very good, thank you.' Declan didn't look up from scrawling his signature.

The holiday atmosphere in Austria was infectious and they made the most of the pure air, the unbroken sunshine and the beauty all around them. Declan savoured the days, organising new excursions, lingering with her over their evening meal, strolling with her in the moonlight, delaying the moment when tenderness would desert her. But in spite of his repeated reassurances, whispered in the darkness, the nights brought no relief from the frozen silence.

Three weeks of frustrated need made him start to shield himself from the pain of rejection. On their last evening it was Judy who suggested they head away from the square where a local band was playing Austrian folk music and go for one last walk alone beside the lake. The bushes grew denser as they walked further away from civilisation. Ghostly silhouettes of trees overhung the path, reaching almost to the water's edge in places, and she moved closer to him as if fearful of the darkness. Declan held her against his side, steering a course between the obstacles. The distant thrum of music was by now barely discernible. It was then that Judy suddenly stopped in her tracks and turned and melted into his arms without a word. His heart thumped painfully. She pressed closer.

'Tell me what you want, Jude,' he whispered hoarsely.

'Will you kiss me – like you did then ... on our wedding night.' Her words were urgent.

He was tentative at first but, meeting no rebuff, became more searching, thrilling to her voluntary closeness.

'Dec. If you want to ... tonight ...'

'Is it what *you* want?'

When she didn't answer he turned her face up into the moonlight. With gentle fingers he wiped away her tears.

'Oh Jude. I wish you'd tell me. What is it?'

'I can't ... I just ... can't. But I know ... it's not fair on you ... You can. You can. Tonight.'

'Maybe. But I won't. Not in these circumstances. You've got to trust me, Jude.'

'I hate myself for ... spoiling everything.' Fresh tears spilled down her pale cheeks.

'You haven't,' he said, drawing her close again. 'It's been a magical three weeks for me – just having you all to myself. There's no urgency. Just give yourself time. I'll still be here. Loving you.'

In some ways it was easier when they returned home and took up the threads of routine life again. They applied themselves wholeheartedly to renovating their new home, a quaint but spacious cottage in Roslin, just outside the city, tiring themselves out with the hard physical effort. Judy returned to her work as a midwife and Declan saw at first-hand the quiet fulfilment she gained from her work.

A new job in the Scottish headquarters of his old firm provided Declan with interesting as well as promotional opportunities which he seized with relief. He'd jumped at the chance of moving away from the Bristol office. There, his line manager, Frank Williams, had been a bully who despised any sign of 'weakness' in men. Declan became his principal target. By his resolute refusal to chase the female staff, or exchange dirty jokes, or bend the office rules, he challenged Williams' code of behaviour daily. The older man wasted no opportunity to taunt him: 'You're nothing but a filthy poofter.' 'Think you're Mother Teresa.' 'Got victim stamped all over your cowering body.' 'Stand up and fight, man, or are you one of those friggin' transvestites?' But no matter the provocation, maddeningly, Declan did not, would not, retaliate.

Instead of aggression he felt nausea and mounting stress. He steeled himself for each day and compensated by single-mindedly applying himself to each new project, developing imaginative and efficient software packages that soon earned him commendation from the managing director. An increasing number of clients asked for him by name; he welcomed every opportunity to travel away from home to meet them. Stung further by Declan's success even in the face of harassment, his tormentor stepped up the taunts. Forthcoming marriage gave Declan the perfect reason to transfer out of this hellhole.

Edinburgh welcomed him wholeheartedly and he was quickly absorbed into the fraternity of an office shared by four young men of similar age and seniority in the company. In the run-up to the wedding he soon became the butt of endless jokes but recognised that these were different, they stemmed from friendship, and he took them in good part, glad of the promise of greater camaraderie. But following his marriage, the jibes began to develop edges of steel. It became an ongoing battle to parry them with humour.

It took a particularly difficult morning to reverse the trend. The day began badly when he was held up on the bypass by heavy traffic, and late in for work. All three of his colleagues treated his excuses with derision.

'We all know it's still honeymoon fever!'

Later, passing his desk with a cup of coffee, Simon suddenly shot him a question: 'D'you know why IT men make hopeless lovers?'

'No, but I'm sure you're going to tell me,' Declan sighed, not looking away from his screen, his fingers suddenly heavier on the keys.

'They think software always goes into hardware.'

'Hah, hah.'

'Eeuuuw. Who stole your handbag?' Simon shrilled. 'The missus giving you grief?'

Pretending his mind was wholly on his work, Declan swung round to Mark on his far side.

'Did you find any gremlins in that program we tested yesterday? I can't get it to run properly here.'

The leaden feeling in his stomach belied his outward nonchalance.

Tired from a bad night where his fevered mind could find no end to his personal torment, he struggled to remain attentive during the team meeting that afternoon and brought down the wrath of the team leader on the whole office when he was forced to confess he hadn't been listening to what was being said. Sore from the unwarranted comprehensive rebuke, Alan fired a broadside at Declan as soon as they were back at their computers: 'Crikey Moses, mate. Cut down on the sex and get more sleep!'

'Cretin!' Declan exploded. 'Get your mind out of the gutter. Everything doesn't revolve around sex!'

He promptly stomped off to the photocopier until he'd calmed down.

All three men looked shamefaced by his subsequent apology; but his uncharacteristic outburst had clearly jolted his colleagues. The ribald jokes ceased and Declan could once more find solace from his domestic frustrations during working hours.

As the weeks went on both Judy and Declan colluded in the creation of a façade: busy, contented newly-weds.

FOUR

An hour. Two hours. Where could she be? He'd surely have heard if there'd been an accident. After another thirty minutes he rang the hospital.

'She's still here. We've had a difficult case.'

'Oh, that's fine, as long as she's all right. Would it be possible for you to ask her – would she like me to come and pick her up?'

Waiting in silence Declan heard the sounds of bells ringing, voices calling, the sudden sound of a baby crying. Judy's world.

'Hi Dec. I'm so sorry. I just couldn't leave this family.'

'It's OK, Jude. But shall I come and pick you up? You must be shattered.'

'No, I'll be fine. But thanks. I'll be here about another hour I should think. Sorry about this.'

'No probs. See you later. Love you.'

She picked at the salad he'd prepared.

'I listened to it die, Dec. A little baby. Before it's ever lived.'

'How's the mum?'

'Distraught. Hysterical. They sedated her in the end.'

'And the dad?'

'Raging mad. Threatening us with everything he could think of.'

'And could it have been prevented?'

'I don't think so. It's natural, though. Lashing out. Wanting to blame something – someone. There'll be an investigation, of course. We always have a team conference afterwards. Pick over the bones. See if we missed anything.'

'I didn't know it would affect *you* so much – you as in the staff, I mean – not necessarily you Judy.'

'Oh, we do feel it – everybody does. You can cut the atmosphere with a knife when you walk into the place.'

'Must be hard to be cheerful for the other families in at the same time.'

'Well, we try not to have the actual staff who've been involved with the death taking on new cases during that shift. But everybody does their best not to let it affect other people. You can't spoil the best moment of their lives for the other families.'

She shivered, shrugging her cardigan around her.

'You need another hug.'

'Please.'

Declan held her tightly, his hand caressing her back, watching the shadows flicker across her face, knowing she was in a world he couldn't enter.

Judy seemed subdued all that week.

'Somebody called Dick rang. Just before you got home tonight,' Declan said lightly, ten days later.

'Ahh. Dick. I'll ring him in a mo.'

'Who is he?'

'Just a colleague. He's been nice about that death we had the other day.'

'You still struggling with that case, Jude?'

'A bit. The dad's kicking up a real stink over this one.'

'But ... *you're* OK?'

'Well, I'm implicated. It was my case. I was monitoring the baby and looking after the mum.'

'And are you anxious – about what *you* did, I mean?'

'Not in my heart of hearts. But all the questioning, it makes you anxious. You feel like everybody's watching you ... wondering. And you keep going over it all. Could I have noticed something earlier? Should I have got help sooner? That kind of thing. And you feel so sad for the parents. Even though it wasn't anybody's fault. You feel responsible because they expect you to hand them a perfect baby.'

'So ... Dick was the doctor – in charge?'

'Oh no. It was my case. He's a fertility doctor. Different department. But this couple had seen him earlier and he'd helped them to conceive, so he came to see them ... when things went wrong, you know? He's the kind of person who really cares. He was lovely to the mum. And I was there and ... well, he was nice to me, too. He understands, you know?'

'Mmhhmm.'

She made the call from the study.

'Better?' Declan asked, looking at her intently when she returned.

'Nothing's changed. He was just ringing to cheer me along.'

'That's kind.'

'Yes. He's like that though. People don't usually see that side of him. *I* didn't know he was like that ... before, I mean. Just doing things quietly – nice things. Things nobody else knows about.'

'Is this business about the baby going to go on for ages?'

'Don't know. Depends on how long the dad keeps fighting, I guess.'

'Poor old you having something like that grumbling on.'

'Poor *family*. It must be ghastly. All that time looking forward to the baby, planning, dreaming, hoping. Then wham. Nothing. And for this couple, after all these years of trying, knowing they might not get another chance ... oh, it's just grim.'

The ongoing investigation took its toll. Declan knew better than to offer hollow reassurances, but she seemed to seek affirmation of his love; she even welcomed his arms about her through the long hours of wakefulness. He clung to her need.

The sound of her laughter was the first thing Declan heard as he let himself into the house. Ahh, at last. Good news.

'Better watch it. People get clapped into the loony bin for less! …You're mad! Perfectly, stark, staring, raving mad … I'll pretend I didn't hear that! …Yeah … I couldn't have done it without you … No, seriously. You've saved my sanity these last few weeks … Yes, you are … Me, too … And you … See you tomorrow … Thanks again … I owe you, big time … OK. Bye … Bye … Watch out for the men in white coats!'

The bright trill of her giggles interspersed the words.

She was smiling broadly as she turned from the phone.

From the darkness of the kitchen Declan watched her. Whoever it was had brought a sparkle to her eyes, a spring to her step.

She started as he suddenly stepped out of the shadows.

'Oh hi! I didn't hear you come in. You're early.'

'The roads are quiet. Half-term, I suppose.'

He held out his arms and she stepped towards him. But instead of pulling her close he held her at arm's length.

'You look pleased with yourself, young lady. Good day off?'

'Average. But I'm feeling a bit smug, I must confess. Did you see I've at last cleared that bad patch down behind the holly bush? No? Looking good. Come and see.'

She made to lead him into the garden but he pulled her back.

'First things first.'

He held her gaze for a long moment. She stood perfectly still, a vaguely puzzled look lifting her eyebrows.

There was nothing unusual in her kiss.

Not until they were walking outside did he venture a casual question. 'Who was that on the phone just now?'

'Oh, just Dick. Checking I'm coping. He's a lunatic. Dah-de-daaaaaah!' She flung an arm wide. The patch of freshly dug earth was indeed a big improvement.

At the sound of her car scrunching to a halt in the drive Declan lit the candles. He stood with his back to the fireplace, wanting to see her first reaction.

She paused for a long moment, scanning the room – the roses, the wine, the decorated table.

'Have I forgotten something?' she ventured hesitantly.

'Maybe.'

'It's not a special date, is it?'

'Not that I know of.'

'You're making me nervous. What should I have remembered?'

'Come here and I'll tell you.' She advanced cautiously. He held her silently.

'Dec ... put me out of my misery. What have I forgotten?'

'How much I love you.'

'Ohhh. You had me really worried there.'

'Isn't a fellow allowed to woo his own wife these days, then?'

She suddenly buried her face in his chest and held him tightly to her. Her voice when it came sounded forlorn.

'Dec ... I said you could.'

'Hey.' His tone was bracing. 'There's no ulterior motive here! You've been a bit low since that baby died – I thought it might help. Just a nice little romantic evening. Just to remind you of how much I love you. No strings. Honestly.'

When she didn't look up he released her enough to smile at her.

'Away you go and dress for dinner, madam. I need time to rescue the potatoes and my culinary reputation from imminent incineration.'

His heart leapt in spite of his stern warnings to himself. She was wearing his favourite dress. The perfume was the one she had worn on her wedding day.

'Mmm. I'm the luckiest guy in this restaurant tonight,' he murmured as his eyes roamed over her.

'Why, thank you, sir. You're most gallant. You scrub up rather well yourself.'

The candlelight turned her eyes into huge pools of mystery. Declan found himself drowning.

He reached across the table to lay a hand over hers.

'Jude ...'

Her expression was unreadable.

He twined his fingers through hers.

His heart missed a beat. Surely not. He looked down at their interwoven hands.

'Judy?'

'Mmmhhmm?'

'Have you lost your wedding ring?'

Her startle appeared genuine. She withdrew her hand and looked at it for a long moment.

'Oh blow! I must have left it at work. I was scrubbed for a Caesarean section today. Must have left it pinned to my uniform. Never mind, it's perfectly safe, in my locker. I'll get it tomorrow.'

He fought the sinking feeling.

'I didn't know you took it off.'

'Oh yes. For theatre work. It's best to. I always do. You can't scrub effectively with rings on.'

It was perfectly understandable. A simple oversight. But he couldn't stop looking at the naked hand. And the light in her eyes seemed now to be veiled by her lashes.

All the sparkle had suddenly left the room. The roses, the candles, seemed trite, passé.

Declan joined a gym, lightly telling Judy he was determined to fight the scourge of all sedentary workers before it manifested itself. She glanced at his firm, flat stomach involuntarily but said nothing. The hard physical activity gave him an outlet for his pent-up energy and he made new friends. Competitive elements crept in and he set himself personal goals which gave added momentum to his efforts.

Warren Newton, who worked in an adjoining office for the same company as Declan, became an unexpected ally. Depressed by the recent acrimonious split from his girlfriend of fourteen years he made no secret of his need to thrash something and he was always on the lookout for a challenging opponent. His aggression made him formidable but Declan found release himself in the compulsion to win through against the odds. The two became regular sparring partners.

After a particularly gruelling game of squash they were showering when Warren suddenly and unexpectedly slid a knife into Declan's unprotected weak spot.

'You in a relationship yourself, Declan?'

'Yep. Married actually.'

'Ahhhh. Heavy duty stuff, eh? How long?'

'Four months, three weeks, five days.'

'Still counting, huh? Lucky sod.'

'But you had fourteen years.'

'Aye. Aye, I did. Never married though. My ex – well, not into official commitment, our Julie. "What's the point of a silly old bit of paper," she used to say. "You wanna be here wi' me or you don't. Simple as that."'

'You can see her point.'

'Aye. But nothing to stop her walking out when she'd had enough.'

'But a certificate wouldn't necessarily stop her either, would it?'

'Maybe not. Maybe not. But …'

A heavy silence hung over the sound of thrashing water as the two men scrubbed their weary muscles.

'How long did you live with her before you married her – your missus, I mean?' Warren called, his words echoing around the tiles.

'Actually, I didn't.'

'Blimey! No dummy run, eh?'

'Mmmmmhhhm.' Declan switched off the water viciously and grabbed his towel. 'I'm done. See you in the café. Five minutes max.'

Towelling himself vigorously he wondered what Warren would say if

26

he knew it was four months, three weeks and five days of marriage without sex. One hundred and forty-nine days. One hundred and forty-eight nights. They could commiserate, at least. But as he watched the older man weaving his way towards the bar, his sports bag swinging loosely from his broad shoulder, his right hand slapping chairs as he passed them, he knew he couldn't share the secrets of his own bedroom with anyone but Judy.

'Two coffees, black, and two doughnuts with cream,' he ordered with defiance. 'I feel a spirit of rebellion coming on!'

Warren grinned as he flung his leg over the adjoining stool.

'You'd better run all the way home then, or this last hour's been pretty pointless!'

'Oh, one of the doughnuts is for you. Can't give the enemy an advantage next time!'

'You already have the advantage. At least ten years of advantage, I'd say!'

Whether it was his youth or the increasing frustration at home, Declan did find himself winning more frequently. He began to extend his time at the gym – lunchtime visits, an additional hour on Friday evenings. It helped superficially, whacking balls, pounding the treadmill, lashing through sixty lengths of back crawl.

Georgina's visit was fleeting. She was up in Scotland visiting an exhibition of furniture from Sweden and making contacts useful for her growing business in kitchen design, but managed to fit in one free evening with her brother.

'Wow! Domestic bliss or what?' she said, leaning back in her chair and surveying the leaping flames in the hearth. 'Has he got you warming his slippers yet, Judy?'

'No. Nor ironing his newspaper.' Judy grinned back.

'Give it time. Just give it time!'

Declan leapt to his feet.

'That's right, you girls just gang up against a defenceless male, why don't you? I'm off to make some coffee. Black no sugar still, Georgina?'

'Heck! My Sunday name. Things are definitely looking ominous.'

'Despots don't fraternise with the enemy.'

Although he had no intention of eavesdropping he couldn't help overhearing Georgina's comment as he paused outside the door, balancing the tray of drinks against his hip.

'You're very good for Dec, Judy.'

'You think so? I ...'

'He's crazy about you. Nice to see. He's been a cautious Cuthbert where girls are concerned. But no question he's besotted with you!'

'Ohh.'

27

'He's the best, Dec. Deserves to be happy. I'm glad he found you.'

'OK, OK, OK,' Declan entered the room noisily. 'Stir your stumps, little sister. Not every day your big brother waits on you hand and foot.'

'Crumbs! They say every man's home is his castle but you needn't be quite such a warlord!'

The easy banter continued and it was some time later that Declan realised Judy was taking an excessively long time preparing a second pot of coffee.

He found her in the kitchen, scouring a roasting tin vigorously.

'Hey, leave that, Jude. We'll clear up later when Georgie's gone.'

When she didn't look up he moved closer.

'Jude?'

'Just give me a few minutes. I'll come through in a minute.'

He peered round to see her face and his eyes widened.

'Jude …'

'Later, Dec. Please. Not now … Georgie …'

'Later then. But *definitely*. Promise me?'

She nodded, redoubling her efforts in the sink, not looking at him.

When Judy reappeared with the coffee, there was no evidence of her earlier distress. Declan let out his breath slowly. He maintained a watchful eye but she seemed to avoid his gaze and to concentrate all her energy on entertaining her sister-in-law.

Talk soon turned to the Robertson family and Georgina regaled them with recent tales of their nieces and nephews. Declan realised with a pang how easy it was to lose touch. Since Judy had come into his life, he'd not maintained the same level of contact with the rest of the family in New Zealand. Georgina knew about the little things that brought them closer. He must make more effort.

Declan insisted he run Georgina back to her hotel but once she was in the car he whispered to Judy, 'We'll talk when I get back. Promise?'

'Promise.'

Georgina was silent as he negotiated the awkward angle out of the drive, but once on the open road conversation resumed.

'Thanks heaps, Dec. I've had a great evening.'

'Thank *you* for fitting us in to your whirlwind schedule. Super to see you.'

'It's lovely to see *you* in your home setting. Quite the family man!'

'We love the cottage. And it's great doing things together on it – making it *ours*.'

'Judy OK?'

'How d'you mean?'

'She seemed a bit subdued.'

'She's just tired. We've had a lot of late nights lately.'

'Ahhh … '

'Besides, it's not easy for her – when you and I get together.'

'I guess so.'

'I *know* so.'

Judy was sitting in the dark beside the dying fire when he returned. He flopped onto the floor beside her chair.

'What a madcap my crazy sister is! Thanks for tolerating all the nonsense. We revert to kids when we get together, I know.'

'It's nice that. The closeness.' She sounded suddenly wistful.

'But it can be overwhelming, I know. Mum was always telling us to calm it when other people were around.'

'I like to see you ... happy.'

'I *am* happy, Jude. I've got you.'

He reached across to stir the embers and throw on some sticks. They both watched in silence as the flames rekindled and curled around the half-burned log. Then Declan swivelled around to face her, taking her hands in his, looking directly into her eyes.

'But, Jude, I know something happened to upset you today. What's wrong? Tell me. I so much want you to be happy, too.'

She dropped her eyes, her jaw tightening.

'It's more than just that business with the baby dying, isn't it?'

She nodded.

'Was it Georgie? Did she say something?'

Her eyes were glued to her fingers restlessly kneading his.

'Jude? I know she can be brutal in her opinions. But she doesn't mean anything.'

'She was right though.'

'About what?'

'You deserve to be happy.'

'Did she say that? It's just Georgie. She's always been prejudiced in my favour. Clucking round like a mother hen. Thirty-one going on sixty-one at times.'

'But you do.'

'Well, I *am* happy. Did she imply I wasn't?'

'No.'

'Good. So what's the problem?'

She suddenly pulled her fingers away from his.

'Do you want a divorce?'

'What?!' The word exploded from him.

She seemed to cower back into her chair.

'Are you crazy? *Divorce*? Nothing is further from my mind.'

'I'd understand.'

'Well, I wouldn't!'

'I'm not ... a good wife for you ... you deserve better.'

'What twaddle! What on earth has Georgie been saying?'

'It's not just Georgie – I *know* I'm not. *You* know I'm not.'

'I know nothing of the kind ... unless ...' Declan sat back on his heels and took a long painful breath. 'Jude ... is there ... someone else?'

Her sudden frowning look seemed genuine.

'Someone else? What d'you mean, someone else?'

'Somebody at work maybe ... somebody who makes you feel happier ... than you are ... with me?'

'You are joking ...?' It was her turn to stare at him with an intensity that seemed to bore into his brain.

'Well ... lately I've wondered ... if you can't bear to be close to me ... maybe ...'

'Oh Dec! Noooooo!' She reached forward and took his face in both her hands. 'There isn't – there *couldn't* be – anybody else for me.'

Declan let out his breath slowly.

'Nobody could ask for a better husband than you. It's *me* – not *you* – that's the problem. That's why I have to give you the chance ... to go ... if you want to.'

'I don't *want* to go. Ever. I love you, Jude. I want to spend the rest of my life with you.'

'But ...' She broke off, her forced calm deserting her suddenly.

He gathered her close.

'But nothing, you goose. Oh, you don't know how good it feels hearing you say that.'

'It's not because I can't bear *you* ...' She broke off on a quivering breath.

'Then that's OK.'

'But it's *not* OK. I know it's not. But I can't ... I just can't ...'

'Listen. I know you can't bear the thought of sex. But as long as you really do *love* me, I can deal with that. It doesn't stop me wanting to be with you. I love you for who you are, not because of what you do for me.'

'But I know *you* want to ...' She couldn't even say it.

'Yes. Of course you do. And I've never denied it. I want you. All of you. Sometimes I admit I'm struggling. Sometimes I think I'll go mad! Heck, sometimes the punching bag at the gym thinks I *have* gone mad! I blame you entirely. You shouldn't be so gorgeous.' He gave her an affectionate shake. 'But no matter how much I have of you I'd still want more.'

'But not to give you ... anything ...'

'You give me plenty. OK, yes, I want more. But just because I want you, doesn't mean I'm going to make you do something that's obviously distasteful for you. Nor does it mean I want a divorce unless I get what I want. So put that little notion right out of your mind.'

'You could get an annulment ...'

'I don't *want* an annulment! We're married. You're my wife.'

'But I'm *not* ...'

'Technically all right, maybe not. But this is between you and me. Nothing to do with anybody else. So if *we* regard ourselves as husband and wife that's the end of the matter.'

'But I know it's not fair on you.'

'I'll live. I just wish – well, sometimes I wish you weren't *quite* so … tempting …' His voice thickened. 'More rounds with Warren Newton called for – heck, I'll be thrashing him every game soon! More cold showers on the agenda! Might even send off for a hairshirt!'

Instead of smiling she crumpled into the chair. He pulled her forward and cradled her against his shoulder, waiting.

'Hey, I'm only teasing you.'

She mumbled something against his jumper.

'Uhhm? Didn't catch that.'

'I think you should just … do it anyway.'

'What …? Divorce you? No way!'

'No … have … sex.'

'Nope. That is not an option in my book. Georgie might call me a Victorian despot but *you* should know better. It has to be what we *both* want.'

'I'm so … sorry.' Her voice died away in a choked whisper.

'Jude, this is obviously a big issue for you. I wish, I really do wish, you could tell me what it is that troubles you. But I know – I can see – it's too painful. If you can't tell *me*, could you talk to somebody else – a counsellor or somebody? Maybe somebody at work? Just to help *you* with it, I mean. You needn't tell them … about *us*, I mean. Not if you don't want to.'

'I *can't*. I can't talk about it.' She was choking on the thought.

'Fair enough. It was just an idea. I hate to see you so upset.'

There was a long silence. Declan stroked the hair tickling his chin.

'Can I say something?'

'Uhhuhh.'

'The thing that hurts me most is that you still don't seem to trust me. It kills me seeing you all screwed up over on your edge of the bed as if you're afraid I'll pounce on you if you so much as relax a muscle. I've told you, I've *shown* you, I won't. It would make all the difference if you'd just let me hold you, love you. If I felt you were happy just being near me. If you trusted me.'

'I *am*, Dec. I *do*! And I *do* like being near you.' She wriggled close, throwing her arms around his neck. 'I really do. I love being close to you.'

'But not in bed, not undressed.'

Silence again.

'If I promise … on my honour … on my life … on anything you like … not to take advantage of you, couldn't you just let me hold you?'

'It doesn't seem fair.'

'If *I* think I can handle it, isn't that a good enough reason to give it a whirl?'

'It would be worse if I … encouraged you … and then I wouldn't …'

'But it's *me* encouraging *you*. Just let's be as close as we can be. As close as you feel safe with. I'll let you know if it's too much my end. If I start taking more than six cold showers a night we'll review the situation!'

'Well … if you're sure.'

FIVE

She was lying fast asleep in his arms when the sudden shriek woke him. A midnight marauder. Cats seemed to be multiplying in their neighbourhood. A violent hissing sounded close by. Then silence.

He looked across at her without moving. In the faint light her skin looked ghostly pale, almost translucent. He watched her breathing, rising … falling, rising … falling, so evenly. Her right leg was warm and soft against his thigh. It had taken time and several false starts but gradually she'd learned to relax and a new closeness had grown between them at night. Suspicion nagged less viciously. But he stepped up the pace at the gym until even Warren cried out for mercy: 'Blimey, mate, for a quiet bloke you're an aggressive beggar in shorts!'

She turned in her sleep and her trapped nightdress pulled tightly across her chest. He reached across instinctively to release it but instantly snatched his hand away. He dragged his eyes up to her face. How trusting she looked in repose.

After a few minutes he eased his arm from beneath her, slid out of bed and moved across to stare out of the window. Two wide amber eyes glared back at him from the garden. That tortoiseshell from three doors away – far too comfortable on their territory. He shook his fist at it. It didn't even blink.

He heard the rustle of the duvet as she turned in the bed but resolutely kept his back to her.

Suddenly and without warning, her breath was whispering against his neck. Her arms slid around his waist from behind. He drew in his breath sharply.

'You all right?' she murmured, resting her cheek against his back as if she was only half awake.

'Uhhuh. That blessed cat from number forty-two woke me. It doesn't even have the grace to scuttle off when you threaten it these days.'

'Mmmm.'

She snuggled against him, her breasts softly crushed against his back. He stood perfectly still, holding his breath, feeling her hands sliding over his skin … glancing over his nipples … down over his abdomen … softly, tentatively …

He closed his eyes. It was what he'd asked for … tenderness, love, closeness. The surge of excitement made his throat constrict.

'Jude … Go easy.'

He guided her hands back up to his waist, stepping away from her.

'Come back to bed, Dec,' she whispered, pulling him back against her body.

'I can't ...'

She nestled closer.

'Judy ... This is too ... I'm only human ...'

He wrenched himself out of her clasp and backed away towards the door.

'For goodness sake,' he ground out. 'You just aren't playing fair. I'm not made of *stone*. I can't take much more of this.'

Without waiting for her response he strode to the door, slamming it behind him and took the stairs two at a time.

It was dark in the study but he didn't pause to turn on the light. Kicking the door shut behind him, he dropped heavily into the swivel chair. His fingers clenched in his unruly hair.

The slight noise of the door handle turning arrested all movement but he didn't look up.

'Dec?'

He held his breath.

'Dec ... please.'

'You can come in ... I haven't blown my brains out.' Declan recoiled from the harshness of his own words.

'I'm sorry. I didn't mean ...'

'I know. You never *mean* to. But you just don't seem to have any idea what you're doing to me.'

'But ... I wanted to ...'

'Please, Judy. Just leave me alone for now. I need space. I need to sort things out in my head. Please. You go back to bed.'

He already knew she felt guilty. He didn't need to hear it again.

There was silence.

He didn't look round. He daren't look round. But not until he heard her footsteps overhead did he let out his breath.

The seething emotions mocked his efforts at rational thought.

I promised her! I *promised*! If she can't trust me, what use am I to her? What kind of a hell are we creating?

What if he had stayed ... and started ...? A vivid picture of her frozen expression made him recoil into the chair, a powerful shudder running through his body. It would be tantamount to rape.

When he woke it was almost eight o'clock. A shaft of light lay in a pencil strip across the desk where his head rested on his cramped arms. For a moment he remained motionless, the gradual realisation of discomfort inching through his brain. Memory flooded in like a torrent of flood water.

He scraped back the chair. He must go to her. What must she be thinking?

The plain postcard was propped on the kitchen table.

Dec: On an early shift. PLEASE, PLEASE don't leave me. I love you so much. I'll do anything you want. PLEASE. J XXX

Declan slammed his hand hard against his head.

The midwife who answered his first call was apologetic.

'I'm afraid she's already in with a mum. Is it urgent? I don't like to call her out – the lady's close to delivery.'

'OK, thanks. I'll try later.'

It was almost impossible to keep his mind on work but scheduled meetings kept him fully occupied until eleven thirty. The hospital switchboard took even longer to reply.

'I'm sorry, Judy Robertson's in theatre,' the unknown voice said. 'With an emergency section. May I ask who's calling? ... Could it wait? ... Can I give her a message?'

'Could you tell her ... just say her husband rang? Please.'

The third attempt at two thirty gave him an impatient voice. Labour Suite was 'going like a fair'. Judy Robertson? She didn't know. Probably attending another delivery. They could give her a message. When there was a lull.

'No, it's OK, thanks. I'll see her at home.'

The hours ground painfully by for the rest of his day. He lost an hour of unsaved work by absently hitting the wrong key. He snapped at the secretary who innocently asked twice for his contribution to the Christmas night out. He was out of the door on the stroke of five thirty, not even stopping to rinse out his mug – and that in spite of last week's circular about the cleaning staff's rebellion. Mercifully the car started first time – it had begun ageing protests about the cold of late. And, he thought ruefully, it had every right to hit back after this morning's uncalled-for kick to a hub cap.

He wove carefully out of the car park through the mocking fairy-lights the admin staff had strung round the pillars, but once on the bypass he put his foot down with uncharacteristic force. The sudden need to brake made the seatbelt saw painfully against his collarbone. With mounting impatience he craned to see what was causing the hold-up but for mile after mile there was nothing but cars, stationary or crawling, without explanation. He jerked on the radio. After twenty minutes of the local news he was none the wiser.

An hour passed. Then another. Over and over again he cursed himself for leaving his mobile phone at home. Today of all days.

The accident was clearly serious. Twisted wreckage still littered the carriageway when Declan eventually inched his car through. Four police vehicles and two ambulances cordoned off the victims.

He found her in the study, ashen faced, shivering in the chair he had vacated only that morning.

'Jude. Jude, darling …'

Dropping to his knees he gathered her into his arms.

'Oh Dec … I thought …' The hoarse whisper shrivelled into silent heaving sobs.

'I'm so, so sorry. I forgot my mobile. There was an accident on the bypass.'

'I thought …'

'I know. But there was no way I could let you know.'

'After … last night …'

'I know. Jude, can you ever forgive me? I've been beating myself up all day. I can't *believe* I fell asleep and spent the rest of the night in the study! I went crazy when I woke up and found you'd already left for work. And I hadn't even explained. I rang the hospital four times. They said you were busy.'

'I thought … they said … they only said … you'd rung …'

'Well, come on,' Declan said in a rallying tone, leaning back to look at her, 'I couldn't very well say, tell my wife I'm not leaving her, could I? Imagine how much explaining you'd have had to do then?!'

He looked for an answering smile. Instead she shrank away from him.

'Jude! You weren't serious? You surely didn't seriously think …? Good grief … you … did …'

Declan suddenly got to his feet and reached down to pull her out of the chair. His hands cupped her face for a long moment as he stared down into her eyes.

'I just don't understand what's going on in that head of yours. We've got to get to the bottom of this. But right now, you feel frozen. How long have you been sitting here in the cold?'

She shrugged her shoulders.

'Well, come through into the kitchen. You need a hot drink.'

She sat huddled in the rocking chair, unmoving, staring at the kettle as if it was dependent on her energy to boil the water.

Declan cast furtive glances at her as he busied himself preparing the drinks but made no effort to say anything until she had drained the mug and stopped trembling. Then he dragged his own chair across the hearth until it was directly facing hers.

'Now then, Jude. I'm not moving until you tell me exactly what's going on here.'

'I thought … you'd left me.'

'For goodness sake … why on earth would I *leave* you?'

'You said … you couldn't take … any more.'

'Last night … ahhhhh! Jude. I'm so, so sorry. I didn't mean to speak to you like that.' Her eyes seemed enormous in the half-light. Declan hitched his chair even closer and leaned forward to take both her hands in his. 'It was just … Your nearness, your kisses … your hands … It was tearing me apart, Jude. It was hard enough seeing you lying there in bed – that's why I got up in the first place. But then when you started … It was heaven … it was hell … I don't know. I was just so tempted. I wanted you *so much* I very nearly … Jude, can you forgive me? Jude?'

'It's my fault, not yours.'

'No! I *promised*. On everything sacred. I promised you. And I almost broke that promise last night.'

'But I *wanted* you to.'

'Don't, please. Don't try to let me off the hook. We agreed. I don't know what's really going on in your head but you've let me know without a shadow of a doubt, sex is a big no-no for you. I have to respect that. What kind of a husband would I be if I forced you into something you hate? You'd end up hating *me*. And I couldn't bear that.'

'I won't, Dec. Not now.'

'I can't take that risk. But it's my problem. *I* have to sort it out. I was the one who encouraged you to be close to me at night. I have to find a way of dealing with it. I don't know yet how I'll handle it. But I will. I just need time.'

'You … won't … just leave?' It was scarcely audible.

'Where is this coming from?' Declan stared into her face, her huge eyes like gimlets boring into his, searching, haunted. 'I. HAVE. ABSO-LUTELY. NO. INTENTION. OF. LEAVING. YOU. I love you, Jude. For goodness sake, I love you so much you're driving me crazy! Why would I *leave* you? Hey, you can't get rid of me that easily, young woman!'

'Will you hold me?'

'Of course I will. Come here.' He stood up and pulled her close against him.

The sudden shrilling of the phone made her move back.

'Leave it. Nothing is more important than this,' he said.

The dishwasher needed to be emptied. There were papers to assemble for tomorrow's meetings. A late programme on an ongoing pension debacle would be a useful way to gen up on new financial developments. It was easy to find legitimate excuses to delay going up to bed.

Judy seemed to be fast asleep when he slid warily beneath the duvet.

He took long slow breaths, keeping his eyes shut, willing his racing thoughts towards safety.

It had been an exhausting day after very little sleep. His body ached for rest; his mind denied it solace.

'Am I allowed to hold you?' The whisper came from far away.

'Jude … I just … don't know any more.'

'If I just put my arm around you …' She didn't wait for permission. Declan lay perfectly still.

'I need to explain … Dec, you have to believe me.'

'All right. Try me. But just stay still. Like this. OK?'

'At first … I was so scared. But lately … since you helped me to be close to you … in bed, I mean. Well, lately it's changed. I want you … so much. These feelings … I just ache for you. Dec, will you … now?'

Declan felt a choking sensation.

'This is because you're still afraid I'm going to leave you. I'm not. Really, I'm not.'

'I *knew* you'd think that. I knew it.'

'You've had a fright today – two frights – last night too.'

'It's not that. Last night … it was deliberate … I *tried* to make you want me … I *wanted* you to …'

'Jude, you're still too mixed up about everything. You have to trust me if it's ever going to work. What if we start … and then you change your mind? Oh, it's all too fraught.'

'It's not fraught … not if you want me as much as I want you … it's just … natural.'

'*If* I want you! Heavens above, girl! Don't throw that one at me!'

'Please, Dec … please.'

She inched closer and he held his breath.

'It's partly why I was so miserable last night. I felt … rejected. I wanted you so much. But you wouldn't listen.'

Flopping over onto his front he lifted himself up on his elbows, staring down at her.

'I have to be brutal here, Jude. Look at me. I'm going to put on the side light. Ready?'

She blinked rapidly and he waited until her gaze was unwavering.

'Tell me again … looking into my eyes … why you've suddenly changed your mind.'

'Because I love you … Because I want you … so much … there's no other way I can show you how much.'

He stared still.

'And because my body aches for you.'

'Really? Truly?'

'Really, truly, and … Oh, you *have* to believe me.'

When he still made no move, she suddenly sat up and dragged her nightie over her head, dropping it on the floor. She slid over until her face was under his.

'Please. I won't change my mind. I know I won't.'

Without taking his eyes from her body he reached across to switch off the light.

'Help me, Jude. Show me what you want,' he said hoarsely.

Afterwards they lay in the darkness, neither moving, neither speaking. The first blush of dawn was staining their sheets pink when Declan stirred. Memory rushed down the receding valley of his dreams. Without moving he glanced across at her ... long lashes sweeping her cheek, one hand tucked under her face, her shoulders relaxed in sleep ... bare shoulders ... He let out his breath slowly. It was no dream.

When he finally awoke it was well into the morning. He emerged slowly to the softest of touches. She was leaning on one elbow, trickling one finger over his chest.

'Dec, you'll never know how much I owe you. But one day – soon – I'll try to tell you. I owe you that, I know.'

'You don't owe me anything. Last night cancelled any debt you might have *felt* you owed. But hey, if you feel like making further payment ...'

They melted down under the covers and lost all sense of time.

SIX

But the promise borne of her happiness showed no sign of being fulfilled in the ensuing days and weeks. Declan made no reference to it. It no longer mattered.

Twice she started to tell him.

On the first occasion she was lying across his lap one Sunday evening. They had just finished watching a video and the light had faded naturally, leaving the room almost in darkness.

'Dec,' she began tentatively.

'Uhhmmm?' His fingers traced her contours.

'I need to tell you …'

'Tell me what? Is it urgent? Could it wait … perhaps an hour or two …'

'I need to explain … why I couldn't …'

Catching sight of her face he was instantly contrite. 'Sorry. My mind's on other things. I'm listening. Take your time.'

Wrapping his arms around her, he faced her squarely.

'I … it was … I was only …' she began.

The trembling grew in intensity. Declan tightened his hold.

'Take your time. I'm not going anywhere.'

Silent sobs shook her whole body.

'Ssshhhh. It doesn't matter, Jude. As long as you're sure it's OK between us … you know … You are … *sure* … aren't you? You're not just saying it?'

'Oh yes! You make it … so … so …'

Great barren sobs were wrenched from some fathomless waste.

'Sshhhh. Ssssshhhh. Don't distress yourself about it. Sssshhhh. It's all over now. You're fine. We're fine, now.'

By the time he had quietened her terror he was in no hurry to return to a subject that brought such a violent reaction.

Quietly, steadily, they adjusted to their new happiness. The shadows receded in Declan's heart. He began to relax and little by little the old teasing returned.

He spent more time at home, less at the gym, and their efforts to renovate the cottage took giant leaps forward. A favourite room was the second bedroom with its deep terracotta walls and reclaimed timber. The day the curtains were hung they stood together in the doorway admiring the finished product.

'We make a winning team I think, Mrs Robertson.'

'Indeed we do. What shall we call ourselves? Robertson and Robertson Limited: Interior Designers?'

'Sounds pretty good to me. You were right about this colour. Perfect choice for the light on this aspect of the house.'

'Maybe we should take over this room in the autumn.'

'What's happening in the autumn?'

'No, I meant just because the colours will be brilliant in the autumn light.'

'Oh, I thought for one minute you meant ... it was your way of telling me you might be pregnant.'

She laughed.

'Nope.'

He gave her a sudden hug.

'What was that for?' she asked, looking at him curiously.

'Oh, do I have to have a reason to hug my wife nowadays?'

'No. But there was a reason.'

'You are getting to know me too well for my peace of mind.'

'And ...?'

'Well, since you insist ... I was just remembering a time when I thought there was no danger you'd ever be pregnant. And feeling so lucky now.' He reached out to draw her against him, rubbing his cheek softly against her hair.

'I'm the lucky one. Lucky that you didn't give up on me.'

'Not a chance. I know when I've found what I want.'

'And children? You do still want children?'

'One day. But we agreed not for at least two years, remember?'

'That was before ...'

'Before we were married, yes, I know.'

'No, I meant before I ... gave you such a hard time.'

'Well, if you're going to give me another hard time maybe I should just crack on while I can,' he said, sliding his hands over her hips.

She resisted his efforts to turn her to face him.

'I won't, Dec. That's over.'

'Is it, sweetheart? Quite over?'

'Except for telling you ...'

'You don't need to. It's enough for me that everything is OK between us.'

'It is, Dec. More than OK. You know it is. But I *have* to explain why I was ... like that ... I have to tell you.'

'Well, if you must. When you're ready.'

'There's never a right time. It will always ... spoil things.' The words seemed to strangle in her throat.

'Then let's not spoil this moment of glory. After all the hard work, you just enjoy looking at another room completed by Robertson and Robertson Limited to our entire satisfaction.'

'I do love this colour. And shall we? Shall we sleep in here some time? Just try it out?'

'This sounds like a proposition I'd be an idiot to pass up on!' he murmured in a sultry voice in her ear.

'If you think I'm going to fall for that old line you've got another think coming,' she retorted with feigned affront and twisted out of his arms before darting from the room. He shot after her and the ensuing chase left the last vestiges of her pain far behind.

They lay in the massive four-poster bed listening to the silence outside. The complete absence of sound made Declan want to hold his breath. He let it out noiselessly.

It had been a perfect weekend, a spur of the moment decision to take up a special offer of three nights in a retreat in the Lake District, far from the bustle of tourist attractions and busy commuters. They'd gone for long walks, swum lazily in the hotel pool, fooled around at crazy golf and lost themselves within the great brocade drapes of the ornate bed.

'Dec,' her voice came to him haltingly.

'Mmhmm?'

'Will you hold me very tight.'

'*Again?* No problem!'

He slid his body over hers.

'No, not in that way – not yet – just hold me tight. I need to feel safe.'

He moved to lie beside her, arms around her.

'This time I *must*, Dec. I must tell you. If we're ever to have children I must tell you first. Before we try for a baby.'

'OK, sweetheart. If you must.'

'I need you to be strong for me. Don't let me give up. Please, Dec. *Please.*'

'All right, Jude. I hear you.'

'Even if I get upset. Promise me! Promise you won't stop me?'

'Promise. I'll do my best, anyway. Take your time. I'm here. You're perfectly safe.'

Gone now the soft curving into his body, the thrill of intertwined limbs. She lay stiffly, straight out in the bed, legs clenched together, upper arms rigid across her chest. Her fingers pulled at a paper handkerchief. Declan felt her taking gulping breaths of air.

Her staccato voice was devoid of emotion.

'I must have been … about eleven when … when it started. The first time he just came into the bathroom when I was in the bath. He just sat on the toilet talking to me. He said he would help me dry but I didn't want him to. And I said so. So he left. After that I locked the door.'

The tissue was in two pieces. Still her fingers shredded.

'Then one night I woke up and he was … he was sitting on my bed.

42

He'd turned the bedclothes down and he was just staring ... at my ... breasts. You know, they'd just started to develop. As soon as I woke I snatched the bedclothes up and wrapped myself in them. He made some feeble excuse about making sure I was tucked up. But I knew. Even at that age, I knew.'

Declan tightened his hold, fearful of what was to come but every instinct reaching out to protect and comfort her.

'Then one night ... Oh Dec, hold me, hold me! I need to tell you but ... it's so hard ... I don't want you to ...'

'Take your time, darling. I'm here. I'm not going anywhere. Take as long as you need.'

He held his breath, waiting.

'Mum was out at the Christmas do for one of her societies. I'd gone to bed but I was reading, wanted to finish off a book I was nearly through. Dad came in and he ... he ... got into bed beside me. I shouted at him, but he turned it into a joke – you know, like families do. He tickled me, tried to make me laugh. Then he said he knew a better game. It was a lot of fun but it was a secret game. He started to feel my breasts and he ... he ... rubbed himself ... against my leg.'

Judy shredded the remains of the handkerchief and reached for another. Declan lay silent, stroking her hair as he might a child who had woken from a bad dream. His heart seemed to him to be pounding in his chest so loudly Judy would surely be distracted. But she was lost in her nightmare.

'In the end I kicked him till he got out. Then he said ... I remember every word ... he said: "Remember, don't tell Mummy. It's our secret and if you tell Mummy, Daddy will go away for ever and ever, and there'll be nobody to love Daddy's little Princess. Nobody loves his Princess like Daddy does."'

The silence seemed interminable.

'It was several weeks before it started again. Mum was usually around so he didn't have much opportunity, I suppose. But the next time he said Mum had sent him to have a talk with me about the birds and the bees. He told me about the birds and the bees all right – but he *showed* me too ... you know. I was only a kid. I wanted to be sick. I made an excuse and went to the loo and stayed there for ages. But he was waiting for me when I got back and he started again telling me all the details and showing me how it worked and everything. He said fathers were supposed to tell their children ... and show them ... that's how they learned. And always, always he said if I didn't let him do these things he'd leave and nobody would love me.'

Declan cradled her as she wept.

When she was still again she continued between sobs.

'He never actually ... you know ... raped me or anything. But he ... touched me ... and once he made me touch him. But I screamed and

cried and he must have known he couldn't risk that again. I remember
that time he said it was OK, he wasn't really my Dad, he was my lover, so
it was OK for us to do things that real dads and daughters shouldn't do. I
was his Princess. Lovers could do anything and it was OK. He'd look after
me always and protect me because he was my lover.'

Shivers shook her whole body and Declan pulled the covers closer around
them both.

'Then when I was just turned thirteen he came in the middle of the
night. He must have thought Mum was safely asleep. I was – asleep, I
mean – but I woke up when he got into my bed and I started to cry and
beg him not to. I didn't want it to start again. Mum must have heard me
crying and she came to see what was wrong.

'When she found him there and ... and ... you know ... naked, aroused
... she went totally white. I remember thinking she was going to die standing there. It was like seeing something in slow motion – the life was just
draining out of her. Then she just said – and I can see her now, her teeth
were gritted – and she just said, "Get out!" And ... well, he did. And he
looked pathetic really. He was gone by the morning and I never saw him
again. She never talked about it. The only thing she said to me was ... it
was next morning, she didn't even turn round from the sink when I went
into the kitchen. She just said, "Judith, I want you to forget what happened. Just put it out of your mind. And don't tell a living soul about it.
He'll never hurt you again. He won't be coming back." She never ever
spoke about it again. Nor did I. And I never did tell anybody about it ...
until now. Oh Dec, I'm sorry, I'm so sorry.'

A fresh wave of anguished sobs wracked her body. Declan rocked and
soothed.

'*You?* Why should *you* be sorry? You poor darling. And carrying that
burden all these years.'

'But I feel so ... so ... *soiled!*'

He tried in vain to still the shuddering.

'And I know ... I hurt you – when I wouldn't – couldn't let you near
me.'

'Well, I'm not surprised you couldn't! It must have triggered appalling
memories.'

He held her close for a long time in silence.

'So *that's* why you pulled away ... before we were married, too,' Declan
said slowly, remembering.

'But I thought ... once we were married, it'd be different. I loved you so
much. I just never expected ... those awful feelings to rush over me when
you touched me. They just sort of wiped out everything else.'

'Oh, I wish you'd told me! All those months ... thinking you were
repulsed by *me.*'

'It was never *that!*'

'But that's what it felt like.'

'I'm so, so sorry.'

'I don't really understand, though – after all that time – what made it all right in the end?' Declan asked.

'Two things really. Well, *three* I suppose. First of all, you showed me that you loved me – whatever. I didn't have to do things I didn't want to do. It was unconditional. And then when you held me, loved me, especially at night, when we were close, you made me want you more and more. And then in the end, *I* came to *you*. I initiated it. That made it different. You see, it was too much like ... those other times ... at first ... when you got into bed beside me, you being naked, when you moved against me, when you touched me, in *that* way. It all reminded me – of my *father* coming to me and starting those things.'

'Of course. It would. If only I'd known. We could have saved ourselves so much heartache, so much doubt.'

'I couldn't – I *couldn't* tell you. I thought you'd be so disgusted. I thought you'd leave me.'

'Ah, that's another thing. What's all this stuff about me leaving you? I've never understood that, either.'

'That was my Dad, too. That's what he said. If you don't do what they want, men do go away. They don't love you. And I thought that *was* true. Other men – there haven't been many – but the ones I have dated, well, they've usually tried to rush things and I've just gone all frozen and ... well, they don't hang around, do they?'

The jigsaw was falling into place.

'You were different. From the beginning. You told me: no sex. Nothing. You never tried anything. I felt safe.'

She struggled with her thoughts during the long agonising silence.

'And even when we were married – when you could have insisted – we *should* have – you accepted that I wasn't ready. You didn't try to force me. Or even persuade me. I counted. What *I* wanted counted. You promised you *wouldn't* go away. You showed me my Dad was wrong. Lovers don't leave if they don't get what they want. You *did* still love me. You *didn't* go away. Oh, it all sounds so childish ...'

'No, it's not. It makes perfect sense. I understand what you mean. But Jude ... bless you for finding the courage to tell me now. It's better that I know.'

'I *had* to – for *you* as well as for me. For us. I see now, I should have told you from the beginning. But I ... just *couldn't*.'

Occasional sobs still caught in her throat as she tried to continue.

'It's daft, I know, but I feel so ... *responsible*. If I hadn't cried that night, if I'd just done ... what he wanted ... he wouldn't have gone away. We would have been a family. Mum wouldn't be on her own now. It was my fault he went away.'

'It was *not* your fault. He was entirely to blame. He was abusing your trust and his position. No, whatever else, you were completely innocent. He brought it on himself.'

'I wish I could believe that *in my heart*. But … I think I can live with it now … now you know why I was so afraid to let you near me. I just hated you thinking it was because I didn't want *you*.'

'Jude, can I ask you again? Now we're being brutally honest – is it *really* OK – making love, I mean – now? You're not just saying it to make me happy?'

'OK? No, it's not *OK*. It's just … *magic*! I wanted to tell you, that first time, when we just lay there – afterwards. I didn't want to move. I wanted us to be that close always. Before … I had to scrub myself … I felt so … *dirty*.' She shuddered. 'But *this*' – her arms slid along his back – 'oh Dec, I can't tell you. It feels so *right*.'

He held her close.

'But now I do know – well, you know I'd never deliberately hurt you, but I can see I might do something – inadvertently. So please, *please* tell me. You know I shall always love you, *never* go away. Whatever.'

'I will. Promise.' She snuggled up against him with a drawn-out sigh. 'It hurts, Jude, when you shut me out.'

'Oh Dec, I'm so, so sorry. Forgive me.'

He stopped her words and her breath as he crushed her fiercely against his chest.

After a long silence she began again.

'Dec, I need you to understand. You know what happened now, but it *isn't* over. I've read stacks of books on abuse since, and I thought I'd sorted most of it out in my mind. But there are these guilty feelings, buried inside me somewhere. And they just bob up – unexpectedly. When I'm not looking. And I know I've probably still got heaps of confused feelings about sex and families and trust and, well, all kinds of things.'

'I'm not surprised!'

'No, but you see, I thought they'd gone. I thought I'd got the old stuff out of my system. I felt so safe with you. Then – well, our wedding night, it took me by surprise. Perhaps I never will entirely get rid of it. And when those old feelings came flooding in … I just hated feeling that again so I … well, I tried to avoid … a … situation … anything … that might start it up again.'

'Like my being close to you in bed.'

'Mmmm. I didn't want those horrible feelings to spoil what we have.'

'They can't. Not where it matters. We both know – those other things – they've nothing to do with what *we* have – with *this*.' He enveloped her again in a strong embrace.

'This is the best therapy for a damaged girl that anyone could ever ask for!' With that, Judy curled her body into his and wrapped her arms tightly around him.

'Hmmm. Never heard it called therapy before!' he teased gently.

Desire stirred within him as they lay silently in the great bed, their bodies speaking a language that needed no words. It would always be a marvel to him. After all the months of doubt and suspicion, he would never take it for granted.

But somewhere in the darkest recesses of his mind a sneering voice mocked his efforts. Could the spectre of her father ever really be erased?

He pulled the bedding up over their heads, obliterating all light.

SEVEN

It was three weeks before their second wedding anniversary. Arriving home from work, he caught her in his arms and whirled her round until her feet left the ground.

'We're going away to celebrate two whole years together,' he informed her, breathless from the effort.

'I thought you'd forgotten!'

'Forgotten? Me? For shame, Judith Robertson. As if!'

'Where? Where are we going?'

'Far from the madding crowd! It'll be a sort of second honeymoon.'

'What do I need? What should I pack?'

'Oh, a toothbrush!'

'And what sort of clothes? Is it somewhere hot? Cold? Here? Abroad?'

'Warmish. Abroad. Oh, you don't need anything exotic. Just a few odds and ends – nothing much. Walking boots. But there again …' – his grin was lopsided – 'maybe that skimpy black number I liked you in at Christmas time! Mmmmmm, yep, slip in a bit of glamour. I want to be tantalised, bewitched, *slain* by your charms!'

'Befuddled and zonked by the booze sounds more like it!' she retorted.

The gîte he had booked in Vézelois, on the French border, gave them easy access into Switzerland. They drove through the majesty of the Ballon des Vosges mountains. They browsed among curiosities, dowsed their tired feet in fountains, giggled through wild pronunciations of the local names, and tried out their rusty French in the local baker's.

They discovered a quaint little German-run restaurant not far from the gîte, and booked a table tucked away in the corner of the courtyard for their evening meal. They spoke little, preferring instead to intertwine fingers across the table, raising their glasses in an unspoken toast. Romance was in the very air of this place.

At night there were no sounds, no street lights, nothing to distract them from each other.

It was Declan who broke the silence of their second night. His fingers played with the soft curls at her temple.

'Jude?'

'Mmm?'

'What about babies?'

'What about them?'

'Remember we said two years? Then we'd think about children?'

'I remember.'

'D'you still want that?'

Judy snuggled closer against his neck.

'More than ever. Having *your* baby – holding it inside me, loving it, caring for it – that would be a perfect sequel to our love. For me. What about you?'

'Me too. I want so much to have a baby with you.'

'And you are so good with kids. You'll be a brilliant Dad.'

'I was wondering – just wondering – if we could maybe try this week? Only if it feels right to you, though. No pressure. If it worked it'd be a ... well, sort of a symbol – of everything this week stands for. Am I being soppy?'

Judy leaned back to look deep into his eyes.

'Soppy? No. Romantic? Yes. Impossibly so. I can't think of anything more wonderful to commemorate all this. Every time we looked at him – or her – we'd remember.'

'It might not work, of course, don't know how fertile we are!' he grinned.

'Virility will do for me right now! Fertility, well, that's in the lap of the gods.'

It seemed the gods were on their side when Judy missed her next period. She bought a kit and locked herself in the bathroom while she did the test. Declan sat on the edge of the bed, feeling suddenly breathless. His eyes flew to her face when she emerged but her look was inscrutable.

'*You* do it. Here's a new kit,' she begged, not daring to watch him.

He was silent as he walked across the room to where she stood with her back to him, hands up to her face.

'Bingo, Mrs Robertson,' he whispered in her ear, sliding his arms around her to place his hands over her abdomen. 'Somewhere deep in there a miracle has begun.'

Four months of constant nausea and frequent bouts of vomiting left her feeling permanently exhausted. She grew weary of everyone telling her how ill and tired she looked. Didn't she think it would be a good idea to give up working full time now she had the responsibility of a home and a husband? Was she working too hard on renovating the cottage? Shouldn't she go to the doctor? She probably needed a tonic.

'Any chance you might be pregnant?' Tess, her best friend, was the only one to ask directly.

'I see enough of squalling infants in my job, thank you very much, not to want to introduce them into my home life!' she retorted.

'But I guess it'd be different if it was your own kid and you loved the little beggar?' Tess persisted.

'Maybe. Maybe. Best to wait till they come in self-assembly packs, I think!'

'Yep, best way. Off the shelf in a plastic bag! No varicose veins or heart-burn. No pain. Ready weaned and potty trained!'

Their giggles relieved the moment of tension. If Tess continued to sus-pect she kept it to herself.

The nausea vanished suddenly at the beginning of the fifth month. Judy started to bloom. The reason became obvious. Declan repeatedly told her how alluring her pregnant body was to him. Together, excitedly, they prepared for parenthood.

Once she could tolerate the smell of paint Judy threw herself into decorating the nursery. Betty was the first visitor. Judy flung the door wide with an extravagant flourish, loving the impact of the delicate white drapes of the cot against the deep blues and purples they'd chosen for the walls and curtains. Her mother's reaction took her by surprise.

'Hmmm. Looks a bit like a setting for a royal baby! Sort of thing you see in glossy magazines.'

'Well, he … she'll be every bit as precious as any princess,' Judy retorted swiftly.

The force of the constriction in her stomach doubled her up. There was no warning.

'What is it? What's happened? What's wrong?' Betty was all flustered concern.

'It's OK, Mum. Honest. Just a spasm.' Judy tried to sound calm. She made her excuses and went to the bathroom, locking the door and sinking down onto the floor.

Princess. Daddy's Princess. The word, her own word. But how bitter the memories cascading through her thoughts. They were still there. Sub-merged most of the time maybe, but there. Lurking. Waiting. No, she couldn't – she *mustn't* – let herself dwell on that. Not now. Declan's love had healed so much. She owed it to him. To his child.

By the time she emerged she was herself again to all outward appearances. She forced herself to sit with her mother, knitting a shawl; her mother crocheting a coat for this, her first grandchild. But today the shadow loomed unnaturally large between them. Did her mother assume she had forgotten?

'Tell me about my birth, Mum. You've never really talked about that.' Judy tried to open up safe ground.

'It was a long labour. Thirty-six hours. I was just glad when it was all over,' her mother said, counting stitches.

'Did you love me at first sight like they say? I know it doesn't always happen – lots of the mums I see say they're quite disappointed at first. And too exhausted!' Judy smiled.

'I think I did actually. You looked just like my sister Helen. And she was always a favourite.'

'Did you see any of Dad's side of the family – then, at first?' Judy took a tentative step onto eggshell.

'Never. You were always a Laidlaw.' It was a clear do-not-continue-with-this-point reply.

'Was I an easy baby? Did I feed well?' Judy rushed on. 'I wish I had a pound for every mum I've helped who was told breastfeeding is natural, you won't have any problems if you do it the right way, but who's then had to struggle to get going. I'm going into *that* with my eyes well and truly opened anyway.'

'Well, actually you were good. Sucked well from the beginning. It was nice that bit. I liked the feeling of … being close. Being needed.' Betty's voice had softened. She had stopped crocheting, and was staring into the dancing flames in the hearth. Judy looked at her with sudden tenderness. Her mother so rarely expressed any emotion; it was reassuring to know she had had these good feelings.

'And the terrible twos? Was I a pain then?'

'Not that I remember especially. But, of course, we didn't have all these labels when you were little. We didn't *expect* trouble at each stage. We just got on with it.'

'Yes, I think you've hit the nail on the head there, Mum. I think perhaps we know too much nowadays. It freaks me out when these mums appear in labour with their great sheet of wants. How *can* they know whether an episiotomy is going to be best, or whether they might need a painkiller or forceps or whatever? Whatever happened to trusting the professional?'

'Hmm. You sound a bit reactionary.' Betty smiled.

'Well, OK, I'm old-fashioned! And, of course, in my professional capacity I *have* to ask them to tell me what they want and go along with it. But it's a nonsense! Bring back the good old-fashioned midwife-knows-best, I say! You won't catch me dictating to the midwife who delivers *our* baby, I can tell you. If she says he's better off out now and an episiotomy will do the trick, an episiotomy I shall have!'

'Good for you, dear.'

It was warming, this new closeness, the shared experience.

'Well, I mean, I don't go into the garage and tell the mechanic to repair the sump – whatever that is – in a certain way, do I? I haven't got a clue! I rely on him to do it the best way he knows. I know he knows far more about cars and how they work than I do. I don't tell an airline pilot what route to take or what to do if he's forced to abandon a take-off. I expect him to use his knowledge and experience. But these girls come in having read a few books and think they know it all and they can dictate. It's mad.'

Judy poked the fire with energy and the flames leapt up.

'Judith, would you like me to come and help – afterwards, I mean? You know I'm willing, but I – I don't want to …' Betty left the sentence unfinished.

'Thanks, Mum. I really appreciate that. Actually Dec wants to look after us at first. He's taking a couple of weeks off anyway. And it'd be nice just having the baby to ourselves – just at first. While we make all the mistakes!' Judy tried to soften her response. 'But what you *could* do – and I'd really like this – could you make us some of your super soups and casseroles and things? So we don't have to worry too much about food. That would be really great and a big help. Then a bit later, when Dec has to go back to work, then I'm sure I'll be glad of somebody to flick a duster, or do the ironing or pacify the screaming infant!'

'What screaming infant is that?' asked Declan, arriving home from work in time to hear this comment. 'Are you casting aspersions on my child already? There will be no screaming in this house, I can assure you. I forbid it!' He dropped to the floor at Judy's feet with a broad smile. She leaned forward to exchange a kiss. His hand patted her abdomen in silent greeting. Betty averted her eyes.

'And how are Mum, babe and Granny today?' Declan looked towards each in turn.

'Mum is fine and happy to see you home, thanks. Babe is oblivious as to your presence as yet but is warm and comfortable and currently napping. So that leaves you, Granny – who, by the way, has just generously offered to help us as raw recruits in the parenting business,' Judy reported.

'Oh, well, it's only if I can be of help. I don't want to intrude, Declan.'

'That's kind, Betty. And did Judy accept your help?'

'I'd be more than happy to cook for you,' Betty replied directly to Judy. 'Just let me know if you'd like anything else – and when.'

'Thanks, Mum, it'll be great just knowing you're there.'

'You could do one thing for *me* actually, Betty. Give me some hints on how not to faint at the wrong moment,' Declan said with a grin.

'Faint? Why would you faint?' Betty was mystified.

'Don't new dads faint all over the place and get under everybody's feet in the delivery room?'

'Oh *then* – I was talking about after the baby comes home!' Betty said.

'No, *then* the dads just die of exhaustion, I know. But during the delivery, any tips?'

Judy watched Betty's face tighten, the shared laughter fading.

'I don't know. Not my field. Better ask Judith.'

'Did Dad faint?' It was an innocent question.

'He wasn't there.' Betty's voice was even, unemotional, but the tight look remained.

'Oh, of course, men weren't involved as much then – they knew their place!'

Declan rounded on her with mock indignation.

'Thank *you*, Judith Robertson! We liberated men know our place! At the sharp end … of our women's tongues!'

He skipped to his feet and wriggled from her flailing arms. She chased his retreating figure.

52

Betty leaned back in her chair feeling suddenly weary. She heard the foot-steps careering through the house, laughter mapping their passage, until silence fell in the kitchen. But her thoughts were in the past.

It was almost twenty years since Jim had left. But she could still not find it in her heart to forgive. It was a heavy burden, troubling her tight Christian conscience. Did Judith remember what had happened? Today was the first time she'd mentioned him since that dreadful night. There had been no hint of any distress in her voice. But children were amazingly resilient.

By eight months Judy was finding it difficult to get comfortable, especially at night time when the baby seemed to come alive. She had already stuffed a pillow under her bump to take some of the weight, when Declan made to climb into bed beside her. There was limited space left on his side.

'Hey, move over, little one! Let Daddy in.'

He felt rather than saw Judy go rigid.

'Jude! I'm sorry. I'm sorry. I didn't think ...'

'It's OK. I'll be OK in a minute. Hold me, Dec. Hold me.'

He took her trembling body in his arms and rocked her, crooning endearments until the tension eased.

EIGHT

Labour started exactly on cue on the due date.

· Bethany Erika slipped silently into the world at thirteen minutes past eleven that evening.

'It's a … girl!' cried Fiona, the night-duty midwife. The last word spun out over an octave, sounding like an exaggerated announcement by a game show hostess.

Bethany lay like a discarded rag doll, inert, grey and floppy. But the two midwives seemed unperturbed.

'We'll just give you a wee look, Judy, and then Gail will take her along for a whiff of oxygen.'

'Is she OK?'

'She'll be OK when she gets over the shock of coming into this crazy old world.' Fiona wrapped the baby deftly and lifted her towards her mother. Judy reached up to touch her daughter's crumpled face.

'Hello, angel,' she said softly. 'Come back soon. Then we'll really say hello.'

'Here I am, Daddy.' Fiona skimmed Bethany past Declan and handed her to Gail. The door swung behind her with a dull thud.

A strange quiet descended. Judy turned glistening eyes to Declan. He buried his face against her neck. The moment was too poignant for any words. After a swift glance, Fiona looked away and laid a hand on the deflated abdomen waiting in silence for the placenta. That delivered, she worked efficiently, completing the process, stitching, cleaning, keeping up a superficial conversation with Judy about mutual acquaintances, baby names, the advantages and disadvantages of being on the receiving end of care from colleagues, holidays. But there was still no Bethany.

'D'you think … could somebody … just check? Sorry, but … d'you mind …? I don't want to be a difficult Mum, but …' Judy said eventually.

'Don't worry. I'm sure she's fine.' Fiona's voice was paced just as Judy's had been countless times in the past. 'We're terribly short-staffed tonight and the place is packed to the gunnels. What *were* you all doing nine months ago?!'

It was a typical remark, meant nothing, intended only to lighten the moment. Under other circumstances Judy would not have even noticed. But now her eyes flew to Declan's. For a long moment they held, remembering. Without blinking, he lifted her hand, held it to his lips.

'There won't be anybody surplus to requirements to pop back in and tell us.' Fiona was still speaking. 'That's all it'll be. Just hang on a jiffy. I'll just get this equipment sorted and then I'll go myself. Can't leave a *colleague* in a room like a tip now, can I? You might send in a formal complaint!'

Judy wanted to scream at her to hurry. What was keeping them? This was her precious daughter. Where was she? What were they doing to her? It was an eternity of anxiety before Fiona left in search of news.

Declan moved to kiss Judy.

'Jude, you were fantastic. Can you believe it? We've got a daughter! But you, you poor thing, you must be shattered! And is it terribly sore?'

'I'm fine. I just want them to bring her back.' Judy tried to keep her voice calm, matter of fact. 'Oh Dec. She even came on the right day. What a star! Remember we said, we'd always look at her and remember?'

'How could I ever forget?'

Fiona re-entered with a bundle of blankets in her arms. She was smiling.

'Well, here I am, folks. Got a wee bit chilly down there but – hey! – the oxygen's pretty good. Might go back for some more once the queue's gone down.'

'Is she OK?' Judy's eyes were on the blankets.

'She's fine. Bit slow to get going but tried out her lungs nicely now and looking for a bite to eat when you're ready, Mum.'

Fiona slipped the baby into Judy's arms and both parents peered inside the covers. The eyes blinked in the unaccustomed glare.

'Let's put off the main light, can we, Fiona? Let her come to gently,' Judy said softly.

'She's so … tiny.' Declan spoke in an awed whisper.

'Do you mind, Daddy! I'm 6 lb 15 oz. That's a very decent weight, I'll have you know!' Fiona said.

'So 6 lb 15 oz, eh? Better remember that, Dec. Granny will expect you to know! Got all her bits and pieces, has she, Fiona?' Judy felt inside the edge of the blanket, drawing out one clenched and wrinkled hand. Together she and Declan examined the minute fingernails, exclaiming over her perfection.

'Yep, ten of everything as per the manual!' Fiona laughed.

'We won't properly unwrap you till you've warmed up, eh?' Judy crooned. 'But Aunty Fiona tells me you're hungry. So let's see if you've read the instruction book, shall we?'

She held Bethany close to her nipple. Beside her she was aware of Declan watching, holding his breath, his tongue unconsciously mimicking the baby's. The small face nuzzled, mouth opening enough to let her tongue lick out twice but she showed no inclination to suck. Fiona held her head gently, coaxing her, letting the nipple brush against her cheek.

It was Judy who put an end to the abortive attempt.

'You're exhausted, aren't you, darling? It's a mighty old struggle scrambling out of there, eh? But your Daddy is just dying to have a cuddle, so you go and say hello to him. He'll keep you cosy.'

As Judy placed the child in his arms Declan experienced a tide of emotion for which he was quite unprepared. This featherweight creature was *his* – his to cherish, his to protect.

Bethany lay still, eyes closed, and he felt the movement of her chest as she took each breath. Unexpectedly a vivid childhood memory flashed into his mind: a fledgling bird fluttering fearfully in his cupped hands, rescued after its fall to the pavement, a little creature struggling to survive in a harsh world.

A single tear quivered on his eyelashes. Judy reached out to touch his cheek tenderly, understanding.

But the dream sensation took on a reality as he repeated the details over the phone: 'A girl: Bethany Erika, born at 23.13; 6 lb 15 oz; 20 inches long. Mother and baby fine.' Betty first. Then Georgina, who wanted the dimensions in metric. His brain struggled to work out the time in New Zealand to check whether it was a civilised hour to phone his father. But Sid soon reassured him. He'd have wanted to know whatever the hour.

Friends, other relations, they'd wait until daytime. He wanted to tell everyone. 'Bethany. Bethany Erika.' She became an individual, a separate entity, with the telling. He was a father. They were a family. Declan, Judy and Bethany.

Within hours the flowers started to arrive. Judy's room took on the trappings of celebration. Her midwife colleagues sneaked in unofficially to congratulate and commiserate in equal measure.

Betty was their first family visitor. She wouldn't let them take the sleeping child out of the cot but stood bent over her, exclaiming. Pretty name. She hoped they wouldn't shorten it. Yes, she had Judith's forehead. Look at her little fingers! So long and delicate. Maybe she'd be a pianist. Was it too draughty with that window open?

Declan popped in and out all day bringing gifts and waves of paternal pride.

The excitement buoyed Judy up even though her body craved sleep. Even at midnight, alone now with her daughter, she was wide awake. She lay looking at the sleeping child. Her child.

It was crazy; she'd been a midwife all these years, but it felt like a great responsibility to have this one precious little person in her sole charge. She mustn't sleep. There would be no-one else checking to make sure the baby was all right. What if …? She mentally shook herself. Six thousand babies were born each year in this hospital alone. They were survivors.

It took Bethany a day to recover sufficiently to suck. In spite of herself, Judy felt anxiety rising. It was a relief when a midwife friend, Maggie, popped in to congratulate her. Just the person to help coax the baby to feed. She was patient and reassuring, and before long Judy felt the infant jaws working rhythmically. She let out her breath slowly. Silly to keep imagining trouble. Heaps of babies were slow to get started. But this was *her* baby.

Her spirits soared as she watched the baby sucking steadily at the next feed. And the next. They plummeted when six hours later Bethany lay limp and made no effort to respond. Judy told herself sternly over and over again: it was only natural to feel these swings of emotion. Hormones were bound to be chaotic. She was just getting it out of her system earlier than most new mothers.

Mary Bellamy, with five years' experience as Ward Sister, was calm and comforting. Judy confided her anxiety: the baby seemed so lethargic. Mary teased her gently. She was a typical midwife: knowing too much, suspecting trouble at every corner, wouldn't feel she'd had her money's worth until she'd had at least one complication. She'd been the same herself. It went with the territory. But just to set Judy's mind at rest she'd ask the paediatrician to call in and check Bethany over. Judy was grateful.

Judy could see the young paediatrician was nervous; it was bound to be disconcerting having watchful experienced eyes on your every move.

'It's early days yet – I mean, what is she? Only about two days old. Nothing obviously wrong but I think it'd be best – just in case – well, Sister tells me you're anxious – it might help to set your mind at ease – if we just pop her up to Special Care for a few hours just to keep an eye on her.'

'Are *you* worried about her?' Judy's eyes were on the baby lying dishevelled now in the cot. 'Am I just being a neurotic first-time mother?'

'No, you're not neurotic. Better to be safe than sorry. We'll just keep an eye on her for you and then you can relax and start to really enjoy her.'

Judy rang Declan to say what had happened, but she kept the tears at bay until he arrived.

It helped both of them to be with Bethany. Away from her, Judy worried incessantly about what was happening.

'The nurses must be cursing me – being here all the time, in the way,' she whispered to Declan, as if anything louder might disturb the sleeping child. 'Especially as, in the total scheme of things, Bethany isn't really ill like all these others.'

'They seem really nice,' he whispered back.

'Yeah, aren't they. But I still need to be here – *myself*. She needs to feel *we* are here for her, loving her.'

'I think you're allowed to feel that, being her Mum!' A teasing smile crinkled his eyes.

'It's amazing isn't it, Dec, what you feel. Nobody could tell you. You have to experience it.'

Josephine Fallon, who was assigned to care for Bethany, was warm and reassuring.

'Isn't she gorgeous? Lovely long legs. But you're both tall. And look at these fingers! Beautiful hands. I love their little hands. So perfect, aren't they? She's going to have big dark eyes too. Eyelashes to die for. Look at them already. Fabulous. Like yours Judy, uh? Or – ah, you've both got them, I see. Lucky girl – couldn't lose. Yep, this little lady's going to break a few hearts, aren't you, sweetie?'

Judy and Declan did their best to stay out of her way while she carried out the routine observations and care. She chatted lightly, whiling away the hours, telling them about her own upbringing in South Africa, how she'd come over to the UK for a year, met a man here and was now living with him, expecting a baby herself in five months' time.

'And what do your parents think of that?' Judy asked, smiling.

'Well, of course, they're disappointed to be missing out on the pregnancy. But they're planning to come over – once it's born.' Josephine's face broke into a broad grin. 'My Dad's funny. He's a gynaecologist over there. When I told him, he said, "Well, makes for healthy stock taking a mate from such a distance!"'

They all three laughed.

'We can relate to that,' Judy responded. 'We come from opposite ends of the country and we met purely by chance miles away from our homes.'

'Walking on forbidden rail track!' Declan chimed in.

They told her the story of their chance meeting.

'Could have been a very brief encounter indeed!' Josephine laughed.

NINE

Judy watched the intravenous infusion feeding her daughter drip by drip and felt a pang of guilt. It was some small consolation expressing her milk every four hours in readiness.

She was just emerging from using the breast pump when Declan came along the corridor. Though he smiled as soon as he saw her, she was conscious of the lines of tension around his jaw.

'You OK?' she asked, looking up at him with concern.

'Yeah, I'm fine. Actually ... Dr Fairweather wants to see us when you're ready. So I guess they've got some of those test results through.'

Judy squeezed his hand.

'It'll be all right,' she said, 'Doug's the best.'

Douglas Fairweather took Josephine Fallon with him into the little room set aside for interviews with parents. He saw her flash them a reassuring smile, and touch Judy's shoulder briefly, as she took her seat beside them.

Even after seven years as a consultant, Doug still sent up a swift prayer before these encounters with anxious parents. It helped having someone there as calm and competent as Josephine. And she'd obviously got to know this couple already. He let his facial muscles relax into a smile, settling himself almost casually in the chair opposite them.

He'd spoken to Judy and Declan several times beside Bethany's incubator explaining what they were doing, but this was the first formal session. It could be daunting for parents.

'Well, how are you both doing? It's tough, I know, having your baby up here.'

'How is she, Doug?' Judy's interruption was natural.

Careful. Watch how you phrase things.

'Well, she does seem a bit sleepy. And she's not tolerating her feeds very well, at the moment. We're not really very sure at this stage what's going on. We're running tests, as you know – bloods, electrolytes, all the usual things. Lumbar punctures, X-rays, EEGs, ECGs.'

They both nodded, eyes fixed on his face. The anxiety was palpable. Nobody liked seeing their baby put through this battery of procedures.

'Now, there could be lots of simple explanations. It's early days yet. And it's only by a process of elimination that we can rule different things out. It's hard to be patient, I know. But we can't hurry this bit.'

'So far though ... what do you *think* it is?' Judy sat forward in her seat, her body tense.

'Well, I must confess, I'm not sure – yet. And I'm reluctant to pin it down to anything – at the moment.'

'D'you think … it's serious?' Declan asked.

They were pushing him. Careful. Stay in control of the information.

'Well, I have to be honest, it *could* be. I'm not sure, but I can't say categorically that no, it's not. We haven't got enough facts yet for me to be sure. There are a number of things which don't quite add up at the moment – vague sorts of things – a combination of little things that just make us ask questions. I must emphasise again, they could just all add up to an infection or something simple like that. But we need more results before we can rule other things out.'

'But if you had to say now, at this moment, what are you *thinking*? What do you *suspect* it is?' Judy's tone was intense.

Doug looked hard at them. Too much information before they were certain could be cruel. Too little, unfair on them. But Judy was a midwife. She must have an inkling of what it might be.

'Well, I might be entirely wrong but it could be – possibly – metabolic.'

Judy was silent.

'What does that mean?' Declan asked.

This was easier – simply state the facts.

'Well, there are conditions which we call inborn errors of metabolism. There are literally hundreds of them. And we keep finding more all the time. Basically they're things that affect the absorption and processing of food. Unfortunately, they can be very difficult to diagnose because the presenting symptoms are pretty vague and each of the symptoms could be due to lots of other things.'

'And are they serious? I mean, can … can you treat them? What's it mean?' Declan's questions tumbled over themselves.

Time for another guarded response. No merit in unnecessarily alarming them until there was more concrete evidence one way or the other.

'Well, it varies. Some are easily treated with supplements, or treatments of one kind or another. Others are less easily managed.'

'And some are lethal.' Judy's voice was flat, expressionless, but her eyes were great pools of darkness. It was further than Doug had wanted to take them.

'Well, that's right, of course, but I think you should try to keep an open mind at this stage.' He met her look squarely. 'I'm only telling you about this … *possibility* because, well, it's only fair. You're asking. You want to know – what we're considering. But it *is* only *considering*. We don't know. We don't know anything more than I've told you. It's nothing more than a suspicion. Nothing concrete that says it *is* a metabolic thing even, never mind what *kind* of metabolic thing. I know it's wretchedly difficult when you're worried out of your mind, but at the moment it's still just as possible that the symptoms are signs of sepsis – some infection – or whatever.'

'And you could treat that?' Declan was searching for something definite to hang on to.

'Oh yes, almost certainly, when we know what kind of infection we're dealing with.'

'So what next?' Judy was rushing him on. Had she suspected?

'Well, one of our colleagues, Ted Elliott – d'you know him, Judy?' She shook her head. 'Well, he's a bit of a whizz-kid when it comes to all things metabolic – specialised in them actually. So if anyone can spot one, it's Ted. And we've got him on board – just in case. In fact we've got a whole team of people – in the labs and in the nursery – all working their socks off trying to find out what's going on. Bethany's getting the very best care she could possibly get. We're monitoring her really closely, watching for any clues, any signs of anything. And at the moment she's stable. So *try* not to worry unduly at this stage. We'll keep you posted. As soon as we know anything for sure, you'll be the first to know.'

'She's so very precious.' Doug heard the mute appeal in Judy's voice.

'I know. I know. She's precious to us too. And believe me, we're doing everything possible.'

'We know you are. And thanks. Thanks a lot.' Judy's voice crumbled. She needed space. They needed time together, alone.

Doug laid a compassionate hand on her arm, and then rose to leave. At the door he paused, turning back, his voice casual.

'By the way, Judy, you don't have a funny diet or anything, do you? You're not a vegetarian? Vegan? Or anything?'

'No. Why?'

'Well, it's just that sometimes things like that produce funny effects in babies. But that's fine. We can rule *that* out at least!'

TEN

The waiting seemed interminable. Judy almost envied Declan his outlet; searching the Internet for information on metabolic disorders, although she stubbornly refused to listen to anything he found. She told him sharply it was too easy to get things very wrong. This was highly specialised stuff, not for amateurs. Besides, Doug would let them know when there was anything to tell. She trusted him completely.

Declan assured her he was perfectly well aware that anyone could add things to these websites without any real foundation, but she knew a moment of pure relief when he stopped searching. He told her lightly that the language was incomprehensible and, besides, his own knowledge base was so flimsy he couldn't discern the good from the ugly, fact from fiction, smiling as he dismissed it as an option. But inwardly she knew his fears too were escalating.

Through endless wearying hours they sat beside Bethany, watching for any glimmer of change, willing her to respond to their enveloping love. They hung on the nurses' superficial reports of physiological stability, sleeping patterns and food tolerance. They told each other the doctors were stalling only because they were waiting for concrete facts.

Josephine was busy tidying Bethany after a nappy change when they arrived in the Unit one week after Bethany's transfer.

'Hi there. Did you get the message? Doug wants to see you this morning.'

'Now?' Judy's voice sounded odd in her own ears.

'Twenty minutes time. Is that all right with you? He's just finishing a round.'

Judy fought back the foreboding. They had no idea what was coming. It was just as likely to be good news as bad. It was just the waiting that got to you. All these hours of watching the baby, wondering, not knowing.

It was good having Josephine there. It was probably just coincidence that her eyes didn't quite meet theirs.

'Let me introduce Dr Elliott – Ted Elliott – the metabolic specialist I told you about. Ted, Judy and Declan Robertson.' It felt odd. The social niceties. Doug's formality.

Doug perched on the edge of his seat, leaning towards them.

'I'm going to give you the hardest news first so you don't sit there dreading what's coming. I'm afraid it is, as we suspected, a metabolic disorder. It's got a ghastly mouthful of a name: methylmalonic aciduria. Ted will fill you in on the details in a minute but I'll just give you a broad picture so you have a framework to hang things on.'

Judy stared at him in silence.

'The tests we ran show Bethany's excreting a large amount of methylmalonic acid in her urine. You've seen yourselves that she's lethargic. Not feeding as we'd like her to. Bit anaemic too. We've done a skin biopsy – just a simple punch biopsy – nothing nasty,' he said quickly as Judy instinctively flinched. 'That will tell us more about what kind of defect it is. What we'd like to try now is a course of vitamin B_{12} to see if we can decrease the amount of this acid that she's excreting. And we'll reduce her protein intake as well. Hopefully the two things together will show a fairly rapid improvement.'

'And will that cure her?'

'Well, not exactly *cure*, but we hope it'll treat it and enable her to develop perfectly normally.'

'But ... it might not.' Judy's voice was flat, devoid of feeling.

'Well, some forms of the condition respond dramatically to B_{12} but unfortunately they don't all. I think at this stage we must just hope that Bethany has one of the ones which do respond.'

'And if not ...?'

The two consultants' voices came from a great distance. Judy heard the words: ketoacidosis ... thrombocytopenia ... plasma ammonia ... but her brain refused to filter with comprehension. Bethany – their beloved baby – a serious defect – might die. She *couldn't* die!

Into the whirlpool of her confusion two words dropped with shocking clarity – 'mental impairment'. There was a possibility their baby might be mentally impaired. The words sank like leaden weights through her consciousness. They must be wrong. This must be a nightmare. Bethany was the product of a love so healing she *couldn't* be less than perfect herself.

Judy's composure crumbled. Biochemistry, physiology – she'd never really taken to the scientific stuff. Mental impairment, brain damage, that she understood. She was silent, withdrawn, in her weeping. Dimly she was aware of Josephine crouching beside her, pressing a bundle of tissues into her hand. She made no effort to use them.

Declan sat rigidly beside her, his hand grasping hers but he seemed totally isolated from her. Poor Declan, he'd be struggling to understand the technical terms. She knew it had irritated him earlier when they gave information at two levels; interpreting things for his benefit. Why didn't the doctors speak to them both as parents, he'd wanted to know. Judy wasn't a colleague, not now. She was Bethany's Mum. They were equally her parents. Both of them. They had created her together; they should understand what had gone wrong together, in the same way.

Somewhere out there Doug and Ted were doing their best. They reiterated clearly that Bethany might well respond readily to the treatment, and be to all intents and purposes as normal. But Judy's heart refused to believe them. Again and again Declan's voice reached her, asking halting questions. Gently, sympathetically, they tried to simplify the complex, help him to absorb the reality. But to Judy their grave expressions spoke more eloquently than their words. 'I'm so sorry', so often repeated and so heartfelt, impinged more forcefully than any catalogue of diagnostic facts. The potential lifelines of hope sat uneasily with their other cues. So what if it had been detected as early as possible because of Ted's high level of clinical suspicion? It didn't alter the facts, did it? Bethany still had this ... this dreadful thing, this rare dreadful thing. Her future was not going to be what they had anticipated. A shadow – a permanent shadow – would be cast over a flawless dream.

Doug was leaning towards her. Saying her name. Judy forced herself to concentrate.

'You need time alone to take this in. Stay as long as you like. But when you're ready, feel free to ask me anything. Anything at all. And ask as many times as you need to. Ask a hundred times if you want to, a hundred and one. Or ask Ted if you'd rather. We'll do our best to be totally honest, share everything we know.'

The door closed soundlessly behind them. Josephine remained, crouched on one knee, not breaking into the initial silence with words.

The look in Declan's eyes as he turned for the first time to look directly at Judy held a pain too deep for expression. Without a word she took his head in her arms, cradling him, rocking him, as the enormity of the revelations washed over them. They clung together. It was a full twenty minutes before Judy noticed that Josephine had slipped out of the room. She felt a momentary sense of gratitude that no-one had suggested a tray of tea. There was no panacea for hurt this raw.

Returning to the nursery was unexpectedly hard, Judy found. Her baby needed them now more than ever, but now they knew the truth, would they see the subtle changes that would reinforce this horror? Was it her imagination, or were the nurses all looking at them with pity now?

She stood close to Declan beside the incubator, glad of his partial protection from her colleagues' eyes. For the first time she noted the tension in Bethany's limbs as she lay sleeping.

'Would it help to cuddle her?' Josephine's voice was quiet, tentative.

Through a blur of tears, Judy looked up to nod.

Bethany lay in her arms, eyes closed, still save for the rhythmic movement of her chest. Folding the blanket protectively about the baby, she left one hand where it lay. Her fingers stroked the soft skin. It never ceased to move her, the feel of a new baby. She placed a finger in the tiny palm, felt the hand close instinctively.

'Oh Dec, how can she be so perfect ... and yet not?' Her words were almost inaudible.

He knelt beside her chair, dropping a kiss on Bethany's forehead. Her eyes screwed up momentarily. They smiled through their tears.

Together they exclaimed over her exquisite ears, her shapely finger-nails, her long legs. They saw Declan's nose, Judy's chin, Betty's frown. They told her over and over again how much they loved her, how precious she was – would always be. Judy insisted that Declan hold her too. Bethany needed to know he was there loving her too, she said.

Josephine took family photographs. Their smiles were natural, sponta-neous. This was their daughter, their firstborn. The bonds were stronger than ever.

Judy grew increasingly irritated as everyone urged her to get some rest. Yes, of course she was exhausted, she admitted it, but what did that mat-ter now? Time with Bethany was more important. That was true, but the baby was stable, Josephine said, and they'd call her instantly if there was any change. Still she lingered, desperately willing her strength into the child behind the perspex barrier.

Why didn't she rest just while he popped home for some fresh clothes, and to make a few phone calls, Declan coaxed. He'd be back in no time. They'd go back to the nursery together then. He promised. Bethany needed her to be strong and she couldn't keep being strong if she was exhausted.

It made sense.

She lay on top of the bed, her mind travelling with Declan. It would be an ordeal, telling people, but marginally easier to ring from the quiet of their own home, with no listening ears. If he broke down there would be no-one to see, to judge, to pity him.

He'd have to contact his work, to tell them he was taking a couple of days off, now rather than later. The baby wasn't so well.

He'd have to tell Betty, ask her not to visit, not just yet. Judy had felt guilty putting that burden on him. But she needed time; time to assimi-late this new reality, time to build up her courage. It fleetingly crossed her mind that it must be hard for a mother to give up her role as chief com-forter to a strange young man who had known her daughter for just a few short years. But she knew Declan would be gentle in his request.

He'd want to ring Georgina. She would let their father and sister know in New Zealand. Would it be his breaking point telling his twin? With each telling the reality would sink in deeper.

What was the reality? Judy realised she didn't know what she was pre-paring herself for. Was it better to have Bethany no matter how serious the impairments or would it be preferable to lose her now and face the rest of life without her? What was she suffering, this tiny creature so lately arrived from the security of her womb? Why, why had this happened? Was it a punishment? Was it …

A light tap at the door brought her eyes flickering down from the pale green ceiling. At the sight of the chaplain hesitating at the door, Judy sat up immediately, reaching out a hand to welcome him in.

Geoff Frazer was unfazed by her tumbling questions.

'There are no easy answers, Judy. I wish I could trot out the old platitudes and mean them. But you know me. I can't. We've both been around too long, you and me, both seen too many tragedies in life. And there can be no easy explanation for why a perfectly innocent wee baby should suffer.'

'And looking at her, Geoff – she's just so perfect. How *could* things go so wrong?' The rawness of the pain was like a physical hurt.

Geoff shook his head. 'It's a question I've asked a thousand times.'

'We wanted her so much.'

His clasp on her hands was comforting as she struggled to suppress her sobs.

'Oh Geoff, I'm so scared.'

'Of course you're scared. Who wouldn't be?' he soothed. 'You've had a terrible shock. For all you've brought hundreds of babies into the world, held thousands of them, there's never been a baby like Bethany. You're only just beginning to understand and really feel the strength of parental love. It swallows you up and eats you whole, doesn't it? The very idea of anything happening to someone so precious, so unique, is so overwhelming that it threatens our reason.'

'I didn't know … *how* overwhelming.'

'Of course you didn't. You hadn't experienced it.'

'And Dec … it's the same for him. It's killing him … knowing she might …' She couldn't mouth the words. Not yet.

'And that huge love you *both* feel for Bethany, that you share, that will get you through this – together. Whatever happens. Hang on to that.'

'It was all so *perfect* … before …' The tears were chokingly thick through her voice. 'Now it feels …'

'Everything is out of perspective at first, Judy. It's the shock. You're bound to have dark thoughts. It's only natural.'

'How could God *do* this to us? You're supposed to be on his wavelength, Geoff. Why? Why?'

'I don't know the answers. I only wish I did. But one thing *for me* makes a difference. You're starting to know what a parent feels for a child. God's love for us is supposed to be even stronger than that. He loves us no matter what – and heaven knows – we aren't the lily-white innocents that your little Bethany is! So I can't believe he'd do something horrible to us, deliberately. I simply can't believe he deliberately created Bethany this way. It just doesn't make sense. There must be some other explanation. And it's probably too big for our tiny human minds to get themselves around. But if he loves like a parent, only much, *much* more – and that's something else we can't really get a grasp on – but if he does, then I think we have to trust that he'll help us – like a parent – to deal with whatever life throws at us. Be there for us. Loving us no matter what.'

'But fathers don't always …'

'No, they don't. That's true. But *good* fathers do.'

'So you don't think – it's a punishment…?' Her voice was small, like a child's.

'No, I most definitely do *not*. There's a surprise, eh, Judy? This old knocked-about chaplain having a definite answer to something! But I *am* sure on this one. You wouldn't do something quite horrid deliberately to Bethany, would you?'

'No, of course not! I'd do anything – so would Dec – *anything* to stop anything horrid happening to her. If we could. If *only* we could.'

'And God loves you even more than you love Bethany.'

'Does he? Then why didn't he stop this thing happening to Dec and me?'

'I don't know, except that this world doesn't operate like that. For whatever reason. Bad things do happen to good people. And he doesn't leap in and stop them. Try asking him. Don't be scared. He's big enough for you to shout at him.'

It helped, voicing the turbulent fears and doubts with this trusted friend who didn't pretend he knew the answers. Geoff stayed until she had exhausted her questions, and was silent in her reflection.

'Will you come back … if … we need you?' Judy clutched his hand as he took his leave.

'Any time, day or night, just get them to bleep me.'

The tears were dry on her cheeks by the time Declan returned to find her dozing.

ELEVEN

The sight of Doug's head appearing around her door next morning made Judy leap up from the pillows. Declan sat forward in his chair, tension etched on his face.

Doug perched on the edge of the bed, one long leg twisted under the other to hold his balance. The harsh hospital lighting caught the glints of silver in his fair hair.

'How're you doing? Managing to get any sleep at all?'

'A bit. We're OK. Everyone's being really kind.'

'Good. I thought I'd come down. I know we gave you a hefty dose of information yesterday. Hard stuff to take in too. I thought, now you've had a bit of time to think, you might like to go over bits of it again – ask questions? Just if you feel like it. Or just tell me when, if you don't want to talk about it just yet.'

Judy was surprised to find Declan was ahead of her. She felt a pang of surprise that he'd made no attempt to ask her the question that now tumbled out.

'Thanks. I do have a question. Can you explain – about – how this happens, what's gone wrong?'

'Sure. I'll try anyway. D'you mean how it happened in the first place? Or what's happening inside Bethany now?'

'No, what happened in the first place. You said it was an "inborn error" – I think? So I guess that means she was born with it. So what happened *before* she was born?'

'OK. Good question. It's not easy to explain. Stop me if you don't quite follow. It's a genetic thing. You'll have heard about genes. Do you know about recessive genes?'

'Mendel's peas!' Declan's response was instant.

'Indeed.' Doug grinned at him.

Judy turned raised eyebrows to look at her husband.

'Abbé Gregor Mendel. Austrian monk. Grew peas and catalogued their characteristics. "The Monk in the garden," our biology teacher used to call him! I did experiments with fruit flies in A-level zoology.'

'Excellent, so you'll both know what I'm talking about here.' Doug smiled. 'The gene for this metabolic condition is usually carried on a recessive gene and, as you'll both know, it's only when two recessive genes come together that a characteristic like this is seen. If it comes together with a dominant gene, it remains hidden.'

'So we both' – Judy gestured from herself to Declan – 'carry this recessive gene?'

'That's the likeliest explanation. Yes. We'll know more when we get more results back.'

'And when we – when Bethany was conceived – we both passed on this recessive gene – to her.' Declan's sentence trailed away.

'That's right. It's a very rare condition this one and it's terribly bad luck that you should both carry this particular gene. It's nobody's fault. We can't choose our genes. But you know that. Those fruit flies you observed, they had a certain colour of eyes or a certain kind of wings – inbuilt – when they were conceived, didn't they? Nothing they did, nothing their parents did, made them like it.'

'But if we' – again Judy gestured from herself to Declan and back again – 'if we hadn't … then she wouldn't …'

'Well, rock bottom, yes. If you two hadn't married each other you'd – *neither* of you would have had a child with this condition. Unless your other partner was also carrying this recessive factor, of course. But other children wouldn't have been Bethany.'

The silence hung in the air. There were some things which couldn't be spoken.

'My next question: what are the chances – of this happening again?' Declan's voice was tight.

Judy froze. Why did he have to ask that? They'd only just had Bethany. It was too soon to think of any next baby. He could have warned her.

'I don't know. Not at this stage. We haven't got enough information. As I've just explained, it's highly likely that Bethany inherited the recessive gene from both of you. You each got your own recessive gene from one or other of your parents. Unless it was some sort of mutation. They got theirs from one or other of their parents. Neither your parents nor your grand-parents knew they even had this gene. There was no indication, just as there wasn't in either of you. But a geneticist would need to sit down with you and spell out all the statistics and odds before you could assess what the risk is for future pregnancies. It's not my area of expertise, I'm afraid.'

Judy felt suddenly cold. Babies were the product of something so warm and private. It seemed somehow indecent to calculate, to have a *stranger* assess, their potential to come into existence. She shivered. Declan leaned across to slip her dressing gown around her shoulders, moving his chair closer.

'Would you like me to arrange for a geneticist to see you?' Doug was gentle, cautious.

Judy and Declan turned simultaneously to look at one another.

'Maybe … later? Wait till … we see what … how Bethany …?' Declan's words were low. Judy nodded mutely. Thank God! He hadn't written Bethany off after all. He didn't want to think of a next baby, either. Not yet.

'We'll leave it just now, concentrate on Bethany. See what happens.'

69

'Fine. I think that's a wise decision. We'll talk again. The offer stays open – as long as you need it.' Doug understood the unspoken.

Long after Doug had left, they stayed cocooned in her room, going over and over the ground. It seemed so hard to take in. The mechanics of what had gone wrong had been straightforward enough to grasp, but the implications touched them at a deeper and more intensely personal level. By mutual consent, they began to face the brutality of life: how they would manage with a child with special needs; if their love was strong enough to cope; if Declan's salary would be sufficient to meet the additional financial burdens; if they should think of leaving their cottage for something more adaptable. But Judy knew she was not ready to do more than skirt gingerly around the genetic implications. She hardly heard the appeal in Declan's words.

'Jude, at least we're in this together. Wouldn't it have been worse if it had been just one of us? That one would have felt so alone – *I'd* have felt so responsible. I know we can't help it – it's not our fault, but even so ... I think I'd have felt – well, guilty.'

She was grappling with other fears.

'I know what you mean but ... Dec, for me ... it feels like ... I'm scared – for *us*. How will we feel about each other ... if ...?'

'If we can't have more kids? Or if any kids we do have have something wrong with them?'

'Either – both. You know what I mean. What will it do – to *us*?'

'Well, we can't know for sure, but one thing I do know, I love you and that will never change. And I love Bethany. And even if she *is* going to have problems, I'll still love her.'

'Oh, me too. Me too.' Judy clutched his hand tighter.

'We're strong, Jude. We can do it. Whatever. If we're together.'

Judy shivered. Declan drew her close.

'Ignore me, Dec. I'm being ridiculous, I know. Left my common sense in the Labour ward! I can't seem to stop my imagination running riot. And I seem to cry at the least little thing. Not like me at all!'

'I know. I understand. Where has my sensible, practical Judy gone? But hey, in case it's escaped your notice, young lady, you have just had a baby. Your hormones are *supposed* to be raging!'

'Well, they are!'

'You're OK. It's been a shock. Bound to do things to you – to us both – but more so to you. You've had all the upheaval of giving birth and everything.'

'It's not like me to be superstitious, is it? But ...' Judy shivered again. Her voice sounded small, afraid. 'It's like ... a somebody's-walking-over-your-grave feeling. Is someone trying to tell us something?'

'Good grief, don't tell me you're hearing voices too! Weeping, I can explain. Imagination running riot – just about legit. But *voices* ... now there you're on your own! The psych hospital's full of folk like that, so you'd better lock your door at night or I might find you gone in the morning.'

In spite of herself she smiled at his comical expression.

TWELVE

The tension felt unbearable. With each set of results their spirits fluctuated exhaustingly.

The levels of methylmalonic acid started to go down in Bethany's urine. Hopes rose. The drop might be just because the protein had been restricted, Doug cautioned; it was too early yet to say the baby was responding to the vitamin B_{12}. Spirits were dampened. It was only fair, he said, to be scrupulously honest at this stage.

Judy searched hour by hour for the dramatic change Doug had told them would signal effective treatment. When it failed to materialise she shrank into herself. Rising doubts crept in through all the cracks in her defences. She stopped asking for information. She tried to avoid seeing the doctors.

But they came to her. Gradually, quietly, Doug and Ted, individually and together, described the evolving picture. She fought to reconstruct their words, to rearrange them into more hopeful messages.

'It looks very much as if there are three things happening here. There's none of the necessary enzyme activity going on to stop the methylmalonic acid accumulating. Bethany's condition isn't responding to the protein reduction. And there's no reaction to the vitamin B_{12}.'

Well, give it time …

'We still haven't seen any reaction to the B_{12}.'

So it needs more time …

But the truth of their diagnosis grew inexorably from a whisper to a roar in Judy's head; this was becoming the worst possible scenario.

Nights as well as days were spent in the hospital. They must not, dare not, be far away.

After three weeks of accumulating strain, Judy was exhausted. A surge of irritation made her flounce away from the hand on her shoulder. But the insistent voice in the semi-darkness dragged her from sleep.

'Please, Judy, Declan. Please. Wake up. I'm sorry. But please.' It was Kirsten, Bethany's nurse for the night shift.

Declan sat bolt upright beside her. She too was suddenly wide awake, staring at Kirsten in silent terror.

'Is she …?' It was Declan who whispered the words hanging in the air.

'No, she's still alive but she's taken a turn for the worse. She's really poorly. We think – maybe you should come – you'd want to be with her.'

Two thirty-five in the morning. Judy was under no illusions.

She knew too that it would be pointless to probe for more information from Kirsten. She was the poor unfortunate who had drawn the short straw, going to the ward to wake them. It would be one of the doctors who would tell them what they did not want to hear. Instinctively Declan was walking close to her, clasping her hand tightly, as they followed the nurse down the long corridor, their eyes struggling to adjust to the increasing light.

Through the window she saw Doug hunched over Bethany's incubator, a registrar and the neonatal sister in charge of the Unit on either side. Their faces, their body language made words superfluous. As if alert for their arrival, Doug threw a quick comment over his shoulder to the registrar, and came swiftly out to meet them before they could enter the nursery. He was shaking his head as he spoke.

'I'm sorry, she's just going downhill. Her ammonia is going up. She's hypoglycaemic. Her acidosis is worse, and her pH levels have dropped like a stone. All these things are having a toxic effect on her brain and I'm afraid she's started having convulsions. That's never an easy thing for parents to watch. So you need to prepare yourselves for what you'll see.'

Judy stared back at him bleakly.

'We've tried all the usual things. And we're just not winning. I've just been on the phone to Ted. He's on his way in. We thought you'd want to be with her. But I have to be honest, it's not looking good.'

All eyes were on Bethany. Judy felt a wave of dizziness sweep over her. Gone now the still form of last night. Instead the small frame was jolted with what looked like hiccups, legs pedalled with relentless monotony, fists punched the air aimlessly as if she were fighting an unseen opponent.

'Can we ... touch her?' Her voice was a hoarse whisper.

Staff melted away from both sides of the incubator. Judy's fingers caressed the writhing trunk in a vain effort to still the movements; Declan's hand cupped the tossing head. Broken whispers shattered inside the incubator.

A few minutes passed in silence. Then Judy shot a mute appeal to Doug. He nodded.

'We'll give her something soon. But we need Ted to see her first.'

Ted Elliott, though dragged from sleep, was deft, thorough in his examination, sure in his touch.

The two consultants conferred before them all. There were no secrets between the players in this hideously real drama. The phrases echoed in staccato bursts. Anticonvulsants. All they could offer. What about haemofiltration? Unfair to keep doing unpleasant things to her. Prognosis grim.

Their voices were gentle as they spelled out the position directly to the parents. The reality of their words swam in and out of Judy's consciousness.

'We've now exhausted all the conventional options … There's one last-ditch attempt… we could try to dialyse her … But is that fair to her?'

Judy dragged her eyes away from Bethany to look directly at Doug, mutely seeking his advice. His look said it all, but she was grateful for his quiet statement.

'I have to say, I personally think it would be cruel to put Bethany through any more delaying procedures. Ted?'

'I agree. Best to let her go peacefully.'

'We're so desperately sorry – we did everything we could to save her.'

Judy stared through a veil of tears at the child whose life was ending before it had begun.

'Judy? Declan? What do you feel? Do you agree?'

Judy clutched Declan's hand, nodding without looking at him. She saw his head nod a second later.

As from a great distance, Judy watched Doug increase the infusion. The violent movements ceased as the phenobarbitone took effect. Doug himself disconnected Bethany from her monitors and carried her, cocooned in a warmed blanket, close to his heart, to the room where he had first told them of her problems. Judy and Declan stumbled behind him and sank heavily onto the sofa.

Doug knelt and eased the child into her mother's arms.

'Your love is the most special gift you can give her now,' he said softly, his hand lingering around the sleeping baby. 'She will feel it. She will know it's different from our touch. Talk to her. She knows your voices. Do whatever feels right to you. We'll keep her sedated. She won't feel any pain. She'll just slip away peacefully, knowing only your love.' His own eyes were bright with unshed tears. 'We'll be around. Don't hesitate to ring the bell if you want us. We'll pop in and out, just to make sure she's comfortable. Otherwise this is your time.'

'How long …?' Declan's voice was unrecognisable.

'Impossible to say, but we'll do all we can to make it dignified.'

The family room at night was lit with soft lamps. Not a sound penetrated this quiet place. They took turns cradling Bethany, treasuring the outward perfection of her body, surrounding her with their love. Judy felt curiously detached at times. She was surprised by their calm. Twice they thought the baby had slipped away, and each time Judy held her own breath as she watched. Twice with a gasp Bethany resumed her tenuous hold on life.

Doug came in once to top up her medication, reassuring Judy with his quiet authority. He gave no sign of weariness from the relentless night hours in the nursery. Kirsten lingered to offer them a different camera, more cups of tea, confirming that they should feel free to do anything they felt was right for them. If she could help in any way …

Death when it came was silent and needed no outside confirmation.

Only then did the tears flow. They could now do no more for this, their precious child. Doug was still outside waiting only to pronounce the inevitable. It seemed fitting that he should be the one to share that bleak moment with them. Judy heard his voice cracking, felt his hand squeeze her arm; there was no need for verbal sympathy.

They stayed in the hospital until mid-morning. Josephine came to express her shock and condolences, hugging them both, genuine in her affection.

Doug gently raised the question of genetic counselling. He could set up a preliminary meeting. If they felt it would help. It was impossible to think of other babies; they only wanted Bethany. But Judy nodded dully. He promised he'd attend to it. Keith Galloway was an excellent chap.

And an autopsy? It would help answer questions for the future. Judy knew it was necessary. But no details, *please*. It did not bear thinking about.

Doug told them an appointment would also come for them to see him again, they should expect it in a few weeks' time, but they shouldn't hesitate to contact him if they wanted to talk about anything before the card arrived.

They walked out of the hospital doors into grey drizzle. Two girls, heavily pregnant, stood leaning on the wall, smoking, giggling. Judy turned her eyes abruptly from them, clenching her teeth. How could life go on after such a tragedy? But in thirty minutes she'd be home; she could retain her composure that long, surely. The taxi driver was mercifully silent.

The church was packed for the funeral.

The white coffin that had seemed to dominate their bedroom during the night before, now seemed so small, resting across their knees in the funeral car, then in Declan's arms for the walk to the front of the church. Judy dared not look at his set face. She kept her eyes on the posy of rosebuds she carried. Bethany's rosebuds.

The sound of suppressed weeping, of noses being blown, accompanied their progress, but their own eyes were dry. They were determined to acquit themselves with dignity, to be parents Bethany would have been proud of.

Judy forced herself to concentrate on every word. She even marvelled at the skill Geoff Frazer showed in capturing exactly what they had asked for. Yes, she wanted all these people to know – to *rejoice* in how much Bethany had been a wanted child, how much they had loved her during her short life, how their own lives were the richer for her having come into the world. They needed to hear it was senseless, how neither Geoff nor her parents had answers. It felt right too, telling their friends and relations how important it was that other people did not try to diminish the enormity of their loss by trotting out 'comfortable platitudes' that were anything but comfortable to those who had loved and lost her.

But the front pew felt every bit as conspicuous as she had dreaded. She gripped Declan's hand tightly. She needed to draw on his strength for this ordeal. His own clasp on her fingers never slackened. She was dimly aware of Betty and Georgina, on the inside of the same row, dabbing their eyes surreptitiously. But it was curiously comforting to hear Geoff's voice tremble, to know that he – one of the few people who had shared Bethany's short life – had been personally touched by her death. His sorrow was genuine. It was for the senseless loss of a beautiful child.

By contrast the sniffs and sobs from behind only irritated her. These people had never known Bethany; why show such emotion? Of course they were crying for herself and Declan, for parents everywhere who knew such sorrow; but she wanted them to cry for Bethany too, for the pain of all she had lost. Out of the corner of her eye she saw Declan clenching his jaw. It was enough. She mustn't crumble for his sake. They'd agreed.

Numbly she watched the tiny coffin disappearing into the gaping hole, the rope seeming to scorch her hands as it slid through her fingers. Together, alone, they stood looking down at the plaque. Bethany Erika Robertson. The dates starkly spelling out the shortness of her life: birth and death in the same month of the same year. Judy knew it would be forever imprinted on her mind. But for now she could not let her brain acknowledge that Bethany herself – their Bethany – was in that box.

No-one else dared approach that hallowed space. They, her parents for so short a time, stood, motionless, beyond tears, not wanting to turn away. How could they leave their baby in the cold earth? Behind them the other mourners drifted away to the hotel for refreshments. The undertaker, the grave-diggers, maintained their respectful distance.

There would be no hurried shovelling of earth today. This was a child.

THIRTEEN

Six weeks dragged heavily by. Aching misery held Judy in its thrall much of the time and it was a struggle to face both friends and neighbours. The ordeal of going to the hospital again loomed ever larger. Much as she wanted to see Doug and talk to him about Bethany, it took all her courage to attend the appointment knowing that Keith Galloway, the geneticist, would be probing painful memories.

It proved to be a bewildering experience. Dr Galloway was nothing like the towering figure she had conjured up in her mind. Everyone in the medical fraternity apparently held him in high esteem, but in reality he seemed to her apologetic, insecure, almost bumbling. Didn't they teach geneticists to maintain eye contact? Didn't he realise his incessant fidgeting was distracting?

Curiously though, it helped that this man, never having seen them before, never having known Bethany, started with a blank slate. He assumed nothing. He took pains to spell out the facts and synthesise them into a comprehensible picture. So what if he hid behind statistics and family trees, diagrammatic boxes, symbols and arrows? When he said the tests showed the type of defect identified in Bethany's case was autosomal recessive, she felt a wave of gratitude. He wasn't involved in the same way as the others were; he wasn't just being a friend, trying to ease the hurt. She believed him. Both she and Declan carried this mutant gene. It wasn't her fault. It wasn't his. It just happened. And she had space to think, because Dr Galloway scarcely ever looked up from his scribbling block and the moving pen.

'There's probably a two to three per cent chance for anyone of having a child with a genetic disorder or a birth defect of some sort. And all of us – Doug here, me – we probably all carry several autosomal recessive genes, potentially harmful but usually remaining hidden – unless we happen to mate with someone else carrying the same mutation.'

So they were not so very unusual after all. Just unlucky.

'Some of the rare mutations can be handed down for generations without anyone ever knowing about them. It's as if they're just sleeping. Harmless. Of course, in some cultures where there's a tradition of intermarrying these things manifest themselves more often. For first cousins there's probably something in the region of one in eight shared genes; uncle and niece probably one in four, because their blood relationship is even closer. See? One in *four* shared genes instead of one in eight.'

The lines on his drawing crossed more closely, more often, as he showed them one in eight, then one in four.

'So in that case there's a much higher risk of any child inheriting the mutant gene from both parents. That's what we call being homozygous for the mutant gene.'

He scribbled the word 'homozygous' along the edge of the paper.

'And if there's consanguinity in *preceding* generations as well, then the risk is probably greater than that. But I take it you're not cousins, or uncle and niece?' He half smiled for the first time.

'Certainly not! Yuck! Can you imagine marrying your *uncle*?!'

The others all laughed at the force of her response. Even Declan smiled. The atmosphere seemed to lighten.

'Any possibility you're related anywhere along the line?'

'Not as far as *we* know!' Declan said. 'We come from different ends of the country.'

'So since there seems little chance of this being due to consanguinity, it's just terribly bad luck, I'm afraid.'

She felt Declan's hand reach across to take hers. He held it tightly. It might be bad luck in medical eyes but Declan never tired of reminding her how incredibly lucky they were to have found each other.

'Unfortunately' – Keith Galloway was still speaking – 'once a couple have had one child with an autosomal recessive condition, then we know both parents are carriers. So there's a higher chance successive children will also be affected.'

'How high?' Declan's voice came out in a squeak. She tightened her fingers on his briefly. He coughed and repeated the question in his usual low register. 'How high?'

'One in four.'

Keith Galloway started a new diagram. Male and female symbols connected with four child boxes. He coloured in the second male child.

'So we ... if we ... there'd be a one in four chance of us ... having the same thing?'

'That's right. Is it OK to ask about your families?'

The geneticist glanced up, looking at Declan, then at her. She nodded.

Dr Galloway started a new sheet of paper, sketching out a family tree. Bethany remained for the time alone at the bottom of the page. He began to probe their genetic ancestry. Any unexplained miscarriages anywhere, babies, children who died? He filled in the boxes where she and Declan could supply information. He was apologetic asking if there was any possibility Declan was not the father; he was careful in eliciting precise relationships and diagnoses. Assessment of future risks, he explained, depended on honesty and precision.

Most of it was mechanical, but she felt Declan's sudden tension when mention was made of Georgina.

'My twin – is there any greater risk for her?'

Had they discussed this, Declan and Georgina? He hadn't told her what the family had said. She hadn't asked. It was as much as she could do to cope with her own pain.

More questions came, this time about Georgina. It was reassuring. There was only a remote outside chance if she chose someone with the same mutation. Most unlikely. But it might have been an issue if they'd been from a culture of consanguineous marriages. Judy wondered fleetingly if Declan would remember all this well enough to explain it to his sister.

Dr Galloway advised him to tell Georgina, if she felt anxious, to go to her GP, explain the situation, ask for a referral to a Genetics Clinic. They'd take a full family history and give advice on the couple's particular risk, tell them about tests they might have and so on. Sensible advice. Safer than relying on information conveyed third-hand, filtered through lay minds.

On and on, round and round, they went. Making links, filling in blanks. But there were still gaps. Declan wrote down the questions – questions that hadn't been questions before Bethany. Questions now that demanded answers – answers to which other people held the keys.

FOURTEEN

Isobel McLean was Sid Robertson's childhood sweetheart. They were inseparable; 'joined at the hip,' their parents laughingly said. At the tender age of nine he'd made a pledge, sealed in his schoolboy blood, to marry her when they grew up. And their friendship had endured, even through their adolescent years when hormones kicked in and other attractions beckoned.

His admiration for Isobel grew with the years. She was not only pretty, but she was never moody like his sisters. And she was clever – much more so than he was himself – but modest with it. And best of all she was devoted to him. She won a place at university, but at the last minute declined it. She couldn't face months without him, she told Sid; the London course might be prestigious but he was more important. She enrolled at a local college, which meant she could stay at home, see him often. He was smugly gratified at the time, not truly appreciating her sacrifice until years later.

Adolescent life for him was much more chaotic. School was something to be endured and abandoned at the earliest opportunity. But life beyond it was a confused and essentially hostile environment. A firm of mechanics gave him a chance but he sneered at their benevolence. He tested their goodwill by being persistently late for work, and knocking off early. As he'd expected, their tolerance had limits but nonetheless he railed against them when they sacked him. For a time life as a forester appealed, but being out in all weathers and a surly boss soon became intolerable. His parents despaired, but always Isobel was there, anchoring him, believing in him.

Isobel was in her last term at college, with a signed contract to teach in the local infant school, when they next spoke of marriage. Both families were less than enthusiastic. What kind of security could Sid offer? Isobel insisted she could provide for them both.

'Oh, and when children come along?' her father said crushingly.

'He's right, lad,' Sid's father agreed. 'You've got to think of the future, too.'

The prospect of an indefinite wait was depressing. For the first time in his experience, Isobel cried. Sid was so shocked that he instantly applied for the first possible job in the first paper he scanned. No-one was more surprised than he when the firm of financiers offered him an attractive package: they'd give him practical experience and pay for him to gain qualifications, if he would study in his own time.

He discovered a natural flair. Night school offered him a chance to regain lost ground, and he obtained his HNC, and started studying for a degree. Only to Isobel did he confide the discovery that the challenge was enjoyable as well as stimulating. Both sets of parents sighed with relief. Isobel looked on with pride.

The job symbolised the beginning of Sid's maturing. He smiled wryly as one by one he espoused the conventions he had derided for so long. Marriage served only to stabilise him further. His hard work paid off – he rose through the ranks, bought a newer car, a bigger house. He was head-hunted by a more prestigious company, and they moved to Devon. Success followed success and he started to travel to London to meet with colleagues in head office.

It was Isobel, watching proudly, who first broached the subject of children. They were established now. Her job seemed pretty humdrum compared with the life he led. Was it time to start trying?

After a year without success, Sid began to notice the changes. Isobel, his steadying influence, his rock, was irritable, depressed. He found it hard to keep up with her mood swings. He dreaded the look on her face when people innocently asked if they had a family. For him it was different, life was exciting, but for her, he knew, each month brought another cause for tears. Other pregnancies, other babies, rubbed salt in the wound. Even being with young children all day hurt. She started to go out less.

Isobel without her sunny disposition wasn't the Isobel he felt comfortable with. He tried to think of imaginative forms of distraction, but she was not easily consoled. She fretted about the lost years of potential fertility using contraceptives; she worried about her biological clock ticking away; she feared they might never have children. He soon ran out of platitudes.

It was hard to keep up the outward pretence of normality, but on one thing they were both agreed: this was no-one else's business. Sid started to steel himself each day for the full brunt of her disappointment. She became obsessive about making love on 'the right days'. He found it inhibiting to be so mechanical. The strain started to show in their relationship. But Sid repeatedly told himself this was his chance to be the stable influence, supportive, understanding. He was extra loving, pampering her. Perhaps she was run-down, needing a tonic: why didn't she pop along to see the doctor?

Dr Gregory was an elderly man who believed in being a family doctor not a medically qualified technician. He made time to listen. He heard the catalogue of vague symptoms, but waited for more. The tears came, the bitter disappointment, the fear.

He comforted and, when Isobel was composed again, took a careful medical history. He sent blood samples for a range of tests. His probing questions were gentle and sensitive. Periods – regular? Normal? Any changes? Did she smoke? Drink alcohol? How much? How long had they used contraceptives? What kind? When did they stop? Had she ever been pregnant? Ever had a termination? How often did they have sex? Any pain? Any problems? Husband ever impotent? Ever ejaculate too soon?

'Well, Mrs Robertson, I understand your worry. And I know the desire to have a baby can be quite overwhelming. But try not to let this get to you too much. If you're too strung up, that in itself can make it harder to conceive. Easy to say, not so easy to do, I know!' He grimaced sympathetically.

Isobel, feeling so much better already for having shared her anxieties with him, actually smiled in response.

'About eighty per cent of couples will conceive within one year of trying, ninety per cent within two years. You've been trying for more than a year now so I think I'll refer you to an infertility specialist. That'll probably be enough to make you pregnant straight away!'

Isobel grinned back at him.

'Before I do that though, I need to see your husband. Can he pop in and see me some time? But unless I find something very obvious there, I'll refer you both to the hospital. It might be some time before you get an appointment, so don't think you're forgotten if you don't hear immediately. They're busy places.'

'And should we ... you know ... keep trying? Or is it best to ... abstain and then ...?'

'I know some people think it's a good idea to store sperm up – have a sort of concerted effort. But that isn't actually the case. Two to seven days is probably the ideal – to produce the best sperm. And days thirteen to fourteen of your cycle are probably your most fertile. So as often as you like is the answer! Good luck! Come and see me when you're six weeks pregnant!'

Sid was so reassured to find his wife her old sunny self when he returned home from work that night that he agreed without hesitation. Yes, he'd pop into the surgery Friday evening after work. No problem. It would be more awkward to take time off to go to see the specialist, during the day, without saying why, but he'd think of something. Besides, the doctor might be right: Isobel might well be pregnant before the appointment came.

She wasn't, but he spun a story of needing to take a day off to deal with a domestic crisis. His boss was a DIY enthusiast. He understood.

The infertility clinic was hard to find and they – well, Isobel anyway – had to ask twice before they found it. Too late they realised they could simply have asked for the Gynaecology Clinic in the Outpatient Department. There was nothing overt to show that this was any different from all the other myriad problems women were subject to.

They had twenty minutes to wait. Long enough to make Sid squirm uneasily in this essentially female world.

Dr Melvin Carr rose to greet them as they entered. Sid felt strangely comforted to find himself towering above the doctor by at least a foot. He had one advantage at least. But the doctor seemed so relaxed and friendly that before long Sid started to relax too. The history-taking was meticulous, covering all the questions Dr Gregory had asked and then more, but curiously matter of fact and unemotional. The examination was thorough and again coolly professional. They'd need more tests too. More blood. More semen.

'We'd like two more samples – one today before you leave. And perhaps you could pop the second one in on your way to work, say in three weeks time? Does that sound reasonable? It takes three to four months to produce sperm, you see. Things like flu or a virus months ago could affect production now. So we like to see more than one specimen, over time.'

Sid calculated he could just about fit in the round trip without anyone at work knowing.

They had expected another long wait, so the rapid second appointment took them by surprise. Sid decided a direct appeal to his boss was best.

'Isobel – she's having some women's troubles. She needs to see a specialist up at the hospital. She's pretty strung up about it – as you can imagine. OK if I take a couple of hours off this afternoon – run her up? I can pop in later and work on tonight to get the papers ready for that client tomorrow.'

His manager was guarded. Well, as long as the job was ready on time. He hoped Sid wasn't going to make a habit of asking for time off. It was a tough world out there. They must keep ahead of the game.

Dr Carr was less forthright than he'd been the time before. He seemed to Sid to be fencing, tiptoeing. The rapier thrust when it came caught him unguarded.

'Well, I have to tell you, we've found the cause of your infertility.'

Sid and Isobel were instantly tense, eyes on the consultant, waiting.

'Have you ever heard of Klinefelter's Syndrome?'

'Nope.'

'It's a chromosomal abnormality. And it means that a man has an extra X chromosome, or very occasionally more than one extra X.'

'So? What does that mean in plain English?'

'Men usually have one X and one Y. In Klinefelter's there are two Xs and one Y.'

'And?'

'You have Klinefelter's, Mr Robertson.'

83

'Me? Since when?'

'Since birth. You were born with it. It just happens. It's nobody's fault.'

'What does it mean?' Isobel asked the question but Sid heard it from a great distance.

'I'm afraid it means that your husband is infertile.'

The roaring in his ears was like an oncoming train in a tunnel, rattling over the track with a relentlessly repetitive in*fer*tile, in*fer*tile, in*fer*tile, IN*FER*TILE.

Sid was vaguely aware of the doctor's droning voice, going over the information, repeating it, different words, same meaning. And with each circle the barb went deeper, the numbness receded.

'It means there are no sperm being produced at all.'

Sid felt the cold fact like a shaft of ice through his heart.

'None? You mean ... *none*? I'm ... firing blanks?'

He saw Isobel cringe. OK, it was crude, but this was no time for niceties.

'I'm afraid so. The condition means you aren't producing any sperm at all.'

There it was. No softening, no disguise. He couldn't give her a baby. No matter how much he tried, how much he wanted to. He couldn't. He COULD NOT.

'And what can you do about it?' Was that Isobel's voice? So matter of fact, so unemotional.

'Unfortunately there's nothing we can do to improve things as far as your husband's sperm count goes, although of course, there are other options we might consider to enable you to have a family.'

We might consider? What the hell did he mean? Was *he* proposing having a family with Isobel?

There was a sickening silence. Then gently Dr Carr continued.

'However, I don't think now is the time to go into the detail. I think you should go away and discuss this news. It's important for you, as a couple, to take time, talk about your situation. Discuss together how important it is to you – both of you – to have a child. This is not something to rush into. Take your time. We'll organise another appointment for you to come back and see me, and then we'll look at the options in more detail.'

The shock of the discovery drove all thought of work from Sid's mind. He completely forgot his promise to go back to the office. He forgot the client due next morning. His manager was furious. The client withdrew his business. Sid hardly noticed. But he was no longer the blue-eyed boy.

Isobel was magnificent, enveloping him in her love. But Sid was shaken by more than his own loss.

'Izzie, I'll understand – if you want a divorce – find somebody else who *can* give you a baby.'

84

'What?!! Sidney Holloway Robertson! Divorce? Never! I married you for *you* – not for your bank balance, not for your sperm count! Not to have a father for my kids, really, when I think about it. And you're still you – the man I chose to spend the rest of my life with. So no more talk of divorce.'

'But, think about it ...'

'Nothing to think about! *You* think about it! How many couples d'you know who're just as daft about each other twenty-five years on – or whatever it is since we crawled out of our cradles into each other's lives – as we are? Uhh?'

'Ummmm. None, offhand – I guess.'

'Well, there you are, then. Enough said. We've been through a lot together. And I can't imagine life without you now – crazy loon that I am! You're part of the furniture! You and me, we're two sides of the same coin. OK, we can't have kids like other folk do without a bit of help, but hey, so what? We're a team, you and me, you old duffer. If we never have a family I'll still want you hanging around cluttering up my kitchen. If we do, well, I'll need you to stir your stumps and do a bit more round the house. So get practising!'

'But Izzie ...'

'Besides' – Isobel cut across his protest – 'nobody else would put up with me and my nagging ways!'

And she remained immovable.

By the time they met the gynaecologist again, they were easily able to convince him that they had taken on board the implications of the diagnosis; they were ready to hear about the different options. He talked to them about adoption, about the delays and the stipulations, the advantages and the pitfalls. They listened attentively. He approached more delicate ground cautiously.

'Of course, since Mrs Robertson is apparently fertile, there is another option. And it doesn't involve unpleasant invasive procedures or hospital stays or anything. And it's got a high success rate.'

Their attention was arrested.

'You could consider having donated sperm and create a child for yourselves that way.'

'You mean ...?'

'Artificial insemination.'

'You mean ... like *bulls*?' Sid was flabbergasted. He had no idea such a facility existed.

Dr Carr smiled.

'Well, same principle. We like to think we're more refined about it!'

Sid grinned sheepishly.

'You know about farm life, Mr Robertson?' Dr Carr asked.

'Oh no, not first-hand. But I know what they *do* – sort of.'

'Well, here we introduce the semen in laboratory conditions – using a simple syringe. It just takes minutes. And thereafter pregnancy is just like normal. No-one need ever know that it wasn't a perfectly ordinary conception.'

'Where … who … where do you get … *it* … from?'

'We have a number of volunteers. And we screen them carefully to make sure they're healthy and there aren't likely to be problems.'

'Would we have to meet …?'

'No, you definitely would *not* meet the donor. Anonymity – not knowing who the donor is – that's part of the contract we have with these men. And they don't know if their donations have been used successfully either. We do our best to protect everyone concerned.'

'Aren't they – *curious?*' Isobel asked.

'Well, we don't hear about it if they are.'

'Just to be on the safe side, could we go … somewhere else, further away, to … have it done?'

Sid knew why she was asking. She knew he couldn't afford any more hassles at work. If they could go away there'd be no danger of the firm finding out, making his life miserable.

'I was wondering … I have an aunt, Aunt Peggy; she lives in Fife,' Isobel was saying. 'Presumably they have these clinics in Scotland? I was just thinking, it'd be good if no-one else suspected … it was … well, you know, different from normal. For the child, I mean. Kids can be so cruel. I've been a teacher all my working life. I've heard them first-hand! But we could go up to stay with Aunt Peggy and it'd just be like going on holiday. No-one else need ever know. Even if anyone saw us at the hospital they wouldn't know us. There'd be no wondering what we were doing.'

'There are indeed clinics in Scotland. The nearest to Fife would be Edinburgh. It's a centre of excellence for this kind of thing actually. If you like, I could speak to my colleagues up there and explore the possibilities.'

Isobel nodded, her eyes bright and excited.

Dr Kerr turned suddenly to Sid.

'How do *you* feel about this, Mr Robertson?'

'It's for definite – us not knowing who – him not knowing us – or about the child?'

'Definitely, yes.'

'And *you* do it – the actual … y'know?' Sid jerked his head.

'Introduce the semen. Yes – well, *one* of us, not necessarily me. And if it's in Scotland, definitely *not* me. But the equivalent. A member of the medical team.'

'And what about the birth certificate?' Sid was thinking fast.

'Your name can be on that.'

'Is that – legal?'

86

'It's permitted.'

'So after that ... that – y'know, putting it in – after that, it's just as normal?'

'Absolutely. You share in the pregnancy. You can be at the birth. You bring up the child in every respect just as if it was your own biologically. And after all, when you think about it, being a father is much more about loving the child, rearing it, and all of that than it is about giving it your genetic material, isn't it?'

Out of the corner of his eye, Sid saw Isobel was nodding slowly at this thought.

'Well, I guess, I always thought you did both, but when you put it like that ...'

Sid turned to look directly at Isobel.

'D'you think ...?'

'If you're OK with it, I'm game.'

Sid turned back to Dr Carr but before he could ask his next question Isobel was speaking.

'If we decided we wanted another one – could we ...?'

'Indeed you could. We could even try to give you a second one using the same donor so that the children are even more likely to resemble each other than if they only shared your genes.'

'Oh yeah – *that*.' A thought struck Sid. 'What if they ... look like ... *him*? Wouldn't that – y'know, make people suspicious? Can you choose – anything? Y'know, height, hair, eyes, anything?'

'Bald spot!' Isobel chimed in.

He grinned.

'We do try to match as far as it's possible,' Dr Carr said, smiling too. 'Not bald spot, I'm afraid! But hair colouring and so on. So you wouldn't, for example, get a black donor. Before you leave I'll get you to fill in a form that says what you'd prefer and we'll do our best. But you know, lots of children don't resemble their biological fathers at all, so I don't think you should worry about that too much.'

Dr Carr arranged for them to go to the Edinburgh clinic. July 7th was the appointment date. July 7th. The date they might start their family. Sid had a funny dropping feeling in his stomach thinking of it. July 7th. July 7th. That'd mean an April baby. Good time to have a baby, Isobel said; she could take it for walks, easily get the nappies dried.

She arranged to have a week away from school, telling the head that she was undergoing specialist medical treatment, but that it wasn't something she could talk about. Sid booked a week's annual leave. He wanted to be there, be involved. Whoever heard of a child being conceived and the dad not being there?

After all the talk, all the imagining, the moment itself was an anti-climax. Isobel lay still for half an hour afterwards and they went back to Aunt Peggy's strangely subdued. The possibility that it might not work had hardly crossed their minds. Isobel insisted she started to feel sick straight away, confident that she was pregnant.

When she phoned Sid at work the day it was confirmed, he couldn't contain his excitement, and the whole office knew within minutes. Everyone congratulated him, nudging him with sly comments about what he got up to on holiday in Scotland. He grinned and winked back. Deep inside himself he felt a pang of something unnamed but, whatever it was, it was soon suppressed by the happiness Isobel exuded.

There was no more proud father in the hospital than Sid the April night Sian Margaret entered the world with a shriek of protest. He even helped with her delivery. From the outset he was her slave. And that devotion continued, genuine and unqualified. Sid it was who changed nappies, gave piggy backs, read bedtime stories, took her for train rides, got up in the night to soothe away her nightmares, patiently taught her to pronounce her 'th's.

So happy were they in their domestic fulfilment that they had no hesitation in returning to the clinic two years later. This time Sid could not risk taking time off, so Isobel travelled north alone, Sid's mother caring for Sian. She was away just three days, telling the family that she was just popping up to see her Aunt Peggy. But that attempt failed. Sid insisted it was because he wasn't there; whoever heard of conception without the dad present!

He contrived a meeting with his opposite number in Edinburgh, and tagged on two days' leave. Going that far he'd be better breaking the journey, taking his time, seeing several useful contacts while he was there, he explained, it'd save a repeat visit. The boss followed his logic. Aunt Peggy was initially suspicious that they were hiding something. Why would they come back to see her so soon after the last visit? But she was won over by the suggestion that she should have Sian all to herself while Isobel and Sid popped into Edinburgh to look at the shops and the famous sights.

It was no surprise to Sid that Isobel was pregnant. He was there, wasn't he? Aunt Peggy took it as a personal tribute that they had conceived a second time while under her roof. Magical water in Scotland, she told them. But it was a shock to everyone to hear they were expecting twins. And as the months passed, Isobel struggled. The extra weight of two babies meant more swelling, more heartburn, raised blood pressure. Isobel's mother came to stay to relieve her of some of the strain of an active three-year-old, but in spite of her assistance, the twins came four weeks early. Declan Andrew and Georgina Marie may have been small but they were textbook babies and quickly began to thrive.

However, despite her stoical denials, it became obvious to Sid that Isobel was finding three young children extremely hard going. Ten months' breastfeeding left her permanently exhausted. The gaunt face, the permanently dark-rimmed eyes, the weight loss, belied her own protestations that she was fine. Eventually Sid overruled her, employing a woman to come in to give her a hand: anyone could dust and vacuum, he insisted, parents had more important things to do. Gradually, imperceptibly, Isobel regained her energy.

After the first year Declan and Georgina became each other's distraction, comfort and friend. Temperamentally they were quite unalike but each complemented the other. Sian adored them both, becoming protective and more independent in her efforts to set them an example. Sid began to relax again and openly revel in his family.

When the twins were five they moved to Kent where Sid was made a partner in the firm of financiers. There was no need for Isobel to return to work and they could afford to pay for a good education for the children, and support them in their varied interests. Life centred on the growing family.

Paternal pride knew no bounds when Sian was chosen for the school nativity play, when the twins sang a song and played their recorders in the end-of-year concert, when Declan won the one hundred metres freestyle swimming badge. All three flourished and Sid rarely ever thought of their beginnings. He accepted the compliments with natural pride. He adopted the responsibilities as his natural right.

Not until Sian was twenty did he ever allude to their biological origins. It was a period in their lives when he was feeling particularly powerless. During her adolescent years Sian had become increasingly rebellious; now

89

she had just informed them that she was leaving home and going to live with Roddy, her bohemian boyfriend from university. Sid shared with Isobel his profound sense of anxiety. What would happen to Sian without any parental restraint?

'Izzie, d'you think … is this something in your genes? How much d'you think the kids had in them – already – when they were conceived? We don't know – *anything* really – about their real father – do we? I worry sometimes …'

'I know. I know.' She reached across to pat his hand soothingly. 'But look at all our friends. Their kids are up to all sorts. We parents can only do so much. They've got to find their own values, lead their own lives. We can't make them into little clones of us. Sian might have been just as rebellious, made exactly the same choices, if she'd been genetically yours.'

'You're right. But … I hate to see them making big mistakes.'

'We can't complain. Not really. They've been good kids basically.'

'So far. I guess you're right. But Sian's got a wild streak in her.'

'Hey, look who's talking! I seem to remember a certain other young person not a million miles from here who was the despair of his parents' hearts in his youth!'

'Point taken!' Sid agreed ruefully.

There was a long silence before Isobel said hesitantly, 'Have you ever … you know … regretted … Sid?'

'Having our three? Not for a billionth of a second. Next to you they're the best thing that ever happened to me.'

His conviction was genuine, indisputable.

When the twins were nineteen and away at university, Isobel suddenly collapsed in the street. She was taken straight to hospital in an ambulance, siren blaring. Sid took the call at work. There must be some mistake; Isobel was never ill, always strong and energetic. He raced back from the board meeting, grateful for once that London drivers were used to speed. Isobel made light of her crisis – just trying to draw attention to herself, she said, now she was in danger of being totally eclipsed by these clever children of theirs.

The consultant was kind. Isobel could go home in a few days. Sid insisted he ring Sian, Declan and Georgina. Isobel protested: it was better not to disturb their studies during term-time; they'd soon be home for the holiday. But for once Sid knew he must countermand her wishes. With cracking voice he told them one at a time: it was ovarian cancer; nothing they could do. In the last few weeks, he nursed her devotedly. The children took it in turns to come home to help at weekends, to be with their mother, sharing their own raw pain with their siblings. Within six months Isobel was dead.

The change in their father shocked all three youngsters. Not only was

Sid inconsolable, but for the first time in their lives, he was unavailable to them. The light had gone out of his eyes, out of his life. They tried to be supportive, loving, there for him; but they couldn't reach him where it mattered. Flatly, without emotion, he encouraged them to get on with their own lives. They took holiday jobs near their universities, trying to be self-sufficient. He proudly attended their graduations but it was at these moments he felt his loss so unbearably.

Sian's decision to emigrate to New Zealand with her boyfriend, Roddy, was another gut-wrenching milestone, but in the midst of his pain Sid marvelled at the confidence of his elder daughter. He wanted to share his anxieties with Isobel; instead he consoled himself with the realisation that the relationship seemed to be strong, and there was no sign of Roddy just 'upping and offing' as he'd feared initially.

It was a special moment when Sian rang him to tell him she was pregnant, that he was going to be a grandfather. Zoë Claire arrived two days before Isobel's birthday. Sid's tears and laughter mingled over the phone as Roddy told him. When could he go out? Sian so much wanted him to see the baby. He'd think about it, he said – but New Zealand? It was a long way away. Just one year and eight months later Rory Henry arrived. More requests from Sian: please come out and see them. Zoë had Mum's smile. She rang often at first but the pressure of two small children encroached and gradually the calls became less frequent.

It came as a complete surprise to them all when, four years after Isobel's death, Sid decided to quit his job and retire to New Zealand. He fancied helping on the ranch, he said, and he wanted to see his grandchildren, share in their lives. Sian and Roddy were enthusiastic, welcoming him into their home until he could find somewhere of his own nearby.

Georgina asked fearfully if he was sure it was the right thing to do; New Zealand? So far away? He assured her he needed a chance to start again. Here he was constantly reminded of Isobel and all he'd lost; he wanted to try to rebuild his life.

Declan organised a special family meal before he left and they all cried when Sid made a little broken speech, about how he couldn't have asked for better children, nobody could be more proud of his family than he was. But he had to move on, not become a millstone round their necks.

He left on a cold windy January day.

SIXTEEN

Self-sufficient in an extension at the back of the ranch, Sid found a new peace. Roddy's uncomplicated acceptance of him warmed his heart and he loved to be 'visited' by his grandchildren who clearly rejoiced in his availability and unstinting devotion.

But he missed the son and daughter he'd left behind.

Georgina wrote him long lively letters, recounting colourful and exaggerated tales of her doings. He replied occasionally, telling her how proud he was of her achievements, how proud her mother would have been. But letter writing was not his forte.

Declan rang every weekend. Characteristically he spoke little of himself, encouraging Sid to tell him about life on the ranch and the children. He flew out himself to see them all for three weeks in the summer after Sid had emigrated. The children adored him and became his daytime shadows, but Declan set aside the evenings for his father and Sid basked in the warmth of their mutual love.

It was Georgina who first told Sid about Declan's budding romance with Judy. He smiled at her exuberant endorsement of the girl. Declan was slower to confide, but Sid noticed that the weekend calls became less regular. Thanks to Georgina, he understood.

'Dad, I've met this girl. She's called Judy.' Declan sounded hesitant, feeling his way. 'We've been seeing a lot of each other. She lives in Scotland but we meet every weekend.'

'Serious, is it?' Sid was trying for encouragement without unseemly curiosity.

'For me, yes. But I don't know about her yet. Haven't asked.'

'What's she like, son? Tell me about her.'

'Well, she's tall, slim, curly auburn hair – *naturally* auburn! Fabulous big dark eyes. Lovely personality. Quiet but fun too. Dad, she's … terrific. I can't explain … I've never felt like this before.'

Sid smiled gently. This was a new Declan. He listened as the younger man told him about her work, their chance meeting.

'Gosh, she must have made an instant impact to have that effect on *you*!' Sid was impressed. His cautious son, chasing up to Scotland after a brief encounter?

'I've always hoped I'd find someone – have the kind of love you and Mum had. Anything else, well, it'd seem second rate somehow. It's made me very choosy.'

'You'd go a long way to find anyone like your Mum.' Sid's voice was suddenly muffled.

'I know. I had to go to Shotton! And to Scotland!'

'So – what next?'

'I'm going to ask her to marry me – when the moment's right. If she hasn't gone off me in the meantime!'

'Think she might?'

'I hope *not*. But you know me, Dad, I keep wondering what she can see in me. She could have anyone she wanted. Still could.'

'Don't sell yourself short, lad. And keep me posted, eh? It's times like this I wish I wasn't on the other side of the world.'

'I know. Miss you, too. I just wanted you to know about her, before I ask her.'

'Thanks, Dec. I appreciate that. Any photos? I'd like to at least know what my future daughter-in-law looks like. Without the rose-tinted spectacles!'

'Yep, I'll send you one.'

'Can I tell Sian?'

'Sure.'

'Keep us posted.'

'Will do. Oh and Dad …'

'Yes, Dec?'

'Thanks for everything. You're a great Dad. I know I haven't often said so. You've always set us such a brilliant example. But I often think, even now, what would Dad do?'

'Do you? Thanks for telling me. Means a lot that. But you've been great kids. Mum and I have always been so proud of you.'

His delight was genuine when Declan rang to say Judy had said yes. He and Sian had already discussed coming over for the wedding.

It was Sid's first trip back to the UK and he found himself relieved to be going to Scotland and not back to the haunts which held such powerful memories of Isobel. He didn't want any sense of his own inner unhappiness to mar Declan's joy. Only as the plane circled over Edinburgh airport did it cross his mind that Declan himself had come into being in this very city all those years ago, but would never know it. It was a curious coincidence.

Declan and Judy both met them at the airport. The palpable love between the young couple churned the simmering sadness within Sid's heart, but he allowed no sign of it to escape his private thoughts. Judy was even prettier than the photograph, he conceded, but more than that she had a warmth and thoughtfulness which charmed him. Her obvious delight in gaining a whole family drew her still closer.

Georgina arrived two days before the wedding and Sid savoured this special time when they could all be together after their lives had taken them so far apart.

The superficiality of Judy's mother he excused as the nervous flutterings of an anxious mother-of-the-bride, and he could see nothing of Betty in his new daughter-in-law. Judy's quiet manner and her obvious adoration of his son reassured him that Declan had made a wise choice. There was a lump in his throat as he watched the car take the newly-weds off into the night. When would they all meet again?

When Declan rang to tell him that Judy was pregnant he felt again the swell of pride he had experienced with each one of Sian's babies: Zoë and Rory, then Carl and Selina. He promised himself he would not leave it so long before seeing this grandchild. An ultrasound photograph of the growing baby Robertson took pride of place on his mantelpiece.

The phone call from an excited Declan announcing Bethany's safe arrival sent him immediately to Sian and Roddy's part of the house to share the genuine happiness he felt. They drank a toast to the new arrival in the Dom Perignon champagne he had saved for a special occasion. Silently he included Isobel in the moment.

He had already forwarded a cheque to pay for the pram but now he had something special to pack and post. The tumble of jewellery on the bed conjured up vivid images of Isobel wearing these necklaces and brooches, and he sorted them through a blur of pain. For baby Bethany he selected a ring; three graded pearls with tiny diamond chips between them. If Bethany grew up to have her mother's colouring they would suit her to perfection. He inscribed the card with care.

To Bethany Erika,
This ring used to belong to your grandmother, your Daddy's mother. She was a most special lady. And I am sending it to you because you are a very special granddaughter. I expect you'll want to have the stones reset to make them modern enough but I hope you like the pearls. They remind me of your Mummy as well as Grandma.
With lots of love
from
Grandad
XXXX

He posted it that same day.

The unexpected phone call from Georgina was distorted by an unusually crackly line.

'Say it again, Georgie. I thought for a minute you'd said she'd died. It's a dreadful line today.'

'I did say that, Dad. Dec's just rung. Bethany's … dead.'

'But she can't be.'

'Seems it wasn't just an infection or something simple. I couldn't ask questions. Oh Dad, Dec was so upset. I feel so helpless.'

Sid's own sense of powerlessness was overwhelming.

'Shall I come over? Can you find out? Should I ring? I'd come like a shot, only I don't want to intrude. Let me know, Georgie. I'll do whatever's right for them.'

'Thanks, Dad. Dec'll understand. I'm phoning him again tomorrow. I'll keep you posted.'

It was only when Declan rang himself that Sid even thought of the wider implications for the family.

They had spared him much of the detail of what had happened; listening to the broken voice giving even a brief fragmented account had been painful enough. His every instinct was to wrap Declan in his arms as he had done so often in his boyhood. Nothing could soothe away this hurt but he ached to show his love.

'We saw the geneticist today, Dad. He's looking at our family histories and trying to work out what the chances are of this happening again.'

'Say that again, Dec? I don't follow.'

Patiently Declan explained about the recessive gene, and how they needed to trace its lineage.

'But there was heaps of stuff I didn't know – about Gran and Gramps, and about Mum's side. Judy was the same. So we both have to find out more about our families and then see him again. Can you start jotting down as much as you know? It'll save time when I phone next time.'

SEVENTEEN

There was a flight available two days later. Sid took it. He told Sian he was going over because he wanted to show Dec how much he grieved for him. To Declan he simply said, 'I *have* to be there, son.'

Sid was unprepared for the toll grief had taken, and at the airport he held Declan tightly for a long moment, searching in vain for words. Declan's voice was choked.

'It's OK, Dad. I know. There isn't anything anyone *can* say.'

On the drive to the house he enquired about the journey, about the children. It felt so contrived, so polite, but Sid understood. The time would come to drop the façade, but not yet.

Judy was warm in her embrace and instantly adopted the role of pleased hostess. Taking his cue Sid exclaimed over the delightful home they were creating, and accepted the offer of a guided tour with alacrity. He was sincere in his enthusiasm for what they had achieved, the care they had taken to restore the cottage to its original design, the strong touches which made it their own. It had both character and charm, a winning combination. He encouraged them to expand on their plans for the parts they had not yet worked on.

They had almost completed the leisurely exploration before Judy's composure cracked.

'And this was … to be Bethany's room.'

Sid could find no words for such a moment. His eyes took in the strong blues and purples, the piles of baby things, the white teddy bear. No-one had as yet made any effort to pack things away. It was as if the room still waited for its new owner.

As soon as the door opened Declan had moved to slip an arm around Judy, drawing her tightly to his side. Two pairs of dark eyes bleakly scanned the empty cot. Sid, at a loss, walked across to take them both in his arms. Now was the time. All three wept together.

'We haven't … thanked you … for the ring … you sent her.' Judy's eyes, magnified with tears, struggled to hold their focus, and her hand trembled on his arm. 'It's absolutely beautiful. And it was the most lovely thought. It came a few days before … she died. May we … keep it? Or …'

'Oh my dear, of course, you may! It was Bethany's. Treasure her in the memories.'

'Thanks, Dad.' Declan's voice was muffled by his handkerchief. 'It will always remind me of Mum as well as … Bethany.'

The shared tears cleared the air.

Declan watched his father carefully. It took him a couple of days to re-adjust his body clock and they encouraged him to sleep as and when he needed to. By the Saturday morning he was looking more rested and Declan suggested that they banish the last vestiges of jet-lag by going for a walk through Roslin Glen, a favourite local haunt.

'If you don't mind, I won't come,' Judy said. 'I've got letters to write. But you two take your time. It's a lovely day for the glen.'

Privately to Declan she added, 'He needs time alone with you. He's come all this way; don't deprive him of the chance to just enjoy your company.'

'Are you sure, Jude? You're my top priority. Dad would understand that.'

'I'm sure. I'm fine. Honestly. Off you go.'

The two men walked in silence for a while as the narrow path took them off the road and down into the glen. Declan always loved its chang-ing moods and different seasons. Today sunlight filtered through the fresh growth, shafts of it highlighting patches of undergrowth, birdsong all around them. And as he had done so often with Judy, he stopped to enjoy the majesty of the ruined castle with its old bridge and huge stones. But there was a heaviness to his thoughts today, remembering the events which had robbed them of that old carefree happiness.

He led the way on down through the trees.

'Thanks for coming, Dad. It's great to see you. But it's a long way to come. I really appreciate it. We both do.'

'I had to, Dec. Not just to see you both. There's something I must tell you. Something I've got to tell you now.'

'Mmhmm?'

'It's about your visit to the geneticist.'

'Yep? What about it?'

'You need to know about your family history.'

'That's right.'

'The fact is, Dec ...'

Declan cast a glance back in his direction – was he out of breath on this slope? He didn't appear to be.

'The thing is ... Mum and me – we agreed we wouldn't tell you. We only wanted to protect you. But the thing is – well, now I *have* to. Mum would understand. I *have* to.'

'Have to what?'

'Tell you.'

'Tell me what?' Declan was completely mystified. Was his father losing his grip? Talk about getting blood out of a stone ...!

'The thing is ... I'm not ... actually ... your father. Not biologically speaking, I mean. In every other way, yes, I am. But not genetically.'

Declan stopped so suddenly that Sid collided with him. They steadied each other, and then he stood staring at the older man in silence. There had been no inkling that this was coming.

Sid fidgeted with the change in his trouser pocket.

'Shall we go and sit over there on that trunk?'

They perched side by side against the tree stump. But, for once, Declan was unaware of the beauty all around them. Not looking at him, Sid was speaking again.

'It's a long story. But basically, well I'm ... I can't have kids. Got some funny syndrome with an extra X chromosome. Makes a chap infertile. That was a shock, finding out about that, I can tell you! We only found out when we'd been married several years too, and no babies came along. But Mum – well, Mum and me – we wanted kids. Always loved kids. Both of us. So we decided we'd have ... well, artificial insemination, in a word.'

Declan felt physically sick. Was this real? It felt more like some slow motion movie.

'Sian. And Georgina too, of course. You all came the same way.'

Declan couldn't bring himself to utter a word.

'But I always thought of you as mine. I loved you as if you were my own. In fact, I didn't really think about ... the beginning ... at all. Until you said about the genetic thing.'

'So ... who was my *real* father?' It was cruel. Declan knew that as soon as the words were said. But it was out.

'We don't know. Thing is, the chaps who ... y'know, do that – well, they want to be anonymous. We only know it was somebody healthy, and young and intelligent. Probably tall and dark.'

'Tall, dark, handsome ... *stranger*, huh?' There was no vestige of humour in Declan's soul.

Sid was silent. Declan couldn't look at him. Not yet.

'And could *I* find out?'

'I doubt it. They do their best to cover the tracks – to protect these blokes.'

'So I can't trace my genetic heritage? Ever?'

'Well, I guess you could ask. Under the circumstances. But they told us back then, you couldn't.'

There was a long silence. Declan dropped his head in his hands, his fingers clenched in his hair.

'Dec ... you have to understand ...'

'Understand what?' It was beyond understanding, surely.

'How much you were wanted. It wasn't some easy decision. It cost Mum – and me ... you'll never know what it cost.'

The naked emotion jerked Declan out of his self-absorption. He sat upright, turning slowly to look at the man he had always thought of as his father. The face was drawn and pale, the expression haggard, the shoulders slumped. He looked suddenly old and worn.

'Try me. Tell me ... Dad.' The name was gentle this time, tentative.

He saw Sid's struggle for composure.

'Give me a moment.'

Declan turned away, looking down the glen, his mind in turmoil but dimly aware now of the ache of the man at his side. What had he been forced to resurrect?

Sid's words when they came were quiet and arresting.

'You know what it feels like to love a girl so much you'd do anything for her.'

Declan nodded. He did indeed.

'I saw it in you – with Judy. That first time. Mum was like that for me. I worshipped her. I'd have done anything for her.'

For the hundredth time Declan felt the raw pain of his father's loss.

'We were so happy. Like you two. So happy. But I watched her changing. She wanted a baby so much. It was agony month after month. She changed. It never occurred to me it might be me. When I found out ... well, I told her she could have a divorce. She wouldn't hear of it. But I couldn't bear to think I couldn't give her the one thing I knew she really wanted.'

'Oh Dad! I can't imagine ...'

'No. Nobody can. Unless they've been there. It's the pits. I felt so guilty. And there wasn't a thing I could do about it. If I'd known about the X thing, of course, I'd never have married her. But I didn't. Until it was too late. She was brilliant about it, I have to say. Brilliant. Never ever blamed me. But Mum was like that. Always there for me. Always. Even then.'

Declan sat perfectly still, waiting for him to continue when he could.

'Then the guy at the clinic, the consultant chappie, said there was a way. Next best thing, he said. There was nothing wrong with Mum. We just needed the other half. At first, I don't mind telling you, I found the whole idea ... revolting, repulsive. How could I let some other man ...? But he talked to us and we realised that it was, like he said, the next best thing. Everything – apart from that first moment – everything would be the same. Mum would be pregnant like every other mum, give birth just the same, breastfeed just the same. And I could be there living it all with her. Yep, even when they ... did *it*, y'know. And all through the pregnancy, at the birth, just like every other dad. And nobody else need ever know. And nobody else ever *did* know. Till today.'

'Nobody?'

'No, only the people at the clinic.'

'Not even the family?'

'Nope. We decided to go up to Fife to stay with Mum's aunt. That way nobody where we lived would even know we'd been to a clinic. Aunt Peggy thought we were going shopping. Everybody else thought we were on holiday.'

'And us? Why not tell us?'

'We talked about it. Over and over in the beginning – before we had it done – y'know. But we figured you'd feel more secure if you didn't know. There didn't seem any reason *to* tell you.'

'Until now.'

EIGHTEEN

The silence became oppressive.

'Dec,' Sid began tentatively, 'it's the worst time I know, to drop this on you. On top of Bethany. I'd do anything not to have to. I've gone over and over this in my mind. But you need to know now. I couldn't risk your future by not telling you.'

'You're right. I had to know. Thanks, Dad. Sorry – about earlier. I didn't mean ...'

'I understand. You're not yourself anyway – after Bethany. Can't expect to be. And hearing this – it wouldn't have been easy – even before. I understand.'

'Thanks.' Declan reached across to lay a hand on Sid's arm. His father's hand covered his. 'Thanks.'

They sat silent again.

'Do Sian and Georgie know?'

'No, not yet. I came to tell you first. You *have* to know. And I wanted to be there, to tell you face to face. I couldn't tell you over the phone.'

'An expensive disclosure, eh?'

'In more ways than one!'

'Thanks, Dad. I don't envy you having to tell us that. I'd be struggling in your shoes.'

'But you'd have done the same, Dec. For your kids.'

The pain was searing.

'I'd have given my life for her,' Declan choked, the bleakness enveloping him in a suffocating grip. 'It kills me to think I couldn't protect her.'

'Dec, I'm so sorry ... I didn't think. Oh, what a stupid thing to say.'

Declan felt the arm round his bowed shoulders, but it couldn't eradicate the desolation. Eventually his father spoke again.

'Just so you know, Dec, I'm going to see Georgie next – so I can tell her in person. I'll tell Sian when I get home again.'

'What a grim task. Three times over. Could I ... to save you ...?'

'Thanks, but no. I must do it myself. Better in the flesh too. But they might need you to talk to – afterwards. Will that be all right?'

'Of course.'

'They'll need someone to commiserate with them. And they'll both turn to you. In the shock of it all they might not remember it's not a good time for you.'

'It's OK, Dad. Really. Other things have to go on.' Declan heard the flat, unconvincing tone of his own voice from the depths of his own personal abyss.

'They're better talking to you about the gene thing too. I don't really get all that hereditary stuff myself.'

'Well, I'm not up to speed myself there either. Even Dr Fairweather – you know, the neonatologist … with Bethany – he said *he* didn't understand it all. Very specialised apparently. So it's OK for us to feel ignorant.'

'This thing Bethany had, was it through … him … y'know … the donor?'

'We don't know yet. It could have been. Or through Mum. They're trying to piece it all together. That's why we need all this stuff about our families.'

A new thought froze Declan.

'There are *two* things now to deal with, though. There's this thing about the gene – which I certainly carry and maybe the girls do, too. And needing to find out just what our chances are of having other kids with – well, like Bethany. But on top of that now, me just not knowing half my genetic history.'

'Sian – she's got the same parents – she seems to be all right anyway – with Roddy. Their kids seem fine.'

'Well, if she's a carrier thank God *she* didn't chance on somebody with this gene too, eh?'

Ironic, Declan thought, the family hadn't approved of Roddy at first. Judy had seemed ideal. But, of course, genetics had nothing to do with suitability or all the things that influenced personal preferences. And deep inside he'd been grateful that she carried it too. At least she couldn't blame him, turn away from him, when she was equally responsible. Not fairly anyway. But this … ah … this blank genetic history, it could only be laid at his door. Would it be the splinter that would grow into a wedge, driving them apart? He forced his thoughts to take a different path. He mustn't let these fears surface. He had to have faith.

'Poor old Georgie, eh? Really in the frying pan with this one!' he said with feeling.

'How d'you mean?'

'Well, she'll know about all this *before* she meets her man. No problem if she isn't a carrier herself. But what if she is?'

'Isn't that good – that she knows?'

'Well, it's good in the sense that she could get counselling. She might want to talk to somebody about it.'

'But …?'

'Well, I don't know, will it mean she's afraid of having kids – in case? I mean, if she *hadn't* known, she might have had them and they were all fine – like Sian – and she needn't have worried at all. That's the most likely thing, Dr Galloway says.'

'Oh.'

'But she *does* know. Well, she *will* anyway. I mean, just imagine, Dad. Every man she dates, will she say, "Excuse me, before we go any further, will you get your genes checked out?" Not exactly the most romantic of starts, eh? Or OK, she gives the guy a sporting chance, falls in love, decides he's Mr Right. He asks her to marry him. Does she say, "Well, yes please, if you don't carry this gene." Or does she say, "Yes" and keep shtum in case she puts him off, and just hope any kids are fine? Or does she say, "Yes, but no kids." Or "No thanks, I'm not the marrying kind" ... or what?'

Sid was staring at him aghast.

'It never occurred to me ...'

'I just don't know what I'd have done – if I'd known what I know now.' Declan was musing aloud. 'I think – I think I'd have probably been too scared to ask Judy to marry me – in case. I might even have been scared to ask her out in the first place – just in case one thing led to another and I ended up in just such a predicament. You know me! Maybe I'd have become a monk!' It was a forlorn stab at humour. But there was too much truth in his words for either to find it funny. 'And I'd have missed out on one of the most wonderful things in my life.' Declan's voice was soft. After a long pause he continued in a harder tone. 'And now, what do we all tell our kids ... if we have any? What does Sian tell her four? "By the way, you might be sitting on a time bomb here?" Is it right to burden them with all this? *They* might all be spared loads of unnecessary worry if *we* didn't know. And if I hadn't married Judy, and if we hadn't had Bethany, we'd none of us have known.'

'I see your point but ... I *have* to tell the girls about not being their Dad – Sian and Georgie, I mean – anyway. I can't *not*. Not now, can I?'

'No, I guess they have to know.'

A thought suddenly struck Declan.

'Georgie ... she *is* my twin ... isn't she? *That* was right?'

'Yes, oh yes. She's your twin all right. Definitely. You've seen the baby photos.'

'And Sian – the same father you said?'

'Yes. They advised it. They said there'd be a better chance of real family resemblances. And you've all got the same eyes and hair. You and Sian've got the same chin and hands. Georgie's most like Mum.'

'But people say I stand like you.'

'Habit. You've copied me, I suppose.'

'So the sixty-four thousand dollar question is, this metabolic gene, did we get it from Mum or the donor? And do the girls have it?'

Sid scraped his foot back and forth on the ground, concentrating on the pattern he was creating.

'Will you tell Judy? Or do you want me to?'

'Oh, I'll tell her. When it feels right. Don't you worry about her. I need a bit of time with this first, myself. But I'll need to let her know before we see the geneticist. Apart from anything else she needs to know we might not be able to trace back my genetic ancestry.'

'I'm sorry, Dec. I really am. We never wanted to cause you kids pain.'

'I know, Dad. I know. And hey, if you hadn't done what you did, I wouldn't even exist!'

He must hang on to that.

'One thing more. If I *am* to be able to find out anything more, I need to know which clinic. And when. Presumably they'll have *some* records. Or maybe they'd tell Dr Galloway even if they couldn't – wouldn't – tell me.'

'Fair enough. It was the infertility clinic in Edinburgh. At the Royal Infirmary. Dr Fraserburgh was the guy who did it. Consultant he was. Australian chap actually. Very nice. Dr Carr – our chappie in London – knew him and arranged it personally.'

'And when?'

'16th May.'

'Funny that – knowing exactly, eh?'

'Yep. 7th July, Sian; 16th May, you and Georgina.'

'And Mum – did she use her real name?'

'Oh yes. And I went with her.'

'So if they've still got records they should be able to trace her.'

'Her, yep. Him – I'm not so sure, Dec. Best not get your hopes up too high.'

'For Judy's sake – for both our sakes – I must try. You understand that, don't you? It's not for *me*. You're my Dad. Always will be as far as I'm concerned. And I don't want to know about the donor. Let him rest in peace, I say! But if we're to have children ourselves, I have to know the risks.'

'Of course. And that's why I had to tell you.'

'Didn't you always dread us finding out somehow?'

'Never thought about it. How could you? Nothing to make you ever question …'

'I suppose not. Clever really. Like a totally foolproof crime. Oh, I don't mean …'

'It's OK. I know what you mean. Yep, it felt foolproof. I just never thought about it. You *were* mine.'

By mutual consent they resumed their tramp through the trees. It helped, it was less demanding, they could be silent together without discomfort. It gave Declan time to reflect on what his father had told him.

'Dad, can I ask you something … about the … the infertility thing?'

'Sure. Ask away.'

'When you found out, who did you talk to?'

'Nobody.'

'What – nobody at all?'

'Who *could* I talk to? Mum knew, of course. They told us together. And she and I talked about it at first. But after that first shock, when I said I'd let her go, she – well, it was like she wanted to avoid the subject. Be like we'd always been. Not let it make a difference. She just wanted me to know she loved me just like before.'

'I can believe that. That was Mum all over.'

'Nobody else knew. It's not the kind of thing you tell your mates, eh?'

'I suppose not. But heck, Dad, what a thing to grapple with all inside yourself.'

Sid whacked a clump of nettles at the side of the path. Leaves scattered as the stems cracked.

'Yep. Knocked my concentration all to pot, I can tell you. I got into a fair bit of strife at work – forgetting things, my mind wandering. And of course, they didn't understand. How could they?'

'And the hospital people? Could you talk to them?'

'Well, I suppose I could have gone back to see somebody. They didn't suggest it, though – well, maybe they did and I didn't really hear it. I was just blown out of the water by it all. And to be honest, well, I doubt if I'd have wanted to.'

'But it's something … so deep … so … I don't know … so *fundamental* …' Declan was searching for the right word.

'I suppose. But I didn't think of it like that. I really don't think I did. It was more a matter of, I was letting Mum down. That was the real killer.'

'And that would have made it harder to talk to *her* about it all – even though she was the one person who knew.'

'Exactly.'

'So you really needed somebody – outside – to talk to.'

'Well, I see what you mean but you know, back then, people didn't talk about everything. Not like they do now. Counselling, all that stuff – nope. You just got on with things, tried not to dwell on them, kept busy.'

'Mmmhmm.'

'Anyway, like I say, I don't think I'd have wanted to. Even if they'd offered. It's … too personal.'

'Thanks, Dad, for telling *me*. Helping me to understand. Sorry I wasn't more sympathetic at first. I see now. Well, better, anyway.'

'It's all right. You're you. That's different. I could talk to *you* about it.'

'Thanks, anyway.'

'Mind you, I'm not sure I could have told even *you* – not really explained anyway – before you knew – before you had Judy. I doubt you'd have been able to understand what it would do to you … if you hadn't felt …'

'You're probably right there. It helped, explaining it like that. Best remember that when you tell Sian.'

'Is it the same for a woman? I don't know. I just wish I could ask Mum. I only hope the girls …'

'I can't believe it'll make any difference to how they feel about you.'

Declan's reassurance was sincere. 'After all, they've had a lifetime of love – a real father's love – from you. That must count for a lot.'

'It'll be a shock. I'm prepared for that.'

'It's bound to be. And they might – say things at first – like I did, just because they're caught unawares. But I'm sure they'll understand, when you explain.'

'I hope so. I really hope so.'

But as they neared home Declan's thoughts were on another girl whose peace of mind he must shatter still further.

NINETEEN

Sleep eluded Declan for a long time that night, Sid's words tumbling over and over in his mind. He forced himself to try to understand.

Judy lay on her back, her hair cascading over the pillow. Her face was towards him, lips slightly parted, eyelids fluttering briefly as she dreamed. Even in the semi-darkness he could admire the creaminess of her skin, the curves of her body. Looking down at her sleeping form, he felt again the knot of emotion she so often generated in him. Now he tried to analyse it. Love? Desire? Protection? All of these things. And an overwhelming wish to be everything she needed and wanted.

He tried to imagine how he would feel lying there beside her knowing he was incapable of giving her the baby she wanted. Knowing that he, the only one who could – no, should – perform this function, could never fulfil it. What must it feel like, knowing that? Would he have the courage to offer to release her? Was his love that self-sacrificing?

He remembered again the feeling of the early weeks of their marriage when he had so desperately wanted her and she had turned from him. That had been hard enough, the sense of frustration, the feeling of rejection. It had started to undermine his fragile confidence. And that was without any sense of guilt on his part. And it had been transient. He had had all the other hundreds of nights since then to eradicate that feeling. But what if it could never be erased? What if it was permanent?

If she were pregnant, if she had children, that would change. He could see that. The pressure would be lifted. The act of intercourse itself would have a different meaning.

But artificial insemination? How would he feel knowing that another man's sperm swam inside Judy? He closed his eyes, burrowing his face into the pillow fiercely. Sid had insisted on being there when they did the insemination. Would he have done the same? Could he have coped, imagining what was happening, knowing – knowing the very moment? He wanted to wake Judy, hold her tightly, confirm his own virility, their exclusive love.

Was it even right? His parents had had such high moral principles; how could they think it was right? Wasn't it a form of adultery? *Adultery?* With the husband a willing partner – consenting, before witnesses – sitting there watching while it happened, willing the other man's sperm to fertilise his wife? Hardly!

Was it right to pursue treatment at all? Should couples just accept their disability and sublimate their needs in doing other things – building careers, helping other people? Why? Why should they? What was so different about seeking treatment for blocked Fallopian tubes, or malfunctioning ovaries or testes, or impotence, from seeking treatment for a blocked liver duct, or malfunctioning lungs, or a gammy leg?

But people got very steamed up about the money involved. Infertility wasn't life saving, they said, people could live without kids. But neither was a hip replacement operation. It wasn't important in the total scheme of things, they said. *They'd* never been infertile!

Round and round the questions went. Unable to bear the thoughts at one point he got up, went downstairs and brewed a cup of tea. His head ached. He nursed the drink in both hands absorbing the warmth, trying to eliminate the cold in his heart.

Taking the utmost care not to wake Judy, he slid back into bed, drawn to her physically, distanced from her by the turmoil of his thoughts.

Just supposing it had been Judy incubating that child – some other man's child. Would he smile to see her smiling in her sleep? Would he rejoice to see her taking every care to nurture this baby in that perfect environment within her – as he had done with Bethany? Would he share so gladly in all the milestones of pregnancy as they counted the days to the expected arrival – as Sid had done?

How would he respond to all those congratulations, those man-to-man jokes, knowing – knowing that he had done nothing – not even that first simple natural thing – nothing to be congratulated for? It had been hard enough dealing with his colleagues' jokes about his sex life when he had a hope of the problem eventually resolving. Would his face betray him? And every time someone commented on the family likenesses, would it be a knife turning in his soul? Would he be endlessly on the alert for traits emerging which betrayed an inheritance not his own? In the heat of a rebellious teenage moment would he blame those other genes? Would he – could he – love the offspring so completely as Sid had loved them?

Judy stretched sleepily, arched her back, one leg sliding across to his side of the bed. He remained perfectly still, willing her not to waken. He wasn't ready for her frank gaze. Looking down at her his thoughts returned to that first morning in the bridal suite. He remembered so clearly that moment when she had abruptly removed her arm from his waist as the door closed, retreating from him to pack her case, trying to make it look normal but not meeting his eyes, not sharing her fear. She had been afraid he might override her reluctance. She had taken evasive action. To him – vulnerable, unsure – it had felt like a lack of confidence in him. As if he might put his fierce need before her wishes. It hurt. She'd explained since that she'd been instinctively trying to give him cues, to protect them both. Would he have been receptive to more subtle messages? Perhaps not – not then. He'd been so inexperienced, so eager. If she'd stayed in his embrace wouldn't he have taken it as encouragement, rushed on, without knowing? He conceded all this now but then – then it had felt like a lack of trust. Trust mattered. She had more than compensated since. Telling him about her father's abuse, that had been a powerful demonstration of her trust. Real love, marriage, it had to be built on trust.

What would it do to them if the whole fabric of their family life was based on a lie – a lie like a false birth certificate? Legal they might be but in truth they were falsified records, weren't they? But his own parents had lived with the knowledge of three such birth certificates. Their marriage had seemed rock solid; Sid confirmed it was. Perhaps if the lie was shared that made it acceptable. After all he knew Judy's secret. No-one else but Betty knew. But the shared knowledge had brought them even closer. Maybe the shared knowledge of infertility did the same, made a couple cling closer. An experience like Sid's though – finding out he was infertile, going for artificial insemination – that was in a different league. That, above all things, must surely test the bonds of love. That would seek out the cracks. If you could weather that storm maybe it gave you an absolute confidence in your partner, immovable, dependable, totally committed.

Was his own love for this girl lying close beside him that strong? Strong enough to withstand all this and so much more? He began to see in a new light the measure of the man who had brought him up, who had been his example. Yes, without a doubt, Declan knew it first-hand, Sid Robertson had loved that much – Isobel first, but also the products of that unnatural union: Sian, Georgina and himself. Sid said he had forgotten they weren't really his own, and all the objective evidence substantiated that claim. Yes, he had indeed loved that much. Declan felt humbled by the thought. He couldn't be as confident of his own strength as he was of Sid's. And if he couldn't do what it took, what would that do to Judy's love for him? The involuntary shudder made him bury himself deeper under the bedclothes.

His thoughts strayed to the donor, his biological father. Curious that, just not knowing anything about him. He had been responsible for creating three lives – probably lots of others too. But he didn't know and didn't seem to want to know. What had prompted him to volunteer to be a donor? It wasn't like going and giving blood, was it? Or was it? You were helping folk in need just the same. You were giving something you had plenty of. What did he get out of it? A few pounds? A sense of satisfaction helping somebody else in trouble? What made him volunteer? Did he appreciate the sacredness of creating a human life? Was it right that men could think only of their own interests? Should his biological father have the right to privacy but he, Declan, not be able to find out anything of his paternal heritage? *Was* he paid to do it? Were his gametes a saleable commodity? OK, women in the States bought semen from famous men or Nobel Laureates, but were healthy sperm from ordinary men also worth paying for?

Would it have been different if he'd made himself available to have sex with any of these women needing to be fertilised? In person. The picture this conjured up was so grotesque Declan had to smother a laugh. Judy turned over in her sleep, snuggling down towards him. He fitted himself around her curled-up body. It *would* make a difference, using a syringe, a doctor inserting it. It became a clinical procedure. So why the aversion? Holding Judy he knew. Their love was so exclusive. Their desire to create Bethany had been an extension of that. It was symbolic. But maybe there were other needs that came with time, more to do with the children for their own sake. Then it might not be so significant if part of them came from outside. After all, people adopted children successfully. But that was different. There was no pseudo-intimacy there. It all seemed to come back to that – the act of union, male with female, sperm with egg. When did the desire for a child – any child – override those other needs? Even his own mother, loving Sid as she did, unconditionally, she'd been so desperate to have children that it had changed her, Dad had said. It must be a basic urge, for some women at least. Lesbians, single women, post-menopausal women even, they were desperate enough to go through all sorts of hoops – risk public censure even – just to have a baby. Would Judy want children if she couldn't have *his* children? He couldn't answer that. He didn't even know if it would matter if she did.

And what if *she* couldn't have them but *he* was fertile? Would she be willing to import another woman's eggs, have his sperm create a baby with another woman's eggs? Was it the same for women? Who knew?

Judy half woke.

'Whattimeisit?' she slurred.

'Four thirty.'

'You havin'a bad night?' She reached out to touch him. They both had bad nights since losing Bethany.

'I'm OK. You go back to sleep, Jude.'

She slid out of bed and, rubbing her eyes, shuffled to the bathroom. When she returned Declan was sitting up in bed, arms around his knees, grinning.

'*That* would have been an unexpected thrill for my Dad!' he chuckled.

Her hand flew to her mouth, her eyes wide. The instant the words were spoken Declan regretted them, but she showed no signs of making the connection with her own father thrilling to her body. It was simply that in her drowsiness she had completely forgotten Sid when she'd wandered off without a stitch on. He let out his breath slowly.

'Crisis averted. I presume anyway?'

'Uhhhuh.' She nodded as she spoke. 'Why didn't you warn me?'

'Well, I thought it might be nice if my Dad saw what a lucky chap I am!'

Her eyes flew to his face.

'You didn't ....?'

'Of course I didn't! I was so busy looking at you, admiring you, I didn't even *think* of him. Come here, you silly goose ...' Her body slid down along his. 'You gorgeous ... silly goose.'

If she wondered at the tightness of his embrace she said nothing. The warmth of her response was balm to his troubled mind and he temporarily forgot the past and the future in the reassurance of the present.

All unsuspecting, Sid lay in the adjoining room staring at the ceiling. His own thoughts were bitter-sweet. The blend of sorrow and of joy throughout the past thirty-five years, poignant with memories of Isobel, he wanted those memories to stay as alive as they were tonight. He did not want to forget the pain; in forgetting he would lose something of her.

Each time the other bedroom door opened and closed he heard it – Declan so late going to bed, getting up once, and again. The news today must have unsettled him. Sid was tempted to go out to offer comfort. An inner voice – Isobel's voice – stopped him: 'Part of being a parent, you have to let them go.'

It was Judy now who was his son's comforter. He had played his part.

TWENTY

The reflection looking back at Declan as he shaved the next morning was wan. He had eventually found oblivion in two hours of restless sleep, but the waking hours brought a return of the seething emotions. Strange, he thought, yesterday morning I knew exactly who I was. Today who am I? He was adrift in uncharted waters.

He knew Judy had noticed his disquiet but he devoutly hoped she would assume he was struggling with his grief for Bethany. They both tried to protect the other at times from the full impact of their personal sorrow. He was grateful for her silent support – the arm slipped around his shoulder as she passed, the kiss dropped on his head, the slow smile across the breakfast table. Her one enquiry was easily deflected. He was standing still, staring out into the garden, when she came up behind him, and slid her arms around his waist.

'You all right, Dec?'

'Yeah, I'll be OK. Just a lot on my mind. I'll tell you when Dad's gone back. I don't want to exclude him.'

They both bent their energies to entertaining Sid, taking him out and about and doing their best to give him happy memories to think of when he was back on the other side of the world again. In doing so Declan found reprieve himself.

On the day Sid left to spend the next few days with Georgina, Declan took him to the airport on his way to work. The next appointment to visit the geneticist had arrived and Judy had hastily arranged to visit her mother to collect information on her own family background, forgetting Sid's flight time. Sid dismissed her apology; there was no point in her accompanying him too, he protested; he'd be through the check-in and gone in minutes, absolutely no point in her hanging around.

Declan held his father tightly for a long moment as the call for boarding came.

'Thanks, Dad. Thanks for everything.' His voice sounded hoarse close to his father's ear.

'Take great care of each other, Dec.'

'We will. We will. We'll come through it.'

Declan watched the retreating figure with a lump in his throat. He'd seen the sparkle of tears.

As he drove into town, his own problems crowded closer. There must be no delay in telling Judy. Sid would inform Georgina, perhaps even tonight. Georgie would be almost certain to ring him to talk about it, and

Judy must know before that happened. He must be the one to tell her. It would have to be tonight. Maybe peace would come from sharing it.

Declan was always cautious approaching Judy when he arrived home now. Work was for him an escape; he could push his grief to the back of his mind and gain some respite from its corrosive effects. He'd been strangely glad his immediate colleagues were all men. They'd offered gruff sympathy initially but then treated him as before. The female staff he saw less frequently but they had served only to keep his wound open at work too. The eyes full of tears, the sudden looks of sympathy, the little cards left on his desk, even the occasional posy of rosebuds; they all undermined his self-control. He wanted to smash the reminders into the wastebin, but knew it would be cruel to dash their good intentions. Instead he draped a newspaper casually over the offending flowers; he let the cards slip under his in-tray. But gradually the tragedy faded from people's consciousness and he found reprieve in the demands of his job.

But for Judy there could be no such respite. She could not face returning to a world of birth and babies. He never knew what to expect from day to day, but did his best to be sensitive to her mood, and let her know how profoundly he still shared her loss.

When he entered the kitchen that night, Judy was standing with her back to him, washing salad. It had been swelteringly hot all day. She wore her white sundress with the elasticated top – her 'accessible dress', he called it. Encouraging. The electric fan lifted her curls and wafted the fabric of her skirt rhythmically as it turned ceaselessly to and fro. Under cover of its whirring he tiptoed up behind her and slid one arm around her waist. She started.

'What a fright you gave me! I didn't hear you arrive.'

'Will these help you to forgive me?'

With his free hand he placed a basket of freesias in front of her, carefully avoiding the running water.

'They're gorgeous! Mmmmmmmmmmm. Smell them! My favourites. They're gorgeous, Dec, *thank* you.'

'Perfect for you then ... gorgeous,' he countered.

'Is this a guilty conscience I smell?'

'Nope.'

'So what have I done to deserve these?'

'Well, where shall I start? What have you done? Been lovely to my Dad ...'

'*That* doesn't count. He's a lovely man. No effort at all to be nice to him. Besides he's *my* Dad too now, you know.'

He tightened his embrace so suddenly she toppled.

'He thinks you're fantastic.'

'Then it's mutual. Good. Point one? Null and void. Next?'

'Been lovely to *me* ...'

'All in the line of duty. Point two, null and void. Next?'

'Been a perfect wife ...'

'Task not complete. Premature to decide. Point three, null and void. We're getting closer to that guilty conscience! Next?'

The light-hearted exchange momentarily lifted his spirits. There had been little cause for merriment lately, and he wasn't about to improve things with today's news. He wanted to cling to the moment. Dropping kisses down her neck, he moved to look into her eyes, but she kept her face turned away.

'How can a man think rationally, in a situation like this?' He slipped one strap off of her shoulder and nuzzled the warm skin beneath it. 'While I think, tell me, is the dress ... telling me something?'

'Now what, pray tell me, might an inanimate object like a dress have to say to an intelligent sentient man like you?'

Declan spent the next half an hour telling her exactly what the dress had to say. Her response was balm to his soul. And it delayed the telling.

It was still so hot they took their plates out into the garden to eat, to the wooden table and chairs shaded by an old maple, vibrant red in the setting sun. Under other circumstances he would have gloried in the colour. Not today. The shadows of his thoughts were already lengthening. He couldn't stall much longer.

Was it his imagination or was she too merging into his darkness? As they ate he watched her surreptitiously, with a sinking heart. The gaiety of the kitchen had gone. Looking back it felt brittle, superficial.

He laid down his napkin, leaning his arms on the table.

'Can you talk about it, Jude? Tell me what's troubling you. Is it Bethany?'

For the first time she turned her full gaze towards him. What he saw froze the words on his lips.

Judy shrank from him. How could she tell him? It was too appalling to think of, never mind repeat. Declan's concerned face dissolved, and she saw instead the cowering, white face of her mother.

TWENTY-ONE

'How could you? How *could* you?' Judy spat the words out. 'Our whole lives – all built on lies. Lie after lie and lie!'

'No …'

'Yes!' she shrieked. 'Lies! There's no other word for it. Lies. All lies. What a sham!'

'No …'

'And you always taught me to tell the truth. What a farce! What a mockery! When the whole foundation of our family life was one colossal lie.'

'I was only … trying to protect you.'

'Huh! Protect me? That's rich! Protect *yourself* more like it! Fine sort of protector *you* are!'

'I was … I *was*.'

'No, you weren't! You were trying to protect your grubby little secret. Yes, I see it all. Well, let me tell you, the way I feel at this moment, *you* are as sordid as *he* was. I used to feel sorry for you, guilty because I'd driven him away, left you on your own. Now? Now I pity you. Pathetic! You and your disgusting secrets. Both of you. You *deserved* each other!'

She saw her mother visibly shrink from the venom, but she felt not a shred of pity.

'And you know the worst thing? The thing I'll *never* forgive you for? *Never!* You – your lies – you made me almost … *glad*, when Bethany died. Can you believe that? I never told a soul. Not that! I was too ashamed – of even *thinking* it – even for a moment. But yes, me – her own *mother* – I was relieved that she was dead. Because she was safe.'

'I don't und –'

'No, how *would* you understand? What do *you* know about a mother's love. Real love.' The scorn she felt blistered her throat.

'Judith, please …'

'Well, I'll tell you – tell you what you've done, shall I? All these years I thought that man – the man who did those things to me – *your husband* – was my father – *my* flesh and blood. All my life I've had this fear – this inner dread – that *I* might have inherited something from him – something that would make *me* do those terrible things – would turn me into a monster who would harm my babies – my beautiful daughter … my Bethany.'

Waves of anguish swept over her just saying the name, but she dashed the tears away with an impatient hand.

'But when she died, I knew she was safe. Safe from *me*. I couldn't possibly hurt her now. I thought perhaps God had taken her away to stop anything happening to her. Or perhaps he was punishing me because of what *would* have happened.'

'Judith – you wouldn't … You don't have it in you.'

'No, of course I wouldn't! I know that now! There isn't a shred of him in me. But I didn't know it – not then. Did I? You didn't tell me. You let me think …'

'But I didn't know you thought …'

'No, of course you didn't! You never asked me what I thought. Ever. Did you? *Did you?*'

'I couldn't …'

'No, you couldn't.' Was this sneering voice her own? 'You couldn't ever talk about anything that really mattered. Even when you found him – that night – in my bed – you didn't ask *me*. You *told* me I should just forget it. You behaved as if you *had* forgotten it. As if he never existed.'

She saw her mother recoil as if hit. She knew it was true. She knew.

'But *I* hadn't forgotten. I lived with it day and night. Even when I grew up and could see it for what it was – a pervert taking advantage of a captive victim – a child. Trading on family trust and loyalty. Even then I couldn't get it out of my system. I couldn't bear any man to touch me. I dreaded ever seeing a man naked. I went into nursing because I thought it might help me get over that. Seeing men as patients not as real men – men who wanted to do things to girls. But I hated it. Even seeing them like that, I hated it. It made me remember. The disgust. That's why I did midwifery. No men. No penises. Well, only baby ones, harmless ones. Yes, mother, I'll say it, *penises*. Shocks you, doesn't it? Nice people don't say things like that.'

Never before in her life had she ridden roughshod over her mother's sensitivities. But now she was compelled by a raw urge to expunge the years of repression. The pent-up pain was like a volcano simply waiting to burst through the rent in her control.

'A penis-free world, that's what *you* wanted, eh? Even to make a baby it seems. A quick injection from a clinical syringe. That'd do the trick. Was that why he came to me? Huhh? No joy with the mother, try the daughter.'

She could see how the harshness, the crudity, appalled her mother. But there was no stopping now. If she stopped she could never ever say all that had to be said if she was ever to find peace.

'He told me once he wasn't my Dad.'

'No!'

'Oh yes. He did.'

'He promised …'

'Well, he did. He told me. He wasn't my Dad, he said, he was my lover

116

and lovers could do those things – things that dads didn't do with daughters.'

Betty stared back at her wordlessly.

'Oh, of course I didn't think he meant it – not literally. It was just all part of the secret game – the game he wanted me to play – that I mustn't tell you about. I didn't think he *meant* it. Now – well, perhaps that was the only true thing you either of you ever told me.'

'Oh Judith, that's not true! You know it's not.'

'Do I? Do I know what the truth is any more? What *can* I believe – after this? Even my birth certificate's a lie. Who am I? I don't know. Even *you* don't know!'

'That's not my fault, it's the system. The donors … don't want …'

'I bet they don't! Who wants other people to know they go into a shabby little room, get themselves excited and squirt into a tube? And go back next week and do it again. And again. Even kids – talking in the playground – they know it's not nice – that kind of thing. If you do it, you don't tell. You know, in these clinics, they used to deliberately keep poor records to be sure these donors couldn't be traced. I know why!'

'It's not like that …'

'Isn't it? Isn't it? What *is* it like then? Explain it to me.'

'It's to protect them …' The voice petered out and Betty cringed before her. How predictable! Not even an attempt at a morally defensible argument.

'No. See what I mean? You can't.' She stabbed her finger close to Betty's face, forcing her barbs deeper.

'Their intentions … are good … to help …' It was pathetic.

'Huhh!' Judy snorted, standing back, scorn pouring down on the older woman. 'Believe that, you'll believe anything! What kind of a man would just give his sperm – what? for a few quid? – and walk away from any sense of responsibility? His sperm! That very bit of him that gives new life. But such a man was *my father*. Well, I don't *want* to have a father like that. He *sold* me. He's my flesh and blood – and he *sold* me. And where is he now, huh? He doesn't even know I exist! His own child. I want to be proud of my parentage. Instead I feel … sick. Revolted. My father was no better than a stud horse!'

She cast a look of loathing in the direction of the woman before her, now huddled into herself, rocking back and forth in her misery.

'And as for my mother? Well. What can I say? Look at you! What kind of a woman would have any old sperm shot into her and get up and carry the child created in that cold-blooded way as if nothing had happened? What did you feel lying there, eh? Having it shot into you? It's disgusting. I hate to even think about it. And I'm here – I exist – as a direct result of that. I feel … soiled, degraded, revolted. I'm disgusted by myself.'

'No, no, Judith. It *wasn't* like that.' It was no louder than a hoarse whisper.

'No? What was it like then?'

'We – we both wanted you – for you. We tried – we tried to have you – normally …'

'Magnanimous of you! But …'

'But he couldn't … it wasn't his fault. They said it was probably the radioactive stuff – when he was at sea.'

'Wiped out his sperm production, huhh?'

'Yes. He couldn't help it.'

'So you thought you'd just go for a squirt of any old sperm. It'd do the job.'

'Be fair …'

'Fair? Where does fairness come into *this*? And what did Dad think of this anyway?'

'He wasn't keen at first but then he said, if that's what I wanted …'

'So it was *you* then, really.'

'It wasn't easy – deciding that – for either of us. But we didn't have a choice.'

''Course you did. You didn't *have* to have kids. You could have just accepted it.'

'We wanted one. We really wanted you.' Betty's voice trailed away.

'Oh *you* wanted, did you? *You* wanted.' The sneer was frankly acidic, just as she meant it to be. 'Never mind what *I* might want, *my* needs, *my* rights. That's OK, *you* wanted, so you must have.'

'No …'

'Did you – did you *ever* – think – about me? What it would mean to me?'

'Yes …'

'False identity. Blank genetic past. Am I even legitimate? Do I have any legal rights? If you had died would … *he* – your husband – have raised me? If I hadn't let him have sex would he have just disowned me? He didn't own me, did he? He wasn't any relation of mine at all.'

'He was …'

'No, mother, he *wasn't*. He even forfeited the right to be my stepfather – my adopted father – whatever this makes him. What does being a parent mean? Is it providing the gametes? Or is it being a guardian, a protector? Seems to me he wasn't a parent in either sense.' All the losses of her childhood washed over Judy again, fuelling her anger. 'No, whichever way you look at it, my rights – my rights as a child – they didn't come into it. It was your need – a sad, frustrated woman – your need to have what everybody else had.'

Betty's silence was maddening. Why didn't she fight back, convince her it wasn't like that?

'The very fact that it's all so secretive shows you that it's shameful. The women – they're too embarrassed to be honest on the birth certificate.

118

Too ashamed to tell the kids. The donors, well, they're too embarrassed to be identified at any stage. The doctors, they collude in all the secrecy, so they must have something to hide too. I was never very comfortable with infertility work, throwing vast sums of money into treatments that rarely work – for people who aren't ill. Now – now I *know* it ought not to be allowed!'

'You wouldn't even be here if …'

'Well, I wish I wasn't! If it wasn't for Declan, I'd probably …'

It was like a bucket of cold water. Declan. His gentleness, his quiet compassion, his love – what would he think of her intemperate language, her tirade, her lack of control. She crumpled onto the floor.

The initial release in tears gave way to harrowing sobs as she rocked herself on the cold linoleum. She moaned Declan's name in her abject misery. But he was not here. Only her mother was here, not daring to approach. Judy felt abandoned, utterly alone, and very afraid.

But she must get a grip. There was work to be done, the work she'd come here to do, the questions that had preoccupied her until this bombshell had exploded around her ears. She heard a different voice, subdued now, cold, robotic. Her brain took time recognising it as her own.

'Everyone knows you're supposed to tell adopted children where they came from. Everybody *needs* to know their origins. But *I* don't know. Even you can't tell me. A few mls of semen in a syringe, that's all you know. And what did he pass on to me? Was it his gene that made Bethany the way she was? Or was it yours? If it was his I can't ever track it, I can't know what the chances are …'

No. And worse still, *nobody* knew. Could they even find out? And it was this woman's fault.

'Weren't you afraid all those years I might find out?' Judy asked coldly.

'There was nothing to … make you … suspect …'

'That's right. Except for that moment, and that was covered up so completely nobody *could* know.'

It was true. It had been foolproof.

'Didn't you worry about family likenesses? Things coming out?'

'You're so like Aunty Helen, it didn't matter.'

'And to think, when I mentioned … him, I thought you clammed up because of the abuse. You know, they say that almost all adults born from artificial insemination sense a family secret? I *knew* there was a secret. But I thought I knew what that secret was too. My Dad was a sexual predator. Of *course* you didn't want to talk about him. It never *occurred* to me that … he wasn't my Dad.'

'So should we have told you – from the beginning? Is that what you would have wanted?' Judy recognised her mother was reaching out to her in spite of all that had gone before. The knowledge made her soften her tone momentarily.

119

'What I would have wanted? I wish you'd never done it in the first place.'

'But we did. And you're here. What should we …?'

'What do I think? Given that I am an AID child? Oh, now I know why they abbreviate it to AID. So much more sanitised than a child born from artificial insemination by *donor*.' An involuntary shudder shook her body. 'The very thought makes me feel sick. What do I think?'

Judy reflected for a long moment. Then she ticked points off on her fingers.

'I think children like me should have rights – if we want to exercise them. What are they? To be told the truth, that's for sure. To have an accurate birth certificate. To have legal status. To have a means of finding out about our genetic inheritance. To be able to find out about our real father. Contacting him if we want to. That's a minimum.'

'But men wouldn't do it. They couldn't take a chance on people suddenly appearing on the doorstep.'

'Well then, they shouldn't do it at all. I'd rather not exist than feel like this. I simply *hate* the thought of having been *manufactured*.' Judy seemed to vomit the word. 'Just because you wanted a kid, and he wanted a few quid, or OK, let's put the best slant on it possible, he thought he'd be big and altruistic and help sad inadequate women. Babies should be the result of passion – of love – not of technology.'

'Aren't you being … hard? … Idealistic?'

Judy felt her anger rising again.

'Idealistic? What if I am? Somebody has to stand up for people like me. Why should innocent children have to suffer because other people lower their standards … to *this*? And just how far would you go, eh? To get what you wanted? How far, eh? Would you have borrowed some other woman's eggs or farmed me out to a surrogate mother to incubate and deliver me, if there'd been something wrong with *you*? Or if you were a career woman who didn't want to go through the fag of carrying kids or losing your figure? Should just anybody be allowed to demand that kids be created artificially if they don't happen to like the way nature designed things? Hey, why not stop this whole sex lark and just go for cloning anyway?' Powerful forces beyond her control fuelled the sarcasm, raising the volume.

'Not everyone's lucky enough to be *able* to have children – as nature intended. You and Declan, you can. But if he couldn't, wouldn't you …?'

She saw Betty faltering, losing her nerve.

'Want his children? Yes, I would. *His* children. But not some other man's, someone I didn't even *know*! It's sick. *I* feel sick.'

'But what if he had some dreadful hereditary illness that he might pass on to his children? Wouldn't you …?' Betty clapped her hand to her mouth, remembering too late.

Reality rushed at Judy like a tidal wave. Unutterable sadness made her lips stiff, her voice leaden.

'That's exactly what he does have, in case you've forgotten. We both have. That's why this has all come out. If we hadn't had Bethany, we still wouldn't know. But now, we do know. And we have to know where this thing came from. What the risks are. We have to think of the child. We can't deliberately put another child through what Bethany went through. We can't. We just can't.'

'Judith, I'm so, *so* sorry.'

But Judy wasn't listening. A new appalling thought presented.

'*What* am I going to tell Dec? I don't know half my ancestry. There's a good chance nobody does. How can we possibly … make a decision – an informed decision about our future?'

'Maybe … the clinic …?'

'I doubt it. I very much doubt it. But just in case, you'd better tell me where, when – anything you do know. But it's a forlorn hope.'

'It was the Edinburgh infertility clinic. And it was a lady doctor, Dr Teresa Fairley, who did it. And it was September 23rd.'

Judy stared at her mother unseeingly. She thought of the richness of her relationship with Declan, his sensitivity, his passion. How could you begin to compare Dr Fairley's syringe on September 23rd with their lingering nights in that French gîte? Yet she, Judy, had been the result of the former, Bethany the result of the latter. Life was so unfair, so bitterly unfair.

Her mother's stricken face receded, the room closed in on her, and she felt herself drowning in the depths of herself no-one could reach.

TWENTY-TWO

Betty shrank back in her seat, her heart yearning to comfort her daughter, knowing with certainty she was powerless to do so. If only, if only she could tell Judy it hadn't been like that. The years rolled back. She was 18 again.

The young Elizabeth Laidlaw – Betty – had been a mousey girl of average height with an old-world innocence resulting from a strictly religious and protected childhood. Her most redeeming feature was her smile which transformed her angular features into something softer – 'winsomely appealing', Jim had called it then.

Jim. James Rhett Burrows (although in later years she became suspicious about the authenticity of the Rhett). Her senior by ten years, he was sophisticated and suave, self-confident, and a great favourite with the girls. His money bought him many favours and, by the age of twenty-eight, he had a richly inflated opinion of his own importance. Even knowing all that, it was still flattering to have him courting her attentions. At first she'd been coy about his advances, asking him to return an expensive bracelet and give the money to help a local orphanage, begging him not to choose such exotic restaurants.

Her parents told her unequivocally not to be taken in by superficial charm; he was a philanderer and there could be no future in it. She wasn't expecting a future; she was simply enjoying an unexpected break in the drabness of the present. They were just having fun, she told them airily. And fun she had.

Jim whirled her to dances and all-night parties. He drove her fast along winding roads. He wined and dined her, wooed and excited her. She revelled in the novelty of a world beyond her imagining but resolutely refused to allow him any intimacy beyond a kiss, little suspecting that it was her very inaccessibility which kept him intrigued.

No-one was more surprised than Betty when Jim proposed to her. She had daily expected to be replaced by some more available girl when he grew bored with her. She asked for time. He laughingly granted her one week to decide.

She wanted to consult her parents but their continuing disapproval of Jim and his lifestyle precluded that. Instead she sat in her solitary bedroom and wrote down a list of his good points and the not so good. When the not so good threatened to overtake the good she justified them on the grounds of his zest for life and willingness to please. She told herself he'd settle down when he was married. *She* could still follow her conscience. He didn't attempt to dissuade her from her own rather narrow way of thinking. Quite the reverse. He said he liked that in her; it made her different from all the shallow girls he'd known.

She gave up the struggle to work through the arguments logically. Instead she wrote out 'Elizabeth Rose Burrows' fifteen times, each time in a different style, a different size. And each time she stared at what she'd written she felt strange flutterings in inaccessible places. She hid the paper inside her Bible and looked at it first thing in the morning, last thing at night, every day, hoping for some sort of a sign.

A week later she said yes.

Betty was totally unprepared for married life with Jim. Experienced as he was with women he expected more than she knew how to give. In the first month he told her roundly he found her inhibitions trying. In the second month he craftily resorted to using her own weapon to insist on his 'rights', pointing to Ephesians 5, and 1 Peter 3, telling her it was her Christian *duty*.

Friction spilled out of the bedroom into the kitchen, the bank, into their leisure activities. Slowly, painfully, Betty became conscious of their total dissimilarity.

At Jim's insistence, they deferred parenthood for three years while he pursued his many outside interests. Betty, growing increasingly suspicious as to his fidelity, resolutely closed her eyes and ears to any possible confirmation. Things improved marginally once they had made the decision to embark on pregnancy, and she became more tolerant of sex; that is, until her failure to conceive drove a new wedge between them. Jim taunted her: she was a buttoned-up little prude, couldn't even relax enough for that; and with each month she grew increasingly insecure.

Secretly Betty made an appointment to see her GP, Dr Evans. But once in the surgery she found herself tongue-tied. Perhaps he could ... give her something? Dr Evans was sympathetic, letting her talk. Inch by painful inch he coaxed out of her the real reason for her visit.

He recommended more rest. Be less intense about getting pregnant, he counselled. Let it just happen naturally. Could they go away on holiday somewhere warm and sunny? Could she give up her job?

Jim was surprisingly amenable to the idea of a holiday. It did her good, relaxing in the sunshine in Spain for two weeks. But she still wasn't pregnant when they returned to the usual routines of work and everyday preoccupations. A spur of the moment decision to hand in her notice made Jim clench his teeth hard.

'Well, we'll just have to hope you're more fertile now!' was his acid response.

But being at home with nothing to distract her thoughts, Betty became increasingly focused on her menstrual cycle. She marked the calendar with red dots. Her spirits plummeted with each one.

'Hell and damnation, woman. For goodness sake get to the quack. Get something for your depression. Your infernal weeping is driving me nuts,' Jim stormed one particularly low weekend.

Dr Evans listened carefully again. He asked her questions about her relationship with her husband, emotional, physical, mechanical. She hated talking about it. It was private, nothing to do with anyone but herself and Jim. But she tolerated the probing, recognising the necessity.

'I'll need to see your husband, too. Can you ask him to make an appointment later this week?' Dr Evans said.

'Well, he's … I'm afraid he's terribly busy. Work, you know. I mean, of course, he's happy for me to try to get this sorted out but … it's not easy to take time off.'

'Evening surgery will be fine. After work.'

'I don't know …'

'You know, Mrs Burrows, I can't refer you to a specialist without at least seeing if there's an obvious cause for your not conceiving. And the hospital will expect to see you both if I do refer you on. So do explain to Mr Burrows. It won't take long. Just a few questions. A simple test.'

'A test …'

Dr Evans smiled.

'I know. Lots of men hate the thought of tests and hospitals but maybe you should point out to him that it's the women who bear the brunt of this whole investigation process. As I've explained, the hospital will do a lot more procedures to try to get to the bottom of this – some of them not exactly pleasant. And you'll be the one to put up with all that. His bit of it is completely non-invasive and over quickly.'

'I'll try,' Betty lied, knowing none of this would cut any ice with Jim.

'Perhaps you need to remind him that it takes two to tango!'

Betty gritted her teeth. Oh, Jim knew all about tangoing! Far more than she could tell him.

At the time he said flatly, 'Don't mention this again or I'm out of here.'

Only later did she realise he must have gone to the doctor without telling her.

When the appointment for the hospital came she knew she had no option but to raise the subject again. Jim was furious. Betty wept. He was adamant: nothing would persuade him to set foot in such a place. It was her problem; she should get on and deal with it.

For three weeks he held out but in the end her constant weeping eroded his resistance sufficiently for him grudgingly to agree to attend just for 'his bit'.

'And then, I can tell you, I'll be out of there like a bat out of hell. You're on your own with this ridiculous farce!'

The experience of going to the clinic was even more embarrassing than Betty had anticipated. Second by second she expected Jim to bolt for the exit. The signs to the Gynaecology, Colposcopy, and Infertility Clinics seemed to be written in luminous paint, their footsteps to leave a trail of muddy footsteps for all to see. They descended into the bowels of the hospital. Her vulnerable mind conjured up an image of a world divided into layers. They were sinking into a realm better consigned to the underground – an undercover, unacceptable chamber others could not, should not, see. The frosted glass at the basement window provided only a vague pretence of privacy.

With every step the dread increased. It was bad enough for her to share the secrets of their private life with a complete stranger; she knew Jim would never forgive her for any scrutiny of his performance.

The undisguised notices littering the shelves, posters blazoning the walls, booklets strewn on the chairs, seemed to draw unwarranted attention to the process of seeking help. 'Place semen sample in box.' 'Need a sympathetic ear? Call 0131 896 1010.' 'Impotence explained.' Whichever way she turned her eye was assailed with embarrassing detail. She reported to the reception desk, muttering her name so indistinctly that the clerkess had to ask her to repeat it, and they took seats in a far corner; huddling together seeming preferable to taking their individual places in this judgemental world. Vague smells of countless bodies all mingled together in the waiting area – the smell of fear or shame, Betty thought privately.

The room into which they were ushered after thirty-five minutes was austere and functional. The slightly yellowed magnolia of the walls made her feel she too was jaded, too second-rate to warrant a facelift. Bright yellow boxes sat on the trolley in the corner, with, in capital letters, PROTECTORS written on the side. Protecting whom? From what? The mismatch of chairs gathered around the desk reflected their ill-assorted status.

She wished instantly that Jim had worn a tie and a smart jacket. His leather jerkin seemed to make him less significant, less in control in that moment. The consultant's immaculate navy suit reinforced his rank although she thought fleetingly it made him too much another man and too little a clinical specialist. She'd have preferred a white coat, immunity, detachment, safety.

The doctor stood as they entered and extended a hand courteously as he introduced himself – Dr Benedict. His voice was quiet but authoritative. Would his words be words of benediction?

The questions began, gently at first, seeking facts. Health, occupation. Operations, illnesses. Parents, siblings. Time together. Sex – how often, any problems. She responded mechanically, flatly. Make it business-like. No emotion. Jim's insolence was enough for both of them.

It was not so easy on the couch. Hospital sheets made flimsy coverings. The torn-off slice of paper lining the surface seemed incongruously thin. Next to nothing between her and all those other bodies that had given up their secrets, revealed their deficiencies, on that very spot. Close your eyes and think of England – that's what they advised, wasn't it? Or, in her case, Scotland.

Producing a semen sample sounded simple enough to her. But she saw the dull rash flood Jim's neck when Dr Benedict mentioned it; she heard the muttered blasphemy when he came out of the cubicle afterwards.

When the letter came asking for another one, he cursed the hospital as well as her. They'd have mixed up the samples. Incompetent fools.

In spite of his protests, she insisted on going back with him, secretly fearing if she didn't he wouldn't. There were more questions – questions that seemed pointless to her – about underwear, hot baths, driving long distances. Nope. Nope. Nope. She cringed at Jim's tone. Any infections in the last three months? He was totally fit, in prime condition. He knew it. They'd soon see. Any exposure to toxic chemicals, nuclear substances? Nope … or … well – there was that time, when he was in the Navy …

More specimens needed. Same procedure. Just leave it in the box.

Dr Benedict saw them together at the next meeting. At first Jim had said wild horses wouldn't drag him back to that place ever again, but the secretary had insisted over the phone he *had* to be there.

Dr Benedict was gentle in the telling. Betty found his quiet tone soothing, but she knew that Jim would hate his sympathy. She wanted to reach out to him, show him she cared, but she knew he'd misconstrue it. He had pinned on his invincible look securely before they left home. Infertile? *Him?* Rubbish! Bloody doctors! What did they know?

Concern for him dulled her concentration. The consultant's monologue impinged spasmodically, staccato words boomeranged off the edges of her awareness.

'Things we can do … Nobody need know … inseminate her … all very private … everyone else think normal … just as if you did it.'

Jim drank himself into a stupor that night. Now *he* became the one avoiding sex. Betty tried to reassure him it was the shock, the ceiling would lift in time, but in her heart other emotions struggled for precedence. Dr Benedict was offering pregnancy without the sex. She wanted to be pregnant; she wanted a baby; she didn't really want the sex. It was an attractive proposition. And now it wasn't contingent on Jim's co-operation. As long as he didn't withhold his consent, she could do this herself. Relief and a growing hope replaced the pain of years and gave her a new determination.

At first Jim flatly refused to give his permission. But Betty's dream was not to be snatched away now. She wheedled, she coaxed. It would look as if he was potent. Because she wasn't working, she could go discreetly. Nobody would know. She'd never breathe a word of it.

In the end he grudgingly conceded: 'If it means you'll get off my friggin' back and stop your infernal whingeing!'

He went away 'on urgent business' the first time she went for the procedure. It didn't work and he flaunted his malicious pleasure: 'It was probably your bloody fault all along!'

The second time it was the same: 'See!'

But the third time he was forced to face the stark truth. Betty was not the one with the problem. He relapsed into the taciturn stranger whose arrogance Dr Benedict had penetrated and exposed for the sham it was.

She sailed through the pregnancy. A new contentment enveloped her, softening her feelings towards Jim. She did her best to involve him in the pregnancy and plans but he was morosely dismissive of her efforts.

She felt his resentment powerfully but did her best to understand it. He hadn't been enthusiastic about having children in the first place. He hadn't wanted her to pursue treatment. He hadn't wanted to undergo tests himself – it must have been a fearful shock finding out he was infertile. He must resent the man who could afford to give away his sperm so easily. But that man was unknown. He must blame her, Betty, for wanting some of that bounty.

She was almost relieved when Jim elected to be away on business at the time of the birth. There was no need to veil her excitement or waste a precious moment worrying about his sensibilities. For the first time in her life she could allow herself to love another person without restraint. This new untainted creature. Her daughter.

Judith was a placid child who caused little disruption to Jim's routines, and Betty expected little from him. His outward indifference was only what she'd anticipated. Totally unexpected was his imperceptible succumbing to the charms of a toddler who innocently scrabbled towards him with a beaming smile when he entered the room; who climbed onto his lap, put her thumb in her mouth, and fell asleep on his chest.

Betty watched with incredulous surprise as he began to read to her, to romp through the house with her. Gladly she sent Judy off with him on excursions, kite flying, building a wooden house together. Through this child they had achieved a degree of harmony that passed as family life. He even took sole charge of bath time at the weekends; he willingly got up in the night if Judy was unwell or had a nightmare.

The shock of the final discovery appalled Betty to such an extent that she remained rooted to the spot for a full minute.

'Get out! And never ever come back,' she ground out. No tears. No screaming. No accusations.

She herself threw his clothes into a large case and bundled him out of the door. Afterwards she was amazed that he had put up no resistance. She burned as many of his possessions as were combustible, dumping the rest in with the household waste. He never contacted her again; she didn't know whether he was alive or dead. Any mail that came she returned as 'unknown at this address'. It was as if he had never existed. Thereafter she followed the habit of a lifetime; by not mentioning what had occurred it was as if it had never been.

But finally after almost twenty years that flimsy façade had been breached. Bethany's death demanded the truth; there was now no hiding place. It was hard enough to mention Jim; having to disclose the manner of Judy's conception in the same conversation was too much for Betty's fragile hold on reality. She knew her words were incoherent. But piece by wrenching piece Judy had slotted them together.

Dimly Betty recognised that the venom expressed the pain of a lifetime as well as the shock of discovery.

TWENTY-THREE

Judy had dreaded Declan's homecoming that evening. She'd put off the moment of truth by keeping busy, avoiding his gaze, welcoming the distraction of his teasing, but her own responses had sounded hollow to her ears. Now with his eyes boring into hers across the wooden garden table there could be no more procrastination.

'Jude, what is it? Tell me.'

She stared at him bleakly. He had always put her on a pedestal, she knew that. She sat uneasily in such an exalted place, only too aware of the cracks which would show if she were subjected to close scrutiny over time. What would he think if he knew just how imperfect she was? Would she have to watch him turn away in disgust, see his love grow cold? But she could not let their joint lives be based on a lie, as her parents' had been. She *had* to tell him, no matter the consequences.

'You seemed fine when I came home. Did I do something to upset you?'

'No. No. It wasn't you.'

'Can't you share it? I only want to help. I hate to see you like this. I know things can never be the same ever again – because of Bethany. But I thought – I hoped – we were starting to get something of what *we* have back again. Was I wrong?'

'No, we were – we *are*. But … Oh Dec, you would have been so ashamed of me today!'

'Why? What happened?'

'I was so horrible. I said such unforgivable things. I hate myself. You would have …'

'Wowwa. Slow down. I'm lost. This doesn't sound a bit like you. Start at the beginning.'

Hot tears scalded her eyes. He rose from the table and held out his hand.

'Come on. Let's go inside and you can tell me all about it.'

His arm around her felt so comforting Judy's courage started to fail her. Could she risk his censure or, worse still, his emotional withdrawal? He led her over to the settee, seating her before carrying the fan in from the kitchen. It was insufferably hot and close without it. He half knelt, half crouched on the floor beside her, the currents of air rhythmically rippling his shirt like an implacable incoming tide.

'Don't look at me like that, Jude. I'm not a Victorian father! I'm your husband, not your executioner! I love you. Tell me what's troubling you.'

His hands held both of hers, his thumbs caressing her skin gently. In the face of his gentleness Judy was crushed again by her own sense of unworthiness.

'I have to tell you. I *have* to. I can't bear to think *our* lives are based on a lie. But ... but ... I can't bear to think things will come between us.'

His fingers tightened their hold on hers. It was meant to soothe her, but the feeling of agitation would not be suppressed.

'I haven't a clue what you're talking about. But nothing is going to come between us. You are my life. I wouldn't *let* anything come between us.'

'You don't know ... this might change everything.'

'Hey, come on. You're overwrought. I'm sure it's not as bad as you're making out. Now, try me.'

'It was Mum – when I went to see Mum. She told me ... things. And I was so angry. I said some terrible things – unforgivably cruel things to her.'

'Was this about your Dad – and the abuse?' he coaxed.

'No. Well, not exactly. It was ...'

For a long moment Judy fought the impulses within. It was unnerving, Declan kneeling there, waiting, waiting ... so unsuspecting. The words suddenly rushed out, stampeding one another in their need to be said before her courage deserted her.

'Dec, I'm not who I thought I was. My Mum had me artificially. She had insemination because my Dad – well, the man I thought was my Dad – was infertile. Something about exposure to radiation.'

She saw his eyes widen, the sudden stillness, but she rushed on. She must explain.

'But they never told me. Honestly Dec, I didn't know. I would have told you. But I didn't know. Until today.'

He was nodding. 'I believe you.'

'I can't believe they thought I shouldn't know! To protect me, she said. *Protect* me? I told her just what I thought of *that*!' She felt the smouldering anger resurfacing. 'All these years – all based on lies. How could they go all this time, knowing it was all lies? That's why I have to tell you all this, Dec. There mustn't be secrets between *us*. I know it's horrible and I know I've been horrible, but we can't – we *can't* let lies come between us! We *can't*!'

'I understand, Jude.' She hardly heard him through her own grim determination to tell all.

'My life, it's been ... so many lies. What my Dad did to me. When she *knew* ...' The word tailed off in a whisper. She shuddered, dropping her head down in her hands.

His arms pulled her against his shoulder, holding her through the intense struggle to regain her composure. When she began again he sat back on his haunches to look squarely into her eyes as she dredged her soul.

'And even when she knew, she pretended. She didn't *try* to understand what it was like to have him … abusing me. She pretended it hadn't happened. It was so disgusting, so wrong, but she didn't ever say anything to make me feel better. I just felt guilty, as if it was my fault. And I felt sorry for her because she was on her own. And I thought it was my fault because if I hadn't hated it, he'd still be there. Oh, I'm just so … angry. And I was so mad with her today.'

'No wonder.'

'Oh, but Dec, I was really, really horrible to her. My own mother. You would have been so ashamed of me. I know you would.'

'No, I think I would have understood, actually.'

'Not if you'd heard me.'

'No. Really, I'm sure I would.'

She stared at him, wanting to be convinced.

'You're not going to believe this, Jude, but *I* have something to tell *you*. I know you haven't finished your story, and we'll come back to it. But I can tell you enough to show you I *do* know what you mean, that I do understand. It's such a shock. I felt something similar – well, at first anyway.' He shook his head as he repeated, 'You are *not* going to believe this. Remember on Saturday when Dad and I came back from our walk, and you thought I was very quiet, and you asked me if I was OK, and I said I had a lot on my mind, but I'd tell you when Dad had gone?'

'Mmhhmmm. I was worried about you. But I presume it was because of Bethany?'

'Well, no, not this time. It was something Dad told me – on that walk through Roslin Glen. Something that I had no idea at all about. Something so important he came all the way from New Zealand to tell me.'

'You're kidding!'

'No. That's why he came.'

'And?'

'It was … He told me that he wasn't my biological father.'

Judy stared at him open-mouthed.

'I don't believe it. You too? And you never knew?'

'It never entered my head.'

'So what …?'

'He couldn't have kids. So my Mum – and this is the uncanny bit – *my* Mum too had – artificial insemination. It's unbelievable, isn't it? Both of us?'

'And … didn't you … *mind*?'

'At first, when he first said it, I felt sick. Actually I think I probably said – or maybe just thought, I don't know – something I won't repeat!'

'But then? It was … OK?'

'Well, Dad explained how it happened.'

Judy listened to his parents' story in silence.

131

'And I remembered all the love both our parents had given us all these years.' Declan's voice resonated with his gratitude. 'And so I stopped feeling sorry for myself. But it was only that night when I looked at you lying in bed beside me, and I held you in my arms, that I sorted it all out in my head. I made myself think what it would have been like if *I* couldn't give *you* a baby. And if *we'd* had to make that choice.'

'And …?'

'I was so shattered by what it did to me – just *thinking* about it – I came to see what an incredible man my father must be. The love of a natural father's something special, but this man – who wasn't my natural father – he showed a depth of love that I don't think I *could* have done.'

Judy's eyes pleaded with him.

'Help me see that, Dec. Tell me …'

'Jude, what we have – you and me – it's so … special, so private. Imagine – just imagine if I couldn't give you a child. You want one and I can't give you one. Do I just say, "Tough. That's life," and watch you pine before my very eyes? OK, I don't want you to pine away so I look into the options. What can we do to sort this out? The safest thing for you – and the best option available to us – is for you to be impregnated with another man's sperm. When I got to that point I wanted to scream. I couldn't bear it. Just thinking of anyone else, anywhere near you – in that way.'

Judy watched intently, not moving, as he relived the horror of his nightmare.

'But then I thought, my Dad did that. He endured that, for my Mum, because he loved her that much. I can tell you, Jude, it made me feel pretty small, that I had – even for a second – been disgusted by what they'd done. Of course, they didn't *want* to have to involve anybody else in the act of creating a child, any more than we would, but they did it. For each other. That's pretty special.'

'And didn't they …?' She couldn't continue.

'Dad said, once that bit was over, the rest of it was just as if he *had* done it himself. That's what it was like, he said. We *were* his. He was involved in it at every stage, in every way, just like normal. Just like I was with Bethany. Except that I had put her there, and he had watched while a doctor put *us* there. Yeah, blow me, he even made sure he was there for the insemination bit so he was involved in that too, deliberately. He was sitting there willing it to work. Imagine that, Jude! The more I thought about it, the more flabbergasted I was by the strength of the man. I just couldn't get my head around it. And nobody but Mum ever knew.'

Judy was looking at him with dawning sympathy for the plight of his parents.

'So you see, I felt the same way as you at first. Sick to the core. Wanting to lash out. So don't be so hard on yourself. And I let Dad see I was revolted too – to my shame. But it's only natural. And just think of the difference. It was so much easier for me – tons easier. I'd had nothing but love and support from my parents. You had all those other horrors. I'm not surprised you flipped. Anybody would. It was the last straw. Especially when you're not yourself anyway so soon after Bethany. So don't be so hard on yourself.'

Instead of warming to his reassurance, Judy felt another chilling wave sweep over her.

TWENTY-FOUR

She had to tell him. She *had* to.

'Ah yes, Bethany. That's another thing. The worst bit of it all. I never told you this. I *couldn't* tell you. I'll never – *ever* – forgive her for this. I told her that. I won't. I can't.'

'Bethany? But she wasn't your Mum's fault.'

'Oh no, I know that. But not telling me that my Dad wasn't my Dad, *that* was her fault.'

'I'm lost again.'

'When Bethany died … Oh Dec, can you believe this? When she died, I was almost *relieved*.'

Declan shook his head, completely mystified.

'Ever since I was old enough to understand about heredity, I've had this terrible dread that I might have inherited something evil from … him … you know, because of what he was like, what he did to me.'

'Oh, Jude.'

'It was like a terrible, terrible thing just lurking somewhere inside me. I used to look at myself in the mirror sometimes and think, was this the face of a monster? But when you came along you made me feel so much better about myself. It was like you – well, you made me start to believe I *was* the lovely person you said I was.'

It was his turn to sit rapt.

'And Bethany,' she said in a hushed voice, caressing the name. 'She was a pure thing, created by our love. Then, when we found out she wasn't … wasn't perfect … like she should have been – then the old thoughts started to come back. Was this the evil from the past coming out now? And was the tendency to abuse still in me? Would I … one day would *I* harm *her*? You know they say abusers beget abusers, don't they?' She heard her voice take on a wild agitated edge, and was grateful for his sudden understanding hug.

'I got very low after she was born, when she was ill. And I had frightening thoughts. Oh, I know new mothers *do* get depressed. It's normal. But this was something more. It was much … darker.' She shivered, remembering. 'So when she died, I felt a great weight lift off me. Now I *couldn't* harm her. I'd never be *able* to harm her. She was safely away from me – for *ever*. I'd *never, never, ever* harm her.' Her voice crumbled away and she sobbed uncontrollably.

He held her, making no effort to still the storm, his tears mingling with hers. When the heaving sobs abated to occasional spasms, her voice resumed, now flat and colourless.

'My mother … could have spared me all that. If only she'd told me … I wasn't his child at all.'

'But you aren't, Jude. Thank God, you aren't.'

'There isn't anything of him at all in me.'

'That's right. And donors, you know, they're screened and everything.'

'But I *am* to blame for being so horrible to my Mum.'

'She'll understand. It was such a shock. It's a natural reaction to lash out. I'm sure she'll understand.'

'Will she? I don't know. I said … Oh Dec, I said such cruel things.'

'But didn't your Mum explain – you know, her side of things? Didn't that help you to …?'

'I didn't give her a chance to explain. I just yelled at her. Accused her of … having no morals, no decency … being a terrible mother … not caring, not telling the truth …'

'That was just the shock. And all the years of pain and fear speaking. She'll see that.'

'Will she? I'll have to phone her, see her, explain.'

'I'm sure she will. She's your Mum. She loves you – in her own way. You'll feel better when you've got it all out in the open with her.'

She sat still in his arms, plucking at the edge of her pocket, repetitively, aimlessly, not as confident of this as he was. Her thoughts moved on. She turned slowly to face him again, her hands now holding his face steady so that he had no choice except to meet her gaze directly. Fear once again had her in its grip.

'And you, Dec, can *you* still love me – now? Now you know?'

'Can you doubt it – for a second? I'm crazy about you. I thought it was totally beyond question. I'm always telling you, showing you, how much I love you.'

'I know you are. But … inside … I feel so scared. I know I don't deserve you. And today I've shown you that – I *don't*.'

'Nonsense! You're just human, that's all. You're right, I *do* put you on a pedestal sometimes – OK, often. But I know really, you're human too. We all have faults. I have loads, and yes, I admit, you have a few too. But I love you, faults and all, you *know* I do.'

She shook her head sadly, remembering her behaviour that very day.

'Jude, you can't really doubt it. You *can't*! For goodness sake! What we have – there can't be a shred of doubt – surely.' He changed tack. 'Do *you* still love *me*?'

'Oh Dec, you know I do!'

'But I'm not the person you thought I was this morning. I'm not Sid's son.'

'But you're still you – the you I fell in love with.'

'Exactly so. So why begin to doubt *my* constancy? If you doubt my love is strong enough to take this simple truth then I must start to doubt yours.

135

We're both in the same predicament here. We neither of us know who our fathers were, who we are. At least, on one level. But we do know – you know and I know – that we're the same people tonight that we were this morning – to each other. OK, we might both have had thoughts we wish we hadn't had, we might have said things we wouldn't want the other to hear, but that doesn't mean we stop loving each other.'

She caressed his cheek gently with fingers that trembled. He caught the hand in his, pressing it against his face.

'Jude, I so much want you to be happy again. I miss your laughter. I miss the way we were together. I know it can never be the same – like it was before Bethany. But we still have each other. And we must hang on to the specialness of what we have. Trust me. Don't shut me out.'

'I've told you everything now, Dec. There isn't anything else … black … in there.'

Their gentle kiss was like a seal on their pact. It was a long time before either spoke. Declan's voice sounded dreamy.

'Georgie once told me I was obsessive in my love for you. I think she was right!'

'It was Georgie who told *me* something like that.'

'Oh, did she now? She's got a lot to answer for, that girl! When did she tell you that?'

'That first time you took me to see her.'

'You mean, *before* I even asked you to marry me?'

'Oh yes, ages before. That first time she and I met.'

'What did she say?'

'She told me that you were – well, *besotted* with me. Her word, not mine.'

'But you knew that anyway.'

'Well, no, I didn't. Not at that stage. I wasn't to know whether you treated all girls – like that.'

'Like I treated *you* …?'

'Mmhmm.'

'Well, blow me! You actually thought … it was par for the course? And I thought I was being so crashingly obvious too.'

'Georgie thought you were too, but then I didn't know what you were like before.'

'Fair enough. So what did you think when she told you that?'

'It gave me a bit more confidence that you were serious about me.'

'You doubted I was serious?' His incredulous look made her smile sheepishly.

'Well, I wasn't totally sure … what your intentions were.'

He took her face in his hands and looked into her eyes.

'I think I have been very remiss from the outset in not checking your perceptions much more closely. I have never in my life thought about, or treated, any other girl in the way that I do you. Not even remotely. You slipped under my guard that first meeting on Shotton station. I can't even tell you what it was that attracted me. It was – well, I don't know. Something just clicked. I couldn't believe myself! Here I was writing an email to a complete stranger within hours of meeting you, trekking up and down the country at every available opportunity just to see you. And my Dad and Georgie were completely staggered by my crazy behaviour! I was always terribly timid where girls were concerned, and now here I was – careful, shy, old Dec – throwing caution to the wind. They were amazed! They'd never seen me like this before. Oh no, *they* had no doubts this was the real thing. I'd lost my heart – and my sanity too, as far as they were concerned! It was blatantly obvious, and still is apparently, to everyone else but you!'

'That's what Georgie implied.'

'Well, promise me, you won't ever – ever – doubt it again. Promise me?'

It was much later before Declan began to inch towards their problem again.

'Jude, we do have one thing we'll have to talk about. And since we've bared our souls tonight, I guess it's best out in the open now.'

'Uhhuhh?'

'Our future. You know … having babies.'

'Yeah, I know. We might not be *able* to find out where that gene came from.'

'That's right. And now, it's *both* of us without half of our genetic background. Dr Galloway is not going to believe this!'

'I'll have to go back to see Mum, to fill in the bits on her side. We didn't get that far. The other things just …'

'Yep, she'll give you that bit.' She was grateful for the interruption. 'And Dad's given me *my* Mum's side. So if it's come through our mothers we'll have a clearer picture. But as far as our respective fathers are concerned, well, I guess we'll need to talk to Dr Galloway, see if he knows how we could find out. That is, if it matters. I mean, if it wasn't through them I guess we can let sleeping dogs lie. D'you think? Or do you need to know anyway?'

'I don't know yet, whether I do or not.'

'I honestly don't think *I* do. I feel my Dad *was* my Dad and the other bit – well, it was just a … a … treatment.'

'I need to think about it for me. And I need time to sort it all out.'

'Of course. It's different for you. And remember, whatever you decide, I'll be here for you. I'll support you.'

But Judy declined his offer of support for her next contact with her mother. This was something she had to do on her own.

TWENTY-FIVE

The imminence of their meeting with the geneticist meant she could not procrastinate for long. But it was with real trepidation that she lifted the phone and her heart lurched when it started to ring.

'Betty Burrows speaking.'

'Hello, Mum. It's me.'

'Oh.'

'I'm so sorry, Mum. About the other day.'

Nothing.

'I really am sorry. It was a shock … hearing.'

Silence.

'I was wondering if I could come and see you. We still need information … you know …'

'I could be free tomorrow afternoon. After two.' There was no warmth, no encouragement.

'Thanks. I'll see you then.'

She heard the click. No farewell. No reaching out.

'Dec, I'm so frightened I'll lose the plot again. Just seeing her. Remembering,' Judy confided, shaken again by contact with her mother.

'Try and hang on to what it must feel like for your Mum, Jude. I mean, it must be appalling to be married to a man and find he could do something so horrendous, don't you think? It would make you want to hide from everybody – especially your daughter – wouldn't it? And what a burden, carrying those secrets around on your own for all those years.'

Judy struggled to let the ideas soften her heart.

As the car crunched to a standstill outside her mother's house she closed her eyes and pictured Declan. Imagine he's standing listening, she told herself. Declan's here, watching. Remember him.

Every guard was up. Her mother's body language told her so. Judy dropped a routine kiss close to her cheek. How she'd always hated Betty's half-hearted offering of the side of her face, never being the one to give a kiss. She just seemed to endure the contact.

Betty led the way into the kitchen. Instantly she was in motion, making a pot of tea, rummaging for biscuits. Judy felt irritation rising within her at the endless fussing. Inwardly she heard Declan calming her: it's only her discomfort, her way of coping. Be gentle with her.

Betty handed her a cup and saucer. Her own she placed at the back of the work surface. If Judy would excuse her, she must get on with making chutney for tomorrow; she'd promised it for a charity sale. She clattered around collecting preserving pan, spoons, chopping board, knife, onions, apples, spices. Judy gritted her teeth hard. Hang in there, Jude. Don't blow it.

'Can I help, Mum? Chop the onions?'

'If you want to. No need though, I can manage.'

Judy turned to the sink, glad to look away from the restless movements. The brown skin peeled away in layers. It was like uncovering the inner core of her own childhood, her own creation, layer by layer. She'd go gently, not too sharp a knife.

'Mum, I'm really sorry. I said some horrible things, I know. But I didn't mean it ...'

'It's all right. No need ...'

'Yes, there *is* a need. I was bang out of order – and unforgivably rude.'

'It's all right.'

Vinegar splashed the sides of the preserving pan. The words were right but the non-verbal cues belied them. It wasn't all right. The last brown skin fell. Judy laid the exposed white flesh on the chopping board, and instantly her mother began chopping it – this way, that way, opposite direction, smaller, smaller, smaller.

'Mum, I didn't give you a chance to explain ... the other day. I'm sorry. Can you ... can you tell me, about then?'

'What about then?'

'I want to understand ... what it was like for you, I mean. What made you decide? What it felt like? Anything you can tell me.'

'I know you'll find it hard to believe, but your Dad – he wasn't ... he wasn't always ... When I met him ... he was...' The chopping resumed fiercely. 'Oh, you wouldn't understand. Declan's so different.'

'This isn't about Declan, Mum. I want to know about Dad – and you – then.'

'But you wouldn't understand ...'

Judy bit her lip hard.

'Try, Mum. Please?' She hoped her voice sounded kind. 'I want to know what Dad was *really* like. You must have loved him once. Tell me about him, when you met him. Please?'

'He was ... exciting. I'd grown up with "don't do this, don't do that". He showed me there was an exciting life out there. I loved it. I felt free. Life was suddenly fun.'

'What sorts of things did you do?'

'He had a fast car, he drove it fast. Just to make me laugh. He took me to shows. I'd never ever been to anything. It was fun. He bought me nice things. I'd always thought it was sinful to have expensive things when there were so many people living in poverty, but he said he could help them and still give *me* nice things. He was quite comfortably off. He wanted to ...' Betty's voice tailed away. Judy slid another peeled onion onto her board. She resumed her chopping.

'And when you got married?'

'He ... it wasn't easy.' The voice was tight. Go carefully, Jude. Respect her privacy.

'Was he ... did he hurt you?'

'Oh no, nothing like that.'

'How ... not easy?'

'He was ... well ... demanding.' It was too hard for her. Judy backed off.

'How did you find out – you know, that he couldn't have children?'

The stinging juices pervaded the air. Betty wiped her eyes roughly with the edge of her apron.

'I always wanted children ... but ... even when we ... it didn't happen.'

The tiny fragments of cold onion shot into the hot vinegar, the noise making speech impossible for a moment.

'So – when it didn't?'

'The GP referred us to a specialist. He found out – about Dad.'

'It must have been a hard thing – for him – for Dad, I mean – to know he couldn't ...'

'Uhhuhh.' Furious chopping demolished another half of an onion.

'And you.'

No response.

'So how did you ... decide to have ... insemination?'

'The specialist said it was the best option we had. Safe. Nobody needed to know.'

'And you? What did you think?'

'I know you think it's selfish, but ...'

'I don't. Not now, Mum. I was angry the other day.'

'I wanted a baby. I really wanted you.'

'And Dad ...?'

'He agreed. But I know he wouldn't have done it ... if I hadn't been ... so ... wanted one so much.'

Betty tipped apples into the sink. Judy started peeling. She slid the blade carefully through the fruit. Would the skin come off in one piece? It had been fun trying this when she was growing up. And if you did manage it, you threw the skin over your shoulder and it would fall in the initial of the person you would marry. No need for that now. It would always be a D.

'But he agreed?'

'Yes.'

'And afterwards? Did he ... mind?'

'At first he didn't really ... take much notice of you. But men often don't really like babies – not *small* babies anyway – not at first, not when they don't *do* anything.'

'True. Even modern new-age men!'

'But then, when you *were* doing things, he – well, he just somehow started to do things with you.'

'What sorts of things, Mum? Tell me about those times.'

Betty finished chopping the apples and scraped them off the board into the pan, stirring the mixture hard. Through the sounds of bubbling she told of the games, the outings, of Jim's increasing involvement. So there had been good times. How sad that child could recall none of them.

Expertly her mother tied the spices in a square of muslin, pulling the strings tightly to ensure nothing of the mix could escape. She dropped the bag into the seething vinegar, added dried fruit, ginger, seasoning. The wooden spoon turned this way, that way. She added extra vinegar, carefully tipped in the sugar, removed the spoon, placed a lid on the pan. The noise of simmering was muffled.

'I'm glad – glad he did those nice things with me. I don't remember. It helps to know.'

Betty was silent, staring out at the swaying trees.

'Have you got photos – of then?' Judy asked.

'There are some. Yes. You've seen them.'

'No, I mean of *him* with us – when I was little?'

'No.'

'None?'

'No, I burned them all – when I found out.'

Judy felt a sense of emptiness. Another big section of her identity was lost forever. She had not a single photograph of the man she had thought of as her father, and it was likely none existed.

'Can you bear – to talk about … what he did … later?' Judy's voice was low, tentative. Betty's back stiffened. 'Did you know, Mum?'

'No! No! Judith, you have to believe it. I didn't!' Her mother turned to face her for the first time, eyes pleading.

'I do, Mum. I believe you. I never really thought you did.'

Betty closed her eyes, her breath exhaled in a long sigh.

'Was he … like that … with anyone else?'

'I … don't know … for sure … I don't think so. But how can anybody really know? But he … I think … he might have been … with other women.'

'Oh, Mum.' Judy involuntarily stretched out a hand towards her. Betty tensed. The hand was withdrawn. 'How awful for you.' What an absurd comment. If Declan … No point in even thinking about it. He wouldn't. She knew without a shadow of a doubt, he just wouldn't.

Betty stirred the pot. The hot sweet liquid splashed, catching her thumb. She sucked it, tears in her eyes, replacing the lid, adjusting the heat before running her hand under the cold tap. The mixture boiled steadily. They both stood inactive for a moment, both facing the window. But it was too painful. Betty began to wash up the utensils, scrubbing the board so vigorously she sent a spray of water over the floor. She grabbed a sheaf of kitchen paper and mopped frantically.

'Did he … was it … often?' Her voice reached Judy as a mere whisper.

'Not really. He knew I hated it. And there wasn't much opportunity.'

'And did he ever …? How far …?'

'No, Mum. Honestly. He never went that far.'

'Thank God. Thank God.' Tears dripped from Betty's nose. She sniffed uncharacteristically, before snatching a fresh sheet of kitchen towel and blowing into it noisily. 'I always thought it was a punishment. Because I wanted a baby so much. Going against nature, doing that. I shouldn't have.' Judy recognised it was the nearest thing to an apology her mother could manage.

'I was wondering, Mum, was it … reaction, d'you think? When he found out he couldn't give you children?'

'I don't think … No. Well, not the other women anyway. It started before he knew … before he found out he couldn't.'

'Oh, Mum …' What was there to say?

'He … he … he always wanted more – more than I …'

'I understand.' Did she? Intellectually maybe, but not emotionally. Declan had been the complete opposite.

'Mum, I'm not really as bitter – not now – not like I said the other day. Not really. Yes, I hated what he did and it frightened me. And it was a long time before it healed. But now, Declan – he's helped me overcome most of that. I don't wish I hadn't been born. I'm sorry I said that. I was angry.'

'He's a good man, Declan.'

'The best.' Impossible to tell her mother just how good he had been.

'Does he know … about your father?'

'I had to tell him. I *had* to, Mum.'

Betty nodded but Judy saw the flush of colour staining her neck.

'So can you forgive me for the things I said? It was the shock. And I know I do get upset terribly easily nowadays. It doesn't excuse my behaviour but … Mum, I'm so ashamed of myself.' The tears fell quietly. She felt her mother's arm fleetingly around her, rubbing her skin briefly, clumsily.

'It's all right. I understand. It must have been a shock. I see that.'

Betty turned to the simmering pot. The acrid smell of hot vinegar was choking. Judy felt a powerful urge to go outside into the fresh air but she knew this moment would not return. She watched as Betty stirred the thickening mixture.

'I do have to find out as much as I can about myself, where I came from. You do see that, don't you? We don't know … if we have other children … we need to know if we *should* have any more. If they'd be like Bethany.'

'I see that. But Judith …' Betty's voice trembled. She took a big breath. 'You're going to hate me even more if you find it was … me … who passed that gene on.'

'Hate you? I don't hate you! And it's no more your fault that I have the gene than it's my fault Bethany had it.'

'But if I hadn't ….'

'If you hadn't had that insemination I wouldn't be here, and I'd never have known all the happy things that have happened in my life. And that includes being a Mum myself, being pregnant with Bethany and loving her.' Judy fought back the tears for Bethany lest they be misconstrued. 'Can you tell me *anything* about my real father – the donor, I mean?'

'Only that they tried to match him to your … to Jim.'

'Tall?'

'And dark, I think. They said that anyway. Jim was very dark. Hair, eyes. But he had a tanned sort of skin too.'

Judy glanced involuntarily at her own delicate creamy skin, a natural accompaniment to auburn hair.

'Nothing else?'

'They said they chose them carefully. Made sure they were healthy. And they were usually very intelligent. Medical students, professional men, people like that, usually, they said.'

'Would you mind … if they try to find out more – just so we know, for future babies? Not for me.'

'No, it's all right. If you need to. But I … I don't want to know.'

'Fair enough. They probably won't be able to trace him anyway. But Dec and I think we should at least try.'

Betty nodded.

'But you *will* be able to tell me about *your* side of the family. Hang on a mo while I get a piece of paper. Dr Galloway showed us how to fill in the bits.'

Perched on the single high stool against the breakfast bar, Judy wrote while her mother worked. Betty answered the questions without hesitation now; they were on safer ground. Declan was right: clearing the air had done them both good.

Betty removed the bag of spices and ladled the hot chutney into warmed jars. She screwed the lids on tightly and added her own neat labels, each a measured distance from the base. Judy admired the finished product. Strange to think all those ingredients processed in this way ended up looking like something completely other. It was a bit like the information Betty had provided; it looked different from the raw picture of that first disclosure.

It was five o'clock when Judy eventually took her leave. She gave her mother a quick hug and was rewarded with a slight squeeze in return. A still warm jar of chutney was pressed into her hand. Judy insisted on contributing something to the charity sale, and Betty smiled fleetingly for the first time as she waved goodbye.

TWENTY-SIX

As she drove home Judy's thoughts returned to Bethany. How different their mother-daughter relationship would have been. If she ever had a daughter of her own there would be no rationing of affection, no dark secrets, no stinting on love. But would she? The sadness cut cruelly through her fragile calm.

She took the first available turning off her planned route.

The grave was an oasis of calm, not another soul present as far as the eye could see. She was quite alone, alone with agonising thoughts of all she had lost. But mercifully there was no-one to prevent the torrent of grief; the tears could fall unchecked.

The stench of vinegar hit her as she got back in the car, and her body craved the cleansing power of shampoo and shower. There was so much to be washed away.

Judy was kneeling on the floor beside the open patio doors, a slight breeze cooling her, when Declan arrived home that night. In front of her was their wedding album. He knew there was even more cause than usual to tread warily tonight, so it was a relief to see her ready smile. Tossing his briefcase into the corner, he laid his laptop carefully on the table.

'Does that mean you're working tonight?' she asked, pulling a face at the computer.

'If there's time. We hit a snag this afternoon but I think I can see a way of fixing it. I just didn't want to stay late at work today – just in case ... well, in case you needed a shoulder.'

'I'm fine. But thanks for that.'

He dropped down beside her, a hug saying more than words. Her hair was still damp and clung in tendrils around her neck giving her an air of freshness and youth. He ran his fingers lightly through the curls.

'Mmmmm. What a fragrant wife!'

'You wouldn't have thought so a couple of hours ago!'

'No? How come?'

'Mother was making chutney. Yuck! I stank of it.'

He grimaced.

'Is this you strolling down memory lane?' He gestured at the photographs.

The album was open at one of his favourites. It was a portrait of Judy looking directly into the camera, the close-up lens showing her clear complexion, the chestnut shades in her hair, the detail on the bodice of her dress. She had such a serene expression. Her eyes were enormous within those long black lashes.

'Just thinking.' She turned the page. Bride and groom stood framed by a huge stone archway, hands lightly clasped, looking into each other's eyes. The line of Judy's dress emphasised her slim figure, the train arranged so perfectly at their feet it looked as if it were pinned.

'Much nicer with you beside me.' She nuzzled against him as she spoke.

Their happiness shone through the pages. There had been no shadows that day.

'How was your Mum?' he ventured.

'Very stiff and withdrawn when I arrived. But better when I left. Thanks to you.'

'Me? What's it got to do with me?'

'I kept imagining you were there watching. It stopped me getting so irritated with her.'

He shook his head at her.

'Actually, for *her* – well, you know my Mum – for her, she wasn't too bad. In the end, I mean.'

'Good. And did you get things sorted out?'

'Well, sort of. She told me what it was like in the early days before Dad … you know. And it was nice that, Dec, hearing that he *had* been a proper Dad for a while. But you know, she's burned *all* the photos of him. Not one left. That says a lot, eh?'

'Poor woman. And we have millions already!'

'Exactly. That's why I got out the album. I was sitting here wondering. These fantastic photos – would I keep them? If you were unfaithful to me, or if you did anything as horrible as he did, would I want to keep them? I don't know.'

'No point wasting your brain space on *that*! Not a chance! Besides, where could I go for anything more exciting than this?' He gave her a tender shake.

'I know you wouldn't.'

'Did you get anything useful for Dr Galloway?'

'Yep, Mum could fill in the things for *her* side. Nothing startling, I don't think, but he might make something of it.'

'So, we're all set then? No more gaps? Well, none we can fill in anyway?'

'Nope. Funny feeling, huh? Telling a stranger all about us – all this stuff we've only just found out about ourselves.' She rubbed her head against his shoulder.

'I'm still struggling with the uncanny bit, really. Both of us with this recessive gene; both of us conceived artificially? But in an odd sort of way it helps. Just knowing we're both equally responsible. We've both got blank bits. Neither of us needs to feel we're letting the other one down. I know it wouldn't really be like that – because we can't help it – but I think I might feel like that inside.'

'I know. I'd be the same.'

'We are *so* lucky, Jude. In spite of everything that's happened.'

'I felt that a lot today, Dec. Thinking about how different it all was for my Mum. Even in the early days, she wasn't happy with my Dad. She's pretty sure he was unfaithful to her – with other women, I mean – even early on. Imagine knowing that! She didn't like the physical side of things; he wanted a lot. He didn't really want her to go for artificial insemination, but she was desperate. Pulling against each other all the time. And that was all *before* he did anything to me.'

He pulled her closer. Yes, they had much to be thankful for.

The telephone was strangely quiet that evening and, his computing problem solved, Declan concentrated on diverting Judy's attention onto plans for the porch they were adding to the back door. They were still outside measuring when the phone rang at ten o'clock. It was Georgina – a very subdued Georgina.

'Dad told me this morning.'

'Ahhh.'

'Isn't it awful, Dec?' Her voice sounded hollow.

'It's a shock, I agree. Are you OK? D'you want to talk about it?'

'I can't get my head round it really. You, me, Sian – all made like *that*. It's so ... *gross*.'

'Did Dad explain?'

'Oh, yeah. I know *why* they did it. I understand. But I still hate it.'

'I did at first, too, but they didn't have much choice, did they?'

'I wish I didn't know.'

'I'm sorry, that's our fault.'

'No, I didn't mean that. It's not your fault. But what am I going to *do*, Dec?'

'How do you mean – *do*?'

'You've got Judy already. Sian's got Roddy. Who'll want me?'

'Heaps of blokes! Hey, you're the same girl you were yesterday. And since when were you ever short of admirers? You've had more dates than I've had hot dinners, as they say!'

'That was then. They won't want to know now.'

'So you think they only found you attractive because of your normal parentage?' He tried to tease her out of her melancholy. 'Don't be daft. What difference does it make to them?'

'What difference? *What difference*? That is such a ... *male* ... attitude! Trust you!'

'Male? Meaning?'

'"Love is for man a thing apart, 'tis woman's whole existence,"' she

quoted at him with a bite in her voice. 'It might not matter to *you* but it matters a whole heap to *me* that I came into being via a syringe, I can tell you.'

'Well, yes, I know. I didn't mean it doesn't affect *you*. But them – the men? What difference does it make to them? You're just *you*. It doesn't matter to them that you aren't really biologically Sid's daughter. Does it?'

'How do I know?'

He wasn't making a good job of this.

'Georgie, what's making you so mad? Which bit of it?'

'Well it's – I don't know who I *am* any more. And I'm scared of what I might be passing on. We just don't know where we've come from now.'

'I know what you mean. But when you think about it, actually, we didn't know what we might be passing on – before – did we? I mean, you don't get handed a pedigree record when you're born *normally*, do you?'

'No, but at least you can look at your Mum and Dad and their families and see that there isn't anything nasty there.'

'Nothing obvious, I suppose. But things do still come out, don't they? And for each new couple it's a gamble. Even when you *know* where you come from.'

'Oh, there you go again! Will you stop being so ... so ... *reasonable!*'

He smiled in spite of himself. Typical Georgina! Always quick to gather a head of steam on emotive issues. Since schooldays she'd been infuriated by his tendency to analyse the arguments and present a calmly rational viewpoint.

'I'm sorry, Georgie, I didn't mean to annoy you. And I'm not discounting your feelings. Honestly. I hated it too, at first. Well, I still do in some ways. But now I've had more time to think, and now I've had a chance to talk to Judy about it, well, it doesn't feel as awful as it did. And honestly, I really don't think you need to worry. You're still you. Chaps will still think you're terrific. And anyway, it looks like Judy and I have drawn the short straw. Must be a million to one chance of it happening to you.'

'Hmmm. Well, I'm still hating the very idea of Mum having ... yuck! It's so ... *animal!*'

'D'you know what made me feel differently about it all?'

'No, what?'

'Remember how much Mum and Dad loved us? Everything they did for us?'

''Course I do.'

'Well, when you think they loved us like that, *knowing* all the time, and they did it in the first place because they loved each other and wanted us kids that much – well, that made me feel very small.'

'How d'you mean? I don't follow.'

'Well, I have to tell you, I don't think I *could* cope with having that done to Judy. It kills me just *thinking* about it. But Dad loved Mum so much he consented. And he shared the whole thing with her, you know, no grousing, no whingeing, just like – well, *Dad*. We never suspected there was anything, because we *were* his kids, he *made* it that way.'

'I suppose.'

'Georgie, why don't you come up this weekend? We're all struggling with lots of big questions right now. It'd be good to be able to talk – you know, face to face. Yeah?'

'Could I? Could you bear it? I'd love to. I'm a mess right now, I know.'

'Then come.'

'But … is it too soon for you and Judy – you know, after Bethany? You need space. Don't worry about me. Always one to blow my stack first and think later.'

'No. Do come. We're not always very chirpy, but you'll understand. And we don't cry *all* the time! It'll do us good having you here.'

Poor old Georgie – always the wild one – now forced to grow up all in a hurry, Declan thought, with a sigh.

TWENTY-SEVEN

All three talked long into the night the day Georgina arrived. Over and over the ground, looking at all their 'if onlys', all their 'what ifs', from every conceivable angle.

Georgina pressed Judy for medical facts but there was much she couldn't answer.

'Dick'll know,' Judy said.

'Dick? Who's Dick?'

'A colleague of mine. He's coming tomorrow to fill us in on some of the facts. He's a fertility expert – he knows about all this stuff.'

There it was again – a sudden surreptitious look. It was the same look Declan had given her when she'd first suggested asking Dick. He'd disclaimed any reason for it at the time but she wasn't persuaded. Had he heard about Dick's reputation somehow? The best remedy was meeting the man for himself.

Darkness crept silently into the room as they talked. The intimacy of the subdued corner lamp was conducive to sharing their doubts and fears.

'Judy, did you know straight away Dec was the one for you?' The sudden question took her by surprise.

'Well, no. Not immediately. I *liked* him instantly, but ... '

'It wasn't love at first sight then?'

'No. But I'm naturally the cautious type. Why?'

'What made you decide he *was* the one?'

Judy glanced at Declan. Where was Georgina leading?

'Is it OK, me asking? I miss having Mum to talk to.'

It was a heartfelt appeal.

'Put like that – yes, you can certainly *ask*. What made me decide?' Judy leaned back in her seat considering. 'He made me feel safe. He always cared how I felt. We just seemed ... right together. Oh, that sounds so dull. But it certainly wasn't dull. Not at all. It was ... I don't know ... electric. But safe.' Her eyes met Declan's.

'And the electric bit – was that always there?'

'Weeeeeell, it was *special* from the start, and different. But I think I was just intrigued at first. Because we clicked. The electric bit? That started the first time we held hands. For me anyway.'

'And you, Dec?' Georgina said.

'For me?' Declan's eyes were still on her, and Judy held her breath. 'From the first time we met the electricity was there. The touching, that just blew my fuse!' Her laughter merged with Georgina's.

'So you knew from the beginning, Dec?' Georgina was pursuing a point.

'I suspected from the beginning. It was different from anything I'd ever experienced before. But I didn't decide Judy was definitely the girl for me till I knew her better – knew the inside person. When I discovered that she was everything I wanted on the inside as well as on the outside, that's when I knew definitely.'

'So if you'd known what you know now, when would you have told her?'

'I can't be certain but I think, probably when I started to feel this might be heading towards permanent.'

'And you, Judy, when would you have told Dec? Or when would you have wanted him to tell you?'

Judy thought for a long moment.

'I think, yes, the same. When we sensed this was getting to be really deep stuff.'

'And did you each know when the other one was starting to think that?'

It was Declan's turn to laugh.

'No! We were talking about this only last week. It seems Judy wasn't sure I was serious till *you* told her I was crazy about her.' Judy saw his eyes were dancing.

'Me?' Georgina's surprise was evident.

'Yep. You.'

'That time in the garden,' Judy chipped in. 'The first time Dec brought me to meet you.'

'But he was dotty about you. It was obvious. Anybody could see that.'

'Not Judy apparently!' Declan assured her.

'So, what if he'd told you about the genes and things *then* – when *he* thought it was serious but you weren't sure?'

'Well, I think, on balance I'd have been impressed that he trusted me with that information. I guess it would have told me that he was serious about us, too.'

'How would you have told her, Dec?'

There was a long silence. Declan's gaze was steady; it was as if he were about to tell her in reality.

'I'd have probably told her how I was feeling – about her, I mean. Then I'd tell her that I was starting to think long term, and because it was all getting so serious for me, I had to tell her something very personal – something definitely not for public consumption but I trusted her with it. And I'd probably say I wanted her to tell me honestly if it would make any difference to her feelings. Something like that. And inside I'd be a screwed-up mess in case I'd completely misread the situation and entirely blown my chances with her!'

Judy, dragging her eyes away to Georgina, was arrested by the intensity of her listening.

150

'Georgie. This isn't about us, is it? Is there someone – someone special – for you?'

'Maybe.' The dark eyes were bright.

'D'you want to tell us about him?'

'His name's Rupert.'

'And?'

'Well, when I set up the kitchen design company I didn't realise how much financial know-how you'd need. I'm not bad on the design side – though I say it myself – just in the privacy of these four walls; but I'm a dead loss when it comes to finances! Yep, Dec, I see you grinning. I was never any good at maths, I know. Well, anyway, Rupert was one of my clients last year. He seemed pretty pleased with the kitchen I did for him and we got chatting and when I said I hated the financial aspect of running a company, he offered to help me any time I needed it. He's an economist by background, you see. And I have to say he's a good operator – he's saved me loads of time and money. Or course, I pay him for his advice. He wanted to do it just as a friend, but I insisted it had to be on a proper footing.'

'But this is something more than work?'

'Well, at first it was just work. But … well, one thing led to another and we found we shared quite a few interests – the theatre, music, good restaurants. London's a great place for shows and we just sort of started going to different ones. And well …' She broke off suddenly with a self-conscious shrug, a faint blush staining her cheeks.

'Thirty-three years old and looking like a schoolgirl,' Declan teased her. 'The original taming of the shrew! Good for Rupert.'

'Ahh well, he probably thinks I'm far too much of a party animal to be serious!' she said dismissively.

'He's still seeing you though, isn't he?' Judy countered.

'It's probably just habit! Maybe he's just at a loose end at the weekends!'

'Georgie!'

'But to return to the real question of the day, supposing – just supposing I was interested enough to think of long term with him, I'd have to tell him about me.'

'The AID and the gene thing.' Judy was nodding.

'Double whammy, eh? I can tell you, at this moment it makes me want to run a mile!'

'But you won't.' Declan's statement sounded definite.

'Won't I? I don't know. I've looked out my spiked shoes … in case.'

'Not if you really care for him, I'd have thought. There's no reason why he'd be put off if *he* really cares. Neither of those things should make a difference to *him*.'

'But if I start talking about heredity he'll think I'm thinking of having kids with him, and heck, even in *my* liberated world there are things girls just don't rush headlong into! You wait for the guy to say first.'

'So if he mentioned the future to you first, it'd be OK to tell him then?' Declan asked.

'Sort of. Although then he might wonder why I hadn't warned him first.'

'Equality rules, but only some of the time, eh?' Declan said, with a quizzical look. 'In your thoroughly modern world.'

'Well, who did all the going in your case?' she shot back.

Judy glanced at Declan. She smiled; he looked suddenly thoughtful.

'I did, I guess.' Declan said. Judy nodded.

'Yeah, you see?'

'But then, we're terribly old-fashioned; *you're* a thoroughly modern miss.'

'Well, modern I may be – whatever that means – but even in my modern thinking, there are things a girl just doesn't do. And talking about having kids with a bloke is one of them! I know it's not rational when we keep banging on about our rights and all that, but that's the way it is. It's-the-guy-who-pops-the-question syndrome.'

'So what are you going to do, Georgie?' Judy was intrigued.

'Don't know. Wait and see how things go, probably. *If* we go on seeing each other and it looks like it's going somewhere, I might feel I have to say something. I must say, it feels bad having something as big as this unsaid. False pretences and all that jazz. But I see what you mean: if he runs away when he knows, his interest wasn't up to much in the first place. But if I'm keen, and he runs away because I told him, I guess I'm going to feel as sick as a parrot anyway! And you'd have a hard job convincing me that it was his fault and not my bad timing! I'll come to you to lick my wounds for me, eh?'

'I think you'll be surprised how little it means to him, actually,' Declan said.

'Even the thought that he might father kids – you know – who ...?' Georgina suddenly stopped in her tracks, her eyes fearful.

'Who have serious abnormalities. Or die,' Judy finished for her, not flinching.

'Sorry, Judy.'

Judy shook her head. 'It's all right.'

'But the chances of that are a million to one,' Declan chipped in, looking at his sister but getting up suddenly and coming to sit beside his wife, taking her hand in his. 'The chances of Judy and *me* both carrying that gene were infinitesimal. The chances of *you* meeting up with someone else with that same thing are even more remote.'

'It's true, Georgie,' Judy agreed.

'Yes. I know that – in my head anyway. But I'd still have to talk about my background to ... well, to anyone I thought I might have kids with.'

'Yes, I see that. And now you *know*, that's bound to be a big thing in your thinking.'

'You can't go back and be the innocent abroad. Not after this little packet falls in your lap!'

Was it her imagination or was there bitterness in Georgina's voice? Judy knew she was super-sensitive to any implied slur against Bethany. She pushed the beginnings of her resentment firmly away. Georgina had no-one else to turn to.

TWENTY-EIGHT

Georgina changed tack abruptly.

'Can you bear to talk about the options? I'm just so pig ignorant. But say, you know, tell me to just shut up, if it's all too painful. You're brilliant. Dead impressive. But don't let me, you know … encroach.'

'It's fine. By me anyway.' Judy's face was tight but she was sincere in her response. 'Yep, it's painful but if you can't talk to *us* about all this who can you talk to? And you, Dec?'

'No, it's fine by me too. And believe me, you won't touch any raw nerves we haven't hit over and over ourselves.'

'Thanks. I don't know how you two do it. It makes me want to cry just being with you.'

Silence filled a long moment. Then Judy leaned forward, frowning.

'But, Georgie, you have to remember, I don't know the answers to lots of this stuff. You think I know it all, but I honestly don't. It's really special-ised stuff. Even our paediatrician was out of his depth with it. That's why we're seeing the geneticist. So don't take what I say as gospel.'

'Right, I hear you. But if I don't know *a bit* it'll be hopeless talking to your friend tomorrow. I don't want to look a complete banana.'

'As long as you understand – to use a horrible cliché – a little knowledge is a dangerous thing. There might be nothing at all for you to worry about. There's no point in you losing sleep at this stage, till we know. We aren't even sure for ourselves, and we know *we've* got a problem. You mightn't have anything at all to worry about.'

'Right.'

'So, what d'you want to know?'

'If, let's say, I did tell Rupert all this and he didn't run a mile. We get together. We decide we want kids. If I haven't got this gene, we're OK. That right?'

'Right – well, as far as *this* condition's concerned. There're never any guarantees, of course.'

'Yep, point taken. If I *have* got it but he hasn't, we're still OK. Yeah?'

'Yes.'

'Can we have a test to see if we carry it?'

'That I don't know. We can ask about that. It's on our list for Dr Gallo-way next week. Dick Halley might know tomorrow, but he might not. These gene things are changing all the time and only the specialists in the field really know the up-to-the-minute knowledge.'

'Fair enough. Hey, this sounds like I'm only thinking about me. I know it's a trillion times worse for you guys. I don't mean to ....'

'It's fine, Georgie, we know. We're all in it together, though. We all need to know so we can make sensible decisions based on the facts. So take that as read.'

Georgina smiled at her warmly.

'So, we find out that I carry it *and* he carries it. What are the options now?'

Judy felt Declan's fingers tighten over hers. This was exactly where they were. 'Well, as far as I can tell, the next question is, can they tell if an embryo is affected?'

'You mean early on?'

'Yeah. I don't know if they can. That's on our list too. If they *can* tell, try to conceive – naturally with him, I mean. They then test the embryo and you decide what you do. If it's unaffected, you just go ahead and all's well. If it's *affected* you then have to decide. You could go ahead anyway, knowing you'll end up with a child with huge problems, or you could have it aborted.' Judy's jaw tightened, giving a hard edge to her voice. She'd wept bitter tears over this prospect.

'And either way – grim, huh?'

'Yep.' Declan's monosyllable was loaded with emotion. 'And we're not militant anti-abortionists. It's just – well, it'd be our child.'

'So, if that's all too awful, or too big a risk, is there anything else open to us?'

'Well, I don't know if they'd do it in these circumstances – we've still to find out – but the logical next step, it seems to me, is to consider conception outside the womb.'

'Yeah?' Georgina's eyes were focused on Judy.

'Well, the important thing seems to be to avoid these two recessive genes coming together. So if you can engineer that from the outset you don't have to think of destroying an embryo that already exists.'

'Right. I see that. And that's a better option, uhh?'

'Well, maybe. It depends.'

'On?'

'Whether the options that allow you to create that embryo are acceptable to you.'

'And they are ... what? Gee, I'm so ignorant. Sorry, Judy. I see this stuff in the papers – surrogacy and the genome project and cloning and all. But heck, I haven't a clue what it means in real life.'

'It's OK. There was no reason for you to know – before.'

'A steep learning curve, eh, Georgie?' Declan gave her a rueful grin. 'For me too.'

She nodded, then looked back to Judy.

'Well,' Judy began cautiously, 'If they could detect the faulty gene in the sperm or egg – before they meet and form an embryo, I mean – then I think it'd be a matter of choosing healthy ones and ensuring *they* are used. But I don't know if they can do that. We've still to ask that question too.'

'And they do that under a microscope or in a test tube, or whatever, yep?'

'Yes. They can do that already for some of the major diseases, the ones that are real killers. And it's a process that's been perfected in IVF treatment in general.'

'So it'd still be *our* genes. But somebody else would be involved in making sure that the healthy ones are selected and they come together.'

'Yes, in a nutshell.'

Georgina thought about this for a moment, then looked searchingly from one to the other.

'Would that be ... so awful? Tell me if it's too painful to talk about it, or too private.'

'For us, yes; me especially, I think,' Declan said. 'I find it hard to think of anybody else being involved in something so – well, private, as you say. But under the circumstances, and if it was *our* genes, we think we probably could deal with that – if it gave us a healthy child. But it still takes some getting used to.'

'But each couple would have to decide for themselves if it was tolerable, yeah?'

'That's right. It depends how you view things – your relationship, having children at all, what's natural, all those kinds of things.'

'OK. So if they *can* find this thing on the egg or sperm, that's an option. But if they can't?'

'Well, if you can't find it early on then you're back to waiting till *after* conception and then having to decide whether you abort the embryo or not. That is, if you're insisting the genes must be yours and – well, Rupert's, in this hypothetical case we're talking about.'

'But ...?'

'Well, you could think, OK, we don't like the idea of abortion. We can't cope with going through pregnancy to term and having babies terribly damaged or dying. Perhaps we should avoid that situation altogether and go for using the genetic material from *one* of us and bring in the other half from elsewhere where we know it's sound.'

Judy saw the realisation dawning on Georgina.

'Sperm. From a donor.' The words were dragged out of her unwillingly.

'Or eggs from a donor.' Judy carried on mechanically.

'It's unreal – this whole business. How're you guys still sane? I'd be going out of my mind. All these arguments and options all coming back to the same issues.'

'Yep. It certainly feels like that.' Declan nodded.

'And are *you* having to think about ... *that*?' Georgina's eyes were wide and dark as she looked from Judy to Declan.

'We don't know enough yet, as Judy says.' Declan spoke slowly. 'But thanks to Judy I do know enough to know we *might* have to make those choices. So we're trying to look at them all logically and see how far we're personally prepared to go.'

'But it might not come to any of these options,' Judy interrupted swiftly. 'Look, don't be misled by anything I say. A lot of this stuff is new to me too. There might not be any tests they *can* do. We might just need to take pot luck. Or decide we won't have a family.'

'Blimey. It's as bad as that?'

'Well, it might be.'

'What would *that* do to you? When you really, really want children, I mean.'

'We don't know. Nobody can predict …' Judy felt the tears thickening her voice and stopped abruptly.

'Let's not go there yet,' Declan said quietly. 'At the moment we have to concentrate on being prepared enough to know what questions we need answered, so we aren't just derailed by the first thing they throw at us.'

'I don't know what to say.' Georgina spread her hands helplessly.

'We're just hoping that the geneticist can spell out what the position is, the risks and the options available. But if it *does* come to donor anything, we just don't know at the moment. But hey, it's funny how it changes how you see things.' Judy heard Declan lightening his tone. 'I was looking at one of those holiday things a couple of days ago. It was plugging holidays in Slovenia as it happens. And it had, you know, all the usual blurb about the weather there, and the scenery, and food and everything. And it had this bit about the language. I mean, who speaks Slovene nowadays, for goodness sake? But it told you how to ask for a cup of coffee, the way to the station, a room for two, directions to the museum, stuff like that. You know, touristy things. And then it had as much again about things to say to pick up a girl! Now normally I doubt I'd have even given it a thought.'

'Well, I'm pleased to hear *that* little crumb of comfort,' Judy said with mock indignation.

Declan grinned back at her.

'Hey, you, don't spoil my story! As I said, before I was so rudely interrupted, this week this stuff just jumped out at me. It shrieks out at you that heaps of other people don't think of sex in the way we do. It just made me wonder. Maybe these things we're talking about … what d'you think? D'you suppose they're as big a deal to your average Joe Bloggs? I don't know. Maybe I'm getting bitter and twisted in my old age.'

'I know what you mean,' Judy agreed, nodding slowly. 'Since I've been at home I've occasionally watched daytime telly. It helps to stop me thinking sometimes. And it's really noticeable how quickly folk jump into bed with anyone who seems to show the first signs of interest. You know, they exchange a look, they kiss, and instantly they're ripping their clothes off and the camera homes in on them in bed together.'

'What rubbish have you been filling your mind with?' Declan's eyes were teasing.

'I know! Shocking, isn't it? But even the so-called professional folk – you know, doctors, teachers, lawyers – folk who you'd expect to have a responsible approach to life – are having sex with different folk, and getting pregnant by mistake, and all that stuff. Well, maybe it's just the sort of thing that makes a story but it seems to me to say something quite frightening about what is accepted, expected.'

'Yoiks! Listen to yourselves!' Georgina interrupted, her eyes suddenly kindled. 'Talk about hellfire and damnation! In case it has escaped your pious attention, we haven't just crawled out of the ark with Noah! It's not just a *story*! These soaps – they're only staying in tune with society as we know it today. People don't hang around denying themselves until marriage nowadays. Get real! I mean, pretty much all my friends just live together. Nobody bats an eyelid.'

Declan shrugged.

'So *do* they think differently about things like artificial conception?' Judy wondered aloud, her quiet tones a sharp contrast to Georgina's abrasive comments.

'I've no idea. I've never asked them. I can't imagine most people bother their heads about such things actually. But listening to you two – well, I mean, I can see that for you – well, like you say, it'd feel like a real intrusion. But if it wasn't so … special, so exclusive? I don't know.'

'And would it bother *you*, Georgie?' Declan asked slowly.

'I don't know. I guess if I got to the stage of wanting to have kids I'd have to be pretty much committed to a bloke, anyway. Yeah, having a family – that's heavy duty stuff. But whether I'd ever want kids desperately enough to go through all that, well, I'm not so sure.'

'That's the real question. I mean, we really wanted Bethany, but …' Judy's voice trembled and trailed away. Declan took over.

'But now we have to ask ourselves how much do we want a child – for its own sake. And we haven't got the answer yet because we end up each time saying, well, it depends. There's a price that's too high and we're not prepared to pay it. We just aren't sure where the line comes for us yet, because we haven't got enough facts.'

Judy fought the tears, not wanting to embarrass Georgina.

'You know, I read somewhere recently – the paper I think it was' – Georgina was doing her best to steer away from danger zones – 'that somebody once said they didn't know what all the fuss was about when the first test-tube baby was created. Louise Brown, wasn't it? Well, anyway, this person thought the real miracle was *every time* a sperm and egg came together naturally and created a new life. Zillions of times without any intervention on anybody's part. You can see what they mean, eh?'

'And it *is* a miracle, *we* know that. We felt like that about Bethany.' Declan's voice was hushed. Again there was silence.

Judy got to her feet.

'Drinks all round?'

'Let me ...' Declan looked up at her.

'No, I'll do it. Please.' She must get away from the intensity. It helped doing something.

Her footsteps were silent on the carpet outside the open door, and Georgina's words carried clearly.

'Dec, I owe you an apology.'

'I'm sure you do! What have you done this time?'

'For getting mad at you – for being so reasonable.'

'Forget it. I'm used to your tantrums by now!'

'No, I'm being serious, Dec. I shouldn't have. I can see ... losing Bethany ... all these questions – it's the most awful thing. And you feel it every bit as much as Judy. Sorry, Dec. I mean it.'

'Thanks, Georgie. Nice of you to say so. But we'll cope.' Judy heard the thickening in Declan's voice.

'I know you will. And for what it's worth, I think you're both brilliant. I don't think I'd be that strong.'

'When it happens, you don't have much choice.'

How true.

'Doesn't it put a strain on your marriage, though? All this grief and all the worry about the future and kids and everything, I mean?'

'Yep.' The monosyllable was flat, emotionless.

'You two going to be OK?'

'I hope so.'

Judy crept away, cold fingers clutching at her heart.

It was Georgina's suggestion to go swimming before breakfast. She always ensured she took regular exercise and told them, bluntly, today she was looking for a diversion from the turbulence of her thoughts.

'Race you! Last one over five lengths shouts the other two coffee!' she challenged. 'On your marks, set, GO!'

At the end of the third length, Declan was suddenly arrested by the sound of his own name being called. A colleague from work, Martin Howard, came swimming across to say hello.

Georgina took instant advantage of the diversion and shot off for the last two laps, Judy a split second behind her. Declan laughingly explained what was happening and both men were smiling broadly when Georgina emerged triumphantly at the end of her fifth lap.

'Coffees are on you, bro!'

'My unsporting twin, Georgina! This is Martin; he works with me and knows *I* would never take an unfair advantage *myself,*' he said, feigning indignation.

Before she could respond, Judy shot through the water to touch the edge of the pool.

'Second!' crowed Georgina. 'Dec gets the booby prize!'

Breathlessly Judy clung to the side, unable to retort for a moment.

'Your other sister. From New Zealand?' Martin smiled at her. 'Hi, I'm Declan's colleague, Martin.'

'No. This is Judy, my wife.' Declan grinned again.

'Apologies. Everybody looks the same when you see them wet, eh?'

It was true, Declan noticed, the girls did look alike when only their heads were above the water, and their wet hair was plastered close to their heads, the dampness darkening Judy's brighter colouring.

'I'm so sorry ... about the baby,' Martin said hesitantly.

'Thanks.'

'I can't imagine ...'

Before Declan could think of anything to say, Judy interrupted. 'Are your family here?' She was looking around at the swimmers for any sign of children.

'They're away at the grandparents this weekend.' Declan saw Martin's discomfort. He was probably wishing himself anywhere but here, talking about any subject but this. It was impressive though, Judy calmly asking about his children's progress at school and in sport. She made it seem so natural. Perhaps only he knew what it cost her. But he could sympathise with Martin too; for him it must feel all wrong. It was time to rescue him.

'Right, you two cheats, last to the other end gets to buy the doughnuts,' he hissed. 'See you Monday, Martin,' and with that he ploughed through the water in their wake.

TWENTY-NINE

Dr Richard Halley erupted into Greenacre Crescent, Roslin, in a riot of sound and colour. A flamboyant figure in his red sports car, dapper moleskin waistcoat, and purple bow tie, his hearty greeting echoed round the quiet cul-de-sac.

Declan watched him with mixed emotions. Judy's warning lingered: 'Don't be put off by his manner, he's a real professional. Just doesn't want people to know he's a marshmallow inside.'

A *marshmallow*? This exhibitionist?

Now Dick followed Judy into the sitting room, and threw himself into the rocking chair.

'What a joy, coming away from that madhouse they call a hospital! And this cottage – wow! Now this is my kind of place.'

'Bad week at the office?' Judy's face seemed lit up and Declan watched the interplay between the two with curious eyes. Dick wasn't the sort of man Judy usually warmed to but he seemed to brighten her mood instantly. He felt a pang of jealousy. If only he could produce such a transformation.

'Insane, my dear, insane!' Dick said with a histrionic clutching of his forehead. 'But the peace and tranquillity of this haven will be as good as any tonic known to the British Pharmacopoeia.'

'Is it the clinical load or the research giving you the headaches?'

'Both. But most of all it's the boys in grey suits. They're the biggest bane of my life at this precise moment. Threatening to ban the introduction of any equipment made since 1901, to stop the pay of all the technicians, to hamstring us doctors until we can't buy so much as a test tube without bowing and scraping and filling in six forms in triplicate. And they're still expecting research results yesterday.'

Judy grinned at him.

'I'm sure you're more than a match for the administrators.'

'I only wish I were. Only wish I were. I can think of heaps of nasty experimental things I'd like to do to unmentionable parts of their anatomy to make them weep for mercy and offer me the moon, but these jumped-up little clerks have no concept of what we're about, and moreover they have no intention of sullying their closed little minds with any attempt to do so.'

'Shaken your pedestal, have they?'

'I was never on one as far as they're concerned, I'm sorry to say.'

'Are all departments in this? Or is it infertility in particular?'

'We're all feeling the pinch, of course. Same everywhere. But this particular thumbscrew is reserved for those of us who have the audacity to think we can fritter funds away on frivolities. I mean … *infertility*? Who cares about *that*? Bottom of the heap, chaps!' Dick's extravagant gestures consigned the whole discipline to the waste-basket.

'It must be galling.'

'Galling? Far too polite a term for it, my dear, but fear not, I shan't sully your chaste little ears with a more accurate description.' He grinned around at them all. 'Let's forget the iniquities of those pipsqueaks and talk about you lovely people.'

Judy handed him a coffee. He inhaled the aroma with an exaggerated gesture.

'Mmmmm. Worth it all for this.'

'You know, Dick, no-one would ever suspect you were a serious academic. You are quite, quite mad.' Judy laughed as she passed drinks to Declan and Georgina.

'Oh, I know I am. But keep that little observation to yourself, I beg you! The admin boys are just waiting for a chance to bundle me up into a secure unit and tie a label around my neck saying, "certifiable". It's my daily labour to steer them away from the evidence! But enough of them. How goes it in this little backwater?'

There was silence for a moment. The gap between Dick's banter and the seriousness of their problems felt insurmountable. Dick himself took the first step to bridge it.

'Georgina … may I call you by your first name?' She nodded instantly. 'Georgina, tell me about you. What do you do?'

She began hesitantly, clearly unsure what reaction she might unleash, but his manner had changed as abruptly as a summer storm gives way to tranquil sunshine. It was as if she were the only person in the room for him. Declan watched mesmerised as his fiery sister visibly relaxed and confided her anxieties. This man had something, indefinable maybe, but powerful in its effect.

'So I really need to know more about this gene thing,' Georgina concluded. 'I'm a complete ignoramus where this sort of thing's concerned.'

'Happy to help, but bear in mind Keith Galloway's your man really. He's the expert. Salt of the earth, Keith. Sound as a bell.'

'He's been really kind,' Judy chipped in. 'But it's all so complicated and we don't know enough to ask the right questions. So it'd be really good if you could fill us in a bit – especially while Georgie's here. There's so much just going round and round in circles because we don't know what's possible.'

'Fair enough. It can be mighty confusing all this hereditary stuff. Try me.'

'Dick, don't take this the wrong way, but Declan and Georgie don't know you as well as I do.' She shot him a look. 'Anything we tell you ...'

He turned from her to look squarely first at Georgina and then Declan.

'I'm not really the lunatic I pretend to be. It's just a cover. Protects me in a way. Rest assured, this is serious business – for me too. Nothing we talk about today will go beyond these four walls. You have my word on that.'

It was like being in the presence of a ventriloquist. He was instantly a different man.

Declan let out his breath slowly.

'Thanks.' Judy was smiling warmly at Dick.

'Now, all I know so far is what Judy's told me. You both have a recessive gene and only found that out when you had Bethany. Has Keith Galloway given you any more info?'

It was good – the way he spoke of Bethany so naturally, no skirting round the subject, no euphemisms, no evasions. Declan felt his own resistance melting.

'He's asked us to check our family trees for anything relevant but says we've probably got a one-in-four chance of a repeat.'

'Mhhmmm. And the family trees? Anything there?' His eyes moved around them all.

Declan looked at Judy, eyebrows raised. She nodded.

'You tell him, Dec.'

'We've found out that both of us' – he gestured from himself to Judy and back – 'we're both the product of artificial insemination ... by donor.' He kept his voice devoid of expression.

'Me, too,' Georgina added in a low voice. It felt as if they were in an Alcoholics Anonymous group, all admitting an addiction. They had come out. They had said it, aloud, to a stranger.

'OK.' The matter-of-fact response was almost deflating. No shocked look, no startled expression, nothing. But of course, it was his job. He must hear this kind of thing all the time. 'Anything else?'

'Not that we can identify as significant.'

'And d'you see the AID as significant?'

'Well, it means neither of us can trace back our paternal ancestry,' Declan replied. 'Not without help anyway. Could we – with help – this far down the line?'

''Fraid not. They kept very poor records back then. Quite deliberately.'

'Don't you still do that, then?'

'No, it's all much more tightly controlled now. In fact, fertility treatment is probably the most tightly regulated area of medicine.'

'Quite right too. You're creating life.' Georgina spoke with some passion.

Dick smiled at her. 'Well, *helping* to create. I think there's a subtle difference.'

'Right. Fair comment.'

'But yes, I agree. I don't think we mind having such tight regulations really, though we do mutter and grumble, of course! On principle! But the controls are there to protect everybody concerned: babies, infertile couples, donors, even us doctors. It's all a matter of respecting privacy and safeguarding interests. Rightly so.'

'And part of that is stopping the children finding out about their donor parent?' There was a slight edge to Georgina's question but Dick didn't seem to notice.

'Until recently, yes. But we've come to see that the children of these treatments might need to know their origins at some point, and since 1990 the licensing authority has required us to keep records. So we now track the results of each treatment. When donated gametes are used successfully, for instance, it's documented ... subject to a very strict code of confidentiality too, of course. But at the moment anyway, even today, the children couldn't find out who the donor was, not his or her name or anything, just a few basic characteristics maybe. Having said that, there *is* a move afoot to make it possible for young people after the age of eighteen to find out more about their genetic parents. I think it'll come. Whether it'll ever be possible to identify them and make *contact* in the future, I don't know. Some people think that will come too. There've been a load of changes since AID was first practised in the eighteenth century. And things are constantly evolving. What about you folk, d'you think that should be the case – the children being able to trace the biological father?'

'I *certainly* do.' Georgina was swift to respond.

'I'm not sure.' Declan was more guarded. 'If I put myself in the shoes of the donor, I don't think I'd be too keen on the idea of a few twenty-year-olds appearing on my doorstep claiming I was their father, freaking my wife out, antagonising my real children, and fleecing me dry for university fees!'

Dick grinned at him, nodding. It encouraged him to continue.

'I don't even think I want to know for *myself* either – trace my own biological father, I mean. This far down the track I think it's probably best left alone. And I certainly don't want to risk hurting the feelings of the man who brought me up as his son.'

'Your point about protection of the donors is the main reason why it hasn't been possible in the past to trace them, of course,' Dick said. 'But it's interesting: there's some evidence, from an Australian survey actually, that a lot of donors – more than half of their sample, but I can't remember the numbers, so that doesn't tell you much, does it? – but a lot of them, anyway, *would* be willing to have their identity made known to any kids born using their sperm *and* provision made for contact if they wished it. Of course, the Scots are a different breed from the Aussies so I don't know if you'd get the same results here. But in any case, I'm not personally so sure it's necessary to go the whole way in identifying them. It'd serve most purposes if the donor was just given an identifying number and gave consent to a list of those characteristics that he was willing to have divulged, don't you think?'

'But shouldn't everybody be *entitled* to know where they come from, who their parents were?' Georgina wasn't going to swim with the tide yet. 'I mean, it's a bit arrogant of the clinic people, or whoever, just to destroy the evidence, isn't it? Should it be down to them?'

'That's a very valid point.'

'I'm sick that *I* don't know, I can tell you.' Georgina sounded so sure again.

Dick nodded slowly, looking directly at her as he continued reflectively. 'But you know, in reality, heaps of ordinary young people, whose parents haven't had infertility treatment, don't *actually* know their origins. And usually it really doesn't matter. If parents and grandparents are all dead there's often nobody who *can* tell them about their past or make the connections. And some of those people, who *think* they know their origins, in fact don't. You'd be surprised how many social fathers aren't the children's biological fathers. Women often don't tell either the father or the kids that they actually carried somebody else's child. Not in AID cases like yours, I don't mean – but just families where the mothers slept with other men and passed the children off as their partners'. We hear these things in confidence, because it sometimes affects what we can or should do.'

'Don't you find it depressing, all the deceit and everything?' Georgina asked, wrinkling her nose in distaste.

'I personally try not to identify with it in that way. It's other people's lives. Of course, I have my *own* set of principles but it's not my job to dictate other people's morals.'

Declan's eyes flicked from Dick to Judy. She was watching Dick, her expression inscrutable. He looked back at Dick, seeing him suddenly in a different way. What must it be like for a man like this, dealing day in, day out with reproduction, other people's sex lives? What would that do to him as a man, a lover, a father? But he seemed pretty slick at moving in and out of roles. Too slick.

'That's a good point actually, Georgie, don't you think?' Declan said aloud, dragging his thoughts back onto safer ground. 'I mean, if Mum had had a fling with the local milkman and had us, we wouldn't have known our background any more than now, would we? So I guess we're no more disadvantaged than loads of other kids.'

'And that same jolly milkman might have had flings with half the bored housewives in the village and you could have seen clones of yourselves everywhere!' Dick grinned. They all smiled back.

'There are even some *advantages* to being conceived by AID,' he went on. 'It does away with some of the random chance of "normal" conception.' His fingers drew the inverted commas in the air. 'We screen the donors carefully. They tend to be in the upper bands of intelligence. In our case we test them for a variety of things before we take them on. If they pass that scrutiny we freeze their sperm and quarantine it for a few months and then do more tests. Only if everything's clear do we use that semen. So it's quality controlled.'

'I'm still not exactly delighted to have been made that way.' Georgina sounded rather truculent, Declan thought. He glanced swiftly at Dick but the doctor again seemed impervious to her tone. In fact his voice sounded sympathetic.

'It's a shock finding out, I know.'

Indeed it was.

THIRTY

Judy's thoughts were moving in a different direction.

'Dick, do most parents tell the children they've been conceived in this way?' she asked.

'AID, you mean? No. Not in my experience. Most *don't*.'

So her mother wasn't really different from the majority.

'No need for them to do so, really,' Dick continued. 'Once the insemination's done, the rest of it – the pregnancy, birth and upbringing of the child – are as normal. In fact, there's a strong argument in favour of just saying nothing.' So it even had medical approval, that deceit. 'It's one of the least invasive, least unnatural treatments we do. It doesn't even really require medical intervention, except that it seems preferable to ensure it's a clinically safe and controlled thing rather than a back-alley job, done by folk in it for all the wrong reasons.'

He hunched down into his seat, furtively glancing from side to side making them all smile again. Declan was impressed by his ability to keep the tone light even when discussing serious issues. It helped them relax. And it no longer seemed quite so indelicate to be talking about such intimate matters in this open way.

'Do you always have to have the consent of the husband or can you go ahead and treat a woman without it?' he asked. Sid had consented, he knew that, but if the husband really objected, like *he*, Declan, did …?

'The consent of the husband is ethically required if he's to have parental responsibility.'

'Quite right too.'

'And can people choose at all? D'you have banks of Nobel prize winners and Mensa champions here?' It was Georgina's turn. Curious thought that. Could *they* have been fathered by a giant among men themselves? Declan smiled ruefully; he didn't see much sign of greatness in himself.

'No! They're not thick on the ground in Scotland, I have to say!' Dick laughed.

'So they can't choose?'

'Well, we do note main characteristics they would choose – usually those of the husband or partner – and try to match them appropriately as far as possible.'

'Are we likely to look a bit like our fathers?' Georgina wondered.

'Possibly. But if you look at lots of folk who know their fathers, there's often no striking resemblance. So it's unlikely you'll walk along the street and see a man who looks exactly like you.'

'That *would* be an odd feeling.'

'Best not to rush up to him and call him Dad!' Dick laughed.

Both girls grinned simultaneously.

'Is it true they used to pay donors – back then, I mean, when we were conceived?'

'Yep. About fifteen pounds I think the going rate was. They used to get impecunious medical students buying their textbooks with the proceeds!'

'Fifteen pounds for a child's life.' Judy sounded so sad.

'Not even that actually. One ejaculate would be used for several treatments,' Dick pointed out.

She shook her head.

'And do you still? Pay them, I mean?' Declan pursued his point.

'Some places do, some don't. Some people feel very strongly it should be a gift. Like blood. You tend to get older men who've had their own families donating for altruistic reasons; the younger guys tend to want money.'

'D'*you* think they should be paid?' Georgina was curious.

'Me personally? I'm ambivalent. There are pros and cons. The main thing for me is having enough semen – healthy semen – from the best sources, for the treatments we need to give. If that supply will dry up if we don't give incentives, then I'm prepared to stoop to payment. But I guess that's not a politically correct attitude, so don't broadcast it!'

'Is there a problem getting enough donors then?' Declan asked.

'It varies in different parts of the country. Of course, it's not a problem in countries where the regulations aren't as rigid. I mean, in the United States there's nothing to stop a private physician using his own sperm.'

'Blimey!' The image this conjured up made Declan's eyes open wide.

'I know,' Dick responded. 'Mercifully *our* job descriptions don't include *that*!'

'It's a relief to hear that, at least!' Declan said and Dick grinned broadly at him.

Judy suddenly jumped up to offer more coffee. In that instant Declan saw her discomfort. He rushed on, deflecting attention away from her, willing Dick not to notice.

'It seems to me there's a huge difference in being the product of AID and wanting it for oneself.' Realising what he'd said he added, 'Or one's wife!'

'Yes?' Dick invited elaboration.

'Well, to be frank, now I've got used to the idea I don't think it actually makes much difference to me personally who exactly my father was. I'm the person I am. Georgie maybe feels differently. I'm just saying how it is for me, now. But the thought of Judy having it …'

Dick nodded.

'Different kettle of fish. I know.'

'Yep. I can't deal with that.'

'It's a very personal thing. Some people can tolerate one thing, others can't. It's fair enough. Our job is to give people the options and help them to find a solution they can live with. If you were sitting in front of me as a patient I wouldn't try to persuade you.'

'You wouldn't? Not even if Judy ...?'

'Nope. I'd say you must discuss this together and work out your own decision. You're the ones who have to live with it. I wouldn't want to be responsible for putting tensions into your relationship. You're a single unit to me in that situation.'

Declan shot him a hard look. What about other situations? But Dick had already turned towards Judy.

'Did doctors always think like that? Even thirty years ago?' Judy asked slowly. She must be thinking of the tensions for her own parents: her mother's eagerness for treatment, her father's reluctance.

'I suspect things weren't as explicit. And doctors probably didn't really get to know what patients thought. Maybe we don't always now, but it *feels* more frank and honest. Of course, the whole ethos was different then. The public weren't as knowledgeable. There wasn't the open discussion about these things there is today. No Oprah Winfreys or Esther Rantzens baring the nation's soul. Back then couples felt stigmatised if they couldn't produce a child naturally. Nowadays much less so. With all the stuff you see on TV or read in the magazines and papers, people know that loads of couples have problems. Something like one in six couples.'

'Wow.' Declan was amazed by the figure. How fortunate he and Judy were not to have had this to face. Their success had been instantaneous.

'That's not to say it's *easy* for couples to seek help even nowadays. It's still not a comfortable thing to be forced to parade your most intimate lives in front of strangers. I feel for them. And they're usually fit and healthy and it's actually quite difficult often for them to give themselves up to treatment. And just the trying and not succeeding can be depressing.'

Declan was beginning to see the sensitivity which drove this man, why Judy had such confidence in him. There was nothing routine about this. Beneath that brash façade he was reaching out to human need, feeling their pain.

'Does it ever worry you? I mean, dabbling in this sort of work? Isn't nature maybe telling you something if you can't conceive without lots of help?' Georgina suddenly shot out.

'I'm often asked that. My answer is to ask *you* a question – if I may? Would you turn down antibiotics if you got pneumonia? Would you refuse an operation if you got appendicitis?'

She shook her head.

'No, and very few people would. When you think about it, pretty much

169

all of medicine's going against nature, isn't it? So why single out infertility as something you shouldn't dabble in on that basis?'

'But it *is* different, isn't it? It isn't just mending a creaking ship. It's creating a new life. And it seems to me that's pretty special. It's sort of sacred – life.'

He smiled at her warmly.

'Right. I think so, too. Partly why I'm in the job I'm in, I guess. It *is* special. But if there's something mechanical stopping two people creating that life on their own, I don't see why people like me shouldn't help to remove the obstacles to that. Just give them a helping hand.'

'OK, I see that if it's unblocking tubes or adjusting hormone levels or whatever. But sometimes it's more than that, isn't it? Take even AID. You say it's the simplest procedure, but you're introducing foreign cells. It's not helping a couple to have a child of their *own*. It's helping them to have *somebody else's* child. It feels different – to me anyway.'

'But it's still overcoming an obstacle, righting something nature hasn't got quite right. And if you put in a plastic hip or a pig's valve, you're introducing something foreign, aren't you? These sperm, they are at least human.'

'Mmhhmm.' Round and round, it went. Declan had the sensation of stepping on and off a roundabout at a fair.

'D'you find it difficult to be the one who has to decide who gets treatment and who doesn't?' Judy asked.

'Sometimes, yes. And the questions get increasingly complex.'

'But d'you think it's right that *doctors* control these things? I mean, there are no controls whatever over who conceives naturally. You can be a multiple murderer with HIV and a history of domestic violence and you can still go ahead and have a baby naturally. But a woman in her fifties who doesn't have a stable partner, maybe drinks socially, will be refused help to have a child in a clinic, even though she might make a brilliant mother.'

'I know what you mean. But I think it's right that when we medical people get involved, we do take the responsibility seriously. And I know one of my priorities is: what would this mean to a child? If I'm going to help in the process of creating him, I have to think whether I'm giving him a good start in life.'

'When you put it like that …'

'And we'd none of us *choose* to have babies fathered by your multiple murderer with HIV, would we? We just don't have any say in that.'

'What about all the other things you do? Like creating extra embryos, but not using them? Does that kind of thing bother you?'

'I must admit, *all* these things bother me. I'm always looking at what I do and asking myself difficult questions. But it's a matter of trading burdens with benefits, weighing them up, trying to harmonise everything

170

so we can live with the end result – with a relatively clear conscience anyway – as far as I'm concerned. And there's a price to be paid for most of what we do. We just try to be sure we're not going beyond what it's reasonable to do.'

'Phew! Nobody would know you're coping with all that on a daily basis,' Georgina said, staring at him open-mouthed.

'Because I come across as such a fool and so devil-may-care, you mean?' He grinned at her.

'Well …' She blushed. Declan knew it was what she meant, but she didn't intend to be unkind or critical.

'Oh, it's OK. I know I do. A bit of it's deliberate, you know. Don't want people dragging all *this* stuff out of me all the time.'

'It's good of you to talk to us like this though, Dick. It's invaluable for us,' Judy said earnestly, leaning towards him as she spoke.

'Oh, in *your* case it's different.' Declan saw the quiet smile. 'And it's good for me actually to be challenged. So don't worry on my account. If I hadn't got a justification or an explanation for what I do, that's when I'd be squirming.'

'D'you actually think about the moral status of the embryo and all that philosophical stuff, in real-life practice?' Judy asked.

'Well, yes, I suppose we do. But that underpins the whole of what we're about – morality, respect for persons, when a person becomes a person, who owns what, what's in the best interests of everyone concerned. But when you have this troubled couple in front of you, that's not the time to start thinking of the fundamentals. That's when you have to look at the options for *them* and give them choices you think are reasonable and fair, and help them to understand the costs to them. Because, make no mistake, most of these treatments are really invasive and the couples – especially the women – pay a high price. When you see what they put up with to get a child it makes you realise what a powerful force wanting children is.'

Declan glanced swiftly at Judy. She smiled back, reassuring him.

'And when you see a new mother with the baby she's gone through the mill for,' Dick continued, 'well, it keeps us guys in white coats fighting the dragons in grey suits for our bit of the money pie!'

'You're a big softie under that shell, aren't you?' Judy spoke with affection. Declan shot her another look.

Dick feigned horror.

'For goodness sake don't spread that rumour around, dear girl! I'll never be able to hold my head up in public again!'

They all laughed together.

'But to be serious,' Dick went on, 'this question of who decides when motivation is good? It's a vexed issue. Is it right for us to decide *for* a twenty-five-year-old married woman who wants a baby but *against* a fifty-nine-year-old widow who wants one? Is it acceptable for a chap with three sperm to go for really expensive ICSI treatment in Area A but another chap with four sperm to be denied access to that treatment in Area B? Who should decide?'

'Icksy?' Declan was lost.

'Sorry. It's maddening when people do that. ICSI. Stands for intracytoplasmic sperm injection. We inject a single sperm straight into the egg. It's useful if the man has very few sperm.'

'Thanks.' Declan was beginning to think it was pretty amazing that any children were conceived naturally. There seemed no end to the problems.

'And we know that couples wait for years for treatment but all the time the old biological clock's ticking away, and success rates diminish with age. And the strain on couples is huge. But other people, outside constraints, are responsible for delaying their treatment.'

'Does it ... drive them apart ... not being able to have children?' Declan hardly dared voice his fear.

'Sometimes, it has to be said.' Dick met his gaze steadily. 'But other couples become extraordinarily close. Sharing the pain and the experience, you know. I guess if the bonds are strong already, it just strengthens them, but if there are underlying cracks there's a risk they'll widen.'

Declan glanced at Judy. She smiled briefly but then turned back to Dick. Declan continued to watch her. She seemed so animated, so at ease with this friend of hers, so different from the sad and troubled girl he'd been tiptoeing round all these weeks. He watched her leaning towards Dick, speaking so earnestly.

'I must say, I have a real problem with just how far you should extend these treatments. Take post-menopausal women, for example, I personally think you doctors have a huge responsibility there. I mean, that fifty-nine-year-old woman – *she* might want to recapture her youth or want to have a baby for her toy-boy or whatever, but it *has* to be wrong to go down that route. Wrong for the child, most definitely, on heaps of grounds. But wrong for the mother too, and wrong for the doctors – *I* think – to even offer it knowing the chances of success are so slim. And even if she does get pregnant the chances of carrying to term are hugely reduced. The whole thing's unethical, in my book. Doctors should do everything possible to dissuade her and her partner against that, I really do think that. She mightn't understand the difficulties and disadvantages if they don't point them out to her.'

'And she mightn't hear them if they do!' Dick countered.

'True. I know.'

'But then there are doctors who think it's not their place to sit in judgement at all. They see themselves as the people with the knowledge and expertise and they're prepared to make it available to anyone reasonable who wants it.'

'Well, I think that's wrong. Medicine without responsibility.' Judy was heated on this subject. 'They're not glorified technicians, are they? I think one of the most important parts of medicine is the ethics behind it all, making those difficult decisions about what's right and what's wrong.'

'I happen to agree with you but then you could argue it's a lottery if the decision rests with the individual, because what I will do, my colleague might not. So if you come to me you get one response and if you go to him you get a very different one. Is that fair?'

'Postcode inequalities and all that,' Declan added.

'Precisely.' Dick nodded.

A ring at the door forced a break. It was only a neighbour collecting for the forthcoming village Gala Day but it provided a chance for them to move and take a break from the intense discussion.

THIRTY-ONE

When they regrouped, Declan took a seat on the settee beside Judy, close enough to transmit his support if the discussion touched sensitive issues.

He'd been glad of the break to focus his thoughts. These were emotive questions, hard to formulate, and he knew he feared some of the answers. Perhaps it was his own need drawing him close to Judy. Whatever, he had to seize the chance to find out.

'Dick,' he said, 'you must've seen thousands of couples. D'you think it makes a difference to how they feel if the child is their own genetic material? I mean, is it harder for them if they have to have donated … eggs or sperm?'

'Difficult to say, actually. You have to remember I'm often seeing people who are depressed and distressed by the infertility itself, all the disappointment, the stress on their own relationship, and everything. And they can be so desperate to have a child that the means to that end can feel very different from the way a normally fertile person would construe the options.'

'Mmmm, I see that. But would you expect it to make a difference?'

'Sorry, this sounds evasive but there isn't a yes/no answer. It would vary from couple to couple.'

Judy was ready with her question as soon as it was apparent there could be no definitive response for Declan.

'What about pre-implantation genetic diagnosis, Dick? Is that an option for us? I mean, could you tell from the beginning there was a defect, and just select healthy embryos?'

'Not for this particular metabolic thing, no. You know, these processes are still very much in their infancy and everyone's very, very cautious. In spite of what the media like to promote, we're not all mad scientists trying to breed a super race!'

'Mad maybe, but …' Judy ventured.

Dick grinned back at her.

'Point duly noted, I'm halfway there! But you know, this idea that folk just breeze in and say, "OK, while you're at it I'll have one with blue eyes, blonde curls, long legs, musical genius, sporting ability, and the IQ of Einstein" – well, of course, it's a load of hooey. Even if we *could* do it, we *wouldn't*. We don't even think we *should* look for minor defects. It's part of the diversity of life. Who wants a world populated by perfect people? And anyway that same outwardly perfect person might be a really bolshy adolescent who just didn't relate to his parents and caused absolute mayhem in the family.'

'You don't even do it for gender here, do you?' Judy asked.

'Not unless there's a medical reason like a sex-linked disease – you know, something like haemophilia. In that case we might just implant female embryos. And most people, I think, would agree, if you can avoid a situation where a child will have great suffering or an early death it's ethically acceptable to do so.'

'Like in Bethany's case.' Judy's words were scarcely audible. Declan felt his own throat constrict.

'Well, yes, exactly.' Dick's tone was gentle. 'How do *you* feel? Would you want to avoid that happening to another child? Or what do you think?'

'We do want to avoid it if we can. What we aren't sure about is how far we'd need to go to avoid it.'

'Well, Keith will tell you more precisely, but I should think it wouldn't involve any donated gametes anyway,' Dick said. Declan let out his breath slowly, feeling the tension in his shoulders ease. 'It's most likely to be a case of testing the embryo early on, soon after conception.'

'And the downside of *that* is deciding if we terminate the pregnancy if it's affected.' The pain in Judy's voice made Declan slide his fingers through hers.

Dick nodded. 'If you want to protect it from that experience, yes.' What a different slant that put on the process of aborting a precious pregnancy. 'You're not totally opposed to abortion full stop, I take it?'

'Well, no, not if … Well, we don't like the idea at all – for ourselves, I mean. But if it's to spare the baby …' Judy's words were halting but Dick was nodding again.

'In that case, I'd personally see it as acting responsibly, in the best interests of the child,' he went on. They needed time with that. He gave it. 'Of course, people argue endlessly about what "best interests" means. And there are all sorts of experiences where the children can live for years with a reasonable, or even *good*, quality of life but they'll die later of the disease. It's more difficult then. And if you know there's trouble ahead it's not easy to say what you'd choose. I mean, if you know you stand a chance of breast cancer in your thirties would you say, "I'd rather not be born"? Or would you say, "It'd be worth having a fantastic life for thirty-odd years, I'll take the life"? And of course, you might fall under a number forty-three bus before you reach thirty. Not easy, eh?'

'None of it's easy,' Georgina said with feeling. Declan shot her a sympathetic look. Just when you felt you'd started to get a grip on the issues and knew what you thought, the counter-arguments took the rug from under your feet.

His thoughts slid to their narrowing options.

'This figure of one in four – that's what Dr Galloway said it'd be for us, one in four chance of a repeat – from what I remember from statistics, that doesn't mean that if we had four pregnancies three would be OK. Right?'

'Right.'

'But if you had a big enough number that's what it would work out at.'

'Exactly.'

'So each time it's a one in four chance, yes?'

'That's right.'

'So next time it could be the same – as Bethany.'

'It could. But hopefully it won't be. There's a stronger chance it won't be than that it will.'

There was a long silence.

'And for me?' Georgina said. 'If I decided I wanted to have a baby – with a particular person. Could we both be tested to see if we carry this thing, you know, Bethany's gene? I *am* Dec's twin sister, so I guess if he has it, I might?'

'Well, yes, you *might*. But you might very well not. And you're not identical twins. Obviously!' Dick smiled at her. 'Keith – Dr Galloway – would be able to give Judy and Declan the odds for *you* personally. Of course, if you decide to have a child with a cousin or a close relative like that, your chances would be higher than if it's somebody completely un-related to you. Is that a possibility?' His question was gently professional.

'No, definitely not.'

'Then I really don't think you've got anything to worry about at all. The chances of you meeting up with someone who carries this same recessive gene – even *if* you carry it yourself – are so remote there's no point in losing a minute of your beauty sleep!' He smiled at her reassuringly.

'That's what Judy said.'

'Good for Judy,' he teased. 'Well, she's absolutely right.'

'But of course, it's much more convincing coming from you,' Judy laughed.

'Mad though I may be!'

'Mad you may be, but you've been fantastic, for us. Thanks so much,' said Judy.

The sun was already sinking when Dick finally took his leave. He could not be persuaded to let them take him out for an evening meal but admitted he'd love to see their garden.

Georgina, preoccupied with her own thoughts, didn't follow them out-side but for Declan it was a relief to turn his attention to rhododendrons, lawn mowers and a new hybrid tea rose. Only as the doctor was leaving did the subject of fertility return.

'I do hope you soon find a way through this that feels right,' Dick said quietly, as they stood in the drive, the sunlight fragmenting around them. 'But don't hesitate to keep asking questions. These are huge things to grapple with, not something to rush into. Keith's a top chap. Don't mind keep going over and over things with him, he'll understand.'

'Actually, you've settled a lot of things in my mind,' Declan said appreciatively.

'And for me,' Judy agreed.

'Keep me posted?' Dick asked her with a smile.

'Will do,' Judy promised.

He grasped Declan's hand in both his, unexpectedly kissed Judy, leapt into the car and, with a roar and an exaggerated turn, screamed out of the drive leaving them helpless with laughter.

THIRTY-TWO

Declan turned to look down at Judy. Her eyes were dancing.

'What a tonic the man is!' she said. 'Isn't he? Mad as a hatter one minute. Father confessor, Mother Teresa, rolled into one the next.'

'A one-off! Thanks for arranging that. Just what we needed.'

'I hope Georgie thought so too. But he was reassuring to her I thought, didn't you?'

'Absolutely. Jude …' He stopped her with a hand on her arm. His appeal was soft. 'Don't go in yet. Stay outside with me for a moment?'

They walked slowly round to the back of the house, stopping in the shade of an old overhanging tree. He drew her close in his arms, and for a long moment they held one another in silence.

'I needed a hug,' Declan said.

'Me too.'

'D'you know what was especially good? Talking about Bethany so naturally.'

'I know. But that's thanks to Dick. We could be natural because we know he can handle it all. It wouldn't have fazed him if we'd got upset. That'd be natural too.'

'And the next baby – he talked about that as if it was all decided. It felt so … right.'

'Does it, Dec? Could we bear it?' She leaned back to look into his eyes.

'Well, it'd be tougher on you. Starting a pregnancy, knowing it might not continue.'

'But when he said, even if we had to … if we couldn't continue the pregnancy, it would be to protect the baby, that made it so much better.'

'How far on would it be before you could tell?'

'I don't know. That's something to ask Dr Galloway. Hopefully not too far.'

'But you think … eventually …?'

'I think it would be worth it to have a child of our very own.' She twined her arms around his neck. Their kiss was a promise of happier times.

'It was just so amazing, feeling like that – you know, when we held Bethany in our arms. It'd be so good if …'

Judy nodded.

'Eventually. We've got a lot of healing to do first. But it helps, Dec, doesn't it, knowing it might happen, one day?'

'I think I feel more at peace inside at this precise moment than I've done since it happened.'

'I'm glad.'

'I was so afraid I might let you down.'

'You? Never, Dec.'

'Well, I'm not so sure. I promised you I'd never let anything come between us. But I just don't know if I *could* have agreed to AID.'

'I know. But that was for the very best of reasons. I'd have understood that.'

'Now maybe, but as the years had gone on? Maybe you'd have come to resent me.'

'Well, hopefully we'll never have to face that. Dick sounded very sure.'

'Mmmm, he did, didn't he? It's like a candle suddenly appearing at the end of the tunnel.'

'And it won't mean we've forgotten Bethany.' Her arms tightened, as she sought confirmation.

'We'll never, *ever*, forget Bethany.'

'And she'll always be extra special, symbolic of something wonderful.'

They stood for a long moment remembering.

'And the next one, it'll be special too. Different, but special.'

They stood in silence for a long moment.

'Georgie! We must go to her.' Judy pulled away from him with a guilty start.

Still he hesitated.

'She was very quiet,' he said slowly. 'But I guess that's understandable. I felt myself sometimes, it's weird talking about all these intimate things so openly, and with a guy we hardly know. And he was, in some ways, too much another bloke and not enough a doctor, sitting here, you know, in this setting. It must have been even weirder for Georgie, a single girl.'

'Hmmmmm. Hadn't thought of that. I suppose because I see Dick in his professional capacity.'

'And he's *your* friend. But anyway you're used to talking about all these things yourself, in your own job. You're not as squeamish about using the words as us ordinary mortals.'

'Am I not?'

'Oh no. I mean, Georgie's job, the people she mixes with, they speak a different language from people like Dick. My colleagues too. He's from another planet altogether!'

'Yeah?'

'Good grief, yeah! Nearest *my* colleagues get to any of this is smutty jokes!'

'I guess it is different. Dealing with the stuff of other people's lives and tragedies, day in, day out. Folk like Dick, well, they have to mature awfully quickly I suppose, doing what they do.'

'Although you wouldn't call him exactly *mature* on first acquaintance, would you?'

They both laughed again at his antics. It felt good now, talking about Dick openly, another brief respite from the pervasive doubts.

'Actually as far as Georgie goes,' Judy said, 'I was thinking along different lines. Wondering if she was asking herself if *this* man would see her differently because of the AID.'

'Dick? But he wouldn't anyway, would he? It's his job, and he was sort of semi-professional today.'

'To us, yes. But I suspect Georgie's a lot more troubled by this identity thing than we are.'

'You're right there. Better go and see if she's OK, eh? Much as I'd love to stay here alone with you.'

Georgina started as the door suddenly opened. Curled up in the chair, alone, her thoughts had been far away.

'You OK, George?' Declan asked, dropping down in the adjoining seat.

'Actually, yes. Thanks. That was useful.' She obviously didn't want to talk. Not yet.

'Fancy a walk?' Judy suggested.

There was ample opportunity to raise the issues they had covered but Georgina made no opening and they strolled along much of the time in companionable silence, soaking up the beauty of the encroaching night and its effect on the changing landscape, free to allow their thoughts to roam.

They lingered in the garden as the colour gradually drained from the day until the sudden ringing of the phone took Declan into the house. It was Rupert, apologetic about disturbing them, but could he speak to Georgina.

She was glad that Declan and Judy were outside in the garden as she took the call. Her emotions were chaotic.

'Rupert, anything wrong?'

'No. I've been thinking about you. Missing you.'

'That's nice.'

'And I guess it's not easy, being with your brother and his wife. Must be upsetting – so soon after the baby. How're you doing?'

'That's kind of you,' she said softly, touched by his thoughtfulness. 'I'm fine, thanks. Judy and Declan are brilliant, coping really well, most of the time. And it's nice to be here with them, better than just talking over the phone.'

'I know what you mean. I'd rather have you here.'

'Mmmm. Me too.'

'I tried several times to ring on your mobile but …'

'Sorry about that. I've kept it switched off. We've been doing a lot of serious talking.'

'Oh dear, was this a bad moment?'

'No, perfect actually. And ... it's really nice to hear your voice.'

'Is it helping, talking to them?'

'Yes, it is actually. But I've still got heaps of things to work out. Myself, I mean. I'll tell you more when I see you.'

'I'm really missing you, Georgina.'

'Are you?'

'Hugely.'

'That's nice. I'm missing you too.'

'Still coming back tomorrow?'

'Yep. That's the plan.'

'Well, I was wondering, would you like to come here instead of going to your place? I could have a meal ready for you.'

'That'd be really nice. Much better than going home to an empty house. Thanks, I'd like that.'

'Monday's too far away for me, tomorrow sounds much more tolerable.'

'Tomorrow it is then. What time do you want me?'

'I want you now! But I'll settle for as early as you can make it tomorrow.'

'OK. I'll try to leave soon after breakfast and I'll give you a ring when I'm well on the way to tell you roughly what time I'll get to you.'

'D'you feel up to that drive? On your own? I could get the train up and drive you back if you're too exhausted.'

'That's a sweet thought but really I'm fine. You know me. A toughie!'

'But you've had a draining sort of weekend.'

'It'll do me good actually. Give me time to think. I should be better company when I see you. But I appreciate the kind offer.'

'You're always good company. But fair enough. Just ring if you change your mind or if you want me to come part way or anything.'

'I will. And thanks, Rupert. Just knowing you're there is a great comfort.'

'I'm here. Just waiting.' He didn't explain. She wasn't sure what he meant but it felt good.

She took her time returning to the garden. Rupert's call had disturbed her more than she expected. He'd just provided her with the perfect opportunity to tell him. She could lead from Declan and Judy's situation directly into her own without making the link to him at all. If she trusted him to keep the information to himself there was no reason not to divulge the facts of her own paternity.

'That was Rupert,' she began unnecessarily as she dropped onto the garden seat again, glad of the fading light. 'He's invited me for a meal when I get back tomorrow. Is it all right with you guys if I leave soon after breakfast?'

'Fine. Just do what's best for you,' Judy responded. 'We'd love you to stay as long as you can manage, but it's a long journey.'

'Will you be all right driving all that way yourself, George?' Declan asked.

'I'll be fine. Rupert offered to come up for me, and I can always ring him if I need him to come part way. But I'll be fine.'

'It's been super having you here,' Judy said, smiling warmly across at her. 'I hope you'll come back again soon.'

'I think I might very well do that – soon. If you'll have me.'

'And next time, bring Rupert – yes?'

'Maybe.'

Declan offered more drinks and while he was in the house preparing them Georgina looked directly at her sister-in-law.

'How do people like you and Dick do what you do, Judy? You live life at a different level from the rest of us.'

'How d'you mean?'

'Listening to Dick today – the guy's been to places we'll never go to. He's thought out all those really difficult questions, got it all sorted. And spending his working life with all those folk with all those messy problems – things I didn't even know existed! And he just seems to know what to say, and what to do to help, and how to cope with people who're upset. And he still has his own principles, things he won't do himself, because he believes in things. I can tell you it's been a real eye-opener, as far as I'm concerned. I've never met anybody like him before.'

'Mmmm. Made quite a hit I see, our Dick!' Judy teased lightly.

Georgina felt the scrutiny but her mind was too preoccupied to analyse it.

'And who else would get away with asking me – when he's just been introduced – if I'm planning to marry my cousin! I mean …! And it seemed perfectly OK!'

'He's a doctor. It goes with the territory.'

'But you know, to sit there talking about – well – all those … *intimate* things. And he wasn't in the least embarrassed. I felt quite ashamed, because I can tell you, I *was* – some of the time anyway. I mean, the guy's in a different league.'

'I know what you mean, Georgie,' Declan sympathised, returning in time to hear this. 'Not the sort of things a guy usually talks to girls about.'

'But we *asked* Dick to come and …' Judy began.

'Oh, I know you did, but even so. I'm just gobsmacked. And you know, all that stuff about those women cheating on their husbands, he knows about it and he still cares for them and treats them and … I'd feel so mad I'd want to do something to show them it's just not on.'

'But it's not like that if they're your *patients*.' Judy looked bemused by her line of thought. Of course, a midwife would understand. It was just the kind of thing she did too.

'And Dick's wife? I mean, doesn't she care about him doing all those things with women?'

'I've no idea. I don't even know if he's married. We don't actually work together – he's in a completely different department from where I work.'

'Could any woman cope with him?' Declan laughed.

'You wouldn't be too keen to introduce him to your Mum, would you?' Judy responded. 'Or even your friends, if he's in one of his lunatic moods. But having said that, actually, I could see him being perfectly charming if you took him home to meet your parents.'

Georgina nodded slowly. 'Oh yeah. He'd charm the birds off the trees!'

There was a long moment of silence in the garden.

'And I guess if you were his girlfriend, or his wife, it'd feel special knowing he was so different with you from the way everybody else sees him,' Georgina said.

Again Declan saw Judy shoot her a look.

'Well, I've never met anybody like him before,' Georgina went on. 'Makes most of my friends seem, I don't know, shallow, I guess. Me too, come to that. It's made me really think, and I guess it's because I *am* so shallow that I was so mad when Dad told me, you know, about the insemination thing. Dec, you were much more mature about it all than me. I should have listened to you properly when you tried to explain. I see that now. I mean, listening to Dick, AID – it's really no big deal. I need to get my life sorted out, think about what's really important.'

'And d'you think that includes Rupert?' Judy sounded odd.

'Maybe. Depends how he reacts when I tell him, I guess.'

'So you've decided to tell him?'

'Yep. I will now. If he can't handle that then, well …' She shrugged her shoulders.

'Do you see him as mature – like Dick?'

'Nothing like Dick at all, but mature? Yes, actually, he is. He's older than me, you know. Quite a bit. And it's one of the things I do like about him, that he's more mature. He's thoughtful and I can talk to him about things. Not like we've been talking to Dick, I don't mean. Crumbs, *no*! But about serious things.'

'But Dick wouldn't normally be talking about this kind of stuff in ordinary social conversation either. It's only because this was a sort of semi-professional visit. He knew we needed information. I'm sure *he* doesn't talk like that with his girlfriends!'

'But if you know about those kinds of things, and think like that, wouldn't it be a real turn-off, you know, in your own relationships with women?' Georgina knew her revulsion at the idea showed when both Judy and Declan laughed.

'I can't speak for Dick, of course,' Judy said, 'but I think doctors can be normal men – or women – too!'

'And you make a pretty good job of it yourself,' Declan grinned at her.

'Well, it'd make me feel pretty screwed up knowing my bloke did those kinds of things.' Georgina shuddered again. 'You'd wonder what he was really thinking when you … No thanks! I'd rather be seen as sexy, not an incubator of ripe follicles!'

Judy's laughter was spontaneous.

THIRTY-THREE

Dick sped down the road to the Borders, the wind whistling in his ears, revelling in the power beneath his hands. He always found the beauty of the open countryside therapeutic after a hard day. Indeed he had deliberately chosen a house some distance from the city, not just because he loved the wide open spaces, but to give him the opportunity to divest his mind of the troubles of work before he assumed his domestic role again. The extra travelling time was for him time well spent.

The property he had bought four years ago was impressive. Being made a consultant at a young age had enabled him to invest in a large rambling stone building with a walled garden, the whole surrounded by the trees and hills he'd always craved.

He stopped on his way home to buy some fresh turbot, chanterelle mushrooms and raspberries. It was another therapeutic outlet, chopping, blending, experimenting in the kitchen, and he had something special in mind for tonight – not perhaps the feast he had produced to win through to the semi-finals of the regional Masterchef competition, but some small compensation for desertion on a Saturday afternoon.

Roberta sat in the canopied sun lounger, a magazine on her lap, brown legs bare beneath her shorts. He flopped down beside her, rocking the seat violently.

'Tough cookie?' she asked.

'Not particularly. Sad in a way but not difficult my end. Nice girl, Judy. Sensible husband too. And they have a lovely cottage.'

She knew better than to ask questions; he was always totally discreet even with her.

'It made me realise, though, you and I, we lead such very uncomplicated lives,' he smiled.

'Just as well, with all the complications you take on board for all these other people. There's no space for us to be in trouble!'

'True. Are the boys in bed?'

'Yep, should be up soon, I imagine, but they were pretty tired after a couple of hours in the paddling pool.' The evidence of their activity was strewn around the lawn in front of them. The lurid royal blue plastic sides of the pool stood at awkward angles where the children had scrambled out; a discarded hose snaked across the grass; buckets and a partially deflated ball lay inert where they'd been tossed.

He leaned back and looked at her.

'You must be knackered yourself. Sorry not to be here.'

'It's OK. I understand. When you're needed you're needed.'

'It's at times like this I know why I married you.'

She grinned back at him.

'Too heavy and hot at seven months pregnant to throw a tantrum, eh?'

He closed his eyes and leaned back with a slow sigh.

'No, I was thinking more of your legendary even temper. Like balm to my soul. I don't always show my appreciation, I know. But thanks, Robbie. You're a blessed relief from the chaotic hormones that dog me all day long.'

'Ah that. My boring predictability, you mean?'

'Definitely not boring. Reassuring, I guess is the word. The last thing I need is a moody woman at home.'

'I very nearly threw a wobbly today as it happens.'

'You did?'

'Remember Francesca Ainsley-Jones? Chairman of some women's club or guild or something in the village? We met her once at the Christmas watchnight service. Remember?'

'Vaguely.'

'She called this afternoon. Wanted me to collect for some charity or other. She obviously hadn't heard I was pregnant again. Anyway, she took one look at my bump and went into a diatribe about the iniquities of men who left their wives with all the work while they gallivanted.'

'She has a point,' Dick said ruefully.

'Call today "gallivanting"? I think not. Anyway, just to get her off my case I offered her a long cold drink. But it was a mistake.'

'Why?'

'Guess what the next question was?'

Dick groaned.

'Yep. What did my husband do? Your blooming job'll be the death of me!'

'And did you deliver your sweetly crushing response?'

'You mean the one about, "My husband? Oh, he just makes women pregnant" – that one?' She laughed.

'I'd love to have seen her face.'

'I didn't, of course. I gave her some vague waffle about you being a gynaecologist. And yes, I got the usual pitying look of a woman who thinks you're some kind of pervert lusting after every female patient's body.'

'You didn't mention the infertility stuff, then?'

'Nope.'

It was agreed. Both knew only too well that the sort of laboratory work he did attracted the attention of a fringe element – the animal protection people, the pro-life supporters.

'I'm sorry you get all this flak. You're a hero really, putting up with it all. I know you are.'

'I can cope. You have your own cross to bear, I know.' She smirked. Dick's own obvious fertility had made him the butt of endless jokes at work.

'This family I was with today – they made me think again, how lucky we are with the boys and now this one. All so naturally and easily.'

'Speak for yourself! I would not class pregnancy in this heat as "easy", exactly. Nor two extremely boisterous small boys.'

'Indeed! You know I didn't mean it like that though. I meant not needing the services of my crew, not wondering if it's fair to drain the coffers at our age. All that sort of stuff.'

'I know, but speaking of resources, I've thought of a brilliant idea.'

'Why do I not like the sound of this?'

'No, listen. You know how these administrators keep threatening to reduce your share of the money pie? Well, when it all gets too much you can just jack it in. I'll augment my locum GP work by being a surrogate mum. How about that for a good idea?'

'You what?' Dick sat up so suddenly the seat rocked crazily.

'Makes sense. I *love* being pregnant.'

'Maybe you do, but one thing I can tell you now, madam, there ain't no way you're going down that line! So disabuse your overactive imagination *immédiatement, s'il te plaît.* And if you so much as mention this matter again I'll make it my personal crusade to ensure that space is fully occupied until you're on the reproductive scrap heap!'

'That a threat or a promise?' she asked, mischievously quirking an eyebrow.

The sound of Michael calling, and the echo set up by Nicholas, cut short his reply, but he shot her a laughing look as he leapt to his feet to go inside to rescue the tousle-headed twins.

Roberta rocked gently on the lounger, watching their energetic rompings with a contented smile.

THIRTY-FOUR

As time passed Judy began to find the days too long for her peace of mind. A pervasive sorrow bled stealthily into her familiar surroundings, infecting even the most mundane of comments or gestures with sinister undertones.

It was during a particularly depressing grey morning that she received an unexpected visit from Geoff Frazer, the hospital chaplain.

'Just calling by on the off chance you might be in,' he said, looking at her closely. 'I was in Dalkeith visiting someone and thought of you.'

'It's lovely to see you. Come on in.'

'How're you coping, Judy?'

'On the outside, pretty well. On the inside, still screaming.'

'It's still very early days.'

'Too much time to think, I suspect,' she said ruefully, 'but I can't face the thought of going back to work. Not yet.'

'Not the best job right now, eh? New mums, new babies. So how're you filling your days? Your garden looks fabulous. Is that your work?'

'Mostly mine, yep. Declan's so busy. But I enjoy gardening anyway. And I've been doing some more work on the house – our hundred-year project! And having friends over. Things I don't usually find time for.'

'What a lovely photograph!' Geoff exclaimed, walking over to examine the framed picture of Bethany on the mantelpiece. 'But she was a lovely baby.'

It was so natural to talk about Bethany with him. He had known her; he had shared their pain. Their mutual reminiscences brought her to life again. With Geoff she found she could look at the photograph album, covering a whole life in eleven pages, without crying.

She confided that the experience had rocked her own sense of personal security; he sympathised. She explained how their own dilemmas had made her question so much that had hitherto been taken for granted; he understood. He told her how his work brought him face to face with challenges all the time and he never felt he had the complete answer; she was reassured. Even his clerical friends made him uneasy, he told her. She probed further, intrigued by this disclosure.

'Everybody knows that some religious folk are dead against abortion for any reason. But some of them are equally strongly opposed to any form of infertility treatment, for example.'

She felt her stomach contract. Had someone told him about their situation? Was he here on a mission? Her saner self told her it was simply an innocent extension of their conversation. She took a long steadying breath.

'You mean those who aren't against all unnatural intervention?'

'Yes. Sometimes they get steamed up about single issues. You know, like destruction of embryos, say, or ...'

'And that's not an issue for you?'

'Well, not especially. Though, of course, I do hold that life is sacred. I am, I hasten to add, speaking as plain old Geoff Frazer here, not as a chaplain representing the church!'

'So ...?'

'Well, it doesn't seem to me to be any worse than, say, using an intra-uterine device to prevent pregnancy, as thousands of women do. That doesn't prevent sperm and egg fusing. It only stops implantation. So if that's OK, I don't personally see it's so heinous to dispose of frozen embryos.'

'But you say you're speaking as yourself here. How d'you manage when you have to talk to *patients* from all these different standpoints?'

'And try not to tread on their sensitivities, when you don't really know what their values are, you mean? With difficulty! I try not to say what I personally think unless pressed. I just give them a context that hopefully makes things understandable or bearable or whatever. It's different talk-ing to *you*, of course.'

'And can I ask – but you needn't answer – do you have views yourself on infertility treatment?'

'You may certainly ask.' He smiled at her warmly. 'I don't personally see any religious objections. There's not much guidance in religious writings on the topic. But my own view is that there are two main injunctions: to respect life and to show compassion. The problem for me comes in decid-ing which one takes precedence sometimes.'

'So why do these other folk object?'

'Some of them see tinkering with procreation as undermining family values.'

'And you don't?'

'Nope. For me things like divorce, casual sex, single parenthood, are much more undermining of family values than IVF.'

'You're a pro-marriage man then?'

'Old-fashioned, eh? And you might wonder how I survive in my job being so out of step with my clients!' His self-mocking tone made her smile.

'No, I'm smiling because my sister-in-law recently accused *me* of being old-fashioned and out of touch with today's values!'

'Well, I confess, for me personally, marriage and family are important components, part of the fabric of society. And marriage is a public declaration about responsibility for the children of that union. Goodness, how pompous I sound!'

They laughed together.

'We have laws against incest, rape, adultery, under-age sex – to protect that society as well as individuals and specific families within it.'

It was not just Judy's stomach which contracted violently this time, and it took all her willpower to dismiss the vivid picture of her father in her bed. Her mind closed down and she missed Geoff's next comments.

'… they say you shouldn't separate reproduction from the loving sexual act. But *I* see the purpose of the sexual act as twofold – reproduction *and* an expression of the love the couple have for each other. It doesn't necessarily follow that procreation is *only* an expression of marital love, nor the *only* purpose of sexual love. Loving and nurturing a child doesn't depend on the sexual act.'

Her father's face receded; Bethany's took its place.

'So you don't think it matters if the child is created outside the womb, or using donated gametes or anything – to the child, I mean?' Judy wondered if he could hear her heart thudding, see the sweat gathering under her fringe. He was trained to be perceptive.

'I don't see why it should. Not of itself. Because the child doesn't have any experience of being actually conceived. What matters to him is how he's raised.'

'And to the parents?'

'Well, then I think there are different needs. In my experience there are three different needs. Three Bs. To beget. As in the Biblical sense! To produce a child with the same genetic make-up as oneself. To bear. As in to give birth. And to bring up. As in to raise or rear the child. Usually, of course, we don't think about separating them. They're all part of the same package. But in the infertility context I think maybe it helps to separate them out. And you can ask a couple, what is it that they principally want? And that might help them to make choices.'

'Wow! You've got this all sorted! I'm impressed.'

He laughed.

'Actually it makes me want to say stupid things like: two Bs or not three Bs, that is the question!'

Judy giggled.

'Maybe not!'

'Indeed.' He grinned back. 'I don't need to make myself any more a figure of ridicule than I am already!'

'Surely not.'

'Oh yes. The youth of today aren't respecters of the cloth like they used to be in the bad old days. But I have to confess that it's actually doing sessions on these things with the medical students that's made me try to analyse it a bit.'

'And are they persuaded?'

'You are joking! The older I get, the more I suspect a conspiracy amongst young students to give their lecturers as hard a time as possible. And *I'm* a sitting duck before I ever get into the lecture hall. The Reverend? The dog-collar brigade? A religious nut? Bring your pillows and rotten tomatoes, boys. This could be fun!'

They laughed together at the caricature.

'No, but seriously, of course, you're always going to get vocally powerful factions. You know, the radical feminists who're against it because they see modern reproductive technologies as a "male conspiracy" to devalue women, to turn them into walking incubators. Or the religious zealots who will never move on this because the church tells them that things involved in infertility treatment – like masturbation or the use of donated gametes or the destruction of embryos – are wrong, full stop.'

Judy's conscience was pricked. These were just the sorts of wild accusations she'd thrown at her mother. This discussion was more close to her own struggles than Geoff could know. But it was his very innocence of her situation that made it possible for him to talk about these matters so frankly.

'It's not a religious thing for me. I must confess my mother gave me a lasting mistrust of religion – well, the organised variety anyway. I have a personal faith – of sorts, I guess. But I do worry about the *resource* implications,' she said.

'Oh, I know. I sympathise there.'

'So how do you justify that?'

'Well, on the basis that we don't live in an ideal world. In an ideal world we wouldn't tackle infertility problems until we'd eradicated all the preventable diseases and illnesses. But because it's not an ideal world, we have to accept that there are certain injustices and inequities. Even on a simple level, when you think about it, we still go around in our large fuel-guzzling cars consuming more than our fair share of the world's limited reserves. We still eat our way through banquets.' Geoff patted his ample girth with a wry smile. 'Even though we know millions are starving. I know our sins don't excuse it or make it right but I think the idea gives us a context. My taking a week to walk to Nottingham won't actually help our friends in the developing world. My starving won't actually put rice in their bowls. And both will render me less effective in my own ministry. I'm not personally convinced that we shall get a better balance by diverting fertility funds into cardiology, for example. Lots of cardiology patients still drink and smoke and eat too many fatty foods and so on.'

'Eeeh dear, life's so *complicated*,' Judy sighed. 'Maybe it's a kindness *not* to have children!'

'Hard decisions. Is that where you are – after Bethany?' he asked gently.

'Not exactly. We know we *want* children. But it's whether they'll be like Bethany. We don't want to put another child through that.'

'Painful things to think about.'

'Mmmm. And I have to say, Geoff, I know life's unfair and nobody

191

promised us anything different, but when I think about all those unwanted kids and the thousands of pregnancies that are aborted and all that stuff – well, it isn't easy just to accept it.'

'Knowing how much you'd love a child and what good parents you'd be. I know. It *is* unfair.'

The sudden welling of tears made Judy fumble for her handkerchief.

'It's a terrible strain on you both, as individuals and as a couple. How're you two doing, Judy?' It was a gentle caring enquiry, but it still probed areas Judy preferred not to touch.

'Most of the time, I think, we're OK. But … sometimes … It's hard, Geoff.' Tears flowed afresh. He reached across and laid a hand briefly over hers.

'I know. It's inevitable. You're both grieving. You haven't got the space for your own grief and each other's. It can feel desperately lonely sometimes. But hang in there. It will get easier.'

It was too painful to pursue this line of thinking. Judy jumped up to offer him another biscuit. Under cover of the clattering she abruptly changed tack.

'D'you ever worry about the slippery slope, Geoff? Is all this tinkering with reproduction the thin end of the wedge?'

'Not if we're responsible about it all, and have the appropriate insight and integrity and sense of responsibility. Slopes are only dangerously slippery if you're not properly prepared and dressed for them. In this country it's all tightly regulated, as you know. It's up to these official committees – and all of us, I guess – to monitor progress and ensure we don't venture onto slippery slopes unwarily. We must have sufficient resolution and integrity to pull back if we feel there's a danger of it getting too skiddy.'

'I like that idea.'

'Well, we don't say no to contraception in case the human race is extinguished, do we?' He grinned at her. 'So for me the thing is we need to have the courage and strength of purpose to know we'll do the right thing when the next moral choice has to be made, not sit there feeling so weak that we say no to any progress.'

'Gosh, Geoff, I wish I'd had you for our moral philosophy lectures. They were dire!'

'Well, it's nice for *me* to have an interested listener. I get disheartened when I see students asleep in my lectures, I can tell you. Makes me wonder if I'm getting too old for all this.'

Judy knew a moment of dismay when Geoff said he must go to his next appointment. There was so much reassurance she needed. But he promised to return – 'Just give me a call. Any excuse for one of your butter cookies!'

Silence once again settled over the cottage. There was no escape now from the relentless questions darting in and out of her mind.

Would she personally seek help to conceive if it became necessary? Both Dick and Geoff had reinforced her own growing sense that there was a case to be made for couples receiving treatment; it wasn't some frivolous pandering to women's wants, not some therapy for a disordered mind. If you had a disability – in this case an inability to have healthy children by the normal route – it was perfectly reasonable to try to overcome it. That growing inner peace Declan had felt after Dick's visit, she'd begun to feel herself. But – oh God, will there never be an end to the buts? – actually committing herself to another pregnancy – no, she knew she wasn't ready for that. And the horror was whichever way they went there were black holes waiting to swallow them.

Supposing they decided they wouldn't try again. Could she cope with the longing to be a mother, with all her peers becoming absorbed in domestic matters and leaving her behind, with friends asking her when she was going to start a family? Would she alone – this new, maimed Judy – be enough to keep Declan at her side?

Supposing they did go ahead and try again. If they could conceive naturally, it would always be difficult to have people asking how many children she had; if this pregnancy was her first. She couldn't hide away for ever. If they needed outside help to conceive, there would be all the stress of submitting themselves to procedures of the most intimate kind; maybe, too, the additional struggle adjusting to the inner knowledge that the children were not all they seemed. It was a minefield.

A great feeling of sadness swept over her. Life had seemed so breathlessly wonderful when she had conceived Bethany. There had been no questions, no reservations. Even the huge shadow cast by her father's abuse had faded under the influence of Declan's love. That innocence, that taken-for-granted feeling, had now gone. Even the deep satisfaction of physical intimacy would be edged by fear if it might result in a baby; a pregnancy would always now hold that dread of possible tragedy.

How much did she really want a child – even Declan's child? She knew in her heart that she still retained that romantic idealism which demanded it be the natural result of their love. But she also knew that if Declan were to die, if he contracted some dreadful disease which would take him from her, she could have no more beautiful treasure of his than his child.

It was one subject where they had not agreed. They'd discussed it only once – long before Bethany – when a high-profile case of posthumous conception had been debated in all the papers.

'Would *you* want your sperm stored and used after your death?' she'd asked him curiously.

'No way!' The force of his reply had surprised her.

'Why not?'

'Because I wouldn't want you dwelling in the past.'

'But I'd be devastated.'

'Well, I'm arrogant enough to hope you wouldn't forget me and I'd want you to grieve for me. But I'd want you to be happy again eventually. Lingering too much in the past isn't the way to move on.'

'Wouldn't the child help me to look forward – think of the future?'

'It seems to me it's more of an attempt to hold onto the dead person – me. A sort of grief therapy, but an unhealthy one. In a way denying my death. Deliberately trying to make something of me live on.'

'But I'd want to hang on to anything of you that I could.'

'Healthy memories, happy things, yes. But I'd want you to go on and form other rich, fulfilling relationships.'

Far from his unselfish attitude freeing her, she had felt oppressed by the thoughts. Deep down she'd known that she wouldn't want him ever to get over her if the positions were reversed. The mere thought of him with another woman stabbed her jealous heart.

And yet … now, he was the one who couldn't bear the thought of another man's sperm fertilising her. What a complex thing love was. And how fragile it felt now. She shivered involuntarily.

Seeking escape from her troubled thoughts, she snapped on the radio. Her attention was instantly arrested.

'As you say, the genome project, modern reproductive capabilities, raise difficult questions that perplex the lay public,' the interviewer was saying. 'As a professor of medical ethics you delve into these matters at a deeper level than most of us, but what are the issues in a nutshell, would you say?'

As she listened, Judy's own thinking sorted and sifted the comments.

'Children today are facing issues our parents didn't dream of …' the professor said. True.

'They might be able to decide whether or not to use their own unselected genetic material – the old-fashioned way of making babies. Given the popularity of sex it's unlikely to die out completely …' She liked his dry humour.

'If not they might have a number of choices. Having embryos created in the lab; genetically screened – not just for defects but possibly for gender, for desirable characteristics. Having them frozen to be thawed out at a socially or economically convenient time. Having other people's gametes if they seem more desirable for any reason. Using surrogate mothers or artificial wombs to incubate the embryo …' The thought of Bethany's siblings facing these choices made her blood run cold. Was this a world she wanted for her children?

'And medicine in general might in fact benefit from these advances.' Might it? 'There could be an endless supply of material to recreate ageing or diseased organs, extend life, eradicate diseases that have escaped the initial pre-implantation screening. We already have scientists who extol the use of eggs or ovaries from fetuses or dead people for infertile couples,

or the use of various tissues or cells from such sources to treat diseases.'
Judy felt her psychological resilience being stretched too far.

The interviewer dared to question the expert at a personal level.

'Do you have qualms yourself – personally?'

'Oh yes, many.' The answer was too bland. The interviewer pressed him.

'Well, to take one example, we're moving to a point where we can test children for various serious genetic disorders – inherited disorders.' Like Huntington's, Judy thought, or some forms of cancer. Or metabolic disorders. Like Bethany's. 'Do those children have a right not to know? If they know, do they have an obligation to tell others?' This definitely held parallels with their own situation. 'In many cases they could face the possibility of stigma, discrimination, difficulties establishing relationships, psychological trauma.' True, true, true. Better not to know. 'On the other hand if they're tested and know that they're *not* at risk for those diseases they could be given a peace of mind which it seems difficult to refuse them.' Well, put it like that and … 'And I think that's why it's been called "perilous knowledge".'

The interviewer summarily closed the comments at that point. Judy shouted at the radio, telling him how useless he was, not probing further.

Would her brain ever cease its endless questioning of these issues? It was so exhausting, so frightening.

THIRTY-FIVE

Dr Keith Galloway stretched and rubbed his eyes wearily before going out to the waiting area to call the Robertsons into the consulting room. They were the fifth couple he'd seen that afternoon. He'd skimmed the notes again to refresh his memory. Shouldn't be difficult this one.

He proceeded cautiously. The enquiries about how they were coping in their grief were gentle. He listened attentively to their responses, trying to hear the unspoken, detect the chinks in their armour.

'And your family histories? Did you get anywhere?' Sometimes people drew a blank. They mustn't be made to feel guilty too. Declan handed over their neat charts filled in as he'd advised.

Ahh. This wasn't what he'd expected. Artificial insemination on both sides. Unusual. He took notes while Judy recounted her mother's dates and details first. Hmmm. She was obviously finding this uncomfortable. Why? She didn't lift her eyes from his writing pad.

On a fresh sheet of paper he recorded Declan's information. 16th May 1967, in the Edinburgh clinic, twin pregnancy.

'But you come from the West Country. You don't mean Edinburgh, do you?' It was a simple enough error.

'Yes, it was Edinburgh. My mother wanted to protect them from anyone knowing that they were having treatment and that my Dad was infertile. So she came up here for it.'

'I see. Sorry. My mistake. Do go on.' He jotted down two words with a question mark.

OK, that was all they could tell him. Time to tread carefully now, telling them.

'Well, I have to say, unfortunately there's no possibility of tracing donors from that period in medicine.'

They were unsurprised.

'Dick Halley told us that.'

Good old Dick. It helped having some of the spadework done; they could get straight into calculating their risks. Keith raised his eyes, flicking his gaze from one to the other. He'd never liked fixed looks himself, and he didn't want to discomfort these two patients; they looked vulnerable enough already, sitting on the edge of their seats, close together, two pairs of wide dark eyes searching for hope, unusually shaped, unusually large, unusually dark – almost black – eyes.

His roving gaze slowed. Was it his imagination? Did those eyes look the same? Not surprising: it wasn't unusual to find people attracted to those who resembled them in some way. His professional mind sorted the facts. Both conceived in Edinburgh. Both by AID. Both with the recessive gene. Same eyes. Could it be …? He gave himself a mental shake. There was work to be done.

'Have you given thought to future pregnancies?' His voice was gentle. If they'd decided against, no problem.

'We think … we probably will try again – if the risks aren't too high.' Declan spoke with confidence.

Keith took a deep breath. What was too high?

'Right. Well, as I suggested last time, you do have a one-in-four risk of having another child with methylmalonic aciduria.' He paused. Take them one step at a time. Let each point register. 'I'm afraid there are no tests available – at this point in time anyway – which could enable us to identify this gene *before* you embark on another pregnancy. It's just not possible.'

Those two pairs of identical eyes bored into him. Two faces intent on what he was saying. He looked away, pretending to consult his notes.

'The good news is that we *do* have a test we can do early on in the pregnancy which would tell us if the fetus has the condition.'

'When could you know?' Judy's voice sounded shaky. Keith looked up again. This he could meet face to face.

'Ten and a half weeks.' He could almost see their minds calculating. Two and a half months. Seventy-three days. Could they cope with being pregnant for that long and then face terminating the pregnancy? Was it too high a price for the possibility of a further six and a half months of happy anticipation of a healthy baby? It was their decision; he couldn't make it for them.

'And what would the test involve?' Judy was looking straight at him now.

'We'd do a CVS, look at the enzyme activity, see if this particular enzyme is missing.'

'CVS?' Declan was asking.

'Chorionic villus sampling. It's where we take a small sample of tissue from the edge of the placenta and then analyse it in the laboratory.'

'And what would it mean – for Judy?'

'Putting a thin tube in, and sucking a tiny piece of tissue into a syringe.' As he answered Keith drew a diagram to illustrate the procedure.

'It's no big deal for the mum, Dec. Honestly,' Judy said, laying a hand on his arm. Keith noticed that, although Declan nodded, he didn't take his eyes off the drawing. He was resolutely not wanting to be persuaded against his better judgement. Good.

'And for the baby?' Declan persisted.

'Well, there's a tiny risk of miscarriage. Something like two to three per cent above the normal chance of it happening naturally.'

'And the risk of damaging it?'

'We use ultrasound to scan while we do it, to try to avoid that. There's a minute risk of perforating the amniotic sac around the fetus, or of infection, but it's very small – a very small risk.' Keith hoped his voice was even and he wasn't prejudicing Declan's mind.

'But the advantages outweigh the risks – for the procedure, I mean?' Declan was pushing him.

'The major advantage is that we can detect abnormality so early on, avoiding the increased health risk and emotional strain of a later abortion.'

'And if it was affected and we had to terminate it, how long would we have to wait, until we could try again?' Judy's question surprised Keith. Was she already determined to go for another baby whatever the cost? Was he giving too much encouragement?

'There's no right answer there, I'm afraid. It's a matter of individual choice. When each couple feels sufficiently recovered from the loss to embark on another pregnancy.'

She nodded slowly. Of course, she wanted permission, someone else to take the responsibility. But no, he was the geneticist, he gave the facts. He couldn't and wouldn't give them permission. It was their decision. But this time he was feeling the weight of responsibility more than usually; the suspicions wouldn't be quieted.

'We could also test for other recessive factors – just in case – while we're at it. If you want us to, that is.'

Judy shivered. It was a cruel idea to introduce, Keith knew, reassured that the baby was free from one thing, going all that time hoping, and then finding there was something else.

'I'd like to know it was as healthy as it could be,' she said, looking at Declan for his reaction. He nodded.

'You'd have more reassurance early on than most couples have,' Keith said quietly.

'We'll have to talk this over, but thanks for being so honest, Dr Galloway,' Declan said. 'It helps to know fairly and squarely.'

The words knocked against Keith's conscience. 'Honest'? 'Fair and square'? Hardly that! If they knew what he suspected …

'Presumably I should go for an early booking?' Judy said.

'Yes. But, being a midwife, you'd get a few perks, yes? Like going directly to a consultant, wouldn't you?' She nodded. 'Remind me again – who looked after you last time?'

'Dr Yates. Janet Yates.'

'Ah yes. D'you want to go back to her again? Or would that be too painful?'

'No. I'd choose her again. She was brilliant.'

'Fine. But I'll write to your GP anyway and say I've seen you and recommended early referral. We have the details, yes?' He leafed back through the notes. 'Yes, here we are. Dr Farnham. Roslin practice.'

'That's right,' Judy confirmed.

'Any other questions?' It was a vain hope but something else might just deter them.

'Would it be possible to tell if this gene came through my mother or ... the donor?'

'No, there aren't any tests for that. But does it really matter where it came from? The important thing is knowing that you carry it, knowing the risks of a repeat.' He knew in his heart it might very well matter in this case.

'And my twin? Now you know how she was conceived, is she ...?' Declan asked.

'Everyone carries three or four faulty genes. It's not usually of any significance at all. In the case of your sister, well, she has a fifty per cent chance of carrying the mutation but the risk of her having an affected baby is no higher than for the rest of the population. And I'd say, given your own unfortunate experience, it's even less likely that she'll meet up with someone else carrying the same gene. It's only really a problem in communities where there's a lot of inbreeding.'

'And my nieces and nephews?'

'Again there's no test available to see if they carry it. But it wouldn't be worth doing anyway because, as with your twin, there's no real risk for them.'

'So it's just us then.'

Indeed they were the ones with the real problem, Keith thought. And he had just given them a picture of their risks that encouraged them to have more children.

He watched them leave his office with mixed emotions. Then he put his head round the door to ask the clinic staff to give him ten minutes before he saw the next couple.

Georgina let out her breath audibly when Declan reported what they had been told.

'Dick was right, Georgie. No higher risk for you than for the rest of the population.'

She wanted to know about their position.

'So will you, Dec? Will you try again?'

'Yes. In time, we hope so. But there are days when ... but hey, that's our problem.'

'I hope you do. You'll make smashing parents.'

'And how are *you*, Georgie? How are things – with Rupert?'

'I told him. On that Sunday when I got back from Scotland.'

'And ...?'

'He was great about it, actually. Said it didn't matter to him.'

'Brilliant. So you're still together?'

'Yep.'

'And this information – today – that's an added bonus, eh?'

'Actually, Dec, well, he wants to make it official. Us, I mean.'

'And you?'

'I think so. But I needed to know what the geneticist said first. Didn't want him to take me on under false pretences. But he wanted to – regardless of what you found out today.'

'Sounds good to me. I'm glad, Georgie. When are you bringing him up to meet us?'

Georgina smiled at the memory of Rupert's face when she'd told him of the invitation to Roslin.

Solitary reflection during the drive to his house that Sunday had failed to provide any clear solution to the questions raging through her brain. The continuing confusion made her unusually jumpy and shy with him; he became wary, and a palpable tension made conversation stilted and superficial. It was a relief to sit down to a meal with a natural distance between them across the table.

Not until she began describing the cottage and the work of renovation did anything of her customary animation return. In her enthusiasm she momentarily lowered her guard.

'You've been invited to go up and see it – and them – if you're interested.'

'That's kind.'

'You'd love all the nooks and crannies. It's got such character. Just the kind of house you go for. I told them about the things you've done to restore this house to what it used to be.'

'Including your own model kitchen?'

'Well, I may have mentioned it – briefly.'

'What else did you tell them – about me – exactly?' he asked cautiously, putting his plate to one side and leaning forward on his elbows.

Georgina's eyes slid to her fingers, folding and unfolding her napkin.

'That you were a whizz with money!' she said airily. 'And that you'd saved my financial bacon. Dec wasn't surprised that I needed saving!'

He quirked an eyebrow waiting for more.

'That you were mature and sensible.'

'As in eleven years older than you?'

'No.' Her tone changed as, for the first time, she met his gaze squarely. 'As in thoughtful, supportive, reassuring – that I can talk to you about things.'

'Usually, anyway.'

'Touché.'

'And *am* I too old for you, Georgie?' He, too, was suddenly very still.

'Am *I* too young for *you*?' she countered.

'No. In a word.'

'Just too flighty, too opinionated, too bolshy,' she said with a hint of bitterness.

'Just bright and lively and provocative and stimulating.'

'No, I *am* too shallow. I felt that this weekend. I *am*, Rupert. I need to grow up and act my age.'

'Hey, don't grow up too quickly – you make me feel young again!'

'I wish you could have seen this guy who came to talk to us about Bethany and the genes and everything. Wow! He was something else.'

Her gaze was back to her fingers smoothing the folds in her napkin rhythmically, but in her mind she was reliving that discussion with Dick Halley.

In the long preoccupied silence Rupert watched the expressions flicker across her face.

'Should I be jealous?'

''Course not, silly. He was just some medical friend of Judy's. But he made me think twice about shooting my mouth off about things. I mean, he's in a different ball park. When I think of the rubbish I've churned out about things like test-tube babies and cloning and stuff like that – pontificating about subjects I really don't know anything about. What I know would fit comfortably on a postage stamp! Whereas *he* could write an encyclopaedia on the subject but he wasn't in the least pushing what he thought. Why're you looking at me like that?'

'You sound – different?'

'I feel different!' she said, a frown creasing her brow.

'Serious stuff, eh?'

'Totally. Being with Dec and Judy, you know, seeing what all this has done to them – *that* was serious. Seeing all Bethany's photos and her little room and her clothes and her toys – it made me just so sad, realising I won't ever know my own niece. And what must it do to parents to be so excited and preparing for a baby and then, wham, suddenly all the dreams and hopes are shattered?'

She stopped abruptly.

For a long moment Rupert gave her space, then, saying nothing, he got up and, pulling a chair close to hers, put an arm round her shoulders, holding her tightly. As soon as she started to speak again he sat back, watching her steadily. She shot him a watery smile.

'Seeing Dec – my own brother, the same age as me – you know, struggling with all this grief, looking so *haggard* sometimes, and tiptoeing around Judy, and worrying about what else might happen in the future – I thought, this is *real* life. And it's nothing like the sort of life I lead normally. I mean, what does it *matter* if you choose a granite worktop or a wooden one, or whether profits are up this year, or whether you go to a classical concert on Friday night or to the ballet? Being with them, well, it made me think about my own priorities. What do I want out of life? What's important? What are my values?'

'And what *do* you want out of life, Georgie?'

'I don't know. Not exactly. I guess I know more what I *don't* want. But, you know – it sounds daft given everything that's happened with the baby and everything – but in a curious sort of way I actually envied Dec. He's always had a much better idea of what he wants, what he believes in, and what's right and wrong. He's kind of steady and calm and – oh, I don't know, sounds schmaltzy, but confident in his skin, so to speak. And what he and Judy've got – well, you can see it's strong and permanent and they're just so ... good together. They're ... I don't know ... *secure.* I guess, I was thinking, if all that had happened to me I wouldn't be as strong as them in coping with it and making decisions for the future. I'm not ... *anchored* in the way that they are.'

'Perhaps you haven't been ready for anchors before. You needed to free-float first.'

'But Dec's the same age as me and he's so much more – *grown up* about things.'

'This sort of tragedy must age a person.'

'Yeah. But it's not just because of Bethany. He just *is* more steady and reliable and ...' She shrugged.

'And what about your sister?'

'Sian? Well, she was pretty wild in her younger days, actually. I remember Mum and Dad really worrying about her. Especially when she started getting involved with boys. I, of course, looked up to her and thought she was very cool and trendy. And when she went to live with her boyfriend – wow! I mean, we were brought up to think that was really sinful! But then she went out to New Zealand and she settled down and had four kids and, bar the wedding ring, she was as much a regular suburban housewife with conventional values as anyone.'

'So you see yourself as the renegade now, eh?'

'Not exactly a renegade, no. I don't *think*, anyway! But I'm very much the kid sister.'

'In spite of a successful business, a lovely home of your own, loads of friends.'

'It's not about what I've got or what I've done. It's more, who I am.'

'Yes?'

'I'll give you an example. We found out something recently about our family – something ... not very nice. Dec was much more sensible and mature about it than I was. And Sian too, she took it in her stride – after she'd got over the initial shock. But me. Phhheeeeewwwwww!' She threw her arm wide in an explosive gesture. 'All over the place.'

Rupert smiled indulgently. But Georgina shook her head.

'No. I'm not proud of myself, I can tell you. It just showed me how superficial and immature I am.' She paused and then, abruptly shrugging off her introspective mood, she returned to her more customary banter, saying lightly, 'There you are – you asked and I'm baring my soul. Warts and all. Not a pretty sight, eh?'

'I'll pass on the opportunity to dwell on your personal prettiness for the moment in the interests of understanding what's changed. Are you sure it's not just the old men-are-from-Mars thing? I mean, from what you say, your brother sounds like a typical male problem-solver.'

'It's partly that, of course. I *am* more emotional about things. Always have been the volatile one.'

'So is that such a big deal? I *like* women from Venus! Especially the pretty ones!'

Georgina hardly heard the compliment. It was now or never.

'But it's more complicated than that. I mean, it was a *big* thing for me.'

There was a long silence. Georgina turned her dessert fork over and over on the tablecloth, pitting the linen in a myriad of dots.

'Want to talk about it?' Rupert ventured tentatively.

'You'd be shocked …'

'Would I? You sure? I've been around the block a few times. Not easily shocked, me.'

'*I* was!'

'Not as many miles on the clock!'

'OK then. Try this for size. Dec and me, and my sister – we just found out, our Dad wasn't really our Dad.' The words shot out like shellfire in their rapidity.

'Right. So? He was your step-father?'

'Nope. Well, not exactly anyway. Nothing so ordinary. He was our Mum's husband. Oh, and he brought us up. But he wasn't our Dad.'

'So what's the big deal? Loads of folk have affairs.'

'The "big deal", as you call it, is that … all our lives we thought he *was* our Dad.'

'Mmhhhhm.'

'And Mum *didn't* have affairs,' she flashed indignantly.

'OK. Sorry. I just assumed …'

'But – well – she had us by artificial insemination.' Georgina knew she sounded defiant. She kept her eyes glued to her fingers now scribing a figure of eight with the fork.

'Different certainly.' His voice was even and unemotional.

There was a long silence. Eventually she sneaked a look at him out of the corner of her eye. He was looking at her with a strange expression.

Seeing her glance he said, 'And? Am I missing something?'

'Aren't you … shocked? Scandalised? Disgusted?'

'No. Momentarily taken aback, maybe. But not scandalised. Should I be? These things happen. Men who whistle and look the other way, I heard it described as once.'

'There you are! You see? *I* was scandalised.'

'Well, it is a bit different if you're the child of the procedure.'

'But given how hard it was to say it just now, I guess I'm *still* freaking out inside.'

'Why?'

'Because.'

'Because ...?'

'Just ... because.'

'A degree in English from one of our most prestigious universities and the woman's monosyllabic. My oh my! The youth of today!' he chanted, rolling his eyes in mock despair.

'OK. OK. Because I hate to think I started that way.'

'Fair enough. That I can understand,' he nodded.

'Wouldn't you?' She rounded on him with a fierce expression.

'Well, I can't say for certain, since I know I *didn't* come about in that way, but I don't *think* I would be that bothered at the end of the day, no. But fair enough, I can see that initially, finding out, it might take you by surprise.'

'There's something else too,' she rushed on. 'This thing that Bethany had – both Declan and Judy carry some gene or other that caused it.'

'Phew.' He let out the breath softly. 'Now that *is* tough. On top of everything else. That's some burden to carry.'

'And I might too.'

'Yes?' He was looking at her very intently now.

'Well, I'm Dec's twin. He's inherited it so I might too.'

'Right. And what d'you know about it?'

'Apparently it's a recessive thing so it can go through lots of generations not showing itself. But if two people who both carry it get together, and they both pass on that gene, the baby can have the condition that Bethany died of.'

'Mmmmhhhm. So Declan and Judy might have another child with the same thing.'

'Exactly.'

'Geeeeeee. That really *is* a bummer.'

'And I might.'

'But ... only if your partner had the same thing, right?'

'Yeah.'

'And you say it's rare?'

'So Dick said.'

'So ... I don't follow. What did he say about *your* risks?'

'Extremely unlikely, he said. Especially after the million to one chance of Dec marrying someone with it. Unless it was with my cousin or somebody related.'

'So in reality then, no more need for *you* to worry about that than about a helicopter crashing right overhead this minute and falling onto my house, and killing us both, eh?'

'Oh, you! You sound just like Dec. Maddeningly logical!'

'I take it that's not meant as a compliment?'

She couldn't help laughing.

'Now, that's better!' he said, grinning at her. 'More like the old Georgie we know and love.'

'You know what? This is crazy! All the way down I've been wondering how to tell you and in the end I just blurt it out and you don't bat an eyelid!'

'Shall I throw a wobbly just to make you feel more vindicated? I can do a fair impression of a wobbly if I set my mind to it.' He crossed his eyes and jerked absurdly in his chair.

'Idiot!'

A sudden silence fell.

There it was again. That quizzical look.

'What's that look mean? What are you thinking?' she asked, suspiciously.

'I'm just wondering why, Georgie dear, you were so worried about telling me.'

To her annoyance she felt the colour rise in her cheeks.

'Because ... because I thought ...'

'Uhhhuh? By the way, have I told you how adorable you look when you blush? But go on. Be honest. Because you thought ...?'

'I can't.'

'Can't? Or daren't? Come *on*! You "can talk to" me ... remember?' He traced the inverted commas in the air with a look that made her feel suddenly breathless.

'Because I thought ... you might think ... I was thinking ... about ... having children ...' She broke off abruptly.

'With me,' he finished for her. 'And were you?'

'Well ...'

'Well, indeed, I very much hope you were, because I've been thinking along the very same lines for some time now and I can tell you – without jeopardising my chances, I hope – that I can't think of anyone I'd rather make babies with than you.'

She stared at him stupidly for a long moment.

'Not exactly the most romantic response I've ever seen,' he said, leaning back and clasping his hands over his stomach in an attitude of patient waiting. 'But at least it's not an outright rejection. I'll settle for small mercies given the lateness of the hour and your travel fatigue.'

Georgina blinked rapidly.

'But I've just told you ... about ... the genes ... and my Dad ... and ...'

'And so far you haven't told me anything that changes my feelings towards you one scrap.'

'Don't you need time to think about what I've just told you?'

'Nope.'

'But …'

'But it seems *you* need time to think about what *I've* just told *you*. Good thing I'm a patient sort of a chap.'

'I have to know what the geneticist says first.'

'What geneticist is that?'

'The one Dec and Judy are going to see. He'll be able to tell them what the chances are of having another baby like Bethany. And Dec says he'll ask about me – my risks and everything. I'm his twin. I might very well have it too. I don't want you taking me on under false pretences.'

Rupert surveyed her with pursed lips for a long moment, then he straightened up and leaned towards her, holding her gaze with a different light in his own eyes.

'You know something, Georgina Robertson? I appreciate your integrity, but it doesn't matter a tuppenny toss to me what any geneticist says. I want to "take you on", as you so elegantly put it, whoever's daughter you are, whatever genes you've inherited. If you'll have me. But fair enough, for *your* peace of mind I'll wait till you've heard from the geneticist. After that, I give you fair warning I might not continue to be as patient!'

To her utter astonishment Georgina felt tears suddenly welling up and spilling down her cheeks. She raked in her pocket for a tissue but before she could find one she was suddenly enveloped in a tight embrace.

'I hope these are tears of happiness or relief or something positive or I've completely misread the signals here,' Rupert said, looking down at her with a comical expression, using his own handkerchief to wipe her cheeks.

'You're something else,' she said unevenly.

'I can see my first task is to teach you how to respond more appropriately to declarations of love,' he said, pulling her up out of her chair and into his arms.

Her response to his kiss seemed to meet with more satisfaction and it was a long time before he said anything more. His next question took her by surprise.

'Did you by any chance tell your brother that I'm black?'

She grinned up at him and said mischievously, 'No point in crossing hurdles before you come to them – to quote you, logical male problem-solver!'

'Now *there's* a little conundrum for our jolly little geneticist!'

'Well, at least he can't accuse you of being *related* to me!'

206

THIRTY-SIX

Thursday was always a busy day for Keith Galloway. This one was no exception.

He was standing eating a sandwich while he ran off overheads for a seminar he was leading at five thirty. Before then he had a full clinic with some particularly difficult cases. Talking through hard choices with patients who had only a scant awareness of the principles of genetics was never easy; when there were no good options available to them it was emotionally taxing for him as well as them. He could never quite get used to shattering dreams. The years had taught him to keep his distance – he probably seemed like a cold old fish to some of these patients, he thought ruefully – but despite his precautions, pain sometimes crept in through the cracks. There was one case like that this afternoon. He was mentally rehearsing a softened approach when the phone rang.

Hastily swallowing his mouthful of bread he took a gulp of coffee, choking in the process.

'Mmhhh?' he managed.

'Dr Galloway?'

'Speaking.' Not a good impression. Hopefully it was someone who knew him, to whom he could explain his haste.

'This is Dr Henrietta Farnham. GP in Roslin. Have you got a moment?' The name rang a distant bell but he couldn't place her.

'Well, a moment. I've a clinic in twenty minutes though. Will this take time? I really don't like to keep these people waiting.'

'No, I don't think it'll take long. Just a couple of quick questions, if I may.'

'How can I help you?'

He pressed the button for the next three overheads to be printed. The whirring and clicking sounded unpleasantly loud in his ears. It gave a bad impression, showed his mind wasn't wholly on the conversation. He covered the mouthpiece so she wouldn't hear it.

'You've been seeing a couple of my patients. The Robertsons? Live in Roslin. Lost a baby – Bethany – with methylmalonic aciduria a few months ago?'

'I remember them, yes.' Why did some doctors refer to people as *their* patients? She probably called the practice nurse *her* nurse too!

'Well, I was wondering if you could advise me, please. A couple of years ago the husband, Declan, came to see me. He'd had a nasty bout of flu. Complaining of abdominal pain, general malaise. He was a bit jaundiced but I must admit I couldn't pinpoint anything. But my brother works over in Glasgow and he suggested it might be Gilbert's Disease – Gilbert's Syndrome. To be honest I hadn't heard of it. He put me in touch with a team over there who're into this sort of thing, doing some research actually. Under Professor Samuels?'

'I know Ralph Samuels, yes.'

'The team were interested and asked if the Robertsons would take part in their study. I don't remember quite what they were looking at exactly. Anyway they sent the results – for the Robertsons – back over to us and it seems they *both* have Gilbert's.'

'Something like two per cent of the population have it. But it doesn't usually amount to anything. They're usually healthy.'

'That's what they told me. And as far as I know Judith Robertson hasn't ever shown any symptoms. So I didn't think any more about it.'

'And now?'

'Well, I've just found out that it's an inherited dominant condition.'

'Indeed.'

'Well.' She hesitated. 'Put that together with the recessive gene ...'

He didn't help her.

'I think they might be related – closely, I mean.'

'Uhhuh.'

'Well, I didn't make the connection at first but when I phoned the chaps in Glasgow, they told me what it meant.'

'Right. And have you discussed it with anyone else?' He knew he sounded rather acid.

'No. And I didn't name names or anything,' she said, her defensiveness giving an edge to her voice.

'Discretion's terribly important here.'

'I realise that. There's another thing, too,' she rushed on. 'If you look at them both – and the husband's twin sister – there's a strong family likeness around the eyes.'

'And did you notice this *before* you knew about the other things?'

'Well, no ...'

'Hmm. Well, I must say I wouldn't take the family likeness thing per se too seriously. You often find that people are attracted to those who are like them in some way.'

'But all together, the three things ...?'

'Mhmm.'

'Well, when I called to make a visit – you know, a second bereavement visit – routine – Judith Robertson told me about the donor insemination. She thought I ought to know, as their GP. I presume they've told you? So I was thinking, possibly the same donor?'

'It's possible, I agree. The thought did cross my mind, too, I admit.'

'It did?'

'It's a possibility.'

'And what d'you think? Did you say anything?'

'Certainly not.'

'But shouldn't we ...do *something*?'

'Have the *Robertsons* put things together?'

'Oh no.' She sounded sure.

'Just you.'

'Well, and you, I gather.'

'Well, I certainly wouldn't touch it with a bargepole, personally.'

'You'd leave it? Not do anything?'

'Most definitely.'

'Is that fair? On them?'

'I must tell you, I work solely on the basis of medical benefit. That's what I'm paid to do. The social side of all this – well, best not to dabble, I think. Too easy to open a can of worms. Leave that to the TV dramas.'

'But what about the patient's right to know?'

'Depends what there is to know. It's my belief there are some things better not known.'

She'd probably be cursing him for a paternalistic prat, he thought, real old school, needing to leap into the twenty-first century.

'And there's no good outcome if you go down that route for the Robertsons – in my judgement.' He mustn't sound too autocratic. Better she should feel she'd come to that conclusion for herself.

'You mean *we* decide it's better for them not to know.' He could feel her prickliness. She was making less effort to conceal her disdain for his views now. Sounded like she was young. Still idealistic probably.

'That's a paternalistic interpretation, I think. I prefer to think of it in terms of the best interests of the couple. The only *medical* consequence of inadvertent incest is the genetic risk. This couple, they already know they're at risk. We've told them. We've spelled out the precise risk – for a repeat of the methylmalonic aciduria and for other recessive factors too. Spelt it out clearly.'

'And that's enough?'

'I think so. What possible good is there in them knowing the rest? It'd just make their lives a misery. Potentially.'

'I'm sorry, but I'm not so sure it's right for us to know and not them.'

They were plucky, these modern doctors, Keith thought. In his junior days he wouldn't have dared openly defy a consultant.

'Well, I'd advise you to give this very careful thought. I've talked to this couple in depth. Three times now. And it's my judgement that they have all the facts they need to make a decision about their obstetric future.'

'But what if they *do* suspect and they ask me if I knew? It'd destroy their trust in me. And in the profession.'

'Well, it depends how strong your relationship with them is. I think you'd have a good case to argue that you could see no possible benefit to them in knowing. If they know you'd considered it carefully, taken advice even, and come to an informed decision, I think they'd accept that you are indeed trustworthy.'

'I'd have to think about that one.'

'And there's no concrete evidence. Just a suspicion,' he added for good measure.

'But it's pretty strong as suspicions go.'

'Mmhhm.'

'If I think we should confirm it, can I send them to you for a DNA test?'

'Nope.'

'Sorry?'

'No, I wouldn't do it.'

'Why not?'

Keith instantly forgave the impertinence; it must be so frustrating to have doors closed in her face. His reply was even, matter of fact.

'Because I don't see that as my job. There's no medical indication to do so.'

'And if the couple themselves suspect? And they request one?'

'Still no.'

'Not even for their peace of mind?'

'What possible peace of mind is there in knowing for sure what you suspect, Dr Farnham?' He was careful now to distance himself from the suspicion.

'Could I refer them back to you?'

'You could, of course, but I wouldn't myself pick up that issue.'

'So if they request it, what do I do?'

'I personally think it highly unlikely that they will come to you with any such request.'

'But if they do, where would I go?' she persisted.

'For DNA testing? You'd have to send the bloods to a commercial agency. It'd cost them. I'm not sure what the going rate is. But that's the only avenue.'

'That seems a bit steep. When I want to help them to get to grips with their problems.'

'Well, I stick by my earlier position: better not go down that route. Best to avoid any suggestion of anything more than bad luck.'

'Did you think they suspected when you saw them?'

'No, I'm confident they didn't. And I personally gave them no reason to do so. Besides, when you think how much probing *you* had to do with all your medical knowledge, I think you can see a lay person would be most unlikely to put all those factors together and come up with your conclusion.'

210

He glanced at his watch. He really must get to the clinic.

'My advice – my *strong* advice – is, don't do anything to alert them to your suspicions. Just support them in their choice about the next child.'

'Are we colluding in breaking the law here?' She was certainly persistent. And game.

'In what sense?'

'If this is an incestuous marriage? I mean, it's a criminal offence, isn't it?'

'Well, an inadvertent case of incest wouldn't be a punishable offence.'

'And legally?'

'Seems to be some doubt about that. You'd probably have to ask the legal buffs in Civil Law about the specifics of this case.'

'So should I do that first? Or the Medical Defence Union?'

'Well, it's up to you. My own advice would be just keep quiet about the whole thing. For everybody's sake. But it is, of course, your decision.'

Yes, indeed. She was the one fearing the threat of malpractice. But she was only young … and thorough. He was gentler now.

'Look, I'm sorry, I really *must* go. I do understand your dilemma but, for what it's worth, I think there's a time for doctors to skirt carefully around people's lives. If we trample in and out without caution we can do untold damage. We move on. They're the ones left to pick up the pieces. And what good has it done anyone? My philosophy, as I've said, is: no medical benefit? Leave it alone.'

'So you couldn't be persuaded – in this case – just to do the test when they come to see you?'

'I could not.'

'Well …'

'I'm sorry, this time I really *must* ask you to excuse me. Goodbye.'

The Robertsons' predicament preyed on Henrietta Farnham's mind. Keith Galloway hadn't helped at all, hitting the ball straight back into her court with an unreturnable shot. But didn't she have some sort of obligation to do something before the couple embarked on another pregnancy? She needed more guidance: but who could advise her? The more people she confided in, the bigger the list of witnesses who knew of her involvement if this ever came to the scrutiny of the GMC or the courts. Her partners were an obvious choice. But the senior, Harry Tomlinson, was off on extended leave following a stroke. And Randall Squires was already too bumptious for her liking. Give him a loophole and he'd gladly reinforce his view that girls, especially those who'd trained outside London, were second-class doctors.

Opportunity to share her misgivings presented unexpectedly when a new locum GP was called in to deal with Harry's patients. Here was someone who didn't need to see the couple concerned and who had no vested interest in them as patients. Better still, as well as being a woman she was very pregnant herself. Just the person to advise her.

After surgery Henrietta popped her head around the door to ask if her colleague could spare a moment. Dr Roberta Mansfield smiled warmly and invited her in. Henrietta made two cups of tea and flopped into the patient's seat. The usual pleasantries over, she approached her subject with caution.

'I have a very delicate situation with a couple of my patients and I'd be really grateful for any advice you could give me.'

'Fire away. Happy to help if I can.' Roberta wriggled further down the seat, nudging her unborn baby into a more comfortable position.

'Thing is, there's a strong suspicion that the husband and wife are actually half-brother and sister. They've just had their first baby, who died soon after birth – some rare metabolic disease carried on a recessive gene. Now they're thinking of having more, and I don't know where I stand in all this.'

'Gosh! Unusual to say the least. I haven't had to deal with *that* one before!'

Henrietta was encouraged by Roberta's instant response. Some sympathy at last!

'What we know so far is that they're both the product of AID. Both treatments were given in Edinburgh thirty-three, thirty-four years ago or so. *He* actually grew up in the West Country but his mother came up here for treatment just to keep it all hushed up. Now we find they both carry this recessive gene, *and* they both have Gilbert's Syndrome too.' Henrietta paused long enough to see that Roberta understood the implications of this. 'And they even look alike – around the eyes anyway. Enormous, almost black eyes – unusual shape and colour.'

'Jeepers. Quite a series of coincidences if your hunch isn't right.'

'Exactly. But what should I do about it?'

'Have you consulted anybody else about it all?'

'Well, I spoke to some genetics people over in Glasgow initially. And this week I rang the geneticist here in Edinburgh. Keith Galloway. Don't know if you know him?'

'Not personally but I've referred cases to him.'

'He's been seeing this couple since the baby died. But the thing is, the mum, Judith, works in the same hospital as he does – she's a midwife – and my guess is Galloway doesn't want to stir things up for her.'

Henrietta saw Roberta's eyes narrow suddenly, but her voice was even as she asked, 'And what did Dr Galloway suggest?'

'Well, he's heavily into medical paternalism. I must say, I was *not* impressed.'

'But what did he advise in this case?'

'Do nothing. Say nothing.'

'And you don't think he's right?'

'No. I mean, I *know* about this. That makes me liable.'

'Know? Or suspect?' The question was gentle.

'Well, it's a strong suspicion. I think we ought to go for proof but he says he wouldn't do it.'

'Does he give a reason?'

'Yeah. Says it's better not to know. And anyway he wouldn't do the test. They'd have to pay for it commercially.'

'Does he say why he wouldn't?'

'Yeah. Says he's not paid to deal with social problems, only looks at medical benefit. Hell, if we all stuck to what we were *paid* to do, the patients'd get a raw deal!' Henrietta felt her annoyance gathering force.

'Hmmmh. And the Glasgow people? What do they think?'

'Well, I didn't ask them specifically. They told me what the different gene things meant, confirmed that it could mean they're related.'

'So you've only had advice from Dr Galloway on *your* position. Is that right?'

'Yes.'

'And you don't like his advice?'

'Well, it's not exactly "not liking". I just think I'm in a no-win situation here. What if this couple come back to me and say they think maybe they're related, why didn't *I* think of that? I mean, she's a midwife, for goodness sake. She must know a bit about genetics and stuff. I'd have to say, well, I *did* think of it, or what kind of a doctor would I be? So why didn't I say something? Oh well, I thought it was better that they didn't know. I mean, it sounds so *pathetic*! As well as arrogant!'

'So what does Dr Galloway say about your responsibility?'

'He thinks they won't ask. But he says, even if they do, they'd understand I did it for the best of reasons. *He* thinks anyway.'

'And you think they wouldn't – understand, I mean?'

'Who knows? I mean, news like that could send you off your trolley, couldn't it? They might lash out anywhere. And I'd be sitting there waiting for it all to fall on me.'

'Even if you'd shared it all with him and taken his advice? I mean, he's the expert in this stuff, isn't he?'

'Well, I'm not so sure he's an expert in *this* exactly. The chromosomes and hereditary stuff, yes. But this? Doesn't sound like it from where I'm standing.'

'And these reasons for *not* telling them, they'd be … what?'

'Well, he says the only *medical* consequence of incest is the genetic risk, in a case like this. And they already know they're at risk genetically. So there's no reason to tell them. But *I* think there's a whole lot of psychological stuff that you can't discount. But then I don't compartmentalise medical, social, psychological, as much as he seems to do. I mean, us GPs, we have to see people in the round, don't we? More than these guys who see them for half an hour in the clinic at the hospital away from their real settings.'

'I know what you mean.' Roberta was really sympathising. It helped. 'And the possible harm of telling them?'

'Well, I don't know. He didn't spell it out. Just made it sound a dangerous thing to do. But hell, would you want to find out your husband was your brother?'

Roberta grimaced.

'Exactly,' Henrietta said. 'Could wreck their marriage. I don't even know if they'd be allowed to stay married. I mean, incest, it's not allowed – legally.'

'Hmmm. You have my sympathy on this one. There are no easy answers.'

'So what would *you* do?'

'Well, I don't know the family so I can't say for sure …'

'But knowing what you *do* know?'

'Well – don't shoot me! – but I must say I think I'd probably be guided by Dr Galloway here. I mean, he sees loads of tricky cases and he's been around a long time. I hear what you're saying about him being paternalistic. A lot of the old school were. Still are, I know. But you say he knows this couple and he's given them genetic advice himself. Haven't you sort of handed the responsibility to him in a way? He must know at least as much as you do about the worrying things. Mustn't he?'

'Probably more! They're a healthy young couple. I've only seen them a couple of times myself.'

'And you've shared your suspicions with him. So it's not that he hasn't thought of it.'

'Right. Oh yes, he admits he thought something similar.'

'Well, I think I'd probably be tempted to hide behind him on this one.'

'And if the lawyers come after me all guns blazing? Will they buy that he-told-me-to argument?'

'Oh, I think you'd need to have a justification *yourself* for not telling them too. But sounds like you could easily justify this particular non-disclosure, I'd say.'

'Would *you* want to know – if it was you?'

'Probably not, actually.'

'And if you suspected, would you want it confirmed?'

'I don't know.' Roberta thought for a moment. 'It might be better not to know for sure. Then I wouldn't need to decide if I should act on it.'

'Well, it's a bloody awful position to be in. Excuse my French,' Henrietta said with passion. 'My position, I mean.'

'Sorry I can't really help. But you have my sympathy,' Roberta repeated.

'Thanks for listening anyway. It's my problem, I know.'

By the time Roberta arrived home that night, Dick had bathed and fed the boys who were curled up on his lap while he read them a story. They had begged him to let them stay up till Mummy got home so she could kiss them goodnight. She received a rapturous welcome from the two bodies who hurled themselves at her and was glad of the distraction. By the time they sat down to their evening meal she was herself again, if quieter than usual.

'Tired?' Dick asked, a hand briefly on her shoulder as he placed a spicy rice dish in front of her.

'A bit. But this'll perk me up.'

THIRTY-EIGHT

Just when the rash appeared Declan wasn't sure, but within hours the red blotchy patches marked his arms and legs as well as his trunk. Though not normally one to bother about minor ailments, this time he felt a wave of nauseous anxiety.

It was fifteen months since Bethany's death. The first anniversary of her birth had been less traumatic than they'd anticipated. Deliberately, consciously, they had faced the memories together: taken the day off work, visited the grave, walked in the hills during the afternoon, and spent a quiet evening alone with their photographs and memories. By contrast the anniversary of her death took them by storm. Unprepared for the ferocity of their emotions, they were shocked into recognising how superficial was their acceptance of their loss. Overwhelming doubts about their future swamped their thinking.

It was a relief to return to work. The routines, the distraction, helped them to regain some control, but their confidence had taken a battering. Once more they were skirting gingerly around each other. Once more both struggled to hide the worst excesses of their personal pain. It was another six weeks before they could again start to contemplate another pregnancy.

Concern for the welfare of any possible unborn child drove Declan to contact the doctor's surgery immediately.

When Henrietta Farnham saw his name on her list she felt a momentary panic. The Robertsons' situation had slipped out of her consciousness as the weeks and months had passed, but she had still not resolved her dilemma. Did she owe it to her patients to pass on what she knew? Just how much did they know already, or suspect? He was an intelligent man and his wife was a midwife; they'd surely have put two and two together by now. It shouldn't be hard to find out anyway, not with her natural skills in detecting hidden agendas, unearthing the real problems beneath the superficial symptoms.

The rash wasn't serious, she reassured him. Could be a reaction. Any change of soap, washing powder, anything like that? Not that he knew of. Any allergies? None that he knew of. Eaten anything unusual? No. Could it be German measles, he wondered aloud. No, it certainly wasn't that.

Was he under any extra stress lately?

She listened attentively as he explained haltingly how traumatic the past few months had been with the anniversaries.

'Yes, the first year is terribly hard, remembering this time last year.'

'It's like walking on eggshell at home too. I hadn't realised about that before. We're both grieving but in different ways, at different times, for different things. I guess that adds to the stress.'

Henrietta nodded, watching the play of emotions in his face.

'How *is* your wife? How's she coping?'

'She's struggling. It's really tough on her. But she's back at work and I think that helps.'

'And your relationship? Losing a baby puts a strain on couples, without all the other things you two have had to deal with. How are you coping?'

'You mean the AID and everything?'

'Yes.'

'Well, it was a shock finding out, I must admit. But I think we're getting things in perspective gradually.'

'Good.'

'Well, we can't do anything about it now, can we? Water under the bridge.'

'True. Have you talked it through with anyone else? Had any counselling?'

'Apart from Dr Galloway, you mean? No. It's not the kind of thing you exactly want to broadcast, is it?' Ahh, so he did know. 'We've talked about it together, of course. Judy's found it harder to deal with than me, I have to say. But there are reasons for that. Apart from anything else, she knows too much – being a midwife! And these last few months with all the anniversaries, all the stuff about Bethany, and realising that *her* problem was because of *us* – you know, our genes and everything; well, it's rubbed our faces in it a bit. It's been tough. But we're getting there.'

'Quite a packetful all in a oner.'

'That's life, I guess.'

'And when you talked to Dr Galloway, what did he advise?'

'Oh, he was brilliant. And he was really straight with us. Didn't wrap it up. Calls a spade a spade, Dr Galloway. So we know just where we stand with this.' So she *had* succeeded in changing his paternalistic mind then.

'Good. It's better to know. And no-one's to blame.'

'Oh no. We realise that. We don't blame anybody. It's just a weird set of coincidences.'

'Indeed. And now you know?'

'Well, of course, we wish it was all perfectly normal and uncomplicated but we're prepared to take our chances and hope it all works out OK.' He was impressively calm about all this.

'Hope it works out? As in?'

'Trying for another baby.'

Henrietta stared at him for a long moment.

'Sorry?'

217

'We're going to try again – well, actually, we are already.' He looked rather sheepish. Small wonder! 'That's why I came about this rash. Is it something that might affect a baby?'

'The rash? Sorry, I'm confused here. Dr Galloway did explain the risks?'

'Oh yes. He spelled it out loud and clear. I'm pretty scared, I confess. If it all goes pear-shaped, I really fear for Judy. She's been through the mill over all this. But it's what she wants. And if it's right for her, then it's right for me.'

'But *you* have reservations?'

'Good grief, have I ever! I'm fearful for *Judy* as well as about any children we might have. Feels like a huge weight of responsibility. Damned if I do, damned if I don't!'

'The consequences are certainly serious. But knowing that, you're prepared to put your own reservations aside for Judy's sake?'

'Yes. She means everything to me. I owe her that much.'

'And you do understand the legal side of this as well as the genetic risks, yes?'

'Legal?'

'Well, I'm not sure exactly where you stand but if you *know*, it'd be hard to defend ...'

'Know? Know what? I don't follow.'

Henrietta felt a sudden lurching in her stomach.

'I think we may be getting our wires crossed here. What exactly did Dr Galloway tell you?'

'That we have a one-in-four risk of a repeat and we're maybe at risk for other recessive genes ...' Declan's voice tailed away. He was looking hard at her.

She actually felt the sweat gathering on her palms as she teetered on the edge of a yawning crevasse.

'What did you mean ... something legal?'

'Well, it's just ... sometimes these things ... affect different people in different ways.'

'Dr Farnham,' Declan said. There was a hard edge to his voice. 'If you know something I don't know I'd be grateful if you told me. This concerns the welfare of my wife and any possible children. It's hard enough making decisions when we know – what we know.'

Henrietta wished she were anywhere other than in that surgery tonight. Keith Galloway had warned her. Roberta Mansfield had agreed with him. But the patient himself – he *did* have a right to know. Didn't he? She still hesitated.

Declan's unswerving stare bore into her.

'Did Dr Galloway talk about ... your biological father?'

'Yes.'

'What exactly did he tell you?'

'Forget Dr Galloway. What are *you* trying to say? If you know something that relates to Judy or to me I have a right to know.' She'd always said so. Of course he had a right to know.

'Well, it's … it's only a suspicion … no proof … probably nothing.' She had to look away from those penetrating eyes.

'*What* do you suspect?'

'Maybe … Well, your mothers attended the same clinic. You both carry the same gene …' Need she spell it out? Couldn't he just fathom it out for himself, absolve her from blame?

'And …?'

'Maybe … it was … the same donor.' There, it was said. Doctors didn't have a right to keep information from the people it concerned most nearly.

Declan sat unmoving. She watched, mesmerised, the colour draining from his face as the fact sank through his consciousness.

'It's only a suspicion.' Henrietta's voice sounded thin even in her own ears. Too little, too late.

'But you believe it.' The flat statement sounded dead.

'Well …'

'Who else knows?'

'Well, nobody actually *knows* …'

'Suspects then. Who else have you talked to about it?' he snapped.

'Well, I've talked to Dr Galloway, and that's why I thought … when you said … he'd been straight with you … he'd told you …'

'You mean, *he knew* …?'

She was sinking deeper with every word.

'And some colleagues in Glasgow. But they don't know you and I didn't give any names. Just the facts. Because I didn't know what it all meant.' She had to justify telling these people.

'Anyone else?' It was biting. He must be thinking her totally indiscreet.

'No. Oh sorry, just one other person. A locum GP we had here some time back. I didn't know what to do, if I should tell you. So I consulted her.'

'So you've known … for ages.'

'Well, suspected. Because of the baby.'

'But you chose not to tell us.' His icy calm and frozen face were unnerving. It'd be easier to handle if he'd been angry or aggressive.

'No. Well, I didn't know what to do. But Dr Galloway, and the locum, they advised against it.'

'And is there anything else *they've* advised keeping from us?' She couldn't blame him for the sarcasm, but it was cutting nonetheless.

'No, honestly. Nothing I know anyway. And even this, we don't *know*. Not for sure.'

'And could you find out – for sure?'

'Not easily.'

'But you could?'

'It's possible. DNA testing. But it'd have to be private, commercially arranged. And it'd be expensive.' She couldn't feel more miserable but she could save him asking one more question. 'And it might be better ... not to know ... for sure ... don't you think?' She needed to give him something to cling onto.

But looking at him she knew it was a stupid question. For him it would be better not to know *ever* – never to even *suspect* such a thing. And he'd obviously not suspected. He'd come with a simple rash, a rash that would fade in days, and she'd given him this, this horror that would never go away.

'How far will all this have gone?' Even shocked, his brain was thinking logically, methodically. It was impressive.

'No further than I've told you, I'm sure. These people are all very discreet.' There was silence. He was probably wondering what discretion meant to medical people.

She saw an appalled expression suddenly distort his face.

'And Judy – my wife – you haven't ... she doesn't ...?'

'No. No! Honestly. I've not breathed a word of it to her. Believe me. I haven't.'

'Well, make sure you don't.' He spoke so harshly she flinched.

Slowly, mechanically, he rose to leave.

'Are you ... OK?' The question was absurd. His withering look made words superfluous.

'I'll give you a prescription for some cream for that rash.'

She wrote illegibly with a hand that shook uncontrollably. As she passed it to him she knew she must say something.

'I'm so, so sorry. If you need to talk about this, please come back. Any time.'

'I don't think so.' Declan's voice held a sneer there was no mistaking. You've done enough damage to last me a lifetime.

With a feeling of desolation she watched him leave, walking heavily like a drugged man. Keith Galloway had been right; it wasn't a doctor's place to trample into people's lives. They were the ones left with the mess. She'd just seen a man's world shattered into fragments by her insensitivity.

THIRTY-NINE

For once in his life Declan was grateful that Judy was working late; she wouldn't notice his absence.

He went home to collect the car and drove – on and on, unheeding of signposts, unmindful of speed restrictions. He skidded on a tight corner. Merciful really if he killed himself. The fleeting thought was instantly followed by a vision of Judy hearing of his death. Alone with even more grief. He slowed the car, turned at the next junction and headed back, now more cautiously.

Not until he found himself at Bethany's grave did his mind cease its ferment enough to allow him to think coherently.

He sat on the grassy mound with his head in his hands. Sometimes he found solace in talking to the child as he worked, tending the site. Not today. These were thoughts too dark for innocence to hear. Today God only knew – *could* know – what he was grappling with. Since losing Bethany he'd found a nearness to a spiritual presence here at her grave which he found nowhere else, but could he dare to share this, even with God? Was God big enough to take his anger like Geoff had said when Bethany died?

God, how *could* you let something like this happen?

So much slotted into place now. Doug, Dr Galloway, they'd talked of consanguineous marriages right back at the beginning when they'd found out what was wrong with Bethany. The doctors had even asked them outright if they were related, to check their family histories. How he and Judy had laughed at the idea of uncle and niece … but …

God! *Brother and sister?* How *could* you let that happen?

It was unthinkable. Even knowing they'd been conceived in the same fertility clinic – well, it had just been another bond. There was more than a year between them. But, of course, these men – these donors – they didn't just do it once, they kept going back. They fathered loads of kids, probably. And freezing the semen meant they could use each donation more than once …

Oh God! Tell me it wasn't from the same ejaculate.

Would that make them half-*twins* – *triplets* even with Georgina? Georgie! That day in the swimming pool, Martin had mistaken Judy for his other sister. And he'd seen the likeness himself with their hair slicked back, Judy's auburn colouring lost in the wetness, the same enormous dark eyes. And right back at the beginning, that chance meeting at the station, he'd felt a sense of familiarity, felt as if he knew her, that they belonged together. It had stirred his interest, attracted him, made him pursue her, uncharacteristically. And he'd always felt that bond, even when his feelings had changed ... changed ... to those brothers don't have for sisters.

He sank down low over the grave, a groan torn from his lips, fingers wrenching at his hair.

God, why the meeting – so far away – so unexpectedly – if ...?

But that bond was there. Even through the tough times – Bethany's illness and death, Judy's withdrawals – he'd never seriously questioned the survival of their love. Ah yes, Judy's withdrawals. That had tested him. Those first months after their marriage, when she'd been afraid to give herself to him, he'd faced the question: what if she never could? Would it have been better if she hadn't? They wouldn't then have broken any taboos. But it would have been a living hell for him, he knew that, wanting her as he did. And now?

Oh God – what now?

It was incestuous. He shuddered violently. How *could* something as natural, as joyful, be something so ugly? Incest – the very word was loathsome.

God! Oh God! No! Not that! Not again. You couldn't be that cruel.

Judy had been there before. But Jim hadn't been related to her. And he hadn't actually had sex with her – almost but not quite. Declan had repeatedly reassured her, emphasising that very point. And now he himself had gone beyond that boundary, again and again and again. Technically that made him a worse sinner than even Jim had been. And how Judy had loathed what her father had done, what damage it had done to her, damage it had taken him so much love and patience to overcome.

But God, you know it isn't like that. You *know* it isn't!

How could it be loathsome ... if she was a willing partner, a gloriously eager participant? But, consenting or not, they had infringed one of society's deepest taboos – inadvertently though it was – and everyone, every civilised person, would condemn it. If they knew.

They needn't know! Nobody need know. He'd promised to protect Judy, he would protect her from this. No-one should know. But what about Judy herself ...

Oh God! Don't do this to her. You *can't*. Not after what she's been through.

How would *she* react? She had so much in her past that troubled her already. She could never live with the thought that he – her husband – was her half-brother. So must he live the rest of his life with her as his *sister*? No. It was too much to ask.

God, NO! You *can't* ask that!

No, no. She needn't know. They could go on as if nothing had happened. If she didn't know she needn't face these agonising questions. He would protect her.

But if she found out – somehow? Or put two and two together for herself? Why should she? He hadn't. But some other people knew – only a few – but people in *her* world. If *they* knew, *she* might find out. Imagine her finding out. And then finding out he had known all along.

Oh God! Don't, don't, *don't* let her lose trust in *me*!

They could move house, start again. Go somewhere where no-one could possibly know them, or their story. They could go to New Zealand. Start again near Sian and the family, and his Dad. Yes.

Thank you, God. Thank you, thank you, thank you. A way forward.

Nothing to stop them. Yes. Yes. YES! Go to the family. Be near Sian's children …

Oh God! Not that too!

Must they themselves now give up all thought of children? It would break Judy's heart. And what possible reason could he give for denying her that wish? Think. *Think*, man!

He could have a vasectomy. They'd still be 'trying'. She needn't know. But when it didn't happen, she'd want tests. It'd come out. No, that wouldn't work. But could he – would it be right? – to go ahead, have children, knowing what he knew?

He remembered bitterly his repeated promise that he would never, *ever*, let anything come between them, he would always love her, always be there for her. He'd meant it – still did – but what did that promise mean now? Must a secret stand between them? A secret of such appalling dimensions he didn't know if he *could* protect her from it, even if he decided he should. Or was it the knowledge that must for ever lie between them, destroying their happiness, distorting even the basis of their life, their love?

It was after nine thirty when he rose from the grass. He must get home before Judy started to become anxious. He'd rung home at eight to leave a message on the machine to say he was out visiting the grave, not to worry. Leaving the cemetery was always a wrench, but today he hardly noticed. There was no room for his feelings to sink any lower.

Judy looked up anxiously as he entered the house.

'You all right, Dec?'

'Mmmhmm, bit down. Sorry.' He took her in his arms, holding her so tightly she felt breathless.

'Did it help – going to see Bethany?'

'Not really. Bad day, that's all.'

She ran her fingers through his hair, turning his face to hers. He saw her concern. Avoiding her gaze his eyes travelled over her hair, her lips, and down to her body now freed from his own. Must he give up all this?

'Hold me, Jude?' It was hoarse, from the heart. It was her own cry. She held him tenderly, rocking him in her arms, caressing him softly, rhythmically. He clung to her fiercely, unable to say anything.

'Want to talk about it?' Judy ventured eventually.

'No ... I can't. I'm just too churned up. But thanks. Thanks for being there.'

'I'll always be there for you.' His own words, recycled, too late to bring comfort.

After a while he let go of her, protesting that she must be exhausted after a long shift, he'd make her a drink, she could tell him about her day. As from a great distance he heard her voice telling him about the deliveries, the conversations, the minutiae of her shift. But she quickly saw through the pretence, abruptly stopped speaking and walked across to curl up beside him, resting her head on his shoulder.

'You poor love. You don't need all that prattle. It's OK just to be quiet. I understand.'

He felt a choking sensation and buried his face in her curls, fighting the desire to burst into tears. It was merciful that she had nestled down so that he could avoid looking at her directly, but holding her so close, feeling her love and concern, only increased his anguish.

Eventually he suggested she should get to bed. She had an early start tomorrow. He'd be up later but needed a bit of time alone or he'd never sleep.

But there was no respite to be gained from thinking that night and he eventually gave up the attempt to find a solution, and went reluctantly to bed. Judy was sound asleep and he was careful not to disturb her as he slid under the duvet. He kept his back to her, clinging to the very edge of the bed, to be sure of staying well away from her. At five thirty he got up before she had stirred.

He was scheduled to fly to Seattle on business two days later. The staff in his office had been protective of him for the first year, keeping his travel away from home to a minimum so that he could be there when Judy needed him, and take time out himself to deal with the trauma of losing Bethany, but now he had started to resume his normal role. For once he was glad to be going, dreading the return. Two nights avoiding close contact he could excuse, plausibly; more than that she'd start to wonder.

He phoned each day from America. It was easier to keep a pretence of normality from that distance. He enthused over the places he'd seen.

'How would you fancy moving over here, Jude? Starting a new life in a new country?' He kept the tone light, holding his breath till she responded.

'I couldn't, Dec.'

'Why not? It'd be an adventure. Exciting new start.'

'I couldn't, you know that. I couldn't leave Bethany.'

'Of course. Sorry. Didn't mean to ...'

'I know you didn't. It's OK. You couldn't either, I know.' Oh he could! He could – if it meant he could escape some even greater catastrophe.

'Besides it's reassuring being here. For the next baby. With these folk we know and trust, being among friends who know and understand.'

He gritted his teeth. Little did she know how untrustworthy they really were! He steered the conversation onto safer ground. His last hope of escape had been blocked, and that by the one person who stood most to lose from closing it.

Judy drove to the airport to meet him. He hadn't expected to see her at the foot of the escalator; she usually waited in the car to save parking. Instinctively he caught her up in a bear hug. He felt her stiffen and draw away from him. He looked hard at her. Had she heard something? But her smile was warm and wide.

'You all right?' he asked.

'Yep. Why?'

'Just now …?'

'It's OK. I'll tell you when we get home.'

He drove in silence until they were clear of the airport traffic but once on the bypass he glanced across at her. She didn't look like a girl who'd had her world blown apart. And she was talking easily about events in his absence … except … there was something, an undercurrent. Was it his own feverish anxiety? He didn't think so.

He dropped his case in the hall and walked into the sitting room behind her. As he turned her to face him, his eyes searched hers.

'Jude – something happened?'

'Mmmhhmm. Can't you guess?'

He didn't dare.

'Not even when I pulled away from you – at the airport?'

He couldn't speak.

'If I mention tender breasts? Morning sickness?'

He froze, eyes staring down at her.

'You're not …?'

'I am.'

He couldn't move. His emotions were turbulent. All his resolve faded. It was too late.

She looked uncertain, her smile fading.

'Aren't you pleased, Dec? It's what we wanted.'

'Pleased? Pleased? Oh Jude. Words fail me. I can't believe it! Come here.' He gathered her close, holding her tenderly as if she might break. It gave him time, time to rearrange his expression, time to re-organise his thoughts.

'I know it can't be like that moment with Bethany, but it is still a miracle, Dec.' She sounded so forlorn.

'It certainly is. I'm sorry, darling. You just took me by surprise. I hadn't even suspected. Guess I didn't dare let myself hope.' His words were heart-felt this time.

'And you are … pleased?' She leaned away to look into his face, anxiously searching for confirmation.

225

He smiled down at her, his fingers caressing her cheek.

'Pleased? It's the best news I could possibly hear. This little person has the power to change our lives.' He – she – had already done so. There was now no going back.

'We mustn't hope too much, not till after the tests. I need you to be strong for me, help me not get too close till then. But today – this moment – can we just be happy? Like we were last time?' Her appeal touched him deeper than she could have known.

'We will be happy again, Jude. We've been given a second chance.'

'I hated you not being here. Not knowing from the first moment.'

All those hours he had tossed and turned, contemplating giving up the prospect of children, forgoing sex, even leaving her, she had been nursing the knowledge that they had once again created a new life together.

Not until he stood in the shower that night did Declan give himself space to review his own position.

The days in Seattle had brought no solution and he had returned still unsure of just how he should behave with Judy. There was no doubting that his own feelings for her were unchanged. He wanted her – *needed* her – now in his trouble, more than ever. But if she knew, would she still want him to make love to her? Round and round the arguments went. Hearing about the baby had settled one thing: telling her was now out of the question. It was a relief to be spared that. He wanted to protect her; he had a double reason now to do so. But what should he do about sex? What *could* he do? If he refrained she would want to know why. He could only stall for so long. Did it matter any more now anyway? If they had already created this child together, what difference would it make if they made love? But if he did, knowing what he knew now …?

The sound of the water drowned the click of the door opening and he was startled by the sudden feel of her hands sliding around his waist from behind. He turned abruptly, skidding slightly on the wet base.

She smiled shyly up at him as they stood face to face under the cascading water.

'Jude …' He placed his hands on her shoulders. Could he let her innocently …?

She reached up to stem his words with her lips. Then lathering her hands she began to smooth the creamy foam across his chest, his neck, shoulders, arms, down his body.

He stood impassively, watching her in silence. Her touch worked its magic.

'Dec.' The appeal was gentle. His gaze moved from her hands to her face. 'I'm not *crushable* right now, but I *am* touchable.'

Without a word he began to reciprocate. The water fell in a transparent curtain around their glistening bodies.

Only when they were in bed, lying in each other's arms, damp hair sending a creeping watermark across the pillow, did Declan speak for the first time.

'Jude. Thank you. Thank you. More than I can say.'

'Is everything all right again now? Are you OK?'

'Thanks to you, yes, everything is all right again.'

'Oh Dec, I thought ... since that day at the grave ... I was afraid ...'

'What did you think, darling?' He held his breath. Did she suspect?

'At first I thought it was just a delayed grief reaction. But then ... well, I thought perhaps ... you didn't fancy me any more.'

'You ... are ... kidding!' He raised himself on one elbow to look down at her in disbelief. 'Not fancy you? Not ...? You tear me apart with wanting you, Jude.'

'But ... lately ...'

'I know.' He lay back onto the pillow, burying his face into her neck. 'But it was never *that*! I'm so sorry. It was ... I was just all churned up. It wasn't *you*. I never stopped wanting you. It was me. I got lost. But I'm back now, back where I belong.'

He caught her to him fiercely, forgetting her new tenderness. She winced. He was abject in his apologies.

Wide awake, the jetlag dictating it was daytime, he lay looking at Judy sleeping so peacefully beside him. Not for him now that innocent satisfaction.

He had come close to committing the same mistake as Dr Farnham, hinting enough to make questions inevitable. Not by words in his case but in his behaviour. Mercifully Judy had interpreted it wrongly. And by taking the action she had done, she had forced him to overcome the obstacle which kept him away from her. Strange that the positions had reversed. He had never dreamed of that eventuality when he had patiently coaxed her to trust him and give herself to him when they were first married. Then he had been totally unaware of the reason for her inhibition. Now she was the one all unsuspecting. But in both cases the same taboo lay at the heart of their torment. It had been therapeutic for her to share her secret, but she must never share his. He must never again give her reason to question.

It was useless to go over all the 'what ifs'; it just tormented him, changed nothing. Dr Farnham *had* told him. Yes, she'd said it was only a suspicion but he knew in his heart she believed it to be a fact. And Dr Galloway had been right to caution prudence; he did deserve Judy's trust after all. Wisdom had tempered his practice. It would have been better never to have known, as he had advised.

But it was said, and it could never be unsaid.

Declan knew in that moment what he must do. And the baby would ensure his resolve did not waver.

He turned again, sliding an arm around the girl beside him, and waited silently for sleep to claim him too.

FORTY

The first excitement of the pregnancy gave way rapidly to a mounting tension. Over and over again they reminded themselves that a child was only a possibility until they knew the result of the test. The weeks crept by.

Declan felt a surge of relief knowing that Judy's position as a midwife meant she didn't need a letter of referral from Dr Farnham, she could go directly to Dr Janet Yates. She made an early appointment and Declan insisted he would accompany her to the clinic for her first visit as well as for the crucial tests.

Bethany was not far from everyone's thoughts. There was no need to explain their subdued responses to staff. The midwives were gentle in their questioning, smoothing Judy's passage with light-hearted commis-erations about being surrounded by people she knew. Janet Yates was reassuring without offering any false promises: they'd do a scan just to confirm dates, so they could be precise about when to do the next tests. It was a tentative pregnancy indeed.

Declan kept his gaze averted from the screen; Judy lay with her eyes closed. They'd agreed: better not to see this child who might never be. It seemed to take an unconscionably long time for the ultrasonographer to complete the procedure. She was silent as she worked, and they made no effort to engage her in conversation. As she drew Judy's shirt back down over her abdomen, she told them in a level voice, Dr Yates would give them the result.

Janet's words were carefully modulated.

'Sorry. It's probably not a good time to hear this. I think you should brace yourselves for a bit of a shock.'

They held their breath. The silence was deafening.

'I can see two fetuses.'

Declan knew he was staring.

'Two?' He heard his own voice squeaking.

'Twins?' Judy gasped.

'That's right. How would you feel about that?' The consultant's voice was gentle.

Tears filled Judy's eyes. 'After the test – then we'll say.'

Declan gripped her hand hard. To lose two, that would be too cruel.

Janet laid a hand on her arm.

'I understand. It's tough, I know. But not long to wait now. We'll talk more about how we'll take care of you all, once we know all's well.'

They nodded. No-one was smiling at this news yet.

Once in the car, away from everyone else, Declan turned to Judy. 'Jude ...'
He got no further. The tears were cascading down her cheeks unchecked.
He held her close, his own weeping silent, internal. Through the sobs her
words echoed his feelings.

'It's so ... sad, Dec ... Ordinarily we'd have been ... so thrilled. But
now ... we mustn't dare ... start to hope ... for two.'

Declan started the engine and took her home.

The days seemed interminable, the nights too long for all the thoughts
surging and jostling in Declan's head. He worked at staying calm for Judy's
sake but the tension was everywhere. Even their everyday conversation
was stilted as each tried to examine their words for potential pain before
they were uttered.

It was the night before Judy was scheduled to go in for the CVS.

'Dec.'

'Uhhmmm?'

'Could you bear to come up to Bethany's room for a minute?'

'You sure?' he said, looking at her hard. Now they'd packed away the
unused clothes and toys, it was more bearable, but the room was still
furnished for a baby.

'Please,' she said, holding out her hand.

Now they stood together looking at the vibrant walls, the scaled-down
furniture, the soft drapery, the empty cot ... but ... surely that was a different sheet? Yes, the bed had been freshly made up.

Judy's voice was subdued but strong, purposeful.

'Dec, whatever happens tomorrow, I want us to do what it takes to fill
this empty space. If it goes wrong this time I know I'll be a mess, so I need
us to decide now. And then you must hold me to it, right?'

He moved close behind her, wrapping his arms around her, hands over
her abdomen protecting their unseen babies.

'I'm glad,' he said. 'I want that, too – if you can bear it.'

'But I need you to promise – *now*, so if it's tough ... after tomorrow ...
and we have to decide to ... end it' – the words were halting but Declan
knew he must let her say it aloud – 'we won't give up. We'll come back in
here ... and remember that promise.'

He turned her around to face him, taking her face in both his hands to
look down directly into her eyes.

'We will, darling. We will.'

The CVS itself was uneventful and Declan was reassured that Judy had
not found it a physical ordeal. Chaotic emotions kept them silent. They
gripped hands desperately against the gathering storm clouds.

Now all they could do was wait. And somewhere, deep and out of sight,
hope.

News of a coming cyclone – or of a reprieve – lay in a laboratory half a mile away.

The leaden days and hours dragged by. Declan watched the strain telling on Judy with mounting dread. How could he ask her to go through this again if ...?

Her mental state frightened him enough this time around.

Janet Yates was smiling broadly now.

'It's fine. The enzymes are perfectly normal.'

Declan simply stared at her. It took time for the words to penetrate the barriers erected during the weeks of denial and repression.

'The babies are fine,' she said again.

'You mean ...?' He heard the rasping sound and realised it was Judy's voice.

Janet nodded, smiling still.

'We can ... go ahead ...?'

'You can indeed and look forward to two beautiful healthy babies in about six months time!'

Judy turned to bury her head on his shoulder, and he was glad to hide his own reaction in her curls. Janet was forgotten.

'I'm so glad for you,' she said after a while. Declan lifted his head abruptly and shot her an apologetic look. She was handing him tissues.

'Sorry.'

'It's fine. I understand.' Janet gave a dismissive wave.

'Thank you. Thank you for everything.'

'Well, we're only just starting really. Now we must plan how we can take care of these precious babies.'

With a carefully matter-of-fact approach she began to outline a plan of action to ensure the pregnancy stood the best chance of going as near to term as possible. They talked of clinic visits, of diet, of rest. They discussed labour and feeding and possible complications. And through it all, gradually, the reality began to seep into their consciousness.

Janet touched their arms lightly as they prepared to leave.

'It's the best news of the day,' she said simply. 'I'm so glad.'

Declan marvelled at the care of these people for Judy. They were friends indeed. He could safely trust these three lives to their safekeeping.

But it was not until they were alone in the car preparing to go home that he dared to voice his thoughts.

'Oh Jude. Can you believe it? It's over. We can start to be like two normal expectant parents.'

'Tell me I'm not dreaming, Dec.'

'You're not dreaming. It's true. It's brilliant. It's fantastic. It's twins!'

'Well done, you! It's *your* side of the family coming out there!'

By not so much as a flicker of the eyes did he betray anything of what those words meant to him.

All proceeded smoothly until twenty weeks. Then a slight bleed sent waves of dread through them both; it would be too appalling to lose the babies now, to have to go through all that again. Powerful misgivings once again flooded Declan's mind, threatening his stranglehold on that secret information buried within him. The fears became so acute that he put pressure on Judy to leave work and settle down to a quiet few weeks resting at home.

Janet Yates kept a watchful eye on her. The enforced rest paid dividends. But as the twins grew in size and energy, Judy grew increasingly uncomfortable. By thirty-eight weeks she was weary of waiting and it was a relief when she went into spontaneous labour. Declan took three weeks' leave from that moment.

Donella Marianne heralded her arrival with a healthy shriek. The duty paediatric registrar, Sam Reynolds, summoned quietly by Janet to stand by 'just in case', was satisfied his services were not necessary to her. Twenty minutes later Graeme Edward slipped quietly into the world, blinking in the sudden light but seeing no necessity to shout about his coming.

Declan and Judy were each cradling a twin before they were transferred to the ward when Doug Fairweather appeared, his face wreathed in smiles.

'Just heard the good news. Congratulations.'

'Oh, how good of you to come.' Judy held out her free hand. 'And so quickly too! Looks like the bush telegraph is as efficient as usual!'

He moved closer to peer at the baby nestling in her arm.

'We were cheeky enough to ask for regular bulletins on your progress all morning. So we heard when they were both safely here. The flags are out round the hospital today.'

'Thanks for that, Doug,' Declan said quietly.

'Well done, Dad!' Doug grinned, craning to look at Graeme lying with closed eyes in his father's arms.

'Beautiful babies. I'm just so pleased for you. What are they called? What do they weigh? I shall have to give a blow-by-blow account to the team upstairs!'

He wrote the details on a paper towel.

'So now you start the real hard graft, eh? But it's worth every sleepless night.'

Was he remembering that other sleepless night, Declan wondered.

'They look fine. Sam tells me they are, too. But any worries, anything at all, don't hesitate to shout. We know what it's like.'

'Thanks, Doug. Thanks for everything.' Judy spoke with real feeling for them both. Doug smiled again, lightly touched Donella's head, and returned to the sick babies under his care.

231

By day five Judy's room resembled a florist's shop. Cards hung all around the room. Declan struggled to convey the duplicated gifts to the car. With each day he gloried in the normality of the experience this time, even the fourth-day blues seeming as nothing compared to the depression of their first-time parenthood. Judy had elected to stay in hospital longer – 'Just in case, Dec.' But the twins needed no encouragement to suck and, with the ready help of colleagues popping in and out, Judy soon became adept at positioning them so that she could feed them both at once.

Dick called in, in his customary whirlwind way, with a huge bouquet of lilies. He asked tentatively if he might cuddle the babies and impressed Declan with his expert handling of the two together.

'Had twins myself,' he explained.

So he was a father himself. Presumably that meant a wife, or at least a partner.

'Really? Boys? Girls? One of each?'

'Both boys.'

'And are they identical?'

'Absolutely! Couldn't tell them apart myself at this stage!'

'And do they trade on that?'

'Not yet. They're too young. But they'll no doubt try it on before too long. Next time you see me I'll probably look a hundred.'

'Well, you seem pretty sprightly for someone who's survived thus far.' Judy laughed. 'I'll take that as encouragement. We might call on you when the going gets tough. You're obviously a lot better at this than we are at the moment. And everyone gives us dire warnings about how tough it is having two at once.'

'Good things exceed the bad – by about fifty to one,' he responded instantly.

Declan watched his softened expression as he looked from one to the other of the sleeping babies in his arms.

'I can't imagine *ever* being that slick with them,' he said ruefully.

'I give you a few weeks and you'll be handling them as easily as you drive the car,' Dick grinned at him. 'These little people have a habit of sneaking up on you without any warning. Before you know it, feels like you've had them for ever.'

Declan's thoughts were turbulent and he was glad when Dick directed his conversation towards Judy. By the time the doctor rose to leave he was back in control again.

'Well, hey ho, you two gorgeous creatures,' Dick said, 'I'm afraid I must abandon you to these two learners who are proud to call themselves your parents, and go back to ruling the world.'

Deftly he tucked the twins into their cots.

He stood for a moment holding Judy's hand in both his.

'I'm just so pleased for you.'

She smiled up at him; he dropped a kiss on her head and whirled out of the room.

Declan collapsed into the vacated seat.

'It's brilliant eh, Jude, the way all these guys who shared the bad times are so chuffed now?'

'Yes. I've been thinking that. If we hadn't had Bethany, we wouldn't have cherished Donella and Graeme in quite the way we're doing now. And the babies wouldn't have been welcomed in quite such a fantastic way by all these other people.'

'We always said she was special.'

When Kirsten Greenside popped in to visit, Judy was having a shower. Declan was in the room on his own, at a loss to know what to do with two crying babies. He was holding Graeme and patting Donella in her cot, and he looked up sheepishly as she entered. It was a special delight to see Kirsten, who had maintained occasional contact with them since that night in Special Care when she had shared their vigil beside the dying Bethany.

'Sorry about the din!' he apologised. 'I'm not very good at this yet, but I suppose they want their mother?'

Kirsten picked up Donella, who nuzzled against her for a moment but then began to cry again. She tried patting her back, with the child on her shoulder, but to no effect.

'Problem with twins, they keep each other going. One wails, the other joins in.' She laughed across at him. 'The joys in store!'

Declan pulled a face of mock horror. Both children continued to cry.

'D'you want your Mummy, poppet?' Kirsten crooned as she walked to and fro. 'Or are you missing your brother? Let's see if he can make you happy again, eh?'

She laid Donella back in the cot on her side, took Graeme from his father and laid him down facing her. There was instant silence. Declan held his breath, watching. Both babies lay still, blinking as if trying to focus on something too close to see well. Donella's tongue licked out; she turned her head in search of nurture. Her mouth touched her brother's cheek. She made contented sucking noises. Declan watched mesmerised.

'After nine months in a confined space together, they must miss each other first of all, I always think,' Kirsten said quietly, still watching the children.

'I would never have believed that if I hadn't seen it with my own eyes,' he whispered in an awed voice.

'They're gorgeous babies. Look at those mops of dark hair! Going to have dark eyes, too.'

Declan felt his stomach clench.

'Lovely to have one of each,' she enthused. 'Like miniature versions of you and Judy, aren't they? Gorgeous. Congratulations. I'm so thrilled for you.'

'Thanks, Kirsten. Super of you to pop in. And I'm terribly impressed by your diagnosis here.'

Judy returned from the bathroom, her hair wrapped in a towelling turban, a waft of perfume accompanying her. Declan put a finger to his lips and beckoned her closer.

'They were both howling, but as soon as Graeme went in beside Donella they were quiet,' he explained, reaching out to draw her nearer to the cot.

'I hope you don't mind, Judy,' Kirsten said. 'It's not what infection control sister recommends, I know, but I think twins need each other.'

Judy smiled.

'Exactly the right thing to do. Thanks, Kirsten. I hope they'll always be there for one another. They might as well start as we mean them to go on.'

Declan stared down at his son and daughter. Miniature versions of himself and Judy, she'd said. They needed one another. They were there for one another. That bond was stronger than anyone outside of them could see.

He drew Judy to his side protectively.

FORTY-ONE

Six thousand miles away, Professor Dan Allanwood smoothed back his thick grey hair, and sighed. It had been a long and difficult day. First there had been the demanding letter from his ex-wife's lawyer. Then the head of his department had virtually accused him – in a meeting of the whole team too – accused him of disloyalty and of being a 'prima donna'. Petty jealousy, that's all it was, just because his own publication rate wasn't as good; there were no honorary degrees coming his way.

And then Dan had lost a whole afternoon dealing with the third-year student who'd gone to pieces in his office because she couldn't cope with the workload. She had taxed his patience and his ingenuity. If he offered comfort – legitimate, appropriate comfort – would she turn and accuse him of molesting her – like that other hysterical creature he'd tried to help six years ago? It was possible. He couldn't take a chance. With the two departmental secretaries both off, one sick, the other on a course, he'd had to call in a colleague as chaperone. To her credit she'd grudgingly sympathised with his vulnerability, but she wasn't best pleased at the waste of her time either.

The reduced secretarial support meant there was no-one to field the incoming calls. He'd missed lunch altogether in the welter of phone calls he'd had to handle himself. Now he had to content himself with a sandwich and a banana for his evening meal. He sighed. It was going to be a long sitting tonight if he was to catch up on the work he should have been doing. But at least he could now concentrate. Quiet had descended. No-one expected staff to be in their offices at this hour of night. Even the cleaning lady commented. And there was no-one waiting at home to be irritated by his change of plans.

He adjusted his half-glasses, rubbing his eyes. His vision seemed a bit blurred tonight. Did he need new spectacles? Probably only fatigue. He got up and peered at himself in the mirror behind the door. Large dark eyes heavily fringed with coal black lashes stared back at him, a bit bloodshot in one area but no evidence of anything obvious. And his long-distance sight was still excellent. It was probably only the added pressure of this forthcoming tour of the UK.

He returned to the computer. Where was he? He scanned the last few pages. The abbreviated CV made impressive reading, with accolades, distinctions, international recognition. The dean who would preside over his award of an honorary degree from his alma mater, Edinburgh University, was asking for some additional detail – Dan needed to bring the story alive, he'd said. Ah yes, he'd got held up over a word. His brain searched for something more apposite.

He leaned back in the chair, keeping his eyes on the screen while he thought. The precision of the letters became fuzzy as his mind travelled back over the years he'd marked chronologically in reverse order on the document. Eminent professor of forensic pathology now, all the way back to his student days in Scotland.

Happy days, those student days. Uncomplicated. An unknown future beckoning invitingly. How confident he'd been back then – of himself, of his ultimate success. He'd been determined to fly high, single-minded in the pursuit of his own interests.

He shuddered now, remembering his entire lack of humility, his insensitivity, his arrogance. Life had knocked him into better shape since then. Two broken marriages, three children who rarely even made contact, colleagues who couldn't wait for his retirement. Yes, there was plenty of evidence of failure as well as of success. But back then, he'd thought himself invincible. Good-looking, athletic, intelligent, musical, he met his own ideal. Oh, of course, he'd been impecunious just like every-one else in his year, but he'd thought of imaginative ways of earning enough to buy the necessities.

They'd paid fifteen pounds for every ejaculate. Fifteen pounds towards the latest texts – keeping him two steps ahead of the game. And he was arrogant enough to believe that any woman would be grateful to get *his* semen, any child be glad to inherit his genetic material. He'd been gener-ous in the frequency of his donations.

Strange though, he'd never given much thought to what use they'd made of his sperm – if they'd used his contributions at all. He'd needed the money. Odd to think he might have fathered young men and women who'd be pretty much the same age now as he was then. He'd never know, of course. They'd assured him there was no possibility he'd be traceable. He shuddered. Imagine a stream of Dan Allanwood lookalikes beating a path to his door, demanding parental dues. No thanks!

He focused again on the task in hand.

Ah, that was it! The word was 'munificence'.

Other books in the Living Literature Series

VACANT POSSESSION

Vivienne has been in a persistent vegetative state, looked after in a Home, for years. How can she suddenly be pregnant? She cannot speak for herself, so who should decide what happens to her unborn child? What is in her best interests?

Her family, the medical team who care for her, the police investigating the crime – all have different interests, values and opinions on the best way forward. As events gather their own momentum, other people must make medical and moral choices on Vivienne's behalf – choices beset with uncertainty that profoundly affect their own relationships and futures.

ISBN 1 85775 651 7   Paperback, £11.99

DOUBLE TROUBLE (a sequel to *Paternity*)

The Halleys are a close, successful, loving family. But relationships become increasingly complex following the marriages of identical twins Nicholas and Michael. Darker secrets and hidden emotions are revealed when an unplanned pregnancy and a surrogacy arrangement lead to discoveries which challenge their moral values and jeopardise their happiness.

This story probes beneath society's superficial acceptance of fertility treatment, revealing the potential for pain, distorted relationships, and far-reaching consequences, both medical and moral.

ISBN 1 85775 669 X   Paperback, £11.99